KWAKU

Also by Roy Heath

A Man Come Home (1974)

The Murderer (1978) (US 1992)

From the Heat of the Day (1979) (US 1993)

One Generation (1981)

Genetha (1981)

Later published as a trilogy under the title The Armstrong Trilogy *in the United States (1994)*

Orealla (1984)

The Shadow Bride (1988) (US 1996)

The Ministry of Hope (1997) (US 1997)

Roy Heath

KWAKU

Or the Man Who Could Not Keep His Mouth Shut

A Novel

Marion Boyars
London · New York

Published in Great Britain and the United States
in 1997 by Marion Boyars Publishers
24 Lacy Road, London SW15 1NL
237 East 39th Street, New York NY 10016

Distributed in Australia and New Zealand by
Peribo Pty Ltd, 58 Beaumont Road, Mount Kuring-gai, NSW

Originally published by Allison and Busby Limited, London, 1982
© Roy A.K. Heath 1982, 1997

British Library Cataloguing in Publication Data
Heath, Roy A.K. (Roy Aubrey Kelvin), 1926–
    Kwaku, or, The man who could not keep his mouth shut
    1. Guyanese fiction — 20th century
    I. Title
    813 [F]

Library of Congress Cataloging-in-Publication Data
    — available —

ISBN 0-7145-3023-9 Paperback

Contents

Book 1

1	Kwaku's fall from idiocy	page 7
2	The centre of attention	9
3	How Kwaku acquired a sense of responsibility	13
4	The metamorphosis of Kwaku	20
5	Blossom's man-friend	24
6	Kwaku and the one-toothed storyteller	29
7	The delivery of Fabian	35
8	How Kwaku fell foul of his employer	40
9	How Kwaku fell foul of the Party	44
10	Miss Gwendoline's jealousy	47
11	Marriage	53
12	A plague	58
13	The unsympathetic	65
14	A fugitive	72
15	The fancy-dress do	79
16	Kwaku leaves home	90

Book 2

17	The proposal	102
18	How Kwaku acquired a reputation	111
19	A change of fortune	119
20	The healer	125
21	A quarrel	140
22	Talk and drink	148
23	The children	156
24	The hollow ball	170
25	Miss Gwendoline's affliction	175

Book 3

26	A dream of monkeys	182
27	Family troubles	191
28	A conversation overheard	199
29	Rain in the night	212
30	Destitution	217
31	Blossom's visit	230
32	Kwaku and Miss Gwendoline	244

Rain leaves puddles behind
Gauze under the moon
Stray from porch to porch
Settle for the window
With trembling wires
Where abandoned kites
Twist in the wind.

BOOK 1

1 Kwaku's fall from idiocy

THIS IS THE tale of Kwaku, who was reduced to a state of idiocy by intelligent men, but made a spontaneous recovery. A quick look-round at his fellow men convinced him that there was much protection in idiocy, and that intelligence was like the plimpla palm, bearer of good fruit, but afflicted with thorns. So he fell back into a state of idiocy, only to recover again for love of punishment and a hankering after passion. All this took place before Kwaku was ten years old. And his latest remission occurred in the following fashion.

A sadistic teacher introduced boxing among the boys in the school. The arrangement was ostensibly in the interest of the budding character of his pupils, who had taken to playing girls' games like hopscotch in public and doctors in private. This had come to the teacher's knowledge through his class pet; and what alarmed him most was that in these private games the boys were invariably the doctors since the mad rage for the practice of medicine had taken the children. Kwaku – whom he detested from the bottom of his heart – had in his idiocy fashioned a stethoscope from the remnants of an enema tube and had a mind to sound his girl friends under their drawers as they relaxed with a book from the Mobile Library. The teacher enquired carefully into these allegations, which were vigorously denied by all the girls except one, who claimed that she had been so engrossed in the book and that Kwaku had been so gentle in his quest for her heart that she had noticed nothing.

Boxing was the only answer to the sickness, declared the teacher. And it was no coincidence that he had been advocating its introduction for years. He matched Kwaku, who was four foot tall, with an eleven-year-old giant bean-pole of six foot three.

The bean-pole rushed out of his corner and began making pretty patterns round Kwaku. At first bewildered by his opponent's display, Kwaku started to do likewise, but was promptly awarded a fist in full face and stood on the spot, listening to the peculiar sounds in his head. Gradually he recovered to see the bean-pole describing attractive diagrams round him and over him. Then, out of the corner of his eye, Kwaku spied the book-worm who had confessed to her indiscretion. But another flurry of activity from him was repaid by an uppercut to the chin and a rabbit punch which forced him into another lengthy period of inactivity. And when he was himself again the bean-pole was engaged in a dazzling show of skill with his feet and arms, feinting to the east and leaping to the north-west, slapping his gloves together and spinning like Mother Sally in her

Christmas dance. In the end the fight was stopped for want of action, because Kwaku, seeing that his safety lay in doing nothing, allowed the bean-pole to perform round him with impunity.

And from that day onwards Kwaku renounced folly and threw in his lot with Blossom, the book-worm, who was to be his lifelong friend and conscience. In their days in secondary school they became notorious for their attachment, even when Kwaku started going out with other girls and Blossom fell in love with other boys. Often he was to be seen chasing her on the front road, he on a bicycle and she on foot; he shouting after her and she screaming that she would get her father to thrash him. And at other times when the orange trees were in blossom, at the start of the long, dry season, they would walk home slowly from school, with the cycle a good yard between them.

Kwaku was to discover, at the age of fifteen or sixteen, that Blossom was ugly, and that the strange sensations in his loins that overcame him in the company of certain girls were entirely absent when he was with her. And he saw this as perfectly natural and no matter for wonder, just as he saw in her albino skin no matter for wonder. So that when his uncle remarked that he would have to marry Blossom one day Kwaku informed him that she was already promised to someone else.

"O my godfather!" was all the stunned relation could say, while contemplating Kwaku as if he were a freak.

Kwaku shot up between the ages of sixteen and eighteen until, when he stopped growing, he was five foot six inches, with narrow shoulders and slight bow legs. Blossom, a good inch taller than he, had left school at sixteen to work with the Public Transport in New Amsterdam and promised to use her influence to secure Kwaku a job as driver of one of the great buses that crossed the Canje river.

But even then Kwaku believed in his superiority over other men, in a destiny that went beyond driving a bus-load of unthinking passengers past endless clumps of courida bushes to the end of the world at East Canje, where perpetual silence reigned and the only evidence of life were a few barefoot children and the odd one-eyed dog. When the cane fields were set alight to rid them of snakes and the sky was brilliant with orange and yellow, Kwaku knew that there was a profound meaning in the conflagration and the rain of ash that fell in its aftermath. An uncle had died a year before, trapped in a burning field he had set alight inexpertly; and Kwaku believed that there was a meaning to such a death. Did not the Yanoama Indians of Venezuela burn their dead and consume the ashes with crushed plantains?

No, he could not end his days at the wheel of a bus, the hero of small boys.

8

2 The centre of attention

ALTHOUGH Kwaku had left his idiocy behind, there were moments when he said and did things that surprised him and confounded those around him. One evening when the storytelling comrade among the group he used to frequent ran out of stories and the youths took to arguing about the superiority of the members of their respective families, one boy declared that his brother, who worked on a timber grant, had fourteen gold teeth in his mouth, a disclosure which earned him a minute of reverential silence. Then Kwaku, for no reason whatsoever, declared for everyone to hear that his mother had bigger bosoms than the mother of anyone else present. And immediately a commotion broke out, for Kwaku's mother had died when he was an infant.

"But she dead!" one youth shouted scornfully.

"I know," replied Kwaku. "I say she *had*, not that she *got*."

"You mean you remember she bosom, though you was a baby," pitched in another youth who seized the opportunity to put down Kwaku.

"My father tell me," protested Kwaku.

"But he run away years ago," the first youth reminded him. "And you was a lil' boy."

"He tell me *before* he go away."

"You mean," said another youth, "just before he run away he call you and say, 'Son, I runnin' away an' leaving you. But before I go I got something to tell you. You mother had the biggest bubby in the village.' "

Kwaku was now indeed the centre of attention, but not in the way he had expected. The more words he wasted in defending himself, the more impatient his companions became, until one youth said, "Don' worry with him; he stupidy."

So the argument came to an end and the youth whose brother had capped his teeth with gold became the centre of attention once more.

Another time Kwaku was on his way home on Blossom's rickety bicycle, which was making so much noise that pedestrians and vehicles had ample time to avoid him, despite the fact that the cycle was not provided with a lamp as the law required. Rounding the bend on the Public Road he saw a number of lights moving about in the distance and, on approaching, saw that there had been an accident. Two cars were locked together by their front bumpers and glass was scattered on the grass verge between the road and the lotus-covered trench.

"Any witnesses?" Kwaku heard one of the three policemen ask..

He had dismounted and placed Blossom's cycle carefully against a wayside tree lest it fell apart. Then he boldly stepped up and said,.

9

"I'm a witness," though the accident must have occurred some time before he arrived. And he and the others who were on the scene at the moment of the mishap were asked to give their names and addresses.

On the morning of the case, four months later, Kwaku was obliged to walk the eleven miles to court, for Blossom, the previous day, had refused to lend him her bicycle.

"It old," she observed, "and the way you does ride it would die on the way."

Blossom's husband-to-be backed her up, mistakenly seeing in Kwaku a rival for Blossom's affection.

Kwaku set out for court at five o'clock and arrived at ten minutes past nine, just after the hearing began, looking like a cat that was fed at the same time as the dog of the house and out of the same receptacle.

He was made to sit on the bench where the other witnesses were ranged, awaiting their turn to be called into the courtroom.

"How long this thing going last?" a young woman next to him enquired.

But before Kwaku could answer, an old man on her right said, "Can be all day. You bring food?"

"Just as I did think," muttered the woman.

Kwaku had no money. He was to start work as a shoemaker the following week and his uncle would neither oblige by cooking early in the morning nor allow Kwaku to cook a meal for himself, for all his pepper and salt would disappear mysteriously and the food would be inedible.

Kwaku was called at five minutes to four in the afternoon, after the prosecution witnesses had testified and the magistrate had warned that his clerk-of-court had to go home at six o'clock.

By this time Kwaku was hungry and irritable and regretted bitterly his hastiness in putting himself forward as a witness to the accident. And the sight of the well-fed magistrate, who must have been eating fried chicken during the recess, so incensed Kwaku that he decided to teach him a lesson and misbehave in the witness box.

"Will you swear on the Bible, please?" the uniformed gentleman asked.

"I don't swear," declared Kwaku. "My uncle tell me never to swear."

"Your what?" asked the magistrate, his eyes blazing.

"My uncle," said Kwaku defiantly. "And the church say you musn' swear, too."

"You'd better do as you're told," ordered the magistrate, "or you'll take the consequences."

So Kwaku swore. Then he was asked to tell what he saw on the road on the evening of the accident and he spoke his prepared account.

"I was coming down the road on my new bicycle ..."

The magistrate looked at his watch.

"... and slam, the yellow car turn out of the village road and knock into the blue car."

"So one car was yellow and the other blue, eh?" asked the middle-aged counsel for the prosecution sarcastically. "And what was the colour of your glasses?"

"My what?" Kwaku said.

"Your glasses."

"I don't wear glasses," Kwaku protested.

"Precisely! Without glasses the cars were both black!"

"Not when I see the accident," Kwaku corrected him.

The very thing the magistrate feared came to pass. A long-winded witness was going to spoil everything.

And Kwaku did. When six o'clock came the magistrate refused to carry on without his clerk-of-court, and the case was put off until a later date. The driver of the car, who had been charged with dangerous driving and who thought that things had been going well for him until Kwaku came into court, gave him such a withering look he was forced to avert his eyes.

Four weeks later Kwaku had to ask for a day off from his new job in order to attend court once more. It was granted him, without pay. He borrowed Blossom's bicycle, promising to buy her a new one from his wages if it did not last the journey. He arrived at the court-house before the sun came up, when nothing was astir save a flock of jumbee birds pecking in the damp grass, and the only sound was the high, plaintive wail of a bird-call.

Sitting down on the lowest step of the whitewashed court-house staircase he looked about him, at the tiny house opposite with its unpainted shutters, at the boats and the wooden bridge over the drainage canal. The villagers were asleep while he, from another village, was kicking his heels, anxiously awaiting the arrival of a hostile magistrate, who was bent on intimidating him just because he could not hold his tongue. He began to call to mind his follies, which passed before him like a troop of galloping horses. And he resolved that after the court case he would curb his tongue, even if he had to chain it. He would also take care to show Blossom the gratitude she deserved. Which other woman in the world would consecrate a school friendship as she had done, at the risk of her relations with a husband-to-be? And what sort of life lay before his future wife and children if he fell prey to every impulse?

Day broke and with it came the noise and bustle of animals, men and their machines. Asses brayed, dogs barked, goats bleated, buses hummed like giant bees and magistrates slammed their car doors ostentatiously, in the manner of those men who dare not lay a finger on their wives and bang the window instead.

No sooner did the proceedings begin than the magistrate interrupted his clerk-of-court.

"There are those," he began threateningly, "who forget who they are. I am here and they are there; and they forget that. Oh, yes! I warned when the case was last heard of the problems that would arise if it went beyond six o'clock. But certain long-winded people ..."

And at this point the magistrate glared at Kwaku.

"... certain people who don't like taking advice, even when it comes from others in power – *in power* – go on and on and on as if it was morning time. But I'm giving this advice once again. Do not let us hear unnecessary chatter about the colour of cars; because *I* have to go early today. Not the clerk-of-court, but *I*. I hope that's clear."

The magistrate was now sweating profusely and frothing at the mouth as if he had been stung by a scorpion. When he recovered his composure he took up a thick, elegantly bound law-book, raised it and was just about to bring it down on the clerk-of-court's head, as it seemed, but changed his mind and smashed it on to the desk in front of him instead, in order to stress how serious his warning was.

Kwaku was made to take his place in the witness-box, aware that all eyes were on him and that the magistrate was crouching at his desk, ready to spring on him and bring him to order. And in a quarter of an hour the proceedings were at an end. The accused driver was found guilty of dangerous driving and Kwaku was allowed to leave the court-house under the scrutiny of the powerful magistrate.

"Lucky he din' make us charge you with perjury," remarked the constable who had brought the prosecution case. " 'Blue car and yellow car!' You ever see a yellow car in this country?"

Kwaku was about to say that his father owned a yellow car once, but luckily he bit his tongue and put on such a pained expression that the policeman believed he was about to burst into tears for the lies he had told.

On his way home under the heat of the morning sun Kwaku decided that, as he had little control of what he said and did, he would get married and so acquire a sense of responsibility. He was once told by his uncle that the tormented look he noticed on all married men's faces was simply the outward sign of a sense of responsibility. And already, on the way home, he was planning how best he would go about the business of choosing a wife from among the village girls.

3 How Kwaku acquired a sense of responsibility

KWAKU'S UNCLE came into his own in the business of acting as go-between for prospective marriage partners. He took his duties so seriously that when Kwaku was required to explain what he expected his intended to be like his uncle actually listened, something that went against the very grain of his impatient character.

"She got to be tall," Kwaku informed him, "but not too tall. I'd prefer a school teacher, but a dressmaker would do. She musn' get vexed if I come home drunk, but she herself musn't drink. She must know to spell good, but she mustn't spend too much time reading. Unless she's a school teacher. She musn't have a flat chest or a huge batty, like Blossom. Blossom man-friend always falling out of bed 'cause she batty does stab him every time he turn. And now he going around with a dislocated arm, all because of she big batty. She must read she Bible and say she prayers. You remember how Miss Gloria started carrying on when she stop saying she prayers after she grandmother dead and she didn't have no one to supervise she conduct? She musn't make a noise with she mouth when she eating, like Blossom, who neighbours does know when is lunchtime by the slurping and sucking of the soup in she mouth .... Let me see ... aw ... le' me see! Oh, yes! She musn't harass me. That's one thing Blossom don' do, harass me ....'"

"Is Blossom you getting married to?" Kwaku's uncle asked, exasperated by his nephew's exorbitant demands.

"She mustn't be too close to she mother, 'cause that's trouble. I don't got experience but I know that's trouble. And you got to find out if anybody in she family ever practise obeah. I don't want to get married to no obeah woman. It got to be a woman from another village, because everybody here know all you business, if you does pee in the yard behind you house or if you did wet you bed when you small ...."

"You did wet you bed when you were small?" asked his uncle.

"Me? Wet my bed? I never wet my bed! Was Bertram did wet his bed, not me."

"Who is Bertram?"

"The boy at the back of the yard who used to catch the hogs for me father .... If you don' believe me go and ask my father, ne?"

"How am I going to ask him if I don't know where he's living?" demanded Kwaku's uncle.

"Anyway, you finish?" his uncle enquired after reflecting awhile, hard put to remember Kwaku's list of requirements.

"Finish? I suppose so. Let me see ... I did say she mustn't harass me, didn't I? Aw ... Oh, yes! Very important! The most important thing of all. She must respect my friends. My friends must be able to come and go ...."

"But you in't got no friends," his uncle remarked, mystified by Kwaku's unusual demand. Even if he had friends he was not the kind of person to encourage them to come and go as they pleased, he reflected. He considered his nephew to be selfish, wilful and stingy, and was not surprised that no one ever came to see him. Now he was demanding that his wife allow his friends to come and go as they pleased. This bizarre demand, together with the unrealistic portrait of Kwaku's ideal wife, filled his uncle with dismay.

"Is not a wife you want," he observed, despairing of ever getting Kwaku off his hands, "is an angel."

"That's what I want. You did ask me, didn't you?"

"First of all, where you're going to find a teacher?"

"There's ..." began Kwaku, only to be brutally interrupted.

"One teacher's living in this village and she wouldn't spit on you. And which dressmaker would marry you with your reputation?"

"I don' got no reputation!" protested Kwaku, whose blood was now up, what with his inflated opinion of himself and his uncle's low opinion of him.

"You got a bad reputation! You don't have a good reputation."

"I never steal," Kwaku protested.

"I didn't say you ever stole," his uncle said.

"You say I got a bad reputation."

"But even the dogs in the village get out of your way when you're coming down the road; and the children does run from you when they see you in the back dam. They wouldn't do that if you had a good reputation. And the other day when you go past Mr Barzey water tank it suddenly started leaking. And it's a new tank. It's only five years old."

Kwaku's uncle hung his head, ashamed of having to own up to being Kwaku's uncle and guardian. All his consideration in the village had vanished since Kwaku came to live with him; and he, once known for his reliability and uprightness, was now associated with his nephew's misdeeds. He hoped to find a partner for him and start him on the road to responsibility. Or, even better, he hoped that he would marry and vanish. He even prayed that he would go abroad, for those who lived in a village and went abroad never came back, except on a visit.

Kwaku's uncle stood up without giving him the opportunity to add to his list of the virtues he required in a wife. And Kwaku, left alone, was yet unable to make out the true traits of his character in the mirror of his uncle's opinion of him. The only flaw in himself was a weakness for letting his tongue run away with him. He was not the only one who played pranks on people or threw stones at dogs when

14

no one was looking. As for the children who ran away on spotting him from a distance, that had always been a mystery to him.

He watched his uncle through the window and recalled the afternoon when, as a small boy, he came walking down that strange village road for the first time and was introduced to Mr Barzey, whose house stood between his uncle's and the Public Road. He remembered his wonder at Mr Barzey's cylindrical water tank, now replaced by a new one. The old tank leaked mysteriously, rather sweated water on its rusted surface, rich-brown with secret incrustations, where gigantic pawn-flies came to settle and drink and spread their gossamer wings. Time and time again a man emptied that tank and, when it was thoroughly dried out, deployed his tools on the ground before setting about the task of soldering the offending spot. But the tank, as if determined to assert its independence, started to leak in another section; and the golden-brown efflorescences reappeared like exotic petals of new rust-flowers, to spread in triumphant splendour across the round surface of Mr Barzey's tank. The soul of that village was Mr Barzey's tank under the olive-leafed sapodilla tree with its half-eaten fruit, bespattered with bat-droppings and sweating copiously. Then early one morning six men came with ropes and sat on Mr Barzey's stairs drinking rum he had provided and chatting affably. Kwaku sensed that they came straight from hell, despite their laughter and pretence at being humans. And sure enough when the bottle was empty they began trussing up the tank, like a giant they had taken in battle. Kwaku ran into his house, sick at heart that no one else felt like him and was prepared to give his right arm to defend the leviathan.

From his uncle's house he could hear the grunting of the devil's men, like the noises from Blossom's bedroom when her young man was at home. And when they left he came outside to confront the disaster, a gleaming new metal tank, smooth and untarnished, a pot-bellied obscenity.

"The bats wouldn't even shit on it," Kwaku muttered to himself.

From then on he never addressed a word of greeting to Mr Barzey, or his wife, or his lady friend who came up the back stairs when his wife went to her sister's in the neighbouring village, or to his decrepit father, or to his married cousins, who came to air their troubles in his house.

His uncle could at least try, reflected Kwaku. There was no harm in looking for a young woman conforming to his specifications.

And his uncle did try. God knows he had reason enough! He travelled the length and breadth of the country in quest of a woman for Kwaku. In June he was in Morawhanna, in August he crossed

15

the Courantyne river to Nickerie in Surinam. In December he was on the savannah bordering Venezuela, surveying the vast scrub-lands for a likely partner for his demanding nephew. He even stayed a few weeks in the country by the Ireng river, attracted as much by the wild tree-less country as by the prospect of meeting a fatherless girl whose mother was prepared to put her through a course in dressmaking, so that she would be a suitable match for Kwaku. But those he did meet were too short or were poor spellers or read their Bible only occasionally, or ate noisily or were in some other way unsuitable.

But at last he found a young lady qualified, it seemed, in all respects. She lived in Beterverwachting and was seventeen years old, two years younger than Kwaku. Kwaku's uncle entered into extensive negotiations with her parents and finally got them to agree, provided the prospective bridegroom was reasonable looking and was not a boozer. And Kwaku's uncle, making himself out to be not as sprightly as he seemed, assured them that his nephew would inherit his land and house when he died.

The Sunday when the girl, her father, mother and their eleven other children came to the village to meet Kwaku and look over the land he was to inherit, most of the villagers were sleeping after their midday meal. Under the metallic, blue sky a chicken-hawk was trying to steer its shadow over the trees in the windless afternoon. Mr Barzey's father, who was sitting at the top of the stairs of his son's house in the manner of a large bird on its expertly made nest, greeted the visitors with his cavernous smile, from which one tooth winked like a candle-fly at night time. He must have guessed that they had come to see Kwaku's uncle, for he pointed to the yard behind his son's large house, to the small cottage where Kwaku and his uncle lived.

One by one the villagers woke, roused by the chatter of the fourteen-strong family who had arrived at the height of the siesta and by the barking of Mr Barzey's dog. Some of them, too sleepy to care, dozed off again, but others came to see who was making the disturbance.

The tribe tramped up Kwaku's uncle's stairs, believing that they were not expected, for there was no one to welcome them. But Kwaku's uncle, who had been in the habit of taking his nap at that time on Sundays, had fallen asleep in his rocking-chair and was dreaming of a herd of goats walking across his chest.

Kwaku had forgotten about the visit and was playing cards with Blossom and her young man when a small boy came shouting his name and informed him that his uncle was expecting him home because "his lady-friend" had arrived. So Kwaku left, accompanied by the jibes of Blossom and her young man.

On the way he plucked the leaf of a caladium growing near the trench and polished his shoes, which were covered in village dust. He tried to wipe the sweat off his face, but without success, and was obliged to go back to Blossom's house to wash and put himself in a state suitable for the first meeting with the woman he was going to marry and would surely grow to love.

At the house Kwaku found two strange little girls of about three and four sitting on the porch, sucking their thumbs, and he heard the whooping and calling of nine boys despoiling his uncle's fruit trees at the back of the yard. He opened the front door and was presented with the strangest sight a young suitor might ever want to behold as he was about to meet his intended.

His uncle and another man were sleeping in two easy-chairs opposite other, the former snoring so violently that the cloud of insects attracted to his sweating face was blown right across the room, only to be sucked towards him again when he breathed in as violently, and repulsed once more when they were about to disappear into his mouth. The other man, his eyelids fluttering and his mouth drawn across his face in a childlike grin, whistled a popular tune as he exhaled, and followed it with a drum-roll sound while inhaling. On the far side of the drawing-room a strapping lady and a young woman who seemed destined to grow into a creditable imitation of the maternal model were sleeping with their heads against each other as if to advertise their striking resemblance.

Kwaku went to the back of the house, counted the boys playing in the fruit trees, added five to the number and made the total fourteen. One and one made two, he thought; and he came to the conclusion that he and his uncle were no match for the tribe scattered about the house and yard. So he tiptoed past the sleepers, out on to the porch, and in one bound cleared the sixteen steps of his uncle's front stairs.

"Kwaku, is where you flying ...?" one of a group of loafers at the canal bridge called out. But before he could finish his question Kwaku had turned on to the back dam path and disappeared behind a cloud of red dust.

He waited aback until the moon rose above the locust tree and the candle-flies had ceased blinking among the termite hills; then he made his way home, thinking he would invent a story for his uncle in the morning, rather than rack his brain after the strain he had been under during the last few hours. And so as not to wake his uncle, Kwaku crept up the stairs on all fours, gently pushed open the unlocked door and slipped into his bedroom at the back of the house.

But the next day his uncle informed him that everything had been arranged and that the marriage would take place when he was twenty-one.

"But I wasn't there!" protested Kwaku.

"I did tell them you're shy," said his uncle dryly.

"I'm not marrying that girl, you can bet your bottom dollar."

Then his uncle, imagining years ahead tied to his feckless nephew, lost his patience and said:

"You two-mouth idiot! The girl's got nearly everything you asked for! She's a seamstress who used to be a teacher; she does eat like a lady and don't care for her mother."

"I didn't say she musn't care for her mother!" Kwaku said, pouncing on his uncle's words in a dance of triumph.

"You said she musn't be too close to her mother."

"But I din' say she musn't care for her mother."

"Right! I not going argue with you. You either marry her or you leave and fend for yourself."

Kwaku feared it would come to this. His uncle had threatened him with expulsion once before, and with no relations to turn to there was nothing for it but to comply. Now he was doing the same again and was in a position to do so whenever he chose.

"Right!" exclaimed Kwaku manfully. "Since you forcing me I going marry this freak with the wart on her ass."

"Who said she's got a wart there?" demanded the uncle, alive to all his nephew's ruses.

"No, I not talking 'bout it. You want me to married a woman who going parade her warts every time she get undressed, then I going to do it. Let's set the wedding for tomorrow. Come on, ne? What you waiting for?"

"Hold on! Just a minute. We going discuss this business in calm words. Now who said the girl's got a wart on her ... situpon? Who said so? Well, tell me."

Kwaku was looking at him scornfully. "Is common knowledge in BV. Ever since she was a lil' girl and use to skin up her tail 'pon ...."

"Just a minute! Can you produce evidence?"

"Yes," declared Kwaku.

"What kind of evidence?"

"The girl sheself."

His uncle pretended to be amused. "Haw haw haw!" he bellowed unconvincingly, slapping his thighs. " 'The girl herself.' Haw haw haw!"

"Get her back here, ne," Kwaku said.

"What? So that you can make a fool of me again? In any case you can't very well ask her."

"Well, give me her address in BV and I going get her to come and own up to it."

"Ah, ha ha!" screamed his uncle. "If you don't even know where she's living how d'you know she's got a wart and which part of her body it's on?"

18

"Because," said Kwaku, lengthening the word, ostensibly to give it emphasis, but in reality allowing himself time to think up an answer, "because it's common knowledge. Even people who don't know where she living know it. Tobesides, I'm not arguing. I prepared to do anything you say. I not even going to bother to prove it. If you want me to married somebody with warts all over they ass I going to. I not saying nothing more. Just tell me what you want me to do and I going do it."

Kwaku's uncle thought of his dead sister, who had asked him to keep an eye on her son. She would turn in her grave if she knew that he was pushing her son into a marriage with a woman of *that* sort.

So Kwaku had his way and his uncle never mentioned the subject again.

Then one night Kwaku came home and declared that he was getting married to the same young lady from Beterverwachting. She and her father had come that day when Kwaku's uncle had been on an excursion in a launch. Kwaku had been promised two cows and the materials to build a house as a dowry.

"You know I can't understand you," said the uncle, torn between anger and a feeling of enormous relief. "What about her warts?"

"Well," remarked Kwaku, shrugging his shoulders and pushing out his lower lip like a man who knew a thing or two, "that was when she was a girl. It's gone now. These things come and go you know. You never can tell with warts."

"So in years you'll be a married man!" said his uncle, smiling and reaching for his evil-smelling pipe.

"No, they're publishing the banns next month in the BV church. It's in July. I told the minister. You've got to send your consent to him by letter with a duplicate for the marriage registry people."

Kwaku's uncle nearly collapsed with joy, and when he had recovered sufficiently, instructed his nephew on the morality of marriage.

"It's a union for life, and a very beautiful thing ...."

While Kwaku was being lectured his mind wandered; and it occurred to him that it was within the bounds of possibility that Gertrude-Gwendoline had a wart after all. If she had, it was certainly not on her face or on her hands or on her feet or all the visible parts of her fat body. This thought so plagued his mind that he could hardly wait for the day of his marriage and the night of that day when, exercising his rights as a married man, he would be in a position to see whether his anxiety was unfounded.

The day of the marriage arrived and the night of the day when everyone speculated on the possible reasons for Kwaku's preoccupied expression. But when he was asked he only laughed, denying that he was worried about anything.

19

Finally the tribe and their relations and friends abandoned the barbecue fires in the yard and the music of an old violinist, playing for a pound of meat from Kwaku's cow when it was slaughtered.

After the farewells, the departure which lasted as long as the fête had lasted, Kwaku and his new wife bade his uncle good morning and retired to the large bedroom which Kwaku's uncle was allowing them to use until their new house was built.

So the moment that Kwaku had been waiting for came at last, when he would find out whether he had bought his sweet-potato field with his eyes closed. And with the shedding of each of Gwendoline's garments Kwaku's heart thumped violently, so that when the last unmentionable cotton thing was let down he swooned and fell to the greenheart floorboards with a thud.

"Oh! Ah! Hee! Kwaku! Not now!" exclaimed Miss Gwendoline as softly as she could, fearing that her uncle-in-law might draw the wrong conclusion from his nephew's state.

She hurried into the kitchen without even bothering to stick a postage stamp on her navel and came back with a jug of water, which she threw on Kwaku's face.

But Kwaku, believing that somebody had come to steal his new wife, leapt towards her, and in the ensuing mêlée discovered that her skin was as smooth as sidium, without so much as a mole or birthmark, without even the slightest discoloration.

"You skin!" crowed Kwaku. "You got such nice skin."

And the couple started to frolic as if they were still engaged, so that Kwaku's poor uncle, unable to bear the torture, took up his bedclothes and went to sleep at the front of his house.

Truly, that was the way Kwaku acquired a sense of responsibility, out of gratitude that he had got a bargain. He was even able to forgive his father-in-law for delivering to him three weeks later a broken-down cow and its calf, and materials to make a house even smaller than his uncle's.

4   The metamorphosis of Kwaku

EVERYONE commented on the metamorphosis of Kwaku. His employer praised him highly and even claimed that the care and skill he brought to half-soling his clients' shoes had earned him the sort of reputation that attracted custom from villages miles away. He himself came to join the others who were to help build Kwaku's house. Kwaku's uncle, noting the change in his character, allowed him to build on his land at the back of his own yard.

The carpenter in charge of the project killed a chicken and sprinkled its blood in one of the foundation holes for the pillars on which the wooden structure would be built. And only then could the collective task begin, the sawing of imported white pine for the facing boards, the making of greenheart pins for the joints, the planing, hammering, mixing of sand and cement, the drawing up and modification of plans and all the other work necessary for the erection of the most modest dwelling-place.

While all this went on, much rum was provided to keep Kwaku's acquaintances happy, to banish the drudgery of work and convert it into the illusion of play. And during all this Miss Gwendoline came and went, bringing swank for the men and breaking ice, borrowing hats from the neighbours for those who did not normally work in the sun, and generally attending to all the needs to which she could possibly attend.

Since the men could only work on Saturdays – they had their own work during the week, while they spent all Sunday praying, reading the Bible and generally contemplating the condition of their souls – the new house was not finished until the following year. As was the local custom, Kwaku had to find a couple of hundred dollars to throw a house-warming party. But to his uncle's disappointment, and the disappointment of Miss Gwendoline as well, Mr Barzey refused to come, not because he looked down on people living in a smaller house than his or because he could not forget what Kwaku – he suspected – had done to his new water-tank, but on account of the sand dumped in his yard by the lorry driver who had delivered it, and the general confusion caused by the erection of Kwaku's house. His own house fronted the highway and everything delivered for Kwaku's new house had to pass under Mr Barzey's.

But when the house-warming was at its height and Mr Barzey heard his favourite piece of music being played by a makeshift band of musicians he relented and came over to join the revellers. His wife came too, following her husband an hour later. She had had some difficulty persuading Mr Barzey's one-toothed father that the excitement might kill him, and that it was best if he looked on from afar.

Blossom came as well, with her man-friend, who had not yet saved enough money to marry her. He was much more kindly disposed to Kwaku now that the latter was married and frequented Blossom's house less. The postmaster also came, as did the collector of rates and taxes who lived several villages away and hated collecting rates from Kwaku's village, the inhabitants of which were notorious for the abusive manner with which they discharged their debts.

All those who had helped Kwaku build his little house came and spent much time showing their wives which wooden pins they had made and which window-sills they had planed, which window-pane had been glazed with their own hands and which part of the eaves of Kwaku's porch they had helped to pattern with the hacksaw. In fact there were so many guests that some were obliged to spend much of the night hanging out of the window or sitting on a friend's shoulder. (At least that is what a Barbadian guest said. But you know what Barbadians are like when they get drunk, on Mount Gay or any other rum.)

Anyhow, there was a lot of screeching and laughing, much stamping and kicking in the name of dancing, much squeezing and poking in the name of fun, much quarrelling because wives did not wish to go home, and fretting because husbands wanted to stay, and altogether the sort of animation that prompts our newspapers to report, "Much fun was had by all."

Unbelievably, Kwaku's house stood up to the treatment and promised to last through the storms that came from the sea and stand up to the envious eyes of those villagers whose accommodation was rented. And the next day Kwaku moved in with his bride. Her proper name, in the good tradition of our marriage style, was Mrs Gertrude Gwendoline Kwaku Schwarz-Cholmondeley, wife of Kwaku Cholmondeley, apprentice shoemaker of the village of C. But everyone called her Miss Gwendoline, for no other reason than that the inhabitants of C had enough trouble of their own without cracking their false teeth on the name Mrs Schwarz-Cholmondeley. Even Mr Barzey's one-toothed father said "Miss Gwendoline", though the Lord knows that he had enough time on his hands to practise saying her name in full.

So Kwaku and Miss Gwendoline moved into their new love-nest and, as if Nature had been waiting for the signal, the children began to come. First, twins the next year, then a child each of the following five years. And before Kwaku could say "Boogooboo" he and his plump wife had seven children on their hands, four little Schwarz-Cholmondeley boys and three little girls of the same name, all healthy little socialists of a father who had joined the ruling party because he knew where his bread was buttered and who bottled his lemonade.

Blossom reminded him of her promise to use her influence to secure him a job as a driver, which was much better paid then shoemaking. Kwaku had chosen shoemaking in the first place because in the end he would be his own master; but now he seriously thought of taking driving lessons.

"Gwendoline, darling," he said one night, "I going to learn to drive and work with the Transport. I can't support a wife and seven children on what I getting."

"Kwaku, you not serious! I'd be alone till late at night whenever you on duty."

"It won't be so bad, darling, 'pon a starling. Every time I pass by in the bus I going beep my horn so you know I'm passing. And Uncle would be there in case anything happen."

"I know I won't be happy if you not there, Kwaku."

"Well, I couldn't very well take you with me, could I?"

"You don't love me any more," complained Miss Gwendoline.

So Kwaku swallowed his irritation and pursued his shoemaking. The shoemaker with whom he worked, a man in his sixties, was as healthy as he had been in his twenties. If Kwaku set up on his own it would have to be in competition with him, and there was little enough work as it was, since it cost almost as much to half-sole a shoe as to buy a new one. There was nothing left for it but to continue to work with the old man.

Miss Gwendoline, who was in the habit of massaging Kwaku's scalp before he went to bed, noticed his first grey hair one night. He was twenty-seven.

"Look, you got a grey hair!" Plucking out the phenomenon she showed it to her amazed husband.

And Kwaku fell to reflecting on his inability to keep a family, and his conviction that Miss Gwendoline despised him.

"A lot of men does get grey hairs at your age, but nobody does notice," Miss Gwendoline consoled him.

"But once they start they don' stop coming."

Kwaku's prophecy was fulfilled. He rapidly grew grey; and even his distress at being unable to shoe all his family or provide his girl children with more than one dress, or paint his house, which had never been given a coat of paint since it was built, could not match his dismay at growing grey, like Mr Barzey's father. The old rage which had accompanied him throughout his childhood and youth, and which had vanished with his marriage, came upon him once more. For no reason at all he would go past an acquaintance on the road and think to himself, "I feel like getting a gooseberry stick and lashing him!" or, "Suppose I was to tell him that his father was a thief?"

Kwaku's altered disposition showed in the expression on his face, which had turned sour, giving a certain mobility to his features.

"You looking, sour, man. Is all them children you getting. You see you uncle, he face as smooth as he ass. But he not goin' have nobody to look after him in he old age 'xcept you."

These observations were made by the oldest woman in the village, who would not accept that the world had changed for good and prophesied that the days of horse and carriage would come back again. Children would start obeying their parents again and all the derelict sugar estates would one day begin puffing again, fed by the old mule-drawn iron punts rusting away among the water hyacinths.

"It in' good for a young man like you to look sour. When I was a girl I wouldn't go out with a sour-mouth like you. If is you children giving you trouble, put them all out to sleep outside you door one night. An' if is you wife, hand she one box 'pon she face and don' say a word. Long ago ...."

"All right, Mistress, all right," said Kwaku, "I hear you."

That is how he found out what people were saying about him, and the old resentments were rekindled. Why could they not mind their own business? As if he cared about theirs.

Yet, despite his feelings, Kwaku was determined not to fall back into his old ways. He kept watch on those words lurking on the tip of his tongue, ready to tumble out at the slightest provocation, and encircled his temper with a wall of caution; so much so that even when he wished to make a pleasant remark he hesitated in case it was an outburst in disguise. Thus, if his features gave him away, his words and actions belied his expression, and people believed rather that he was suffering than that he was plagued by the old mischiefs.

Kwaku's uncle pitied his nephew for the burden of his children and respected him for his fortitude. He offered him an acre of the land he held aback, to grow something on. But Kwaku reminded him that he already worked from sun-up to sun-down.

"Where I going get the time from to plant land? If I go and kill myself with overwork is what my wife and children going do, eh?"

Kwaku's uncle chewed on his black-sage and reflected that Kwaku was becoming wise. In a way he longed for the old Kwaku who resembled the fisherman's wind, never telling anyone from which direction it was going to blow.

Thus Kwaku came to be sorely tried in his poverty, earning much sympathy for himself from his fellow villagers. But he did not take their sympathy at face value, knowing that if he were well-off those who commiserated with him now would stifle with envy.

5 Blossom's man-friend

ON SUNDAY as the godly were getting ready for church and the ungodly were reflecting on the transient nature of life, Blossom's man-friend Wilfred came over to implore Kwaku for help. Blossom had "pushed him out".

"An' what you want me to do?" asked Kwaku. "Push you in again?"

"Come round and talk to she, ne? My trunk under her house and I in' got nowhere to go. The night air don't agree with me, especially since...."

"She just put you out?" Kwaku enquired.

"This very moment."

The two went on their way without conversation, for Kwaku remembered how, at one time, Wilfred had not a good word for him.

No sooner did Blossom catch sight of her man-friend than she began abusing him again.

"You see this finger?" she asked, pointing to the fourth finger of her left hand. "It make to have a ring put on it. And this house make to have children. Promises, promises! I can't live 'pon wind. I want some action round here."

Kwaku went inside, but Wilfred would not follow him.

Blossom went round the house, pounding the floorboards as if she was testing them for wood-ants.

"He came behind you and got seven already. Seven!" she exclaimed, gesturing towards Kwaku.

"The first two was twins," Wilfred reminded her hesitantly through the window.

"Twins! When you give me *one* you going fall down dead with exhaustion. I don't want twins; one would satisfy me. Even if is a weakling like you."

"Go on!" said Wilfred. "Tell the whole world we business." Thereupon he looked towards the street, uneasy at Blossom's shouted disclosures.

"*We* business? From now on is *my* business, 'cause from now on you not crossing that door-mouth," Blossom said decisively.

"I tell you I marrying you next year."

Blossom flew into a rage. "That's what you tell me nine years ago. But I hear what you tell the tax-collector."

"What I tell the tax-collector?" asked Wilfred.

"You tell him you going marry me when fowl get teeth."

"Me? Me? That's a expression I never use! You ever hear me use that expression, Kwaku? Me? And tobesides the tax-collector don't like the people in this village."

"Well," said Blossom triumphantly, "is not the tax-collector tell me. It was *reported* to me by a third party. You get out of that one."

"Who?" asked Wilfred, visibly anxious.

"I not telling you. It was told me in confidence and I holding it in confidence "

And neither had any more to say to the other at that moment.

"And what you come here for?" asked Blossom, turning to

Kwaku who was sitting in her best chair, his legs crossed. "You in' got no time for me since you get married."

"Shut your mouth," Kwaku said mildly.

Wilfred was vexed that the reprimand brought no reaction from her. After she seemed to have calmed down he had edged a bit nearer to the door, hoping to ease himself through the doorway without her noticing. He was vexed at Kwaku's undemonstrative influence, at her obstimacy in holding on to her job with the Transport and at the photographs of her former men-friends staring down at him from the walaba boards of the partition and walls of the drawing-room. Whenever he objected to sharing her with her pictures she would counter that he lacked nothing and that looks of men in photographs did not kill.

Indeed, Blossom's tidy drawing-room was decorated with the relics from her previous relationships; a Djuka paddle from a friend who laboured on a timber grant in the Courantyne, the wheel of a defunct bus from the young man who had fired her interest in transport, a guard whistle from an acquaintance who worked on the railways and other objects which, according to Wilfred, served no purpose and only cluttered up the spotless room.

Kwaku was racking his brains to find a formula which might bring the two together. A year before, Blossom had given a dinner to which she had invited her former men-friends, the paddle, the whistle, the wheel and the others. But the hint was lost on Wilfred who no doubt considered that his entrenched position was unassailable. In fact, during the dinner he went about the house as if he owned it and, each time he passed the mirror in the kitchen – the house was divided into three rooms, kitchen, bedroom and drawing-room – he stopped to tell his reflection that if Blossom entertained any doubts as to his exceptional looks she now had the God-sent opportunity of judging by comparing him with the freaks eating in her drawing-room.

Suddenly an idea came to Kwaku just as he was despairing of finding his formula, and as he spoke he saw that Wilfred had edged through the doorway and was now sitting in a chair in the centre of the room with such a pained expression that you would have sworn he was still standing on the stairs.

"You want children and Wilfred don' want to get married," said Kwaku. Then, turning to Wilfred he asked, "Why you don' want to get married?"

"'Cause I don't like competition," he answered, casting a glance round the room. "Everywhere I turn, her friends staring at me from the wall."

Then, to Blossom, Kwaku said: "If he married you, you going take down the photographs?"

"I tell him so already!" she exclaimed.

"You *tell* me, but you also say you not doin' it till *after* we get married," Wilfred declared in an unusually wheedling voice.

"And I saying it again, I not taking them down until we become man and wife. You think I stupidy, but I not stupidy."

"Right," said Kwaku, sitting up like a judge about to deliver a judgment. "You not marrying she till she take down the pictures and she not taking down the pictures before she become your wife. Right! I say that you should buy Blossom the wedding ring and then she must take down she men-friends from the wall."

"All right," Blossom lost no time in replying.

She and Kwaku waited for Wilfred to agree to his part of the bargain. By now he had edged his chair right up to the dining table and was sitting with his elbows on it, his hand clasped in an attitude of intense concentration.

"I going buy the ring, yes, but only if she get rid of the paddle and wheel and all them presents I didn' give she."

Blossom thought that he had gone too far. Her secret dream was to have many husbands, all living in the same house, all devoted to her welfare. She had not once met a man with all the qualities she wished in a husband, the mysterious authority of her father, Kwaku's vulnerability and respect for her independence, the paddle's gentleness, the whistle's physical strength and the wheel's indulgence. Here, even before she married him, Wilfred was laying down conditions, behaving as if she was on her knees, begging him to put the ring on her finger.

"I not throwing them things away!" she said firmly.

"Right, right," intervened Kwaku, "you didn't say nothing 'bout that first, you know."

"I din' say that," said Wilfred arrogantly – he was by now standing by the bedroom door – "but I did always object to them things. What she want with a paddle and a wheel in the house? You ever hear anybody got a wheel in the house? Wheel make for travel 'pon the road and paddle make for river."

"Good!" Kwaku said firmly but patiently, sensing that Blossom was losing her temper. "You know what, Blossom? You must get rid of the paddle and the wheel and keep the other things. How about that?"

This time Blossom, lips pursed, was not disposed to give in so easily.

"I got to think about it," she said. She thereupon left the men and went into the kitchen.

"You're a good kunu-munu," Kwaku muttered to Wilfred. "You had she where you did want she and now you spoil everything with you haughtiness. You better agree quick before she

27

push you out for good."

She came back with two glasses of mauby. Serving Kwaku first she then gave the second glass to Wilfred with such an abrupt gesture that some of the drink spilled on his shirt front.

Blossom, out of pride, said no more about the matter, but both men knew that she had given her tacit consent to the arrangements.

Blossom and Kwaku sat in silence, but Wilfred, in an effort to test the seriousness of Blossom's intentions, slipped into the bedroom and began to rummage in the chest-of-drawers, under the pretence of searching for something. He would have liked to bring up his trunk but that would have been pushing his luck, he reckoned. Instead, he settled for a demonstration of his status in the home for Kwaku's benefit. Finding a pipe he had been given by Blossom as a present the year before and which he had never succeeded in getting used to, he put it into the corner of his mouth, disfiguring his lower lip in a manner that gave pipe smokers that particular distinction he so admired. He came outside and joined the other two and, like them, was soon engrossed in his own reflections.

The tinny ringing of the church bell had ceased and the sound of hymn singing from the church just off the Public Road rippled through the village. But no sooner had the voices died away than other noises floated on the morning air, intermittent sounds, the steady pounding of clothes being beaten by women doing their laundry by the roadside trench.

The sun penetrated into the corners of Blossom's dwelling, picking out, high up on the wall, the pupa of some insect that would emerge in a day or a week to fly out of the window, leaving an empty articulated shell behind. The patterns of the partition boards were not hidden by its layers of blue paint and ran in broken, irregular waves across their length, reflecting sunlight as trench water did when disturbed.

In the midst of such tranquillity Kwaku knew a vague distress, not the cares of supporting a wife and seven children, or concern with keeping the unwelcome side of his character in check, but an indefinable unease at his place in the life of the village. On occasions he felt that he was granted a certain time in it, during which he was expected to carry out some mission he had forgotten, while the days and weeks and months went by inexorably. Somehow Blossom was connected with his mission; and once or twice Kwaku felt that she knew more about it than he, and that she was astonished at his inaction. The strange mark of a predetermined course, of a journey to be undertaken, was evident in her behaviour as well, he thought. How else could one explain her preoccupation with the paraphernalia of transport, paddles, wheels, the furnishings of trains and such like? And Kwaku, on suggesting that she did away with her collection, saw in a flash the destruction of her relationship with Wilfred. But if he went back on his proposition and said that she ought to keep her presents, Wilfred would believe that he had done it deliberately, just to cause bad blood between him and Blossom.

He stayed with the couple until Blossom started cooking, but declined to eat with them. Miss Gwendoline could not stand him sleeping out or eating out, he declared.

Blossom made a gesture of exasperation but let him go without a word, since what she wanted to say she would not have said in Wilfred's presence.

Kwaku, half-closing his eyes to avoid the glare of the midday sun, made his way home. He sat down to eat with his family, after the three youngest were fed by his wife and the eldest girl, Rona, who had become the drudge of the house. While eating he surveyed his family and wondered how many children he would father in the end, for Miss Gwendoline was only twenty-seven years old and he was still inordinately fond of her.

"I wonder how many?" he said aloud.

"How many what?" Miss Gwendoline asked.

"Oh, how many days before Wilfred keep his promise to buy Blossom a married ring."

And he told her what had happened that morning at Blossom's house.

6   Kwaku and the one-toothed storyteller

KWAKU TRIED every remedy, tested and untested, to *cure* his grey hair. On the recommendation of the midwife, he rubbed coconut oil into his head during the time of the full moon, followed by a mixture of horse dung and garlic while the moon was on the wane. Though he noticed no observable difference on his head, it did not escape him that fewer customers came into the shoemaker's shop and that those who came spent more time looking for a dead rat than on discussing the state of their shoes.

So Kwaku decided on a much less offensive remedy. He woke up at precisely two o'clock in the morning and got Miss Gwendoline to stimulate his scalp with dried twigs from a young calabash tree, an exercise which gave him considerable pleasure but had no other result than that Miss Gwendoline became pregnant once more. Kwaku therefore decided that it was God's will that he should be grey, and that when all was said and done it was infinitely preferable to be grey than to be bald. Yet when he was told by Mr Barzey that his father was a faith healer who had coaxed back the black colour into an East Indian man's greying hair about sixty years previously, he lost no time in consulting the old man. He had insulted him time and again when he was too young to imagine that Mr Barzey senior could ever do him a favour, but reckoned that the old man was too decrepit to be vengeful. And he judged correctly, for the old man could not even remember who he was and kept calling him "Miss Gwendoline" because he saw him come out of the same house as his wife. In fact he even called Kwaku's children "Miss Gwendoline". No sooner did he see anyone emerge from the house at the back than he called out, "Morning, Miss Gwendoline; I think we're going to get rain." Or, "Howdyedo, Miss Gwendoline. How're things since you buried your husband?" The children giggled at old Mr Barzey's ineptitude, but the humour escaped Kwaku entirely.

Anyway Kwaku visited the old man and, after persuading him that he was still alive and that it was his wife's grandmother who was buried two years before, Mr Barzey senior winked at him with his single tooth and embraced him as if he had just come back from a lengthy tour in the interior.

Yes, there was a reasonable chance to recover the youthful lustre of his hair; but in the end it was all a matter of faith. And, since there was to be no demonstration, the old man and Kwaku spent the better part of the sessions talking to each other.

Kwaku thought Mr Barzey's father to be uncommonly pleasant and liked sitting in the large drawing-room, which possessed that tranquillity that denotes the absence of children. On one wall hung a calendar – known in the village as an almanac – and the floor, polished to a degree, reflected the easy-chairs as indistinct plaques of shadows.

The old man once wore glasses, but since he was never able to find them when they were needed he finally renounced the luxury, to the detriment of his relations with the villagers, who believed that he ignored them deliberately.

"Bring me that magnifying glass on the table," he said to Kwaku, after he had delivered a short lecture on faith as the prerequisite of any cure. "And the book."

Kwaku placed the book and magnifying glass in the old man's hand, and the book, when opened, turned out to be an album of old photographs.

"Ah, you wouldn't have guessed, eh?" said the old man. "Devious, isn't it? Very ingenious, I might tell you. That's how I preserved it all these years. They don't like reading, you see, the people who live in this house and those that come to this house. Most of them don't. So, a book with an old ugly cover escapes their attention. But what riches! What experiences! Do you know how I first became interested in photography?"

"You did take them yourself?" Kwaku asked in disbelief.

"I did, my boy. Look! The hands of an artist."

He held up his hands, pudgy, blunt-fingered hands which Kwaku could not associate with the refinements of the first album page, photographs of St George's cathedral and a lone woman wearing a dress that almost touched the ground.

Kwaku held his breath at the thought that he had misjudged old Mr Barzey, and the exaggerated opinion he now formed of him owed much to the fact that he once stood so low in his estimation. He turned the pages of the album slowly, reverentially, looking up from time to time as though he wanted to make certain that the old man had not gone away.

There were photographs of houses, people, of rivers, of ships moored to wharves, of the trams that once criss-crossed Georgetown before the American company that owned them stopped operating as a result of a strike by its employees.

"You'll never guess who that is!" Mr Barzey exclaimed with child-like glee at the puzzle he was setting Kwaku.

"No, I can't."

"That's Mr Gordon when he was a little boy."

"Mr Gordon across the road?"

"That's right."

Mr Gordon had made his fortune in England and had returned recently to build an imposing concrete house in the village. He now spent his days grinning at passers-by over his garden wall.

"You know how I came to photography?" asked the old man.

"Tell me, ne," urged Kwaku.

"You're going to laugh, mind you. One day – my family was living in Georgetown – I was only about ten. I and my father were walking past Bourda Market. You've never been to Georgetown? Anyway, it's one of the big markets with high iron railings round it. And opposite is a burial ground that's not used any more, all enclosed with tombs and all. It's been out of use for donkey's years. Only English people're buried there, rich people from long ago. Well, one midday in bright sunlight I was walking past the market with my father when all of a sudden I saw a procession of a hearse and carriages going into the burial ground, through the closed gate, as if it wasn't there. I let go of my father's hand and stared at what was happening. I tell you the people in the carriages were dressed like those you see in pictures of the early eighteen hundreds. I stood on the road staring, staring, until my father grabbed my hand and wrenched me away. 'Papa, Papa, did you see it?' I asked him, but he looked frightened and hurried up the road."

"Did he see it too?" Kwaku enquired, glad that night had not yet fallen.

"I don't know. But my mother told me later that a lot of people had seen the procession at one time or another and always at mid-day .... That's how my interest in photography started. I was so stupid at that age I thought I could take a photograph of that procession if I learned to use a camera and happened to see it again."

Kwaku forced himself to laugh, in order to hide his unease.

"Of course I didn't," pursued old Mr Barzey. "But I took many pictures of that burial ground."

Kwaku turned the album of leaves until he came to a series of pictures of the disused cemetery, forming, as it were, a deserted island in that noisy, thriving part of the town, as incongruous as a bed in the middle of a thoroughfare. He stared at the images, some of which were discoloured to a saffron hue, the pale glow of late afternoon; and his head swam at the thought of a shadowy imprint under the surface of the mottled paper.

"You're really impressed!"

"And you been living here all this time!" was all Kwaku could say in answer, convinced that these photographs were the first genuine revelation of his village existence.

"You see," said Mr Barzey confidentially, "in those days people went to the established churches in the day, because it was the thing to do. If they were in a decent job they knew what was good for them. But at night-time they sneaked away to their sect churches and gave full rein to their inner selves .... Ah, but that is only part of the secrets of my album. I've been watching you, at least until I stopped wearing my glasses; and I saw you straining at the leash and ending up a shoemaker."

Kwaku no longer heard what Mr Barzey was saying, for he was lost in a dream of far-away places. He had heard of La Penitence market, but never of Bourda; and this revelation persuaded him that there were many exciting things he was yet to learn about. His reverie was disturbed by a cry from the back yard and he jumped up to investigate, only to see one twin chasing the other towards the road. Rona was sitting at the top of the stairs, plaiting the hair of Irene her youngest sister who sat, head bent and body slightly arched to allow her as much room as possible.

Back in the old man's house Kwaku began to tell him about his anxieties concerning his family.

"And with another one coming up .... I don' know."

"Why not earn a little money on the side?" Mr Barzey suggested.

"Doin' what?"

"Fishing, for instance. You can buy a pin-seine net and try your hand at it with a friend."

32

"That'll take me away from the house at night-time, you see. And Miss Gwendoline don' like that."

"Women, women. Why not try photography?"

The two men discussed the alternatives that would not take Kwaku away from home when he returned from his regular job as a shoemaker. But the old man, exhausted at his unaccustomed effort at conversation, nodded off, leaving Kwaku with the album in his hands.

Kwaku opened the book of memories once more and, breathing life into the still photographs, imagined the subjects stolling along avenues of jacaranda, balustraded where they crossed streets with names he had only read in the papers. The boy rolling his hoop at the edge of the road would stop in a moment and then make for the other side through a break in the traffic.

Kwaku told his wife about Mr Barzey's book of photographs when they were alone, after the children were in bed.

"You like him, eh?" she observed, with that note of encouragement in her voice that, as much as any of her other qualities, made Kwaku appreciate her.

He spoke of the old man's suggestion about taking up photography, not forgetting to mention that the developing of his films would be done at home.

"But you not goin' take the pictures at home, though," she said, while attempting to re-thread her needle.

"Only in the village at first. And then I'd only go off on Saturday afternoon. I mean it."

"I don' mind," she agreed in a half-hearted way.

But Kwaku seized the initiative and promised her a sewing-machine.

"With all the work in the house, how much time I going have to sew?" she said.

"If we get somebody to help out in the house you could even sew for other people again."

Kwaku had not given up the dream of Miss Gwendoline working as a professional dressmaker for all the world to see. He himself had put it out in the weeks before his wedding that he was marrying a seamstress. But apart from a few garments which she had run up for two or three village women while they were still living in his uncle's house, before the children came, she had done nothing to establish herself beyond doubt as a *professional*. Not that Kwaku was complaining! Miss Gwendoline's mother had kept away – except when one of the children was to be delivered – as had the numerous tribe that had come with her. Their cow had died years ago, while the calf had been sold to help pay for the house-warming party, and the only

33

connection with the numerous brood was the materials with which his house was built.

No, if he was disappointed at Miss Gwendoline's record as a seamstress, he was one to count his blessings. Now old Mr Barzey whom he had once despised was treating him for his grey hairs and would also impart to him the techniques behind the secrets of his album leaves. Surely he had arrived at a turning point in his life.

Kwaku, in the course of treatment for the ailment of grey hairs, learnt how to handle Mr Barzey's box camera, with its fixed lens opening and shutter speed. And, as the old man came to like and trust him, he told him more about the pictures in his album.

The young man with bow-tie and moustache curled at the tips had been his best friend.

"A piece of time," said Mr Barzey, "we were inseparable. When we were at school together he used to take out his glass eye and show it to the other children, just to get attention. Looking at him you wouldn't think he had a glass eye. And the women liked him! Never found out what happened to him. And you see that one there, that sore-ass looking fellow? He was a bitch! He was ambition daddy! His father left him a little plot of land when he died and he went to live in the rickety cottage on it, to everybody's surprise – because he was a town man with no feeling for the country. After a time his neighbour's cows began to abort, and no one could tell why. The government agricultural officer came down, the vet, everybody he could get his hands on. But the cows continued to abort. The neighbours thought that somebody was working obeah on him, so he abandoned his land and went abroad. He couldn't get anyone to buy it from him. So you know what that bitch did? He entered into occupation of the man's land! And when the neighbour came back twenty-three years later and claimed his property from him, he lost the case in court because that bitch had got a good title to the pro-perty by adverse possession. The poor man used to come up to look at the place that did belong to him once and used to tell people he'd kill the bitch one day. But *he* didn't get him. It was his own wife who did get him. After he got rich he married a girl eighteen years old. He was in his forties. Brother! He was so jealous of the woman he shaved off her eyebrows, so the poor thing couldn't go out. He told her she didn't need to go out anyway because she had a maid and everything she could want at home. And if she wanted anything else he'd see that she got it .... But she got him in the end."

"How?" asked Kwaku, his mouth half-open.

"So people say, she got him. He died in his bed, in his sleep, with a nail hammered into his skull, people say. That man had an obses-sion with flowers and long words. Funny, eh? The bitch!"

After every faith-healing and camera session the old man would recount a tale from his album, and Kwaku, like a small boy, made him repeat some of them, never tiring of his fluency and the pageant he evoked with his words and gestures.

"Life and understanding of life can be summed up in three words," he once said cryptically. "Clock, book and train. Just three words."

"What you mean?" Kwaku enquired eagerly.

"Never you mind. Knowledge isn't a good thing. Beyond a certain point it can be only destructive. Up to a point creative, yes .... I don't know. What can I do all day, except think, eh? The fools retired me. You ever heard anything as stupid as retirement?"

Kwaku never learned what he was retired from and felt he could not ask.

And in that way a close friendship developed between Kwaku and the old man.

7   The delivery of Fabian

A LINE OF about twenty persons was waiting on the Transport bus. In fourth, ninth and twentieth positions stood three old people, two men and a woman, quietly searching the horizon for the big vehicle. The fields unfolded on either side of the road, concealing the insects that would later defy the night with their shrill cries. In short, all was peace.

In the distance a momentary shaft of light announced the approach of the yellow giant. When, as the bus slowed down, it was evident that there was not enough space to accommodate everyone, the three old people leapt forward, bludgeoned to the ground those who were in their way and clambered into the stationary vehicle. They then settled into their seats as if butter would not melt between their gums.

That incident was reported by a woman from B village, which boasted the most honest people in the country. And, to confirm her reliability as a witness, the lady in question was wearing glasses with very thick lenses whose powers of magnification were great indeed.

The old folk in the village of C were a force to be reckoned with. But people had little to fear from them, since they usually kept to their houses and were only a danger to marauding children and unsuspecting people in bus queues.

However, there were two occasions when they came out in strength, for wakes and births – death and the resurrection of the dead, one old woman explained. And now it was the eve of the day –

or night – when Miss Gwendoline was to deliver herself of her eighth child, and the old women were gathering their strength for the vigil. They would be consulted if anything went wrong; and if the young midwife from Ann's Grove came to supervise the delivery they would see that the ancient traditions prevailed. And the mother would be properly instructed how to protect the new-born child from Old Higue, who would be sure to be flying through the air on the night of the birth as a ball of fire, to settle on the house and wait for an opportune moment to enter and suck the child's blood until it died.

Kwaku very properly interrupted his sessions with Mr Barzey so as to be near his wife when the pains began. His mother-in-law had come to assist her daughter, who could not imagine giving birth without her mother by her side. And although the alarm had not yet sounded two old women were busy around the house, helping to fold towels, to sterilize containers of every size and to clear the big bedroom of any objects and garments not necessary for the delivery. Miss Gwendoline's mother, with Rona's help, was feeding the young children and preparing them for bed.

But the pains did not begin until the day after the following day. And very soon the old women and Miss Gwendoline's mother had their work cut out, for the midwife had not arrived.

Kwaku was sent out of the room; and of the children only Rona was allowed up, to keep two kettles on the boil and supply the guests and helpers with chocolate.

Occasionally the unoccupied guests – Mrs Barzey, a half-dozen women neighbours and two old women who complained incessantly that during Irene's birth they were allowed in the bedroom – fell silent when Miss Gwendoline's high-pitched whine threatened to become a scream. But soon their interrupted conversation was taken up again, accompanying the noises in the bedroom, from which bands of light stretched to the corners of the sloping roof.

"Push! Push, Gwendoline!" her mother was often heard to exclaim. Then in an impatient voice, "You'd think it was the first time! Push, I say! That's it, girl. That's it! You see? You see! Ahhhh!"

"The last time I been in the bedroom with she, Kwaku. Remember?" one of the disgruntled old women said, addressing him. "An' the birth was over in no time. Listen to them now. Is hours!"

"Don' bother, Kwaku boy," the other disgruntled old woman consoled him, "at least the other seven did *live*."

A portentous silence followed this remark, and Kwaku fell to thinking about his perversity in wishing his eighth child to live, despite his inadequate resources.

"I mus' be mad," he muttered.

Then a piercing scream woke little Irene, who began to cry. Rona ran into the smaller bedroom in order to comfort her younger sister and Clayton her youngest brother, who kept repeating that he wanted the baby to be a girl because she would not wear his clothes.

"Rona!" a voice called out.

She hurried across the unpolished drawing-room floorboards into the large bedroom, where she saw her mother surrounded by the women. Her face was covered in large beads of sweat and in her eyes was a look of such terror that the child became afraid, because on previous occasions it had not been so.

"Tell you father to take off his shirt and give you," her grand-mother ordered. "Hurry!"

Kwaku had heard the order, for the partition did not even rise as far as the base of the roof joists; and when his daughter came outside again his shirt was nearly off his back.

Once inside again she handed the shirt to one of the old women, who grabbed it and thrust it under Miss Gwendoline's nose.

"You see? Is you husband shirt," said the mother, trying to calm her. And she herself tried to get her daughter to take hold of Kwaku's sweat-scented shirt. But in her pain she clung to the bedclothes, showing the whites of her eyes and alternating periods of rapid breathing with periods of calm.

"It not so bad if is the child," remarked one of the disgruntled old women in the drawing-room. "But suppose Miss Gwendoline go and dead now, eh?"

Her companion opened her eyes wide, glimpsing the perspective of a much greater calamity.

"You right, you know, when you come to think of it. It wouldn' be the first time." And she sighed deeply, as if Miss Gwendoline were already dead and the delivery had been transformed into a wake.

"It could be the child *and* Miss Gwendoline. They could both dead, both all two," put in her disgruntled friend.

Kwaku's patience was sorely tried and to avoid insulting them he went out into the yard where, above, the universe of stars stretched away on every hand. He realized that the delivery was insignificant in the vast plan of things; but he could imagine no greater disaster than his wife's death. He wanted no one else as a companion and was incapable of trying to please any other woman. If she did go it would be the end of a long journey undertaken unwillingly, but during which he had learned to love deeply for the first time. Often he had wondered what his mother looked like and now he was certain that she had resembled Miss Gwendoline.

Around him were the houses in the village, the smell of vegetation and the night, like some vast, sombre well. A longing seized him to walk along the village road, in the very centre of the empty road, and inhale every breath of air as if it were a gift of such rare sustenance that the sleepers would envy him if they knew.

Thinking he heard someone calling, he went back to the house.

"Kwaku," one of the old women said, "she still there."

He was overcome with rage that he was obliged to remain silent in the face of a ritual which required him to permit people who were not even neighbours to camp in his house and provoke him, just because they were not allowed into the delivery room. Years ago he would have set fire to their clothes or put salt in their chocolate. And even a few weeks back, before he became friendly with Mr Barzey, when his old character seemed to be re-surfacing, he would have had to make a supreme effort to control himself. Now he only needed to think of Mr Barzey's opinion of his conduct, of "letting himself down" as the old man would say, to restrain himself.

It occurred to Kwaku that Blossom was not among those on vigil and he recalled how her presence at the birth of Rona, his second-born, had provoked sarcastic comments from one of the old women.

"Child, you not expecting too, eh?" the woman had enquired, looking pointedly at her belly, and then at Kwaku.

He was wrenched from his reflections by a thin, sharp cry from inside. His child was born. And, inexplicably, he was overcome by an unusual urge; he wanted to kiss the two old women who had just been washing their mouth on Miss Gwendoline and her unborn child. In an involuntary action, he approached them, but held back at the last moment, uncertain as to what their reaction would be.

"Kwaku man," said one of the old women, "everything turn out all right. It's the Lord's will."

Rona appeared with a tray on which were bowls of steaming chocolate, which she handed round to those on vigil.

It was about four in the morning, and already the hum of the odd vehicle came to them from the Public Road. Someone turned off the bedroom light, so that the drawing-room was now in semi-darkness, lit only by a feeble, colourless glow. Indistinct voices in the bedroom gave Kwaku reason to reflect on his wife's condition; but almost immediately his fears were allayed by his mother-in-law, who came out, beaming with satisfaction.

"Is a girl, Kwaku."

"What you going to call it?" asked young Mr Barzey's wife, who had hardly spoken during the vigil.

"How he goin' know that so soon?" butted in one of the disgruntled old women. "How he goin' know that when he din' even know if it'd be a boy or a girl? Some people!"

"We going to call her Fabian," he answered.

"Fabian!" nearly everyone said in chorus, astonished at the unusual name.

Mrs Barzey got up, smiling. "I've got to go to work tomorrow, so I'll go and get some sleep."

Kwaku accompanied her to the foot of the stairs.

"Listen," she said, turning back to address him. "Does the old man say anything about us?"

"Mr Barzey? No!" replied Kwaku promptly.

Young Mr Barzey's wife smiled, and Kwaku saw that she was ashamed at her own question.

"It's only that he's so obstinate," she said, "and he talks his head off, but not to us .... Forget I asked, please."

Kwaku watched her going up their back stairs.

Now that he knew that everything was well Kwaku had no desire to return upstairs. He imagined his wife being bathed in the aluminium tub in which three or four old eight-cent silver bits had been placed. His mother-in-law was sure to have brought these coins along, for the bit had been taken out of circulation since the middle 'thirties and was only kept by some women for that purpose. She was not the witch he had feared she might be and at a time like this who could replace her, he thought.

When the sun came up he would bury the umbilical cord in the back yard, alongside those of his seven other children.

Miss Gwendoline was fond of telling him of the twenty-three people living in her parents' house. Not only her sisters and brothers lived there, but her maternal aunt's family as well. From the way she spoke it was a happy home and Miss Gwendoline's natural distinction was the best proof of it being so. The twenty-three toothbrushes hanging from a rack in the kitchen wall, the constant coming and going in the evening of children from houses around who wanted to buy black pudding made by Miss Gwendoline's mother, the pounding of the record player which entertained not only the children of the house but their friends sitting shoulder to shoulder along the wall – all these things Miss Gwendoline spoke about with affection and nostalgia.

Kwaku was called in to see his wife and child when dawn was already astride her galloping horse. The room reeked of rum which had been sprinkled on the floor at the onset of the birth pangs and in place of the neat array of sheets, towels and garments was the disorder he had come to associate with the aftermath of birth. A pile of linen in one corner of the room rose above the tub with grey water in which his wife and child had been bathed.

He sat down on the edge of Miss Gwendoline's bed and smiled at her, as embarrassed as if she were a stranger. Then he craned his neck to see the bundle lying between her and the partition just where the two malicious old women were sitting, on the other side in the drawing-room.

"Help me with the tub, ne," his mother-in-law asked.

She and he held the tub between them and lifted it gingerly, so as not to spill the water. Having emptied it into the shallow gutter running along the Public Road, he attended to the burial of the umbilical cord, wrapped in thick, greased brown paper.

By this time the guests and helpers had gone home and Kwaku's mother-in-law had made a bed for herself in the drawing-room, next to Rona, who was lying full-length on the couch, her little body heaving and falling in sleep.

Kwaku went and lay down beside his wife, thinking all the while of saffron photographs and the mystery of birth and death.

8 How Kwaku fell foul of his employer

WHENEVER Kwaku managed to put aside a little money he bought a roll of film for old Mr Barzey's box camera. The first time out with the box he wandered around the countryside all day in search of suitable subjects to photograph, and came back late in the afternoon, having attempted to take shots of a sailing boat far out on the ocean, which he was barely able to see with the naked eye.

Old Mr Barzey went out with him the following Sunday and managed – in the space of half an hour – to use up the roll between the house and the bridge over the drainage canal, a distance of only one hundred and fifty yards. He had photographed his son's house, an abandoned dray-cart at the roadside, whose shafts were embedded in the dust, the mosque where the local East Indians worshipped and the bridge itself, which he took from the unusual angle of a bateau moored to the canal bank.

The old man's eyes danced on seeing the film. He developed it himself in his bedroom, converted into a dark-room for the purpose. His large pupils, which left little space for the whites of his eyes, twinkled at the results of the craft he had not practised for so many years.

Kwaku came home the next evening to find prints of the film floating in the Barzeys' kitchen sink. The waves in his two shots of the ocean were recognizable as waves, while a solitary gull riding the warm air-currents over the fore-shore could not be mistaken for a carrion crow. But of the sailing-boat there was no trace.

"Look at that sea, Mr Barzey," crowed Kwaku. "You ever see a sea like that? I'm going to name that photograph 'The Mighty Ocean' and enter it in a exhibition. To think I been wasting my time as a shoemaker all these years! Man! F8 lens aperture; shutter speed 1/60th of a second; standing with my back to the sun; no filter because the sky wasn' too bright. And the ocean surging just like I order it. Cheese and rice! Talk 'bout a natural born talent! Some people would've took some puny subject for a first try. But me! Kwaku Cholmondeley did grapple with the sea!"

And he began to perform a mock battle with the sea. He seized it by the throat, threw it to the ground and then took a snapshot while it lay stunned at his feet. He just had the time to put the camera aside before the sea recovered and surged at him once more. This time it took him by the waist and heaved him up, so that his toes barely touched the ground. Groaning as if his efforts to free himself were vain, Kwaku contorted his body. But suddenly he recovered and heaved so violently that the sea fell back, allowing him enough time to take his second photograph.

"That's why you can't see the ship," he said. "All that foam and thing."

Exhausted from his pantomime Kwaku was breathing heavily while he looked down lovingly at the two prints of his first photographs.

"What're you going to be like when you really take a decent picture?" Mr Barzey remarked dryly. "It's not bad, though, for the first."

The two men went out into the gallery. Mr Barzey told him that his daughter-in-law looked at him in disgust when she found the prints in the sink and had to postpone the washing-up.

"You can't stop women," he remarked softly. "A little thing like that. Her bleddy washing up! When I have artistic fish to fry. God! It's enough to make a man go and buy false teeth. She goes out to work all day and the first thing she wants to do when she comes home is use the kitchen sink. What imagination!"

"You'll have any trouble with them later?" asked Kwaku anxiously.

"No! Trouble? She's so stubborn! She'll turn round and round that sink without saying a word until one day she'll find a way to take it away from me."

Kwaku's passion for photography came to the ears of his employer who was one of these men who felt that his employees were his property and became indignant on learning that they spent money on enjoying themselves. What irked the shoemaker most of all was that Kwaku, with wife and eight children, could find the money to buy a roll of film from time to time. On one occasion he severely reprimanded his young apprentice of six months' standing for going to a dance. Threatening to cut his meagre wage, he said he hoped he could rely on his "sense of proportion" in future.

Well, look story! The shoemaker came in on the Tuesday morning, neglected to say "Good morning" to Kwaku and began to read the "In Memoriam" column in the newspaper. He then passed on to the "Births and Deaths" columns and after that tackled his horoscope, which informed him that all was well with him that day and that anything he undertook would be crowned with success. Needless to say he read Kwaku's horoscope next. "Be polite to colleagues today. Any untoward occurrence will be for your own good. You have strayed from the straight and narrow path."

The shoemaker looked out on to the street, an imperious expression in his eye. He had always been endowed with an insight that raised him above other men.

"Kwaku!" he called.

Kwaku took his time, and when he arrived before his employer found him bristling with anger.

"You didn't hear me call you?"

"Yes, and I come."

The employer flinched before Kwaku's indifference; but recalling the horoscope he went on.

"I hear you've been taking photographs. I hear you've been walking about the village with a camera ... like a tourist."

"You hear right."

"So where you get the money from?" asked the employer.

"From my wages. Where else? I run through my wife vast fortune in the first year of my marriage, you din' hear?"

"Stop this insolence! Stop it!" the shoemaker ordered.

His plan of intimidation having failed, he pointed with trembling hand to the newspaper. But in his rage and confusion he showed Kwaku his own horoscope, so that Kwaku read, "Anything you undertake today will be crowned with success."

"I read it, you dotard," Kwaku told him. "I read it and I can write it. But I hear your wife does write your letters." He laughed out loud, as if he had just said what he had always longed to say.

"Out! Home! Away!" screamed the shoemaker.

"How you mean 'out'?" asked Kwaku, afraid of the consequences of his insolence. "Is who going do the shoes? The apprentice can't do them. And you no ...."

"Out of my establishment!" thundered the angry employer.

"Right! But don' come round begging me to come back. Right! You know my house, but don' come round. Lot 74C, third house at the back is my direction, but don' come enquiring where K. Cholmondeley live. Don' ask Mr Barzey, who does live in front me uncle, who does live in front of me, because he not going to tell you anything. And although Mr Barzey dog don't bite don' pass his house to come in the back yard looking for me because once I make up my mind, my mind is made up! Don' go asking Blossom for me either, because though she's a good friend she won't give anything away."

Kwaku stopped, wondering what effect his words had had on the old shoemaker. They had had some effect, because he did not repeat his order for Kwaku to go.

"To think I give my life blood to this job all these years," Kwaku continued in a more humble tone, "burst up all the fingers of my left hand with your hammer! That's what you get for loyalty. Lord, I does dream 'bout shoes! The other night I wake up in a sweat shouting, 'Shoes!' and nearly frighten my wife and the baby to death. When everybody wearing sandals they buy from the store I got my whole family sweating out they foot and stinking out the house with proper shoes out of loyalty to you .... But if you say I must go, I going go. One thing I got is pride."

Kwaku lifted his head up in the air and placed his right foot in front of his left, leaving his employer in no doubt that his pride would not allow him to beg.

"Well," said the old shoemaker, "you're a grown man and I shouldn't have called out to you as if you were an apprentice. And I can see you've got some qualities. Not that you're good enough to set up on your own or anything like that ... but you're promising. And I've got to admit you come to work early every day ...."

These words were spoken as the young apprentice walked in, a half-hour late. The shoemaker slapped him vigorously on his head as he ducked under the flap of the counter.

"You even too lazy to lift the flap," he shouted. "I can find ten like you every day. Go on! You get my blood up and you'll find yourself on the road, good-for-nothing nincompoop!"

The youngster disappeared into the back shop, leaving Kwaku and his employer to continue their duet.

"All right," said the shoemaker, addressing Kwaku. "I suppose I'm human. I does lose my temper like everybody else. Let's drop the subject."

"Drop the subject?" said Kwaku, beaming like tiger on his first outing with his lady-friend. "No, don't drop it, just let it float gently to the ground."

Kwaku nearly peed himself with relief. He felt like inviting his employer to dinner and regaling him with fermented fruit juice and the jokes he had heard from old Mr Barzey, especially the one about how the elephant came to be endowed with such a minuscule penis and the donkey with such a terrifying weapon.

"You better get back to work then," urged the shoemaker.

Once alone, Kwaku's employer vowed to have his vengeance. He had overplayed his hand. How could he afford to lose Kwaku, especially with a light-headed apprentice coming up? Kwaku was intelligent and could not fail to appreciate that he had bested him in the encounter. He would almost certainly recount the incident to that Mr Barzey, about whom he was forever prattling. And knowing Kwaku he would embellish the incident, casting himself in a heroic role. He, the shoemaker, would probably end up crawling on the floor begging forgiveness. Oh, yes! Kwaku was Kwaku. He would never change. Somehow he must contrive a plan to humiliate him and thereby redress the balance.

"Meanwhile," the shoemaker reflected, "I must get some instant satisfaction. I'm not the type who can wait."

He cast his mind around, so to speak, as a fisherman would on a stretch of water known for its game fish. He thought of his young apprentice, but at once rejected him as being too worthless a catch.

"Ah," he said to himself, "the little ...." Here the shoemaker uttered an unseemly expletive that can be heard on any village street, but which good Christians could not bear to read without fearing for their place in the green pasture of the great beyond.

"Ah!" he repeated, "the little fiddler!"

His mind had hit upon his wife's cousin, who had come, according to him, to stay with them for two weeks. That was two years ago. Not only was he still in the house but he had sent for his lady-friend and little daughter. They were eating him out and were like batty and po with the neighbours he detested. "Yes," he thought, "don't they say that guests and fish stink after two days?"

Then, after a minute's musing, he burst out in a fit of muttering. "Ah! The little f... fanny-doodle! Wait till I get home. If the three of them're there tomorrow I'll renounce all interest in footwear."

And the shoemaker could not wait for twelve o'clock, his lunch hour. He kept asking passers-by what time it was, although he knew that once the top of the bridge was in shadow it would be time to go home. There was a good three feet to go yet.

When a band of light a millimetre broad stretched across the top of the bridge of the shoemaker's shop he stood, poised on tiptoe, ready to take flight.

9   How Kwaku fell foul of the Party

JUST AS Kwaku was leaving for work one morning his uncle met him at the foot of the stairs.

"There's a chap wanting to see you. He's from the Party. I didn't let him knock you up. Miss Gwendoline might worry."

"What he want to see me for?"

"Dunno."

Kwaku followed his uncle up the back stairs and into his drawing-room.

"Sit down, comrade," said the stranger, who had not bothered to get up.

"Sit down? What for? I'm on my way to work."

"Sit down, Kwaku," his uncle advised.

"I don't even know you," declared Kwaku, taking a seat opposite the young man.

"But we know you. You're Kwaku Cholmondeley, right?"

Kwaku did not answer.

"We'd better come to.the point, as you're on your way to work," said the young man, who had crossed his legs and placed his straw hat on his knee.

"According to our information, you've been making disparaging remarks about the Party."

"Me? If is one thing I take care to do is avoid – you understand? – *avoid* talking 'bout the Party, even with Party members. I not stupid."

"Didn't you tell somebody," and at this point the stranger took out a notebook and read from it, " 'Is a lot of nonsense. I don't have to pay for the children school books, but when they hold a meeting I had to contribute money to the Party'?"

The young man looked up expectantly, while Kwaku seemed lost in thought.

"Well, did you?"

Kwaku cast a glance at his uncle, who was sitting on the edge of a chair placed between Kwaku and the visitor.

"I remember saying something like that," admitted Kwaku. "But I don' remember the exact words."

"Good. So you admit it."

"More or less."

"How much you contributed at the meeting?"

"I can't remember. How you expect me to, after so long ago."

"But it was less than the cost of the books if you had to buy them, wasn't it?"

"I suppose so," said Kwaku, angry that he had to submit to this youth's interrogation.

"That is what we call disparaging the Party," declared the young man, like a lawyer who had just put down a witness.

"Wait, man," Kwaku retaliated. "You come to see me early in the morning to tell me I musn't say what's true!"

"What's true?"

"I don' pay for books, but I have to make contributions at meetings."

"Yes, Mr Cholmondeley," replied the young man, with infuriating calm. "But you said it was nonsense."

"So you mean I musn' say what I think!"

"You musn't disparage the Party. It can't be nonsense if you pay less than the books that you would otherwise have to buy. And remember, education in this country is free, from nursery to university. You know anywhere else in South America where education is free?"

The young man tried to stare Kwaku down, but the latter would have none of it and in the end he had to avert his gaze.

"Don't be late for work," said the stranger, looking at his watch.

Kwaku's uncle closed the front door behind the young man and shook his head.

"You have mouths to feed," observed his uncle, "so you've got to be careful."

"But who reported what I said?"

"You stop worrying about that and hush your mouth in future. Go on to work or you'll be late."

"To hell with the shoemaker!" exclaimed Kwaku. "He's another good one. It couldn't be old Mr Barzey. He couldn't care less. But is who?"

Kwaku tried to recall the incident, remembered that it was in the school hall, immediately after the meeting. He was surrounded by a number of the parents, some of whom were making remarks similar to his.

"I don't know why you're working yourself up," said his uncle. "All you've got to do is be careful what you say in future."

"I gone," Kwaku said, nodding as he went out into the sunlight.

He explained why he was late to the shoemaker, who with a curious smile kept saying, "Th! th! th! Such times, such times."

"You can't trust anybody these days," Kwaku remarked. "I wasn't the only one saying it. You mean I can't open my mouth to talk now?"

"Th! th! th! Such times, such times."

"What's the point giving it with one hand and taking it back with the other?"

"Th! th! th! The times, such times."

"Mr Barzey was right .... I swear 'pon the grave of my dead mother I'll break his neck if I find out."

"Th! th! The times, such times," said the shoemaker, knowing full well that Kwaku had no idea where his dead mother's grave was.

"He was only a young fellow," complained Kwaku. "That's what get my goat."

"Such times!"

And Kwaku, directing a contemptuous look at the shoemaker,

went into the back shop to attend to his half-soling.

The shoemaker rubbed his hands gleefully. Now *that* was his idea of bliss. If everything in life went so well, how joyful the evening of his life would be!

His resolution to put out his parasite relations had not gone well. His wife's cousin asked for two weeks' grace, and his wife begged him to agree to the reasonable request. After all, it was her favourite young cousin; he was only fifty-three and had just caught a chill. Anyway, putting Kwaku in his place was enough for the time being.

"I bet he won't be so cocky for some time," mused the shoemaker.

And thereupon he settled down to read the "In Memoriam", the "Births", the "Deaths" and the "Horoscope" columns of his favourite newspaper, which he liked particularly for its objective treatment of the news. Despite its meagre resources it was possibly the outstanding paper in South America and shone with the brilliance of Venus on a fore-day morning. That is why the shoemaker pounced on the "In Memoriam", the "Births", the "Deaths" and the "Horoscope" columns with the avidity of an in-mate of the Mental Hospital who is brought food by a considerate relative.

10   Miss Gwendoline's jealousy

ALAS! Old Mr Barzey's attempts to cure Kwaku of his grey hairs came to nothing.

"It wasn't for want of trying, Kwaku," Mr Barzey assured him.

"I know, Mr Barzey, it wasn't for want of trying," Kwaku conceded. "But you can cure fowl when it got pip, and dog when it got mange; yet when it come to my grey hairs you can't make a impression. You got to admit, is funny. I'm a young man. I just past thirty. A lot o' men not married yet at thirty. I'm in the prime of life, but my hair grey. Something must be wrong somewhere."

"I don't know what's worrying you. You got a lot to be thankful for; and besides, you're coming on as a photographer."

"That's another matter," Kwaku broke in. And he went on to tell him about the incident at the shop.

"The next time he gives you any trouble," said Mr Barzey, "let me know. I'll go and settle him."

"What you can do?" asked Kwaku.

"Plenty."

"Like what?"

Mr Barzey explained that he knew the shoemaker's family. They all had something to hide. The shoemaker's father was always dressed in black, appropriately.

"Why appropriately?" enquired Kwaku.

"The attire of vultures. The man was an undertaker, by nature a scavenger. Even his women he got that way. I've never known him to go out with an unmarried woman. It always had to be a divorcee or a widow or somebody whose husband left her. He'd pose as a protector and as soon as the woman came to rely on him he'd make his move. He even swindled his own wife. Not that she was any better."

The shoemaker's brother was blind, according to Mr Barzey. Nobody knew what happened to him; one night he just returned home, blind as a bat.

"They come from this village?"

"No, from Nismes, West Bank, Demerara."

"Anyway, go on telling me about the blind brother," Kwaku urged his friend.

"Yes, man, he was the most notorious of the lot. He knew everything that happened in the village. If somebody came from outside to find out about the old hand-made bottles he knew exactly where to send a boy to dive for them in Canal Number One. If somebody's daughter did go and get baby he knew who the father was, better than the girl herself. You wanted to emigrate he could tell you exactly how to go about it, whether the country you wanted to emigrate to banned black people or not, how to get around the regulations and so on. If you wanted a job in such and such an office he could tell you if the head of the department would take a bribe or not. He used to sit in his drawing-room with his hands on his head listening, listening."

The shoemaker, Mr Barzey told Kwaku, had not always been a shoemaker. There had been some shady business about his wife. The story went that during the big fire in Georgetown in the early 'sixties she had stolen bales of cloth during the looting and, unable to carry them home by herself, got a little boy to fetch a taxi. The chauffeur helped her to stack away the cloth; but when she went round to the other side to get into the taxi it drove off with her stolen goods. Left open-mouthed at the roadside, she stared after the fast-disappearing vehicle, muttering to herself, "Some people don't got principles!"

"The next time you've got problems with Mr Shoemaker, just come and tell me," Mr Barzey advised. "And meanwhile you go on taking your pictures."

Kwaku was not aware that he had adopted some of his friend's gestures, even affecting that calm exterior that was natural to many old people and which did not correspond with his excitable nature. Kwaku had no illusions about his dependence on Mr Barzey and often remarked to Miss Gwendoline that he would not know what to do with himself if the old man died.

"You got eight children and me," she told him meaningfully. "I don't got any time to be lonely. Apart from his daughter-in-law I don't got time to friends with nobody."

"What about Teresa and Grace? And Charlene?"

"I know. But I say I don't got time. I din' say I don't got friends. Give them a chance they'd be round here all day. But I got eight children."

She did not want to offend her husband by reminding him that he had brought about his isolation in avoiding the company of men his own age.

There was good reason for Miss Gwendoline's testiness. Blossom had just been round to announce that she was to be married, and invited the family to the wedding. She had not yet told Kwaku of his friend's visit and held back out of a vague resentment towards Blossom, who had, nevertheless, always behaved correctly.

"You friend getting married," she said, looking up from her ironing to see what effect her words would have on him.

"Not Blossom!"

"Who else?"

"At last he buy the ring," Kwaku observed, and, inexplicably, began laughing.

"Is why you laugh?" Miss Gwendoline asked, placing her iron on its rest and demanding an answer with her unflinching gaze.

"I don' know," Kwaku answered. "Just so. He's been promising to put that ring on her finger for a couple of years now."

"But what's it to you?"

"Nothing."

In a flash he saw that his wife was jealous of Blossom. Perhaps that was why she hardly ever came around. He had always attributed her neglect to fear of what Wilfred would say.

It was late December and Christmas was only a few days away. Miss Gwendoline saw her husband leave the house and her resentment grew. She placed the iron on its stand on the floor, to allow it to cool before putting it away. Then she took some molasses and honey from the cupboard in order to prepare a Potagee cake, the bol-de-mel that was her Christmas speciality. Her grandmother was of Portuguese extraction, so that many of the customs of her family had passed down through Miss Gwendoline's mother to her household and were now part of the way of life of the Cholmondeley family, like the egg yolk which, on a certain day of the year, was placed in a glass of water, and according to the shape it assumed – church, bottle, tree, hair – pointed to events in the future; or the sharing of aniseed bread by the nuns on a Catholic feast day, a piece of which was kept hung over the doorway for the rest of the year, so that by some notional multiplication the household would never go hungry. Unable to secure any almond nuts, an indispensable ingredient in the cake, she made do with peanuts. But no one except herself appreciated the extent to which the quality had suffered, or the weakening of the tradition.

The half-dozen rice-bowls with their soft, green shoots gave off a rank odour; and despite Kwaku's suggestion that Miss Gwendoline should leave them on a window-sill in the drawing-room, Christmas or no Christmas, she clung to her customs and the memory of her own childhood home, with its antimacassars and flourishing bowls of rice stalks, half-filled with water.

She was not only jealous of Blossom, but of old Mr Barzey and his influence on her husband; and if she was always encouraging Kwaku to associate with the village men in his age group, it was only because she believed that some other acquaintanceship would weaken his ties with the two.

The news of Blossom's impending marriage should cheer her up, Miss Gwendoline told herself; instead, it had had the effect of water on the dormant seed of her jealousy. After all, Blossom was not going to leave the village. Besides, her house with its calabash tree growing, as it seemed, out of the very bridge over the gutter, looked on the Public Road for all to behold; and it was not unusual to see her lying in a hammock slung under the bottom house, waiting – Miss Gwendoline was convinced – for Kwaku to pass by.

The worst of it was that she could not reproach Kwaku with lack of concern for his family or with neglect of his children, or laziness. He was a good man, a much better man than he used to be, according to the villagers. It was this damned photography which, in the beginning, he practised on Sundays but now took up all his Saturday afternoons as well. And Blossom! Ugly, utterly devoid of any quality that might conceivably appeal to a man!

Miss Gwendoline hoped, and even prayed, that Kwaku's hair would fall out, so that he would be unattractive to women. Instead, he had gone grey, a discoloration that endowed him, in her opinion, with still greater appeal.

When, that morning, Blossom announced the news, her impulse was to chase the young woman from her house. She gave her a cup of ginger tea instead and treated her as she deserved, with friendliness, and even promised to show her how to make black pudding, which she had been making lately and selling to her neighbours. The night before she dreamt that she had fallen into the latrine in the back yard, and in her struggle to keep her ahead above the filth she saw an enormous crapaud staring at her with its watery eyes. Suddenly, its already bloated body swelled out, and it began to croak with an in-

50

sistent, terrifying bellow. As a child she used to go in constant fear of falling through the opening of the seat of the latrine in her back yard and of being devoured by the crapauds which spent their lives staring up expectantly from the pit of faeces. Then the first person she was to see that day, apart from the members of her own family, was this Blossom, who came to announce her marriage and awaken in her a violence that was not of her character. She was wearing a bodice of white batiste with sleeves of inset lace and perpendicular pleats down its front. All the accoutrements of an independent woman ... while she, Gwendoline, had to work all day, and much of that day in a kitchen so tiny that she was constantly knocking her elbows against the cupboard, with its legs resting in containers of water to keep away the ants.

Miss Gwendoline's eyes filled with tears at the reflection that her anxieties must be groundless. Everyone knew that Blossom loved her man. Indeed, he was the one who gave her trouble. She made up her mind to banish her fears. Her children were her insurance for the future. Blossom had none, and must be nearly thirty years of age.

"Ma! Ma! Is Mother Sally!" one of the twins shouted.

"Go on then, ne," Miss Gwendoline told her son.

He ran out on to the road, followed by his three brothers, in pursuit of the masquerade band which it had been rumoured would be coming to the village. No one believed, because the last visit had taken place more than five years before.

It was indeed Mother Sally, a powerful man dressed in women's clothes, who was striding along the Public Road on high stilts, casting glances from left to right like a chieftain dispensing wealth. Around him were minor dancers and acolytes armed with fife and drum, seemingly mindless of the crowd following them. Nearly the whole village was there and little Clayton pointed out their father, the shoemaker and the apprentice standing on the shop bridge.

"Look Pa and the fat-up shoemaker," Clayton said, nodding towards the other side of the street.

Old Mr Barzey had come out as well, with his faded cork hat and drainpipe trousers, affecting not to hear Mr Gordon hailing him from just above his concrete wall. Only Mr Gordon's eyes and bald head could be seen and it was easy to pretend that he was invisible.

"Good morning, boys," Mr Gordon said, consoling himself with a greeting for the twins, who started laughing when they were out of earshot.

The crowd followed the masquerade band in awe, impressed more than anything else by the fact that they were not performing. The arrogance of the transvestite dancer on stilts, transformed by a frock, but masterful in his manner, attracted everyone's gaze.

A short drum roll called the crowd's attention to the lowlier members of the band, attired in tunics of rich red and blue and gaudy trousers that came down just below the knees. When Mother Sally stopped on her stilts the crowd stopped as well. And at a signal, fife and drum pierced the afternoon calm, putting to flight a flock of jumbee birds. Then with twitching shoulders, as though unwilling to show their hand, the minor dancers began to perform. Unexpectedly one of them appeared to fall on his side, like an oriole in distress, only to recover before he struck the ground, clutching in his hand the coin thrown by an admiring woman. The crowd roared, forgetting the giant towering above them. And the old were fired by the dancing, recalling the stirring season in their youth, when masquerade bands roamed the countryside before the penance of Christmas Day.

Then, all of a sudden it began, as unexpectedly as the visitation of a dead relative. Mother Sally lifted her skirt and spun miraculously on her stilts, in the manner of a buck-top in its final gyrations. Fife and drum redoubled in intensity, closing their eyes at the blinding sweat that rolled down from their forehead, distorting their features like men possessed by Ogun or the Holy Ghost. One woman in the crowd, unable to contain herself, began dancing and was immediately joined by several children who improvised at the feet of the lofty dancer from an unknown town.

The procession moved slowly, flouncing down the road with a long line of traffic behind, drawing women and old men to their windows and emptying the shops of their customers and owners.

Then it was over, slowly, yet suddenly, leaving children with indelible recollections of a distant past from the African coast and a glimpse of all but withered roots.

The boys were full of the experience for weeks afterwards, so much so that the more enterprising among them made stilts of their own and tried to emulate Mother Sally.

The season fell away into the New Year, when villagers who had quarrelled visited one another in order to become reconciled. And showers occasionally obscured the countryside, disturbing its drainage trenches with momentary circles of shifting light.

With February came the start of the new dry season and the publication in church of the banns of marriage between Wilfred Service and Blossom Dean.

After the expense of Christmas, the villagers were obliged to save for yet another celebration and buy or make presents for the couple.

"Whoever heard such foolishness?" Kwaku's uncle observed. "They've been living together the last ten years. If that's not marriage, what is it then?"

Kwaku explained to him that Blossom wanted to get married in white. "You can't live together in white, can you?" he countered.

But his uncle's view of the matter was more cynical.

"It's the presents they're after, if you ask me."

"They not asking you, though," said Kwaku. "Tobesides, all you got to do is make them something with them waste pieces of wood you always talking about."

Kwaku was referring to his uncle's job as a joiner. He often complained that the country could not afford to throw away the bits of waste wood left lying about the joiner's floor.

But when it came to it Kwaku's uncle was in the thick of the preparations for the wedding and the reception afterwards.

11 Marriage

BEYOND THE trench on the other side of the road a herd of cattle was munching the grass in a field dotted with white egrets. One of the cows knelt gently before collapsing on its side, only to be followed soon afterwards by another, until within a quarter of an hour the whole herd was reclining under the afternoon sun.

Occasionally a couple in their best attire would pass by, the woman with her right hand on her head in an effort to prevent the wind from blowing her hat away. It was the afternoon of Blossom's wedding.

Only two days before Fabian, Kwaku's baby, had fallen ill; and, despite the régime of congo pump tea prescribed by the herbalist, the infant grew worse. The night before Kwaku and his wife slept with the night light burning, as much to find their way about in case they had to get up as to keep away spirits that might harm the child.

Since the racial disturbances, many women recently delivered claimed that they had seen Churael bending over their infants in order to kill them with her touch. Now Miss Gwendoline declared that the night before she herself had seen the East Indian spirit.

All through that brilliant day the children played outside, except Rona, who remained in to do the housework or relay messages to her brothers and sisters. Kwaku wanted to send her to represent the family at the wedding, but Miss Gwendoline would hear nothing of it.

From the window Rona could see the couple on their way home from the church, the bridesmaids and best man behind them, followed by those who had attended the ceremony. And as they turned out of sight up a village road Rona wondered if she would ever get married. She could not understand why her mother was making such a fuss about Fabian's illness, for it was obvious to her that the baby was not very sick.

So it turned out, indeed, for the same night the infant slept soundly and her mother was not required to get up once.

In her canister Miss Gwendoline had saved a few dollars, the proceeds of sales of her black pudding to the people around. The following day she cooked an elaborate meal for her family, to celebrate Fabian's recovery, she told old Mr Barzey whom she met at the tank early that morning. In fact it was a meal of atonement for having duped her family into believing that the infant had been ill, just to take their mind of Blossom's marriage. The infant's illness had been nothing more than profuse sweating induced by a concoction of bush tea she had given it. The tea had done no harm.

After Kwaku said grace the family fell to, chattering and drinking their soup at the same time.

"Nobody running back to school to play marbles," warned Miss Gwendoline. "I got a big surprise for all you."

"What?" demanded one of the twins.

"You can tell me, Ma. I don' go to school," piped little Irene.

"And me!" shouted Clayton. "I don' go neither."

"Come on, tell us, ne?" Kwaku pleaded.

"Is duck!" confided Miss Gwendoline in a whispered exclamation.

"Duck!" came a chorus from the children.

"After this?" asked Kwaku, pointing to his colaloo soup.

"Is duck. I cook two duck with breadcrumbs and stuffing."

"Rubby dubby, jumbee bubby!" screeched Clayton.

"Rubby dubby, jumbee bubby!" Irene mimicked, with no idea what the words meant.

Rona understood that the grand occasion had something to do with Blossom's wedding and the baby's illness, but could not get to the bottom of it. Before she went to school her mother had sent her aback to collect the young leaves of the water bhagee which grew wild in the Conservancy. It took her so long that she was late for school. If she had known of the special meal she would have collected the leaves with more willingness.

Kwaku and the children rushed through their soup so as to come to the duck as quickly as possible; and Rona had to stop Clayton from putting the enamel plate to his mouth.

"What wrong with you? You going spill it."

But Irene, attempting to follow her brother's example, had already spilled hers.

"You see!" Rona declared, angry with her little sister.

"Is nothing," Miss Gwendoline said, in an effort

to calm her daughter.

She set about taking off Irene's dress, while the others fidgeted impatiently.

"Look what you do now," said Damon, the eldest son after the twins, who was the most composed of the children. "If if wasn't for you the duck would be on the table by now."

Kwaku got up to take over from his wife and when she came back from the kitchen with the first duck on the tray Irene was already undressed.

"Rubby dubby, jumbee, bubby!" shouted Irene without Clayton's inspiration.

"Stop it," Rona chided her mildly, envious of the indulgence shown her younger brothers and sisters.

She could not wait to get a piece of the duck in her mouth, but, a model of restraint, she watched while her father carved it on the salt-glazed dish.

"Me first, Pa," one twin suggested. "I'm the oldest."

"You not older than me," his twin brother corrected him.

"I born before you!" came the prompt retort.

"He born before me, Ma?"

But that argument came to an end when Kwaku placed a slice of duck on their plates simultaneously. Each looked suspiciously at the other's plates and would probably have started arguing again had their mother not come in bearing above her head a huge soursop.

Kwaku accompanied the carving with exaggerated miming for the children's benefit. Shaken by Fabian's illness and disappointed that he had missed Blossom's wedding, he had left the house sullen in mood. But his wife's high spirits, the unexpected banquet and the spectacle of his family, united and in rude health, brought out the best in him.

"Well, duck," he said, addressing the remains of the bird on the dish, "you had you day. All them days swimming in the trench, all them nights sleeping with you head tuck up under the wing! Now you cork, duck! Quack, quack! Quack!"

"Make fowl noise now, Pa," begged Clayton.

And Kwaku obliged. He stood up, spread his arms out and emitted the noise of a chicken that had just laid an egg.

"Tuk, tuk, tuk, tawwwwwk!"

"You always ask stupid things," a twin said to Clayton, seeing his father's conduct as unnecessarily childish.

"When I was a girl," said Miss Gwendoline, sitting down at last, "I see a duck dive in the trench and never come up again."

"What happen to it?" enquired Philomena, the girl after Rona, who was as quiet as Damon.

"Alligator get it," his mother said gravely.

"They had alligator in your trench?" Clayton asked, open-mouthed.

"Plenty plenty," replied his mother.

Kwaku, at his most whimsical, then related how he used to court Miss Gwendoline. He would sweet-talk her while feeding the alligators.

"And one day a big alligator did creep up on me. But before he could take a bite out of my batty I see him out of the corner of my eye. You mother stand aside and watch as I struggle with the monster from the deep!"

"But the trench not more than four feet deep," one of the twins objected.

"Bigger alligator come out of that trench, son. They call it alligator trench. But I was telling you ...."

Kwaku related how their mother stood by, hands clasped and face turned aside as he wrestled with the alligator. She kept saying, "Uh! ooh!" in a hardly audible voice, and now and then threw a handful of earth at the brute. But it took no notice of her, so intent was it on dragging him down to its watery den; but in the end he overcame the beast by tearing its head from its body.

Although the older children believed nothing of his alligator talk they were none the less impressed by Kwaku's display and clapped when he sat down.

Finally they came to the soursop, which their mother had been peeling between mouthfuls, each mashing his portion of the fruit to a pulp in milk poured into a bowl for them.

"What about the sugar?" one of the twins asked.

"Oh, yes, the sugar."

"I goin' get it," said Rona, who went to fetch the packet of brown sugar from the kitchen.

The sweet, rich taste of soursop reduced the flow of conversation; and the twins began talking of school and its vegetable garden where the bora beans grew as long as one's arm under the influence of artificial fertilizer. And the meal ended with an explanation from the twins of the advantages of artificial fertilizer. Then the twins and Damon went off to their games of marbles, while Rona and Philomena, the other sister who attended school, cleared the table before occupying themselves with the washing-up.

"Rona!" called out Kwaku from the bedroom, where he had followed his wife. "You and Philomena take Irene and Clayton for a walk in the back-dam."

"The sun so hot, Pa," objected Rona.

"Wear a hat, then."

"Is only I got hat, Pa."

"Cover the others' head with paper, then."

A couple of minutes later Kwaku shouted out, "You gone yet?"

"No, Pa," Rona answered.

"Why not?"

"I can't find paper."

"You got hair 'pon your head."

By this time a sort of hysteria had crept into Kwaku's voice.

"What get into him?" whispered Philomena. "And why Ma not saying nothing?"

"Don' ask me," Rona answered.

But Philomena sensed that she knew more than she wanted to tell.

"You going, girl?" shouted Kwaku once more, almost weeping with impatience.

"Yes, Pa, I find some paper."

Kwaku waited another minute, but not hearing the children leave he called out, "Philomena, girl?"

"Yes, Pa?"

"Is where you there?"

"Here, Pa."

"Why you not gone?"

"The paper, Pa."

"Paper can't walk, paper can't talk, fold it so and put it 'pon your head."

Rona and Philomena were certain that their father was weeping.

"I gone, Ma," Rona finally called out. "I gone, Pa."

"I gone, Ma. I gone, Pa," came Philomena's voice.

"Good!" Miss Gwendoline called out.

Then Clayton and Irene shouted out from the yard where they had been waiting for their sisters.

Two bed-boards went "Budoop", the bedclothes went "Swish" as Kwaku and Miss Gwendoline played a game resembling a combination of "Hide and Seek" and "Doctors", which ended with Miss Gwendoline shouting out, "O Kwaku! Kwakuuuuuuu!"

"Budoop!" came the noise of another bed-board falling to the floor.

"Kwaku, darling."

"Yes, dearest?"

"You did like it?"

"I did adore it ... but number nine child would kill me. We got eight already and I not going for no record."

"What you thinking?" asked Miss Gwendoline after a while.

"I thinking," said Kwaku reflectively, "I thinking we start with soup and end with foop."

"Where you going?" she enquired, seeing him get up from her side.

"I got to work. I got a feeling I late already."

"I wonder if the children clear the table," said Miss Gwendoline, speaking as much to her husband as to herself.

"How they going clear the table when I send them off to the back-dam?"

"That Philomena so lazy!" complained Miss Gwendoline. "She does let Rona do everything."

Kwaku sat on the edge of the bed as if he had the afternoon off.

"You better dress yourself before they come back," advised Miss Gwendoline.

Kwaku went to work and, for the first time in his career as maker of shoes, fell asleep at his bench, no doubt overcome by the excessive heat.

12 A plague

C VILLAGE and others along the coast were singled out, God knows why, for an attack by locusts; and in a matter of weeks the insects' pernicious attentions cost hundreds of coconut trees their branches. At first patches appeared throughout the length of a branch of one tree, like the incursions of some fearful disease. But before it was stripped, gaps opened up in the sheen of nearby branches, and in the end the palm stood denuded, an outcast among others. Then, here and there in the hundreds of fan-like crests of the trees around, the sores broke out, to spread with devastating swiftness until, across the landscape, the skeletons of branches hung like shredded rags, offering no resistance to the wind.

Within months the whole coast was afflicted, so that villages like C, Mahaicony and Hope, which were vast coconut groves, found themselves in serious financial difficulties. Fêtes and celebrations were no longer held in C for many of the inhabitants feared that they would eventually lose their jobs, depending as they did, directly or indirectly, on coconut harvesting.

Kwaku was warned by his employer that if the affliction continued he would have to be sent home until the trees recovered and business picked up. He could not afford to pay him when no money was coming in. The apprentice would have to go next week as things stood.

Everywhere there was despondency.

In order to save money the women of C went aback to gather firewood early in the morning. The man who came round in his cart with his bundles of walaba cursed them and went on to try and sell his cart-load of wood elsewhere.

The villagers of C forgot their differences, and in a display of friendliness born of desperation invented ways of helping one another and made certain that their words, indeed their thoughts, were acceptable to the Lord's ears. Men took to addressing women with excessive respect, calling them "Mistress" and reminding themselves that they were the bearer of children.

At sundown scores of men lined the dam enclosing the Conservancy, clutching a length of baited wire, while at night some of them took their chance in the bush, miles aback, in the hope of trapping labba or some other small animal.

In contrast, Kwaku, who was too lazy to go into the bush to hunt and too impatient to wait for fish to bite, went looking for iguana in the nearby trees but rarely caught any. His lack of experience caused him to go past the trees in which the animals were lying up, and even where their tracks gave them away they were too well camouflaged to be seen.

The first week the shoemaker confessed that there was no money with which to pay him Kwaku lost his temper, remembering old Mr Barzey's stories of his family's notorious reputation. But Kwaku saw how other families were going hungry and agreed to wait. Better that than lose his job, he thought.

With little work to be done in the shop he was home for most of the day and, rather than face Miss Gwendoline, spent his spare time in his uncle's house or in Mr Barzey's company.

Young Mr Barzey and his wife both worked with public corporations, as Blossom did, and were not affected by the blight on the vegetation. But knowing her father-in-law's affection for Kwaku too well Mrs Barzey locked away all the food and drink in her bedroom before going to work.

"I told you about her," said old Mr Barzey, "but you didn't believe me."

Indeed, as the blight-days went by and many families were reduced to hand-to-mouth existence, people ceased to share the animals they caught with their neighbours. One man was stopped by an acquaintance on his way to the Conservancy.

"You catch anything?" he asked him, looking down at his closed basket.

"Nothing, man! Fish not biting. Real hard times, ne?" In his basket were a score of huri he had taken in three hours' fishing.

Miss Gwendoline thought it best to send Irene and Clayton to her mother's home and Kwaku himself took his two youngest children there. He came back late in the afternoon with two parcels of food and high praise for his in-laws.

"Nice people. I did always say so, from the first time I set eyes 'pon your mother and father sleeping with they mouth like that!" he declared, snapping his fingers. "I'm a good judge of people. You remember what I tell you about Mrs Barzey? Remember I tell you she and she husband like dogs? Remember? She come over here with she soft voice and fancy manners the night Fabian born. And you know what she does do? She does lock up her food so that her father don' go giving people round about. They don' even got a chick or a child. Look how the teacher does help she neighbours! And she got she sweet-man to feed *and* his outside children. *And* his alsatian dog. And I'll tell you something: that's no rice dog! *He* don' live on leavings from the table. Is meat he does eat every day. Offal, my dear. Hm! When last we eat offal? I hear she ordering offal from the travelling butcher with the twist-up hand who does scratch he nose while he waiting 'pon his customers. If you see me bring home offal one night you'll know where I get it from. And it won't be from the butcher in Ann's Grove either."

Kwaku let out a suck-teeth to denote his disgust at the state of affairs and the behaviour of some of his fellow men.

"To think I got to feed my family on cuirass and skin fish! Skin fish! My kinna! The thought alone of eating skin fish used to make me come out in a rash. The teacher sweet-man always out of work, but he don' eat skin fish. Is scale fish for him, and when it got too much bone he does threaten to beat she."

"Is a good thing we didn' move to Mahaicony," said Miss Gwendoline, referring to an invitation Kwaku had received three years back to help pioneer a leather-cutting business in Mahaicony. "I hear the drainage canal there clean out of fish."

Kwaku, after a meagre lunch, went to Mr Barzey, and on returning found Blossom speaking to his wife.

"Is you, Mrs Service?" he addressed Blossom mockingly.

Both women fell silent and would not look him in the eye.

"What happening?" Kwaku asked. "I does smell or something?"

"I bring some money," said Blossom, "but Miss Gwendoline wouldn't take it."

She undid the knot in the string round the notes.

"I can afford it!" Blossom declared, offended at Miss Gwendoline's refusal to be helped by her.

She was not aware of the effect her expensive clothes had on Kwaku's wife.

"Tell me at least why you wouldn' take it," Blossom pleaded.

"I don' have to tell you!" Miss Gwendoline exclaimed. "Why I have to tell you? Thank you very much, but take your money somewhere else."

Kwaku, ashamed that he could not provide for his family, dared not intervene. Heaven knew what Miss Gwendoline thought of him as things were.

Blossom looked at him for support.

"It's her pride," was all he could contribute to the argument.

"But is good, honest money," she repeated. "Think of you youngest, at least. *She* don' got no pride."

The baby was on Miss Gwendoline's arm, being gently swung to and fro to keep it quiet.

"One day you might be able to help me, you know," Blossom said, in an effort to be conciliatory. But Miss Gwendoline shook her head decisively.

"Go somewhere else. *He* might want to accept your gifts," Miss Gwendoline declared, nodding towards Kwaku, "but not me."

Blossom bit her lip, mortified at Miss Gwendoline's uncompromising attitude.

"Well, I tell you something," she said finally. "If you don' take what I bring I never going set foot in this house again."

Miss Gwendoline smiled in singular fashion and Blossom understood. At that moment she felt that she hated Kwaku's wife.

"Goodbye, then," said Blossom with a nod. "Nobody ever insult me like that before. I suppose they got people who set out to insult others. But I want you to remember that *I* didn' do you nothing. Is *you* that do me something."

"I goin' talk to her when you gone," suggested Kwaku.

But Miss Gwendoline reacted like a whip-lash.

"I don' want you to talk to me 'bout her! And I don' want you to talk to her about me neither."

Then, not caring to dissemble any longer, Miss Gwendoline said to Blossom, "What you waiting for? You can't tear yourself away? I don' like your money, I don' like you, I don' like you cl .... Is what you waiting for?"

Blossom left without a word, clutching the offending parcel to her bosom.

Kwaku went to the door, not daring to go after her, nor wishing to face his wife either.

"I can't help it if I not earning," Kwaku told her, when he turned round.

"*I* din' say nothing."

"But you thinking it. If I was still bringing in money she wouldn' have come here."

"She come here 'cause she sweet on you," said Gwendoline. "And if you can't see that you got cross eyes!"

"Then why she been running after Wilfred?"

"Don' ask me," said Miss Gwendoline, in a tone of voice which dismissed Kwaku's question as irrelevant.

"What itching you is that I not earning."

"No. You're not the only one," answered Miss Gwendoline, little comfort in her voice.

"Then why you going out of your way to make my life miserable? I din' invite the locusts to come and eat the coconut trees. I hear that in Mexico when they finish eating up the trees and bushes they does set about devouring the people. If they start doing that here I suppose you going blame me for that too."

"I din' say I blame you," she said quietly, looking away into the distance as if the house had no walls. "I thinking, that's all."

"See what I mean. I did tell you! Well, what you thinking then?"

"I thinking it's up to a man to feed his pickney. My father never had to send any of his children away because he couldn' provide for them."

And a long silence came between the couple who, in their fourteen-odd years together had rarely spoken a reproachful word to each other. The calm manner in which his wife had spoken hurt him deeply. He had sensed that she held it against him for not bringing money into the house, but the proof was infinitely more hurtful than the suspicion. He had no desire to reproach her, for she missed Clayton and Irene and had spoken from her heart. But he was misunderstood. Behind it all, he was certain, lay his friendship with old Mr Barzey and Blossom's attachment for him. She herself had said that he was not the only one in the village who was not bringing home money. Indeed a number of men had left the village to find work, and many more were thinking of doing so. But what could he do? She would not permit him to seek work outside the village.

"I'm going down to the shop to see if there's any work," he said, and left her sitting alone with the baby on her lap.

He knew that there was no work in the shoemaker's shop but went all the same, just as children were pouring out of the primary school at the corner. And to avoid meeting any of his own he turned off the Public Road and headed for the back dam, with no particular object in view.

Out of a dead tree lying athwart the drainage canal were growing monstrous fungi, excrescences of an indeterminate colour which, as a child, he was taught to avoid. They were a meal for spirits, round which they gathered on dark nights. That was one of the delicious terrors of childhood, made bearable because they were shared by his acquaintances who, like himself, had no idea how their parents provided their meals or the clothes on their back. He used to envy them mother and father, visible emblems of their superiority. Now as a man, those who still lived in the village envied him in turn Miss Gwendoline, who accommodated, in his mind, the vision of mother and wife, the personification of childhood dreams.

A row of eucalyptus trees had been planted on each side of the canal to arrest the erosion of its banks. Already full-grown, their peeling barks shone, now grey, now blue, like extraordinary ornaments in a derelict cottage. Beyond the koker a winding path led aback; and as Kwaku flattened the grass with his heavy step the noise of a fleeing lizard would cause him to look down. The bottom of his right trouser leg was covered with sweetheart seeds, telltale evidence that he had been aback. It would take him a good half-hour to pick them off.

"What you been aback for? You could've at least bring home some huri or hassa!" he imagined Miss Gwendoline saying to him when he got back.

"Probably she wouldn' say that at all," he thought.

He was taken by a sudden desire to rush home to discover whether his wife had regretted speaking like that to him.

"It's only be worse," he decided, pressing on towards the coconut groves.

In a flash Kwaku saw the answer to his predicament; he must go and find work in Georgetown. A friend of his had once travelled there on an excursion while still a child, and had spoken of the other-worldly scents from a coffee-grinding shop and the iridescence of rain-spattered pitch roads. Others from the village had gone and come back smoking perfumed cigarettes, and their pockets bulging with dollar notes. The ring of their coins was more opulent, even though they were identical to the coins used in C village; and those who had sojourned there for a few years walked with their feet pointed in the direction they were heading, a feat beyond most physical achievements.

The shadows began to lengthen as Kwaku approached the Conservancy, and at the sight of two fishermen with their baskets over their shoulder his awareness of his hunger grew. He had eaten nothing since lunchtime and that meal had been frugal.

Kwaku went out of the men's way, not wishing to become involved in conversation. He knew what he would say and what they would answer; and with each word he would swallow more air and aggravate his hunger pangs. He would look at the stricken palms and say, "Things couldn' be worse," one would answer: "You right, man." Then they would assume an appropriately haggard look to avoid any suspicion of harbouring a concealed supply of food. Kwaku would then tell them how a cousin of his in Mahaicony was living on wild coffee, nettle leaves and burra-burra berries, while the people in town were dining on sweet potato and tripe. And, increasingly nervous because he was anxious to impress, Kwaku would utter some foolish remark which would give rise to talk. "In my opinion," he would say weightily, "is some kind of worm. It isn' locust at all ... ." And the men would gnash their teeth in rage, believing that either Kwaku regarded them as ignoramuses or that he was wrong-headed enough to think up such nonsense. However one looked at it, the outcome of the conversation would not be happy.

So Kwaku hid behind a carrion-crow bush and only came out when the men were well on their way.

Why did he come there, after all? he wondered. He had no rod, no line. It was getting dark and the way back was long. Perhaps it was to look at the reflection of the moon in the Conservancy or to listen to those mysterious sounds that fill the air over land uninhabited by humans, where green lizards paled under an early moon and night grew soft on wings of thyme and lavender.

Kwaku reflected that if he were a giant he could easily have uprooted the eucalyptus trees growing beside the canal. Then, armed with a ladder, a supply of paper and paint and unlimited time, he might restore the coconut trees to their original splendour, so that those coming aback would run to the village, announcing that they were saved by a miracle. He could even hear them shouting: "The locusts gone! They gone! Is a miracle! God hear we prayers. Come and look if you don't believe."

In labba time the village would empty and even Mr Gordon would come out from behind his garden wall and show the whole of his body. They would all flock to see the trees fanning their curved trunks in the leisurely winds that blow out the flames of candle-flies.

In the ensuing excitement the shoemaker would probably pay him his back wages and restore his dignity in the eyes of Miss Gwendoline. She was right: man was put down on earth to earn wages. Look how handsome the men from Georgetown were. They earned big wages! Who ever heard of a man from those parts building a house and leaving it unpainted for so many years? Those were happy people, fortunate people, who looked well and dressed well, and talked with authority.

"Even when black people and East Indians are at one another's throats they do it with more authority and conviction in Georgetown than country people who does earn low wages," thought Kwaku.

"All the misery in this world, people wasting away 'cause their father and husband din' bring home enough food." There must be some secret that put people beyond the changes of fortune, the possession of some potent object, probably. Knowledge, yes. But it was too late to acquire knowledge. And old Mr Barzey's words came to mind, "Life and an understanding of life can be summed up in three words, clock, book, train."

Why did those words appear so mysterious then? They were plain to him now. Book meant no more than knowledge, which Mr Barzey possessed in abundance. Clock must surely be time and train a journey. A journey to where? When he asked Mr Barzey to explain, the old man was annoyed. But if he was talking about life then everyone made this journey.

Could Kwaku's troubles have come about because he had been disrespectful to the man from the Party? Could the man be in league with the shoemaker in order to teach him a lesson? No, no. Families were being dispersed on account of the plague. People were visibly thinner and the village had the air of someone in mourning. Kwaku thought that if he really believed that he was being victimized he would seek out the Party man and prostrate himself before him.

"Kow-tow? I would show them how to kow-tow! Boot-lick? When I finish with his boots he would be able to see his beautiful face in it. Prostrate myself? I would make comoodie look like a matchstick! Smooth words they want? I would make Japanese man sound as if he quarrelling with you."

But when all was said and done he could see no connection between his plight and the youthful Party representative.

Kwaku sat down on the dam surrounding the Conservancy, now thick with the reflected shadows of surrounding vegetation.

Darkness had fallen and a yellow moon rose to preside over the kingdom of the night.

13   The unsympathetic

EARLY THE next morning a car horn was heard to sound, a long, wilful moan that brought many people to their windows.

"The Conservancy breach! Somebody breach the Conservancy!" a man's voice thundered.

The same call was repeated over and over again; and when a large enough number of people had gathered on the road, the man stood up on the roof of the car and began speaking to them. It was Three-Foot Joe, the local taxi owner, who plied the coast between Ann's Grove and Georgetown.

According to Three-Foot Joe, the cane fields and other cultivated land fed by water from the Conservancy were flooded. The Conservancy had been deliberately breached.

Those who owned plots aback lost no time in rushing away to see if their fields were affected, for in many cases it was the cassava, sweet-potatoes and beans harvested from their plots which stood between them and starvation. Girls with only one side of their heads plaited rushed after their mothers; men ran inside to put on their shoes, while women with infants, whose husbands worked outside the village, ordered one of the family to remain with them or left them in the care of the next-door neighbour.

65

Their worst fears were confirmed. The Conservancy was nearly empty, breached in several places by someone who must have worked for several hours over the operation. In the surrounding land the stalks of cassava rose above the muddy water in oblong patches, but the heart-shaped leaves of the sweet potato had disappeared under the flood water. The villagers knew that the badly drained land would hold the water, for beneath the top soil was impervious clay, and they stood looking at the water, only yesterday a boon in the confines of the artificial dam.

People kept arriving from the villages, some making bitter observations, while others, for the most part, just stared in disbelief. One man confided to someone next to him that late the previous afternoon he saw Kwaku hiding behind a carrion-crow bush but did not call out to him, thinking he was up to one of his tricks. And within minutes everyone among the onlookers knew of Kwaku's trip to the back and his odd behaviour.

Why should Kwaku crouch down behind a carrion-crow bush if he had nothing to hide? Besides, where was he now? He did not own a plot, but that would not prevent him from coming to see the state of the fields if he had nothing to hide.

Five burly men took it upon themselves to go and look up Kwaku. If he was the culprit he would have to pay for it. The whole village was now threatened by his behaviour.

On arriving at Kwaku's house they found that he had gone out. His wife claimed that he had left for the shoemaker's house to pick up some leather; but a woman who was selling fruit by the roadside declared that a few minutes earlier she had seen him running off in the direction of Ann's Grove.

"Is he, yes," one of the men said. "Else why should he run away? Le' we go to the police station."

The men went in a body to the police station two miles away.

More than an hour before, a youth had come to warn Kwaku that he was suspected of making a breach in the Conservancy and that some men were coming after him. Miss Gwendoline urged him to stand his ground, for an innocent person had nothing to fear.

"You tell them that for me," Kwaku said to her.

He had got dressed early and was sitting in his drawing-room when the hue and cry was raised. But he did not react.

"Go and see what happening," Miss Gwendoline had said. "Is probably a fire."

"You ever hear about fire early in the morning?"

"Must be a fight then," Miss Gwendoline suggested.

"I don' got stomach for fighting at this time of the morning."

"Somebody beating his wife, then," Miss Gwendoline went on,

66

wondering at his apathy.

"Let him beat her, ne. Is none of my business."

"Some people! You got the pip or something? If is constipation I can give you a enema."

"I not constipated. How can I be constipated when I not eating? Nothing can come out that don't go in."

"It can be a accident," Miss Gwendoline said, after a moment's thought. "Go and see if is a accident. Somebody you know might gone an' get run over."

"I not going, I tell you," Kwaku protested. "I don' want no enema. I don' want no excitement."

"And why you been sitting at the window since four o'clock cocking you ears?"

"I not been cocking my ears. I been thinking."

That was the end of the matter until the youth came. When Kwaku ran off, Miss Gwendoline knew that he was the one who was responsible for flooding the cultivated land.

Now she left the children in Rona's charge and went to see old Mr Barzey.

"Did you hear the news?" she asked young Mr Barzey, who had opened the door.

"Yes, somebody let the water out of ... ."

"People say is Kwaku. They see him hiding behind a carrion-crow bush near the Conservancy."

Young Mr Barzey gave her a cool look, then remarked, "He should've been put away years ago."

"You father there?" Miss Gwendoline enquired.

"Do you have to bother the old man at this time of the morning?" he asked, wishing that Miss Gwendoline would take a sensible view of the matter and let Kwaku go to hell.

"I do, Mr Barzey. Is not you going put bread in my children mouth."

Young Mr Barzey left her to call his father, after offering her a chair near the door.

It was the first time that she had entered the Barzeys' house, but so preoccupied was she with her husband's plight she saw neither the handsome furniture nor the calendar on the wall, nor the polished floor. Nor did she hear the tick-tock of the grandfather clock, out of sight behind the alcove wall, against which grains of dust were already visible in the early morning sunshine.

"Mrs Cholmondeley," old Mr Barzey greeted her. He had put on his cork hat as if he were about to set out on a journey.

"Oh, Mr Barzey. You hear what happen?"

"Only just now, from my son. Sit down, sit down," he said, almost pushing her back into her seat.

She then told him what had happened.

"I don' know what I going to do. And everybody so unsympathetic."

"What you expect, Miss Gwendoline? Especially at a time like this."

"But he got so much on his mind, Mr Barzey. He don' like seeing his flesh and blood suffer."

Mr Barzey listened to her defend her husband with a certain perverted satisfaction, for it only confirmed him in his opinion of womankind.

"And after all," she observed, "is the first time he do something like this for a long while," she observed, convinced that the observation would put Mr Barzey on her side. "But people so unsympathetic!"

"He does have a thing about putting holes in tanks and such like, Miss Gwendoline."

"But he not a delinquent, you know, Mr Barzey. You of all people ought to know that."

"Well, people're funny, Miss Gwendoline. They get vexed for little things nowadays."

"I hear the cassava still standing," Miss Gwendoline reminded him. "The boy say so himself."

Mr Barzey could hardly believe his ears. "What you want me to do, Miss Gwendoline?"

"You can talk to the people in the village and tell them what a good man Kwaku is. They goin' kill him if they catch him."

"No, no," Mr Barzey assured her, "they might break one of his legs or put him in the pen with Mr Gordon's prize bull, but they won't kill him."

"Oh, Mr Barzey, you mocking me! You unsympathetic."

"Well, you won't face facts. Kwaku's ... funny-like. He's got a screw loose."

"Mr Barzey! How you could say a thing like that? He as sane as you or me!"

"As you, probably, Miss Gwendoline. But not as me. I have my two feet on the ground. Not that I don't want to puncture people's car wheels or do other funny things. It's just that I like my freedom."

"I can see how unsympathetic you getting, Mr Barzey."

"Anyway," continued the old man, "you don't like him doing his photography, you don't like him friendsing with Blossom. You're not too sympathetic yourself."

"That woman!" she burst out. "Scheming and scheming! Not content with she own man. You know she had the gall to come and offer us money? Is she who cause all the trouble. If she din' try to give us money I wouldn' have quarrelled with Kwaku and he

68

wouldn've do something like this."

Mr Barzey was astounded at his visitor's insight. Like many apparently simple-minded people she possessed the ability to get to the heart of the matter with an unreflected remark.

"You're not as simple as I thought, Miss Gwendoline," Mr Barzey could not help saying. "But I can't do anything for Kwaku. Talking to other people won't help."

"You can't say that he been here – with you – when it was supposed to happen?" she pleaded.

"I can't do that, Miss Gwendoline. He was seen hiding behind the bushes near the Conservancy, according to you."

"Couldn' you ... you could say is you who breach the dam, Mr Barzey?"

Mr Barzey stared at her, flabbergasted at her boldness.

"I thought my daughter-in-law was bad! No, Miss Gwendoline, I couldn't say I did it."

Miss Gwendoline, in a last effort to impress old Mr Barzey, began wringing her hands. She recalled that her aunt, whose husband had died early in their marriage, used to preface every request for help with, "I'm a widow!" And even when she was quite well-off, out of sheer habit she would beg shopkeepers for credit, saying, "I'm only a widow."

"My children are almost fatherless, Mr Barzey," pleased Miss Gwendoline without looking up at him.

"I would help if I could," he answered, touched by her words. "But I don't have money. Why not ask my son?"

"He can't say he did it, Mr Barzey. You can, because you don' got nothing to lose."

"You'd better go home, Miss Gwendoline," Mr Barzey told her, inwardly cursing her stupidity.

She got up reluctantly, believing that she had not tried hard enough. Mr Barzey's unreasonableness, his refusal to sacrifice himself for her husband and his family, did not square with Kwaku's opinion of him.

He accompanied her down the stairs and crossed the street to go over to see Mr Gordon's head, in order to find out from it more about the events of the night before.

From the teacher's house came a flood of music, a popular record which could be heard in the pool halls in town.

"There's a brown girl in the ring,
    Tra la la la la,
    There's a brown girl in the ring,
    Tra la la la la ... ."

Kwaku did not know at first where he would go. One could only

69

hide aback, and that was where people had congregated. In his haste to get away he had taken no money and only carried on him some loose change. He took the risk of waving down a taxi, but once inside broke into a cold sweat, for a woman sitting next to him began staring at him unwaveringly. Desperately trying to ignore her, he looked straight ahead, but in the end could not help turning towards her.

"What wrong, lady?" he asked, his tongue almost cleaving to his palate.

"You sitting on me dress."

"Oh," said Kwaku, "that's all? Oh, life!" he exclaimed, easing himself off his seat, in order to give the woman time to pull her dress from under him. "Oh, life! That's all."

"Is what you did think?" demanded the woman. "You thought I was in love with you?"

"I din' think nothing, lady. I just thought." He wiped his brow with his bare hands.

"Now you want to drown me," she told him in the same unemotional voice.

In his nervous relief Kwaku had drenched the women with the sweat from his brow.

"Sorry, lady. Is the heat."

Then, thinking that she might be an educated woman, he added, "It is the heat, theee heat, Madame."

"Some people," she muttered.

Then, unaccountably, she turned to stare at him once more; and in no time the sweat started pouring down Kwaku's face once again.

In an attempt to put her off he began whistling. However the woman just continued to stare, as if he were a two-headed harpy eagle or Moon-Gazer himself.

"Is what wrong, lady?" he asked, when he could no longer bear the suspense. "You know me or something?"

"I think so," she answered dryly.

"Look, Madame, I'm of a nervous disposition. If you got something to tell me, then tell me, instead of looking at me as if I had me hand in your handbag!"

"You in' name Kwaku?" the strange woman asked.

"Who? Me?" the outraged Kwaku protested, on the point of fainting. "I thought you was a educated woman."

"Well, what you name then?"

Kwaku could kick himself for not anticipating the question.

"My name is John," he answered, after fumbling about for a suitable one. "Me mother christen me John and my father called me Kwame, 'cause I resemble my father friend who did name Kwame."

"Just like my husband," the woman told him.

70

Kwaku had intended getting out three or four villages from C. However, further conversation with the woman could do him no good, so he stopped the car at the head of the main village road of R, only two villages from his own.

He gave the chauffeur two ten-cent pieces, and while waiting for his five-cent piece change felt the woman's gaze on him.

"Is why you sweating so, mister?" she asked him. "You sweating like pig."

"I don' feel too good, lady," he answered, taking his change from the chauffeur's outstretched hand. He wanted to tell her something flattering, but was afraid that he would only draw more attention to himself.

As the taxi drove off Kwaku groaned, "O me God! The fright nearly kill me."

And he was obliged to sit down by the wayside until he recovered the power in his legs.

"Some women!" he muttered, unconsciously echoing the woman's expression. "Is where she come from? God must've send her to torture me."

Kwaku took to thinking that his encounter with the woman might be a sign that he ought to go back to C and confess. By now the police must be looking for him. If he saved them the trouble the court might be lenient. But the sight of another taxi approaching from the direction of C made him jump up and hurry away up the village road towards the back-dam, where he intended to conceal himself in the bushes.

The village road was similar to that in C, except that there were many more cows grazing by the wayside. On the left-hand side of the road was the cemetery, its graves half engulfed and its gravestones all standing awry, Kwaku reflected that the villagers must be strange people to live cheek by jowl with their dead. He would not like to nod to his dead relations every time he had to take a taxi or go on a short trip outside the village.

Further on was the school, raised high above the ground on concrete pillars, while in the plot next to it was the church with its tiny belfrey and low pillars.

In short everything resembled the layout of C village, except for the burial ground, a morbid aberration, to say the least.

After about twenty minutes' walk the houses became smaller and the gaps between them bigger. Black sage bushes taller than he had seen anywhere else grew in profusion on the edge of the now deeply rutted road, which had narrowed, so that two cars venturing that far would have great difficulty getting by each other.

Then where he least expected to find a shop there was a shop! Even if he dared to show his face in the establishment he would certainly not have ventured across that bridge, which was in such bad repair that the customers and creditors who took the risk of crossing it would have no chance of coming back again.

At last Kwaku caught sight of a koker ahead of him, its sluice-gate open. It was an unusually ambitious structure for that village, and he was encouraged by its size – and the fact that it was topped by a corrugated-iron roof – to shelter under it a while from the sun.

What was his darling wife doing? he wondered. And his children. Rona must have gone to school by now. The twins and Damon must have been there before anyone else, with their passion for games. And Philomena, withdrawn, unlike her other sisters, what was she thinking? Was she cursing him? How were Irene and Clayton faring at their grandparents'?

Dotted about this village were coconut trees, their branches stripped, forlorn pillars in an otherwise flourishing landscape. There were far fewer coconut trees than in C, so that the dilapidation was hardly noticeable.

Kwaku set off for the backdam, hatless under the broiling sun.

14   A fugitive

LATE THAT night Kwaku arrived back at C village. Praying that the dogs would not recognize him and would refrain from barking, he crept over Blossom's bridge and up her back stairs. He rapped feebly on the shutter and waited, but no one came. There was no doubt that she was at home, because the night light was burning. Kwaku called softly, but to no avail. He was exhausted and hungry, for he had eaten nothing all day.

For a moment he wondered if he should not take the risk of going to his own house, but rejected the idea. Even if he were not seen by one of the villagers it would be next to impossible to keep his presence a secret, for one of the children was likely to give him away inadvertently, either by word or conduct. Besides, the police were likely to search his home more than once.

Kwaku crept back down the stairs and lay down in the hammock under Blossom's house, where he fell asleep almost at once.

"Is who that?" Blossom called out, when she saw the form in her hammock on her way down the stairs to the rainwater barrel the next morning.

"Is who in the hammock?" she shouted.

She approached, shook the hammock and saw Kwaku fall out, in full view of anyone who might be passing on the road.

"Jesus! Is you?" she exclaimed, glancing on all sides to see if any neighbour or passer-by was looking in that direction.

"You want to break my back, woman?" Kwaku asked indignantly.

"Come quick! Up the stairs," she ordered.

Kwaku, seeing that it was broad daylight, immediately sized up the situation and followed her, hands raised to his face to avoid being recognized.

"Where you come from?" she asked, once they were upstairs. "You din' sleep in the bottom house all night! Wilfred gone to work," she added, noticing how nervously he was looking about him.

Blossom closed the two shutters on each side of her house and opened the back and front doors instead to allow air to circulate freely.

"Girl, I can't talk. I so hungry!"

She began preparing him bread and butter and ginger tea, telling him all the while what he had already guessed. The police were looking for him and had even been to her house.

"Here? What I going do?" he asked.

"I don' think they'll come again. They didn' even come in. You know they're watching your house."

"But I pass by last night and din' see nobody."

"The man must've been asleep."

Blossom put the plate of buttered bread on the table and started pouring the ginger tea from one cup to the other in order to cool it enough for Kwaku to drink. The vapour radiated from the long column of brown liquid, miraculously suspended in mid-air each time she emptied one cup, raised at least three feet above the other. Kwaku had already eaten his bread when she placed the warm tea before him.

"You not working today?" he asked, after the first mouthful had brought an unusual warmth to his stomach.

"Yes. That's why I up so early. Second shift. A bus picking me up in about two hours."

She instructed him on how to conduct himself while she was out. He must not make the slightest noise, nor was he to attempt to cook. Her neighbours knew what shift she was on and also that Wilfred was at work all day.

"I coming home about eight tonight, and we can talk then. Don' bother! Wilfred won't dare give you away."

Blossom made him a meal which he was to eat cold when he became hungry. Besides, there was bread and butter and guava jelly in the cupboard.

He heard her taking a shower and wondered at his indifference to her as a woman. He recalled how he used to chase her on his cycle when they were still at school, and the astonishment of the villagers when, as young people, they went their separate ways. People were convinced that he had wronged her, just as he had offended so many others.

When Blossom was dressed and made up she bolted the back door and went to sit at the front of the drawing-room to await the arrival of the Public Transport bus.

"You see; if I had a dog you couldn't have come into the yard last night," Blossom said, with one eye on the road. "And I going to have to get one, 'cause people thiefing even in the villages now."

Kwaku nodded off and only woke when he heard Blossom shouting out to the driver of the bus, which had stopped in front of her house. He heard her close and bolt the window.

"Go inside," she came over and whispered, "and don' forget what I tell you."

Blossom then locked the front door and hurried down the stairs.

Kwaku slept for a few hours after Blossom left for work, and on waking made himself a snack with white bread and guava stew he found in a glass bowl in her cupboard. Tired of hiding up in the bedroom, he scraped just enough paint from one of the window panes to allow himself a view of the street, for the glass of all the four front windows had been painted to reflect the sun. By way of distraction he took to counting the taxis and buses and cars that passed; and once in the afternoon he even thought he spotted Blossom in a bus that went by at high speed.

Soon after that he saw two women stop at Blossom's gate and look up. He could not hear what they were saying, but thought that their conversation had something to do with the house. Kwaku drew back as they disappeared from view on their way into the yard, and hearing footsteps on the stairs he fled inside on tiptoe.

"Blossom!" one of the women called out.

"Go round to the back. She probably at the back," the other voice suggested, only to be followed by another call for Blossom.

At the sound of retreating steps Kwaku was just preparing to come outside again when he heard the cry from the back stairs: "Blossom? Is Thelma, Vibert wife!"

"She not there," the same voice said, apparently speaking to the other woman.

"Is funny," the first voice said in turn, "I got the feeling somebody home."

Kwaku felt a chill down his neck. His discomfiture grew when the silence became prolonged. Neither of the women spoke, nor did they go downstairs. The screech of a car horn, long and strident, shattered the silence. For a moment be believed that one of the

74

women had got into the house and, discovering him, had let out a shriek. He dared not sit on the bed, lest the creaking of the springs be heard, nor on the floor, out of fear that the sound of his joints might carry in the total, uncanny silence. He, in turn, felt like shouting out, in order to bring the tension of waiting to an end.

"Come, let's go," one of the two women said.

"I can't come back. Is Vibert send me. He going think I din' want to come."

"You can't talk to she if she not there."

"All right ... but I sure somebody or something in this house."

Footsteps on the stairs announced the departure of the women.

"Blossom was right," thought Kwaku, trembling in every limb. "I better stick to the bedroom."

He went to sleep once more and was awakened by someone turning a key in the front door. He was curiously relieved, certain that it must be Wilfred.

He got up and stood waiting in the bedroom.

"What you doing home at this time?" asked Wilfred, thinking that the noise from the bedroom had been made by Blossom.

"Is not Blossom," said Kwaku, barely showing himself at the door. "Is me."

"What the ass ...?"

"Blossom know I here. I see her this morning." And Kwaku told him how he had slept under the house the night before and how Blossom had found him.

"I din' see you," said Wilfred suspiciously.

"That's not my fault," declared Kwaku, remembering Blossom's assurance that Wilfred would be obliged to co-operate with her in harbouring him.

"Go and sit in the drawing-room or the kitchen," Wilfred ordered. "You can't stay in the bedroom."

"Somebody might see me!" Kwaku objected. "Two women did come earlier on, and if I been in the kitchen they would've be able to see me through the chinks in the window."

"After what you do to the Conservancy they should haul you ass off to jail. I don' know what you come hanging round here for. Your name is trouble."

"You think I want stay in the same house as you?" asked Kwaku.

"Stay?" said Wilfred. "You not staying here! That's something I can tell you now."

Kwaku went inside and lay down on the bed, leaving Wilfred to gnash his teeth at the prospect of having to put up with him in the house. He was married to Blossom now, Wilfred reflected. It was not like the old days.

"I going to put my foot down!" he decided.

At five minutes past eight a bus stopped outside the house, and moments later Blossom was heard climbing the stairs.

"He's there?" she asked Wilfred, who was waiting for her at the window.

"He who?"

"Kwaku," she answered, knitting her brow at the thought that Wilfred might not have found him in the house.

"He there, yes!" burst out Wilfred. "But he not staying in the bedroom! And tobesides he got to be out of the house by tomorrow morning. I not keepin' no criminal in my house ...."

"Talk," Blossom interrupted him in a calm voice. "But keep your voice down. Talk as long as you want and I going listen."

"Listen! I din' marry him, I married you! I din' put no ring 'pon his finger ...."

Blossom stood listening, staring at him all the while; and when he finished saying what he had to say she went past him and into the kitchen. A few minutes later the scent of onions filled the house, then the sound of fierce hissing as fat was dropped into a hot pan.

Wilfred stood alone in the drawing-room, his teeth bared and his fingers splayed as if he were rehearsing the act of strangling someone. He had always disliked Kwaku. Now he detested him with all his heart, his lungs, his liver, his kidneys, indeed with every organ in his body. Now he understood why cannibalism was once practised throughout the world. Undoubtedly the victim was hated by his devourer with a hatred so all-consuming that his death alone could not have brought sufficient satisfaction. If he could he would rip off Kwaku's nose and watch him squirm at his feet. And as he lay there, screeching for mercy, he would tweak off his little balloons. Whereupon Wilfred gave a little tweak with a pair of imaginary pincers in his hand, his face bathed in a king of angelic radiance. "Then I'd flick off his ...."

Just at that point Kwaku presented himself at the bedroom door and, on seeing Wilfred's expression of complete absorption in what appeared to be reflections of a most elevated kind, he was so reassured that he seized his right hand and shook it.

"I'm glad you don' hold it against me," he told him. "Is only in the day I goin' use the bedroom. In the night I goin' allow you and Blossom to sleep in the bed alone while I sleep out here."

"You! You blasted ...!" exclaimed Wilfred, spluttering in his search for suitable words.

"Don' curse him!" It was Blossom's voice from the kitchen.

Then she came out to face Wilfred. "He din' do you nothing. When you give you good-for-nothing uncle money I don' complain. When he come and put his hand in the pot and ask what cooking I don' say nothing. You leave him alone."

"You realize we could get in trouble for keeping a criminal?" asked Wilfred indignantly.

"How you know he's a criminal? He thief anything belonging to you or your family? And in any case we not discussing the resolution no more, 'cause I don' want nobody coming up to ask what we quarrelling about."

She had said not a word to Kwaku since she came home, had not sought him out to find out how he had managed while she was away. Now she stood, a carving knife in her right hand and her eyes blazing with anger at her husband's conduct.

Not certain whether the role of the knife was confined to carving whatever Blossom was carving in her preparations for the evening meal, or whether, as in his own fantasies, it had a more sinister function, Wilfred recoiled, at the same time looking round to make certain that there was ample room to manoeuvre should she go for him.

Their meal was eaten in silence, as much out of fear that a child or even an adult could come up the back stairs without being heard as because of the row Blossom and Wilfred had had. There was only the noise of spoon against plate, the cracking of chicken bone, followed by the hissing made by Wilfred in an effort to suck marrow from the small bones. He ate with a sort of rage, a furious determination to extract everything useful from his meal, so that in the end his empty plate glistened before him, as if food had not yet been placed on it.

At the start of the meal he had silently made the comparison between his heaped plate and Kwaku's, only starting to eat when he was certain that his own plate could not accommodate a single grain of rice more. Then his confidence was restored when Blossom brought in the chicken and crowned his mountain of rice with both drumsticks.

Blossom got up and came back soon afterwards with a bowl of toothpicks which she placed in the centre of the table. Wilfred promptly took one out and vied with her to rid the interstices between his teeth of bits of food; and another hissing began and continued intermittently as each tested his and her handiwork.

Kwaku had enjoyed his fried chicken, but felt that it was not the moment to say so, even in a whisper.

Wilfred, outwardly calm, was inwardly contriving the destruction of his wife's friend. People ought to act in the interests of the collective. He, Wilfred, was no informer. Anyone who attended school with him could vouch for that. When Vibert passed around the drawing of the naked woman in the fourth form of secondary school he took the wild-cane rather than inform on him. Putting aside the fact that Kwaku was a threat to his domestic bliss, the man was a public enemy. The security and livelihood of the whole village was at stake. His preoccupation with the Kwaku problem stemmed from a well developed civic consciousness that told him, "He must be denounced!"

Wilfred decided that he would let the sergeant at Ann's Grove know what the position was ... yes, on the following Friday. He could then stay home on the Saturday morning so that if they came to take Kwaku away late that Saturday Blossom would not suspect that he was involved. She would assume that the police had acted as soon as they were informed.

The whole plot was hatched out during the picking and hissing and before they rose from table to wash their hands. Meanwhile, thought Wilfred, he must not show any hostility towards Kwaku. Mind you, he had to be discreet. If he fell around his neck and kissed him ... well, Blossom was no fool. She would sense that something was cooking and the plan would backfire. He might even be thrown out, for the house was hers. He would be a fool to give that up because he was unable to control his feelings; but he would be just as foolish to have Kwaku sleeping in his house forever. The first night he would sleep out front, the next night by the door and the third night he would take his place in the bed; by the wall if he had the chance. And who could tell what that sort of thing might lead to?

Wilfred's dismay was deepened when Blossom brought out a pack of playing-cards and set them down on the table she had just cleared. Without a word she and Kwaku started a game of bishka.

"I goin' play too," said Wilfred. "Just to show I don' have no hard feelings."

This unexpected concession pleased Blossom, who smiled faintly at his direction and reshuffled the pack before sharing for three.

By Saturday morning the atmosphere in the house was relaxed. Tell a lie – it was heady! It was so heady that Wilfred, before going downstairs to work on a chair he was making, shared a shot of rum with Kwaku. Neither of them had had tea yet. He called him "brother" and vowed that he would have given the remainder of his packet of cigarettes to Kwaku if it were not so risky.

"I got to think of your safety, you know," he said. "You can't have smoke rings coming out of the house while I downstairs, because even fowl-cock would get suspicious and come up the back stairs to find out what happening."

He went downstairs, leaving Blossom and Kwaku together.

"I did misjudge him," remarked Kwaku to Blossom.

During a conversation with the teacher a couple of days back Blossom was surprised to learn that the woman did not dislike Kwaku. Of course her livelihood did not depend on the success of the harvest, and so the breached Conservancy affected her in no way. Delighted that everyone else in the village was not Kwaku's enemy, Blossom confided in her that he was hiding in her house.

The two women planned a surprise party for him that Saturday, to which they would invite old Mr Barzey If they wore fancy dress and Kwaku put on a mask there would be no risk of his being discovered.

Wilfred's high spirits were partly due to the prospect of having the attractive teacher in the house. The fact that she had an unsanctioned relationship with a man, like other lowlier women in the village, gave him some hope of success in a flirtation. Besides, she had the reputation of being an atheist – a fact that caused other villagers to temper their respect for her status with a certain mistrust of her person, but which, in his opinion, should make her even more vulnerable to his advances. And he rated his chances with the teacher so favourably that he offered to make Kwaku's mask himself.

Blossom left for work as usual, after telling Kwaku that she had a surprise in store for him that night. Up to the day before, he could talk of little else except his family's plight, but Blossom set his mind at rest by giving the money his wife had refused to old Mr Barzey, who in turn gave it to Miss Gwendoline as if it was a present from him.

The old man, on hearing from Blossom that Kwaku was at her house, agreed readily to come to their get-together, for the idea of putting one over the rest of the villagers appealed to him. He spent the first half of the day thinking up ideas for a costume and the second making it from the black cloth he used to darken his room when developing photographs. And nothing pleased him more than to see his daughter-in-law hovering round him, intrigued by his occupation. Finally, when she could bear it no longer and asked outright what he was making, he answered brutally:

"It's none of your business!"

She had put an end to his use of the kitchen sink as a bath for his photographic prints and, like a small child, he was delighted at an opportunity to get his own back. In fact he looked forward as much to seeing Kwaku as to mystifying his daughter-in-law about his destination that night.

15   The fancy-dress do

KWAKU, after his initial astonishment at the daring invention of the two women, agreed to take part; but it was the teacher's willingness to come that pleased him most of all. She was unjustly regarded as a snob, and the thought that she was to furnish proof of her sociability had an affect on him similar to Wilfred's fascination. He tried on the horse's head Wilfred had made for him under the house, and, to guard against losing it during the celebration, he made Wilfred attach two strings to its base; these he secured under his armpits.

Blossom was dressed as Old Higue, who attacks infants and pregnant women, sucking their blood through punctures in their neck and leaving them fatally ill. This irreverent attitude towards a lore figure that still held terrors for Kwaku silenced him a while, since, in the village from which he originally came, Old Higue's victims were mainly men. Wilfred disclosed his plans at the last moment. He would wear a dress, like Mother Sally at Christmas time. Blossom clapped her hands in delight and said that it was a pity he could not have stilts to go with it.

To improve the lighting in her house Blossom borrowed an old gas lamp from the teacher, which she still used in preference to electricity, on account of its pervasive brightness. Wilfred pumped it, lit it and hung it from the roof, so that the whole house was bathed in a white glow, broken by shadows where the path of the lamp's light was obstructed by the low partitions.

Blossom had taken home about eight feet of black pudding, bought from Miss Gwendoline. Some impulse had made her go down the road to Kwaku's house, for in the beginning she had not thought of having black pudding.

She found Miss Gwendoline and Rona folding a sheet between them and had to wait to be served.

"You want me to cut it up for you?" Miss Gwendoline asked her.

"Yes, thanks."

The other children must have gone to bed for the house was unusually quiet.

"The children in bed already?" Blossom enquired.

"Yes," replied Rona.

"They got to get up early tomorrow," said Miss Gwendoline, "for Fabian christening."

"Fabian christening tomorrow?"

"Yes," came the grave reply.

And Blossom sensed that Miss Gwendoline wanted to add, "And I don' even know where my husband is."

To herself Blossom said, "Where he is now you don' want him to be. But if he was with you he wouldn' be bringing any money into the house."

"Goodnight, then," she said aloud, in as off-hand a manner as possible.

Blossom's sympathy was not for Miss Gwendoline but for Rona, whose breasts had begun to swell under her bodice and whose hips were those of a grown woman. Her waking hours were devoted to school work and housework. At that age Blossom had already sat on her uncle's knee and experienced the faintness that caused her to sink, as it were, into the earth. She was certain that Rona had not had any sort of preparation for adult life in that way. When she was allowed some freedom she would probably take the first man who came along.

"I buy the black pudding from Miss Gwendoline," Blossom told Kwaku, but said nothing about his daughter's christening.

On learning that all seemed well at his home Kwaku prepared to enjoy himself in earnest, banishing the guilt that often made him ponder on his worth as a husband and father.

"What about the policeman who been guarding the place?" he asked her.

"Wasn' a policeman," Blossom told him. "At least he din' got on a uniform."

"But was he there?"

"No, he does start about ten, when people gone to bed."

Kwaku took a shower, polished his shoes and put on his shirt, which he had washed in tepid water that morning. He hoped that the magnificence of his horse's head would draw attention away from his evil-looking trousers.

While he and Wilfred sat chatting in the kitchen, the horse's head on the dresser nearby – to be donned at the slightest noise on the stairs – Blossom was taking infinite pains on her Old Higue make-up. One would have thought that she was dressing as a film star and not as a hideous lore figure.

Although Blossom had given strict instructions that they should not start drinking before the meal – the curry was still simmering in the pan – Wilfred poured out a shot each for himself and Kwaku.

"To face the teacher," he confessed.

Earlier on he had begun to regret the conspiracy with the sergeant; but the longer Blossom took over her make-up, the closer he came to feeling as he did the day he found Kwaku standing at the door of his bedroom.

"What I care for?" he told himself. "He not my brother."

The first of the guests to arrive was old Mr Barzey.

"Here I am!" he shouted through the open window. "You asked for me and now you've got me."

Kwaku quickly put on his horse's head and ran to meet him, hardly prepared for the sight Mr Barzey presented. He was wearing his cork hat and a black tunic with gold buttons, and carrying a butterfly net with which he made a mighty swipe through the window, before entering the house through the door. Mother Sally and the horse's head roared with laughter at his knee-length short pants, which left his spindly legs and outsize knees exposed.

"Is that Kwaku?" he asked, looking intently at the horse's head.

"Shh!" enjoined Kwaku. "Call me Horse for tonight. Walls got ears, man."

"Oh!" groaned the old man, pulling a chair towards the kitchen. "I've got to sit down. My right foot does run faster than the left, and the left foot can't keep up. Oh!"

He took a seat and downed the shot of run Kwaku poured for him in one gulp.

"You glad to get away, eh?" Kwaku taunted him.

And immediately Mr Barzey launched into a denunciation of his daughter-in-law who, he claimed, had made him join the Burial Society to hasten his death. Then, turning to Wilfred, he said, "So you're Wilfred," ignoring his Mother Sally get-up. "I hope you're keeping Blossom happy. She's mmmm!"

Mr Barzey made a gesture indicating the size of Blossom's backside.

Left in no doubt as to the relationship between Kwaku and the old man, Wilfred took fright at his plot and wished he had not thought it up. Mr Barzey was respected in the village and feared by some people for his sharp tongue and his courage.

"So you catching butterflies now," Kwaku said. "I bet you can't catch the teacher with them knees though."

"Ah, boy," Mr Barzey replied, taking off his hat and wiping his balding head, "if I catch her I wouldn't know what to do with her. I could tell you stories though. But this isn't the place with ...."

"I don' mind!" Blossom called out. "Go on! Tell them. I goin' block up my ears."

Mr Barzey got up, crept towards the bedroom door with his net and, without entering the room, made a sudden swipe as if to catch a butterfly.

"Hi!" Blossom shrieked at the unexpected appearance of the net in the bedroom.

"Did you know," said Mr Barzey in a bantering voice, "that the butterfly was once called the flutterby?"

"What get into you, Mr Barzey?" Blossom asked. "I never see you like this before."

"Because I'm a prisoner in my own house," he complained almost speaking in earnest.

But the tone of the conversation changed when there was a knock at the door and, on the invitation to come in, the teacher entered, dressed as a nun.

"You know, Sister," said old Mr Barzey, "if I was a younger man ... I don't know what I'd do."

He took both her hands in his and kissed them in turn.

From the kitchen on the far side of the house Kwaku and Wilfred nodded, reduced to silence and utter confusion by the appearance of the teacher. Since Mr Barzey's arrival they had both been eyeing the door.

"Is you, Teacher?" Blossom called out. "Come in, ne, and leave the men to talk name and tell dirty stories."

Teacher stood in the doorway of the bedroom, unable to get by, for her headgear – made by her primary school class during a handicraft lesson – was too wide.

"Cock your head, my dear," suggested old Mr Barzey. "Like this!"

And once in she was greeted by Blossom's high-pitched shriek.

"You don't got to listen to what we saying," said Blossom from over the partition. "All-you go on with you talk."

But the men had difficulty continuing their conversation after the apparition.

Wilfred poured rum for each of the other two and Mr Barzey again lost no time in emptying his glass.

"I hear you!" exclaimed Blossom. "I did tell you not to start drinking before you eat. Teacher not accustomed to no bad behaviour."

"Don' bother with she," Kwaku said to Mr Barzey.

"Why he musn' bother with she?" Wilfred said sourly. "She making a intellectual observation."

Wilfred watched Mr Barzey, in order to observe the effect his high language had made on him. Jealous of his friendship with Kwaku, he was determined to impress the old man.

Mr Barzey then began talking about the 'twenties, when he was in Georgetown. And inevitably he came back to Bourda, the district in which he once lived. After recounting his experience with the funeral procession he told them of the day the bulls escaped.

"The bulls were on their way to the slaughterhouse. I can't remember whether it was a dray-cart or what they were on, but there was a door at the back of it. All of a sudden the door flew open, 'Woof!' I don't know what happened next, but I remember clearly seeing this half of a bull's body appear and it stood like a god in the doorway. The animal looked to the left, then looked to the right. Then before spit could reach the ground this bull was in the middle of the road. And I tell you, he wasn't going to any slaughterhouse! Then people started bolting north, south, east, west. It was like a race meeting of a very high standard. But you didn't see anything yet! When the four other bulls got out, people even started screaming from their windows, because they expected them to climb up their stairs and gore them. It was pan-de-monium, I tell you. One old man'd scaled the wrought-iron railings of the burial ground and was springing from one tomb to the other as if he had St Vitus's dance. And a woman, she couldn't have been much younger than he – it was probably his wife – shot up Orange Walk like a bullet; and, hearing hoofs tramping behind her, instead of taking the bridge when she came to South Road, she bent to the left and in one mighty jump leapt over the canal like if it was a gutter. But wait, ne! One bull just stood in the middle of Regent Street, not sure what to do. Brother, he suddenly took it in his head to make for the cemetery. Whether it was this man leaping about the tombs that attracted his attention or what, I don't know, but he lunged at the railings and God! I've never heard a sound like that in my life, a terrible bellowing and wailing; and on the pavement was a pool of blood, getting wider and wider, until it started spilling over into the gutter. His neck was impaled on the railings and every time he made a lunge there was a spurt of blood spattering the pavement."

"Where you was?" asked Wilfred.

"I was in the market itself. Two men managed to close the Regent Street gates when they saw the bulls in the road. One of them kept shouting out, 'The padlock! Who got the padlock?' But whoever had the padlock must have disappeared long time. So men went round the market tying up the wrought-iron gates with leather thongs and hoping for the best."

At that point Blossom emerged from the bedroom, her face masked by a layer of white rice powder, expressionless and menacing. The men were stunned into silence by the transformation.

"Like it?" she asked.

"Is what you put 'pon your face?" Wilfred wanted to know.

"Is rice powder. It frightening, eh?"

Then, when she had been admired by all, she said to Wilfred, "Teacher want you to go and get her record player. Take the hand-cart under the house."

Wilfred complied, taking the key from the teacher. The anticipation of dancing with her was enough to make him go to the end of the world to fetch her record player.

"The records are in a case on the floor next to it," she called after him from a window.

He was soon back, bearing the sizeable record player on his shoulder; and at once Kwaku set about installing the apparatus while Wilfred went to fetch the box of records, which he had left on the cart under the house. Then to the Saturday night sounds in the village was added the voice of the teacher's record player blaring out a popular song.

The men dragged the table to the centre of the drawing-room then went downstairs, under the house, to wait until they were summoned.

Kwaku, for the first time in several days, had an unobstructed view of the road, as far as the horse's head would permit. He strutted about the yard, stroked the mora pillars, sat on the hand-cart and examined the yard as if he had just left prison.

At the knock on the floorboards the three men went up the back stairs to start their meal.

The nun had taken off her headdress and seemed to have lost her inhibitions with it.

"You sit next to me, Mr Barzey," she said, bestowing on him a warm smile.

"As if I'm in church!" he observed.

"And me, what about me?" Kwaku pleaded.

"You sit next to me, Kwaku," ordered Blossom. "Wilfred can sit on the other side of the teacher."

And so the dinner began auspiciously, with the men a little drunk and the women pleased at the way things were going.

Mr Barzey had placed his butterfly net on the floor next to him while Kwaku, still unaccustomed to his headgear, struck Blossom with his muzzle every time he turned to speak to her. Wilfred's jealousy of Kwaku vanished at Blossom's suggestion that he sit by the teacher, and every time she addressed him he shuddered a little and found himself unable to hold her gaze.

"Is time you had a drink, Teacher," he finally found the courage to say.

"Me too," chimed in Blossom. "It'll be good for my complexion."

They laughed at the mention of the word "complexion", recalling the effect she made on them when she appeared in the doorway, like a ghost from the wood-boards.

Wilfred served the ladies, then went to fetch ice from the Frigidaire, for the ice in the bowl had nearly melted, the night was so warm.

The teacher noticed that Wilfred had poured more rum into her glass than into Blossom's. He evidently had no idea of her drinking prowess and was astonished that, long after Blossom began giggling and forgiving him for the things he had done her, the teacher's remarks remained measured and her guarded smile never altered.

"You do me a lot of bad things in the past," Blossom told him, "but every New Year I forgive you and start all over again. All over."

"You getting sentimental now," Kwaku said.

"I wake up on New Year's morning bursting with forgiveness. I was born on New Year's morning, you know. It was raining, my mother tell me. And when I was struggling to come out my father come home drunk and ask for his dinner. He was standing in the outside room in a pool of water, shouting, 'Is where my dinner?' My two aunts drive him out of the house with a hose-pipe and tell him to

85

come back when the baby born. He been out drinking all Old Year's night; he leave my mother though he knew that I was on the way. When he leave to go out drinking with his friends my mother did already begin having birth pains, and when he come back he did want his dinner. My mother forgive him and I was born on New Year's day, a child of forgiveness. That's why that one there does take advantage of me." She nodded towards Wilfred, who was on the point of pouring the teacher another shot of rum.

"You not going to get her, though," Blossom said meaningfully. "She know all about you."

"I must admit," said Kwaku, "I don' forgive so easy. I does bear a grudge." In saying this he wiped his mouth with the back of his hand in a theatrical flourish.

"And I does watch that grudge grow," he went on, "and bear flowers and thing. I'm like that. I can't help it."

Mr Barzey sighed. "I can't remember what I'm like," he said, shaking his head. "I'm not allowed to be what I am. She doesn't let me."

"Who?" asked the teacher, turning towards him with a solicitous expression.

"My daughter-in-law. I'm thwarted. Nothing in my character can flower, because I'm thwarted."

There was no sweet, nor savoury, and after the huge meal the five remained at table drinking rum and talking. Blossom from time to time expressed maudlin sentiments directly or indirectly aimed at Wilfred who, each time he came back from the refrigerator, edged his chair a little closer to the teacher's.

Blossom was leaning against Kwaku, and looked up whenever he spoke, so that the corners of her eyes showed large patches of white.

"Come let's dance." she said of a sudden.

Each took his glass away to allow Wilfred and Kwaku to lift the table, with its dirty crockery and cutlery and remains of food, into the kitchen.

Wilfred went through the records and chose a slow piece; but before he could turn round Blossom was waiting to dance with him.

As Kwaku passed by, the teacher's chin resting on his shoulder, Wilfred tried to catch her eye; but she would not look in his direction. However, old Mr Barzey, who was sitting on a chair against the wall, winked at him furiously, possibly wishing him luck with the teacher when he managed to have a turn with her. Thoroughly out of his element now that the dancing had begun, the old man sat against the wall, his butterfly net on his lap, his tiny glass in his hand, and with a look of expectancy whenever Wilfred or the horse were on the point of turning towards him.

When Blossom went inside to see if any of the rice powder had come off, Wilfred seized the opportunity to dance with the teacher. He held her close and, in his Mother Sally costume, they looked like two women in an embrace.

On coming outside Blossom found them dancing near the front windows, so she consoled herself with Kwaku; she rested her head against his shoulder and they remained on the same spot, cradling each other slowly.

The gas lamp had begun to burn low and now with its light nearly gone the house was almost in complete darkness.

Wilfred's left hand, while being lowered to his partner's waist, brushed her breast as if by accident, and feeling no tension in her body he raised his hand and placed it squarely on her breast. And so they danced in the dark, riveted to each other.

At the end of the record Blossom came to claim him and it was nearly a half an hour before he could dance with the teacher again. This time, with little ceremony, he tried to undo her brassière through her nun's habit. But she took his hand away.

"Wait!" she whispered in his ear, holding him as tightly as she could.

The wind freshened, shaking the two casement windows; and soon the portent was followed by a drizzle, so fine that it crept through the windows, like a thief unnoticed, a breath of the sea or crushed flowers from some offended heart.

Then the rain began to fall in earnest and Blossom stopped dancing in order to close the windows.

"Who's that?" she asked.

"Who?" asked Wilfred.

"There's a car parked in front the gate."

"Who you want?" Blossom shouted, but could not be heard above the downpour.

They were now all looking through the window at the mysterious vehicle parked by the gate.

"Probably somebody had a breakdown," Kwaku suggested.

Just then the car door opened and three men stepped out of the vehicle, through the two doors facing the house.

"Who're you?" Blossom called out, alarmed by the men's silence.

They came up the stairs, opened the front door without knocking and stood in tiny pools of water, just as Blossom's father had done when he came home after his revels.

"We're looking for Kwaku Cholmondeley," said one of the men.

And involuntarily Mr Barzey looked at the horse's head.

"You're Kwaku?" asked the man.

Slowly he undid the string under his armpits and took off the head, which he gave to old Mr Barzey.

"Is me."

"What you going to do to him?" Blossom demanded.

"He's got to come down to the station to get charged."

"What for?" she persisted.

"You didn't hear?" the man said, irritated by her manner. "People say he breached the Conservancy."

"You can't see?" Blossom asked, almost choking with emotion. "We're having a party."

They took Kwaku, and Blossom remained silent. Eventually she got up, went to the record box and chose Joan Armatrading's "Show Some Emotion", to which the four listened in silence, without a thought of dancing.

Blossom sat down next to the teacher, the horse's head on her lap. Then, without warning, she shook her head. And even she did not know how much of her sorrow was for Kwaku and how much was on account of the way Wilfred treated her.

Mr Barzey said he was going home.

"You don' get a umbrella. Wait."

Blossom fetched him a huge umbrella.

"You better go with him and bring it back," she told Wilfred. "And Teacher can then borrow it to go home when you come back."

Wilfred did as he was told, after changing his Mother Sally dress.

"Who could have told the police he was here?" asked the teacher, left alone with Blossom.

"That's what I ask myself," Blossom retorted. "Nobody know he been here except us .... Unless one of the neighbours hear us call his name."

Blossom sat with her legs crossed, staring out of the side window at the rain. On her white-powdered face her pale skin had begun to show through in darker patches, and her hair, carefully done for the party, now hung in unequal tresses from the soaking she had received while talking to the men in the car.

On Wilfred's return he gave the umbrella to the teacher, who embraced Blossom and said a few comforting words to her before leaving.

She and Wilfred went back to their seats to find that the record on the pick-up had come to an end and was making a regular clicking sound. She stood over the spinning turn-table for a while before taking off the record, which she replaced with "Back to the Night" by the same singer.

"I think I'll go down to the station to find out what they do to Kwaku," Wilfred suggested.

"We forget to ask where they take him."

"It's probably Ann's Grove," said Wilfred.

"Tell him I going to see a lawyer, don' forget."

When he was out of the house Blossom said, half-aloud, "She

forget the lamp .... Wilfred can take it with the records tomorrow."
And she had not even noticed that her husband had gone out without
an umbrella.

Wilfred went straight to the teacher's house and knocked on the
door.

"Who's it?"

"Me, Wilfred."

She opened the door without putting on any light. "It's you," she
said. "You'd better come in before someone sees you."

"Yes. You see ...."

"I ... can make you a cup of chocolate."

"If you want." Wilfred stood in the middle of the drawing-room of
the dark house, hardly believing his luck.

"Come this way," he heard her say.

She was mortally afraid of Blossom but did not think it proper to
mention her name.

Wilfred followed her into the dining-room, where he found her at
a cabinet filled with scores of glasses of different shapes and sizes.
He put his arms round her waist and, taken by a sudden impulse,
ripped her nightdress from her back. She turned and held him as in
their last dance together.

"Let's go inside," she said.

But no sooner had they entered the bedroom than there was a
knocking on the door.

"Stay here!" she ordered him.

Quickly she opened a wardrobe next to her bed, took out a dressing gown and put it on.

"Teacher! Open up!"

The teacher flew outside, recognizing Blossom's voice. Half-
opening the window, she asked without looking out, "Who is it?"

"Me, Blossom."

"Come in! Come in!" she exclaimed, drawing the bolts for her.
"You come in this rain? Something happened?"

"I looking for Wilfred."

"I left him with you."

Blossom was impressed by the speed with which the teacher had
opened the door and her invitation to enter her house. She therefore
hesitated before offending her.

"It's just that I'm drunk, Teacher. And Wilfred's not a one-
woman man. I thought he might've come here to say he wanted to
collect the umbrella."

"You didn't think ..." said Teacher, putting her hand to her
mouth.

"With what they do to Kwaku and everything ..." Blossom said
apologetically. "Anyway, I gone."

"Don't forget the umbrella," the teacher said, taking it up from where it lay open on the floor. "You're all right?"

"Yes, I'm all right."

The teacher secured the door and went inside, her heart pounding.

"I'm frightened," she whispered to Wilfred, who, taking advantage of her fear of making any noise, obliged her to let him remove her clothes.

Ignoring her unwillingness to lie with him, he forced his attentions on her until, only minutes later, he lay prostrate beside her tense body.

She had taken no pleasure in what had happened, and now that it was over she was worrying, not only that Blossom might be watching the house but also that her own man-friend, to whom she had given a key, might turn up unexpectedly. The sight of Blossom, her vivid white face covered with blotches and her hair plastered by the rain, haunted her in the darkness of the room, bereft of its trunk and limbs. While dancing with Wilfred she could ony think of his hand in her drawers, but now she regretted bitterly that she had encouraged him.

"If I go now and she outside, we done for," Wilfred told her. "It's best to wait about a hour. She can't very well stand in the rain."

"Suppose she's in a bottom house opposite?" the teacher suggested in an altered voice.

"Possible."

"She can't see you if you go down the back stairs," said the teacher, anxious to have him out of her house, even at the risk of him being seen as he left it. "You can then find your way out through Mr Davey's yard."

"But is best to wait a hour or so," Wilfred objected.

"Suppose she came again?"

The possibility had not even entered his head, but he could not deny that Blossom might come back again.

In the end Wilfred left by the back door, and it was only while he was halfway down the long staircase that the idea came to him that Blossom could have returned to the yard and might be waiting for him under the house. But it was too late to turn back; and under cover of pitch darkness he descended the stairs and headed towards the yard behind the teacher's, jumping the weed-covered drain that divided the two plots of land.

16   Kwaku leaves home

KWAKU·PUSHED open the front door of his tiny cottage and stood in the doorway. The whole family looked up and for a moment just stared at him.

"Carumba!" exclaimed Miss Gwendoline, falling back on her dead grandmother's favourite expletive.

"What happen?" Kwaku asked. "I in' no boo-boo man. I'm you husband, you father. Is me!"

"Is Pa!" whispered Rona.

Miss Gwendoline suddenly jumped up and took him by the arm.

"Is where you been?" she demanded. "Is five days!"

"I been hiding!"

"All this time? Where?"

"Aback."

"Rona, make your father some tea and hot up some black pudding."

"I goin' do it," Philomena said, attracting everyone's attention by the unexpected offer.

The children soon lost interest and returned to what they were doing, the twins to testing each other in arithmetic tables, Rona to fitting two pieces of cloth together with pins, which she took one by one from a tin lying on the floor next to her. Now and then she looked up, whenever her father said something that caught her attention, but looked down again to avoid his eyes.

Kwaku told his wife that he was picked up by the police and taken to the station. But old Mr Barzey, having heard what had happened, came and confessed that it was he who had breached the Conservancy.

"Mr Barzey do that! The old man! Well, I never!" For a while she heard nothing of what her husband was telling her.

"You should see how he treat me at the the station," Kwaku declared.

"Who?"

"Mr Barzey. You should see how he go on when he and me was alone."

Kwaku related how Mr Barzey told him that he had acted not out of friendship but on Miss Gwendoline's account. In any case he would not have done it if he thought they would keep him at the station.

"An' he was right. They let him go on condition that he din' go out after dark. If he did they would charge him with malicious damage to property."

"Where he is now?"

"Home," replied Kwaku. "He jus' come home with me."

Miss Gwendoline opened the front door to see if she could detect any unusual activity in the Barzeys' house, most of which was blocked by Kwaku's uncle's cottage. But apart from the light in the kitchen, unusual even for that early hour of the night – it was about eight o'clock – everything seemed as it had been the day before.

"I hear he been to a party," Miss Gwendoline told her husband when she came back.

"Was a fancy-dress one at Miss Blossom house," one of the twins butt in.

"Have manners!" Miss Gwendoline enjoined. "You can't see your father talking?"

"It ready, Pa," Philomena said to Kwaku, and smiled in a way that suggested that she had missed him.

A little thing like that, which escaped everyone else's notice, filled her father's heart with contentment. Going by her he placed his hand on her head and said jokingly, "Stillomena!" And she wished he would once and for all abandon his rôle as a buffoon.

Miss Gwendoline followed Kwaku into the kitchen to continue their interrupted conversation.

"I hear old Mr Barzey been to a party," she repeated, standing over Kwaku, who had installed himself at the table.

"What it got to do with me if he been to a party or not?" asked Kwaku, hoping that his irritation would be enough to discourage her.

"It wasn' a ordinary party. He been walking about with a net and his bug-house on his head."

The mention of Mr Barzey's cork hat called to mind the appearance of the police at the party.

"I see his net before," Kwaku lied. "And everybody see him in his cork hat."

"Is not only that," added Miss Gwendoline. "There was a nun at this wild party. Two people see she going into the house. A nun! An' she din' even have the decency to take off she clothes."

"Take off she clothes?" Kwaku asked, now thoroughly alarmed.

"I mean change she nun's clothes. She din' even have the decency to go in ordinary clothes. Nobody know where she come from 'cause they in' got no Catholics living in the village. She just appear out of the blue and go straight to Blossom house."

Miss Gwendoline lowered her voice, so that what she was to disclose to her husband should not reach her children's ears: "I hear they do things!"

"What things?" asked Kwaku, with a look in his eyes very nearly resembling that of a hunted animal about to be caught by its pursuers.

"Things! They *carried on*!" Miss Gwendoline confided.

"Who say so?"

"The neighbours say so. Two women was dancing together."

Here Miss Gwendoline's voice fell to an almost inaudible whisper, and her face was so near to Kwaku's that he felt the heat-radiation from her overwrought imagination.

"Two women dancing close together, I tell you. I never hear of that sort of thing happening in this country. You ever hear such a thing happening in this country?"

Kwaku shook his head vigorously, but even this gesture failed to dislodge the lump of black pudding stuck in his throat. "O me God!" he thought to himself. "If she mention the horse my heart goin' drop out."

"And there was a horse!" Miss Gwendoline said a little more audibly.

Kwaku bestowed on his wife a look of such agony that she stopped to examine him.

"Kwaku, what you been eating while you was in the bush?"

"Nothing!" came the reply in a genuine falsetto voice. "Why you tell me all this?"

"The horse!"

"What horse?" he pleaded.

"There was a horse at the party. And it kept jumping up and braying."

"Then it was a donkey!"

"No, a horse!" she insisted.

"Oh, God, woman, leave me alone. I hungry."

"Then eat, ne? I not stopping you." And she pushed the plate closer to him, so that it now touched his dirty shirt.

Miss Gwendoline told him how the horse was jumping at the ladies when they were not dancing together.

Kwaku recalled his subdued role at the party and how, had he not been invited to dance by Blossom, he would have sat by the wall talking to old Mr Barzey instead.

"That's how Blossom behave when you been hiding in the bush," Miss Gwendoline declared triumphantly. "She been rejoicing. Rejoicing! She come here with she hypocrisy and she hypocritical money, but as soon as they start hunting you down she start rejoicing. I did see through her long ago. It take a woman to see through a woman.... Anyway, now you know."

Kwaku, thoroughly demoralized, raised a desultory hand to his mouth. He was now in no doubt that the world was ruled by women. When they were not protecting him they were frightening him to death. Sometimes he was convinced that there was a curious affinity between Blossom and Miss Gwendoline. Outwardly, the only thing they had in common was their portly figures; but their very dislike for each other was complementary, like two metal tracks of the same railway, always near one another, but never meeting.

Other things had happened in the few days that Kwaku had been away. The sanitary inspector had been around, egged on no doubt by the rates collector. He told Miss Gwendoline that the latrine in the yard would have to be moved to a spot a suitable distance from the gutter that ran between her yard and the neighbours'.

"How we going to do something expensive like move a latrine when we can't even eat?" Miss Gwendoline remarked.

And the idea that had taken root in his mind while he was staying at Blossom's stirred once again: there only remained for him to go and seek work outside the village, to New Amsterdam perhaps, or to Kwakwani, the bauxite town on the Berbice river. He would have to make the break – no matter what his wife said – in her interest, in his own and in the children's. A good third of the men had already left, some as far away as the Mazaruni. Tomorrow he would discuss the matter with old Mr Barzey, who would not fail to make some profitable suggestion.

That night the children were sent to bed earlier than usual, so that their parents could exchange confidences and tell each other stories from the Bible, the usual occupation of Guyanese adults between the hours of eight and midnight.

Old Mr Barzey's anger had abated. And the news that Kwaku was going away led him to be less harsh with him. The occasions that he met Kwaku's wife in the yard were painful for, having refused to acknowledge to himself that it was she who – in her crude and forthright way – had suggested the idea of confessing to a crime he did not commit, he feared that she might remind him of their conversation.

Since his return from the police station his daughter-in-law smiled whenever they sat down at table, as much as to say, thought old Mr Barzey, "Now I've got you, you old fraud! No more of your airs with me!" Even his son, who was normally calmness itself in the middle of a thunderstorm, would cast nervous glances that said: "What you expect if you do things like that?"

No, he could never live it down with those two and, in fact, had his work cut out to maintain his psychological advantage over his daughter-in-law. He noticed that she was abandoning her crab-like tactics of caution and circumlocution in favour of a frontal attack. By God, he would soon show her where the psychological advantage lay! He would drive her back and reduce her to a state of cautiousness she only dreamed of before. He would wipe that smile off her face and make her wish she had not seen in his discomfiture an advantage for herself.

When she told him of the talk of the wild party at Blossom's house, he brought out his butterfly net and attached it to the wall as a sign of his defiance.

"You're not going to leave it there," she remarked.

"Yes," came the laconic reply. And old Mr Barzey saw this as the first step in recovering his old position of near inviolability in his son's house.

Kwaku came to consult Mr Barzey about his departure and to collect the old box camera the old man had promised him, together with a tripod, some spare rolls of film and a developing tray.

"Well, things won't be the same without you, Kwaku .... What a party that was, eh? Just as I was getting my blood up those four men came for you. If the thing hadn't come to an end I would've shown you young fellows a thing or three."

"No point staying," Kwaku told him. "I hear some coconut trees aback dead already and the locusts attacking other plants. And tobesides I got to feed my family and can't do it by staying in the village."

Mr Barzey asked if the shoemaker had paid him his back wages.

"He tell me to come today."

They talked of one thing and another, of old times, of the village, its insect and other afflictions, of the rates collector, whose exasperation with the people of C village had grown to unheard-of proportions, fired by their inability to discharge their obligations to the district council. They talked about the project to build a new secondary school two miles away as part of a new self-help scheme, and about the shortage of margarine and other foodstuffs.

"Ah!" sighed Mr Barzey. "The passing days."

He began telling Kwaku of his boyhood in Georgetown, his favourite subject of recollection. His family used to live in a house with a dormer window, the only such window in the whole town, he believed. At nights he could hear the whirring of his mother's sewing-machine, while he lay awake and spoke to all sorts of characters who marched through his room, people he had seen in the streets and whose presence he could conjure up simply by closing his eyes. There was Alan, a tall ageless man whom very old men had known as boys. He was blind in one eye and wore glasses which he could not resist washing whenever he went by a public standpipe. And Turtle, a ponderous talker, renowned more for his manner of talking than for what he said. There was Banga Mary, who followed the masquerade bands in their journeys across the town. She was unable to resist the sound of their drums and on hearing the *bong-dup, bong-dup* floating on the wind she would stop whatever she was doing and say, as if she were in a trance, "Santapee band!" She would listen to the drumming in order to discover

95

from which direction it was coming, and then would be off like a hunter in pursuit of wild hogs. There was the schoolmaster, once head of a well-known school, who had been dismissed on account of some obscure accusation of embezzelment of his pupils' bank-money. He told stories, improvised at the snap of a finger, and collected money from his listeners afterwards. A man of such quality haunting the barber shops and tailor shops, all the establishments with a captive audience, brought a catch to old Mr Barzey's voice. And Kwaku felt that the old man must have known this schoolmaster very well indeed.

"Such injustice! Such injustice!" he muttered, and then looked at Kwaku as if he were a stranger.

When the sun set the two men went out to sit on the porch and watch for the twin lights of cars in the distance, which appeared to grow like the eyes of fabulous animals from bushmen's tales, then went out in a whining of engines. The calabash tree that partly screened the house was heavy with enormous, inedible fruit, hanging over the slack trench water, from which a strangled gurgling of frogs rose. Fragments of talk from neighbouring houses clotted on the cool evening air, hardly understood by the two men, who sat next to each other, inventing new subjects of conversation.

Kwaku thought he could see Wilfred crossing his bridge in the half-light and might even have detected a slight wave of his hand. He had seen Blossom early that morning to explain that it would be unwise for him to come visiting for any length of time. But she had said little, hardly more than to remind him that the bus terminus was at Rosignol, just over the river from New Amsterdam, where he would be living.

If only Blossom and Miss Gwendoline were friends there would be no want, no need for remose, for guilt, for any of the emotions that plagued him without end. On the face of it he was leaving the village to find a means of maintaining his family; but at bottom it was his inability to deal with his wife's unspoken scorn that was driving him away.

"You packed already?" old Mr Barzey asked, breaking the silence.

"All done. Tomorrow I just up and take the bus."

"You'd better pack the camera in straw," Mr Barzey told him. "And put the cap over the lens."

"Why in the name of God you chose New Amsterdam?" asked the old man eventually, after a long silence.

Kwaku shrugged his shoulders in answer. In fact he knew perfectly well why he was going to New Amsterdam instead of the capital, with its unlimited opportunities for freelance work. Mr Barzey's stories of life in the big city had so impressed him he did not believe he was up to living among those larger-than-life characters who inhabited his friend's boyhood memories against the background of whirring sewing-machines. He did not even know what a dormer window was! No, he would be like an ant among marabuntas. New Amsterdam was his town.

"New Amsterdam's a town, isn't it?" he said aloud.

"A dump!" Mr Barzey dismissed his question.

"Well, I goin' to a dump," Kwaku gave in. He would have liked to reveal that that was precisely why he was going there.

"I'm warning you," said Mr Barzey, "there's nothing you can do there."

Kwaku, on the point of confessing his anxieties, was summoned by one of the twins to come home for dinner. He went off, accompanied by the old man's promise to see him off the next day.

That night Kwaku lay awake thinking how thin his children had become. The plague of locusts was for them just another event, as was the fact that they ate little else but black pudding. And if the grown-ups talked mostly of their misery, the boys devoted their spare time to playing with friends, while Philomena and Rona held endless conversations about their admirers; at least that was what Miss Gwendoline had told Kwaku, because more than once when she surprised them they fell silent. Rona never tired of begging her mother for permission to renounce her ribbons and twin plaits in favour of a more grown-up hair-do; but Miss Gwendoline insisted that she was still a girl.

Since there was no work and Kwaku had so much time on his hands, he had come to know his children well, through his wife, who relayed to him the things they confided in her and would not have dreamed of telling their father.

That night Kwaku dreamt that he was drawn to the front road by a strange sound, almost a *call*. Dressing hurriedly he rushed outside, past his uncle's house and under Mr Barzey's, until he came to the bridge, past which a silent procession was marching. In it each person was carrying a lamp and each lamp burned with its own bright ness. When the procession arrived at the road in which the church stood, it took that road, but not to the north, where the church was, but to the south in the direction of the back-lands and eventually the bush, the inpenetrable forest. On waking Kwaku recalled this detail with especial force, for it seemed to him that the direction the procession took was fraught with significance. But above all he was overwhelmed by a feeling of abandonment as he stood alone on Mr Barzey's bridge with the field opposite and empty houses stretching away on both sides of the road and in every direction before and behind him.

The next morning he lay in his bed thinking of the vividness of the dream, of the details that filled his mind as if the procession had only just gone by: the shoes worn by one man, the hunched back of the woman behind him, the child with its own little lamp and the mass of a four-deep throng, heading purposefully for a pre-arranged destination.

"Las' night I dream," he told Miss Gwendoline, after the children had gone to school.

He told her of his dream and she said that since he was about to go away he should consult the old woman living by the locust tree to find out its meaning.

"I don' got time," he told her. "For a start I got to see the shoemaker to get my wages."

"They say when you dream 'bout bad things is good and when you dream 'bout good things is bad."

How could Kwaku explain the flood of tenderness for this woman, the sudden, bizarre intensity of his awareness of the bond that held them together? Sometimes, while he lay on the bed during the day, the sight of a shoe of hers, its tongue rising gently, leading away from the shadowy cavern where her toes dwelt, gave him ideas no other human was capable of having. He was convinced at such times that he could achieve anything he aimed for, provided he bore that shoe in mind, its joints, its stitches, its heel and sole, and its mysterious protuberances.

"Gwendoline," he called gently.

"What?"

"Come, ne."

"For what?"

"Come, ne?"

"In broad daylight?"

He kissed her on the mouth and knew, from that oyster-like touch of her lips, that she was as keen as he.

"Put your shoes on," he said.

"Me shoes? Why?"

"I don' know."

"Me shoes?"

"Yes."

Kwaku followed Miss Gwendoline into the bedroom and watched her rest her right ankle on her left thigh before slipping on the right shoe on her foot. Then she bent down to pick up the other shoe; but he held her wrist and began kissing her again. Fabian, wondering where her mother had gone, crawled into the bedroom and sat down in the middle of the floor, on one of the girls' sleeping mats, to witness her parents' love-making with wide, inquisitive eyes. And at the sight of her mother's breasts the infant raised its hand, smiled fleetingly, then fell back into its squatting position. Everything appeared to her eye in a vermilion hue: the entwined limbs, the bed, as overwhelming as her parents, the towering window and above all else her mother's face, which kept staring beyond her. She sat looking at that face, waiting for the sound of its voice. Then, unexpectedly, she began to cry, unable to make anything of her mother's silence.

Miss Gwendoline glanced at her daughter, but when Kwaku bit her on the shoulder to regain her attention Fabian began to bawl at the top of her voice.

"You got to hurry," Miss Gwendoline said. "She not goin' stop."

And Kwaku consummated his passion in brusque, rapid movements, so that his wife could console their offspring.

"In any case you in' got a lot of time," Miss Gwendoline reminded him.

It was so. His suitcase was resting on its side to take up as little space as possible in the small room. But apart from his visit to the shoemaker's shop certain matters had to be checked; his wallet, identity card and the little things, his uncle claimed, that were unknown in his youth.

Kwaku fetched a bucket of water from the drainage canal and, with a calabash of rainwater for rinsing, shut himself up in his uncle's bath hut at the foot of his stairs. He could hear one of his neighbours singing. She was certainly not suffering on account of the locusts, Kwaku said to himself. If only, long ago, he had accepted Blossom's offer to secure him a job with the Transport when he was capable of taking on anything! Now you could not get work like that for love or money. He sighed at his folly as a young man and at the way things had turned out for him.

Kwaku asked the cake-shop man what time it was and was told that ten had just gone. With only two hours left before his departure, he hurried to the shoemaker's shop, which stood empty, its door wide open. Judging that the shoemaker must be about, he lifted the counter flap and penetrated into the back shop, which was empty as well, then he pushed the door leading into the yard and found his former employer over a tub of liquid, a kind of small paddle in his hand.

"What ... what you doing here?" asked the shoemaker, casting an anxious glance at his tub. "Let's go out front." Dropping the paddle on the floor he led Kwaku through the door, which he slammed shut.

The shoemaker had been experimenting with a new tanning process, the secret of which had been passed on to him by an old porcknocker. It was common knowledge that he bought cartloads of walaba bark, but no one knew for what purpose. His experiments had proved so successful that all his leather came from his own yard, thus saving him the expense of purchasing shop-leather; and the thought that Kwaku with his legendary propensity for free speech might have discovered what he had been doing threw him into confusion.

"Why you don't knock? You must knock the next time."

"Nex' time? I come for my wages. I going away just now."

"Ah, your wages ... . I don't have it."

"Whàt? I goin' away and I don' got any money."

"You only gave me five days' notice, you know," objected the shoemaker.

"But you don' have no work for me."

"The law's the law. You should give me a full seven days' notice. Go and ask any lawyer."

Kwaku grabbed him by the collar.

"I know all about you an' you family of swindlers. I know how you does make the apprentice run errands for your wife. Where he is now, eh? I bet he cleaning her brass or scrubbing down the steps for her. I want my money now!"

Kwaku let go, but, to prevent the shoemaker from calling out, he closed the door and bolted it.

"All right," pleaded the shoemaker, "don't hit me. Is my pressure. This morning when I got out of bed I could hardly walk, my head was spinning so. Wait here."

But Kwaku accompanied him through the door leading into the back shop where the shoemaker opened his writing-desk with its roll-on top and began fumbling in it.

"Here, here ..." he muttered to himself, his hands trembling as he tore the elastic band from a wad of notes. "Don't tell anybody about the desk," he begged. "I trust you. You're decent! Not like the apprentice who would bring his friends in here and clean me out if it wasn't for those padlocks. They tried to break in once, you know, but they couldn't get past the padlocks."

He counted out Kwaku's wages and handed the notes to him, hesitating even at the last moment.

"Good," said Kwaku, after he had checked the money.

Then looking him up and down Kwaku smiled. "I wanted to curse you many times. You forget how you shout at me in front of the apprentice ... ."

"I told you that was an accident," protested the shoemaker, raising his hand. "I even apolo ... ."

"You forget. But I din' forget. That sort of thing I does remember for years and years. 'Kwaku!' you shout out. 'You din' hear me call?' And the apprentice start grinning all over he ugly batty-face; and you think you could make me forget by apologizing! No, man.

'Kwaku!' you shout out. Well, let me tell you something, Mr Shoemaker, I going do now what I been dying to do all these years I been with you in this smelly shop an' got nothing to show for it."

"What's that?" asked the shoemaker, praying silently that someone would knock on the door and save him from this maniac.

Kwaku opened his flies, took out his penis and started spraying the walls with his urine.

"What you doing?" called out the shoemaker. "You gone mad? I going to tell the police."

"Tell them, ne, you swindler, you thief!"

Then, with a little urine still left, he leapt on to the counter and aimed his fire at the shoemaker himself, who, hardly believing his eyes, could only lift his arm in an involuntary gesture of self-defence.

Kwaku then tidied himself up and jumped down to the ground.

"You tell you swindling family," Kwaku said to him, "I do that to you. I urinate 'pon you. I pee 'pon you. I piss 'pon you. An' if you call the police I going tell you apprentice how I piss 'pon you and you wall and I'll spread it round how you come from a family of swindlers .... Ahhhh! That's a load off my mind!" Kwaku declared.

He opened the door wide, inhaled deeply the morning air, struck his chest with his right hand and said, "Ahh!" as he breathed out. "What a morning!" he exclaimed. "Listen to the birds. And I even hear somebody on the road say the locusts going away. What a thing! But we'll never get rid of them. Insects, I mean."

Without bothering to look at the shoemaker, Kwaku strode off with long, triumphant steps into a morning that had brought him unprecedented satisfaction. In less than two hours he had screwed his wife, heard the news about the locusts, recovered his wages and pissed on the premises of his workplace. Was all this not a good augury for his enterprise? Did it not mean that he would conquer New Amsterdam, that a new life was opening before him, like a broad avenue after years of tramping on narrow, overgrown paths? Did his name not mean something special? Kwaku Cholmondeley! Did it not contain the promise of undiscovered worlds, like an egg or a head of hair? The heart was never at rest; but perhaps that was because he had not released those dogs of conquest that kept growling within, demanding that he assert himself in their name. He would look back at this bright morning and use it as a balm on his future wounds, the morning after a dark, foreboding dream.

Kwaku strode homewards, rolling the sights and sounds of his village round the palate of his memory.

BOOK 2

17   The proposal

KWAKU WOKE up in the shed next to the New Amsterdam stelling, where had gone to sleep the night before, after his enquiries had failed to bring him information of a cheap lodging-house. There were so many holes in the roof of the shed that Kwaku at first believed he was looking at the branches of a tree through which the sun was shining.

"You look like a bridegroom," a voice said to him.

Without realizing that the voice had spoken for the second time and that he had in fact been awakened by it, Kwaku blinked and sat up but saw no one.

"I'm here, behind you."

Turning round Kwaku saw a strapping woman of about thirty-five smiling beningly at him.

"You not from around here, eh?"

"No," answered Kwaku, at once thinking of the woman as a possible helper.

"If I was you," she told him, "I'd get up. There was a choke and rob on the stelling last night and the police in' catch the man yet."

Kwaku jumped up and grabbed hold of his tripod and his grip, which he had been using as a head-rest.

"Choke and rob?" he asked. "You got that around here too?"

"That's national disease. It all over. You don' got nowhere to go?"

"No," replied Kwaku hurriedly. "I'm a decent man, but my house get blow down by a hurricane and my poor wife and children ... ." He hung his head disconsolately.

"Hurricane? I din' hear of no hurricane. Tobesides, I thought Guyana was outside the hurricane belt."

"No, lady. Wasn't in Guyana. Is one of them small islands. My wife was a doctor and she and the children been swept out to sea."

"My father was from one of the islands," the woman said, smiling oddly. "Come and talk to him. He like to talk to anybody from the small islands. And he won't let you go away without a clay pipe or something. Come to think of it, he might even put you up for a few days."

Kwaku could not believe his ears. He had intended to stay in the shed as long as the authorities would let him. It cost him no money; and with the dry season only a few weeks old he would only need to buy his food. At the worst he could even cross the river and get in touch with Blossom in Rosignol. Now, out of the blue, had come an opportunity to break into New Amsterdam society. He followed the woman out of the shed, the earth floor of which was covered at intervals with plaques of oil. Once in the street, she stopped a taxi and after a brief exchange of words with the chauffeur, got in and signalled to Kwaku to follow her.

Despite his misgivings about the cost of the journey Kwaku could not help gaping at the buildings they went past, the market, the fire-station, private houses of imposing size and design, all of them painted. "There's not a poor man in this town," he thought to himself.

"Which island you come from?" the woman enquired, taking him by surprise.

"Grenada," came the reply. He had intended saying Barbados, but did not know if it was out of the hurricane belt or not. Grenada was obscure enough to pass muster.

"Ah! That's where my grandfather come from," said the woman.

Kwaku ceased admiring the buildings and began constructing for himself a life in Grenada strongly resembling his own in the village. If he were questioned about street names and suchlike he would have to make out as best he could.

After much turning and twisting they got out at the head of a bridge which led to a long street overgrown with grass, with houses on either side.

To Kwaku's surprise the woman paid the chauffeur.

"Put your money away," she told him. "We don' allow people to pay in these parts."

Once away from the main road they might have been in C village or any of the other villages along the coast which Kwaku knew. The houses were numbered, 1, 1A, 1B, 1C then $\frac{1}{2}$, followed by the A, B and C until number 3 was reached. It was at Lot No. 56B, painted clearly, but in poorly written script, that the woman turned into the gate. Kwaku climbed the tall stairway and followed her into the drawing-room, where she invited him to sit in a deep Berbice chair, which was newly upholstered.

Despite the open windows there was a faint musty reek which Kwaku associated with the indolence of the street up which they had walked, and the peculiar silence of the house, an odour of passivity he recalled in a home he once visited for a short time when a youth, to look up a young lady distinguished by her bovine acquiescence of his advances.

Shortly afterwards a man about the same age as the woman who had befriended Kwaku came out and greeted him, speaking in a soft, ingratiating voice. He was slim and hawk-faced, but with the kindly expression of someone who was accustomed to being trusted.

Hearing that Kwaku was anxious to meet his wife's father the man said, "He's gone out. He not coming back till this afternoon,

103

but I'm sure with you coming from the islands and all he'll take to you."

He was about to leave, but turned to face Kwaku one more. "Ada making you something to eat ... and then we going to talk."

Kwaku smiled and, as the man disappeared, thought that it was just as well that they should talk after they ate. If his hosts found out his lie about the hurricane he would at least have got a meal out of them. Then he fell to thinking that the lady had been greeted by no one as they walked up the overgrown road, nor had she even bothered to look up at the houses past which they had come. But then it was the hour when the men, at least, were at work and the children at school.

As the smell of cooking reached him Kwaku prayed that the meal would not take as long to prepare as those Gwendoline cooked. She behaved as if her life depended on the quality of her cooking.

Some time afterwards the tall lady brought him a bowl of water and a cake of soap and remained by his side until he had washed his hands and wiped them with a white cloth she had hanging over her arm. Then she left him alone once more, only to reappear a good half-hour later with a tray on which was a bowl of boiled shrimps and a plate of steaming hot rice.

"You din' tell us your name," she said, putting down the tray on a centre table a few feet from Kwaku.

"Cholmondeley," Kwaku replied, and stood up for a moment to show his gratitude for the couple's extraordinary hospitality.

"In this house we eat with our hands, Mr Cholmondeley," she declared in a tone so natural and inoffensive that Kwaku felt that a privilege was being bestowed on him.

"That's how God intended us to eat, Mistress. We don' touch the floor no more with our bodies. We must have bed. We don' touch our food either; we must have spoon or knife and fork. Yet the earth is our mother and food is our sustenance."

The tall lady approved of Kwaku's inspired outburst with a warm smile.

"Our ancestors did break their bread just like Jesus did do," she informed him. "In the passage from Africa we learned lots of bad things; and different sounds too, Mr Cholmondeley. We learned 'bout the sound of bells. That's not a African sound. But wha' fo' do? The road back is a long one."

"And painful," added Kwaku, sprinkling a handful of shrimps on the coconut rice.

"It needn't be," said the lady. "It can be beautiful."

Her husband reappeared and, without a word, sat down opposite Kwaku, a few feet from his wife. Then he said:

"You're enjoying your food, Mr –"

"Cholmondeley," his wife put in.

"Mr Cholmondeley?" the man, completed his question.

"Yes, very much," Kwaku replied. "Very much."

"Enjoy it, Mr Cholmondeley," the man exhorted him.

After a long silence, broken only by the whining of a bee seeking a way out of the sun-drenched room, he added, "For in the midst of life there is death."

A shrimp fell from the handful of rice Kwaku was holding. Irrationally, the picture of a train emerging from a mist assailed him, followed by a jumble of unrelated images. Once his uncle, hearing that a cow had been killed by a passing train, hurried to the spot and claimed his part of the carcase, just in time as it turned out, for the animal had already been carved to the bone. He thought of the first gift he ever received, and of his intense disappointment that it was a pencil case. He thought of Blossom's rusty bicycle and his disregard for her concern lest he misused it.

Kwaku was no longer enjoying the meal he had begun with so promising an appetite. Doing his best to avoid his host's gaze he kept his eyes on the ground and discovered wide chinks between the floorboards through which he could see bundles of firewood piled in stacks, and an earth stove with grey ashes. Now that he was nearing the end of his meal he could no longer recall the satisfaction of the first mouthful and began to regret having accepted so readily the offer of a meal.

"You enjoyed it?" his host enquired of Kwaku, who answered that it was the best meal he had ever had.

Once more he was offered a bowl of water and a towel by his hostess, who stood guard over his ablutions as solicitously as she had served him.

"That was good, Mr Cholmondeley, wasn't it?" asked his host.

"That was exceptional," Kwaku agreed.

And his hostess, as soon as she rejoined them, said to him, "Would you do us a favour, Mr Cholmondeley?"

"Anything."

"It's quite a big favour," the man said.

"Oh, yes," Kwaku acquiesced with a gesture of protestation that his hosts should make so much of a favour he welcomed, if only to pay off his debt to them.

"Not very big," the hostess corrected her husband.

"Mr Cholmondeley is a gentleman," said the host, "and is better to exaggerate the size of the favour. It's not too big, nor yet too small either."

"What is it then?"

Husband and wife looked at each other.

"Mr Cholmondeley," said the woman, "when I did look down

and see you sleeping in the shed, pricked by the sun, I was touched to remember the story of the Good Samaritan. I couldn' leave you there, a prey to bad men. And is not only the men! They got women in New Amsterdam who would strip you of your belongings. And if you wearing a gold ring they would rip it off your finger and even take your finger with it ... ."

"It's our daughter, Mr Cholmondeley," the host broke in. "We want you to married her."

The woman, evidently worried at the effect of her husband's words on Kwaku, added hastily, "Is only a formality, Mr Cholmondeley."

"But I'm married," Kwaku managed to articulate.

"What?" exclaimed the man, as stunned by Kwaku's announcement of his civil status as Kwaku had been by his wife's request to marry their daughter.

He transfixed his wife with such a look of despair that she avoided his eyes.

"Excuse me, Mr Cholmondeley," the man said, standing up at the same time. He touched his wife as he went by, and she rose and followed him into the bedroom.

"What we goin' do?" he asked her in a whisper. "She start to stink already."

"It don' matter," she said. "What it matter if he married or not?"

"You think so? It wouldn't be a marriage by law."

"That's man's law."

"You think so?" he asked again, just so that she might repeat those reassuring words.

"I know so!" she declared.

"I suppose you're right ... . All right."

They rejoined Kwaku, who was so downcast at his predicament that he was resolved to say boldly that he was leaving.

"I'm sorry, can I get my grip?" he asked them.

"Mr Cholmondeley," pleaded the man. "We beg you to do us this favour. Is a straight formality. Nobody would know ... not even our daughter."

"But ... ."

"Come ... come and see her."

Kwaku followed the man past the door of the first bedroom and through the open door of the second, where an overpowering stench made him look aside. The woman took his arm and it was only in turning to look at her that he saw the coffin of unpolished wood in which a girl of not more than fifteen was lying, dressed as a bride, in white organdie, with a bouquet of white flowers on her stomach.

"O God!" Kwaku muttered under his breath.

Noticing his revulsion, the lady whispered to him, "She's a virgin,

Mr Cholmondeley."

"But I'm a sane man," Kwaku protested desperately, searching for an excuse to leave, even without his grip and his photographic equipment. "If she's dead why you want her to get married?" he asked, professing an interest he did not feel.

"It's just that," said the man. "She's our only child. We can't let her go without ... ." And the man, overcome with grief, was unable to finish what he was saying. Instead, he just shook his head.

Kwaku could not understand how they could endure the stench and pleaded, "Can we go outside?"

"Just touch her, Mr Cholmondeley," the woman suggested.

But at the thought of approaching the dead girl Kwaku recoiled.

"Touch her and then we'll go out."

Kwaku allowed himself to be led forward by the woman, who was still holding his arm. He put his hand forward and touched the lifeless hand.

"You see?" she said. "That's done. You touched her and it was all right."

But Kwaku had already turned to leave the room when the man grabbed hold of him.

"I don' understand you, Mr Cholmondeley. Look how lovely she is!"

"But I'm married. An' your daughter dead!"

"Not dead, Mr Cholmondeley," said the man, "only sleeping."

"Sir," declared Kwaku, "you're a good man. You so generous I going remember you when I'm old and doddering. And when I get rich I goin' give you half of everything I own. But try and understand my situation."

"Why don' Mr Cholmondeley just slip the ring on Adele finger and nothing more?" suggested the man's wife. "He needn't go through the full ceremony."

Kwaku, almost overcome by the stench, was ready to do anything short of marrying the girl.

"Bring the ring then," he asked. "Quick, please, Mistress."

From a casket on a chair in one corner of the room the man produced a plain gold ring, which he gave to Kwaku, who stepped boldly forward and attempted to slip it on the fourth finger of the dead girl's left hand. But the rigidity of the joints, the coldness of the dead hand and the odour from the coffin made the task exceptionally difficult. Both the girl's parents were bending over their daughter, anxious that Kwaku should succeed.

"Don' try to bend the finger, Mr Cholmondeley," the woman told him. "Just slip it on."

Kwaku steadied his hands, attempted once more to ease the ring gently over the middle joint; and only when he was about to give up, driven to distraction by the stench, did the ring pass the protruding joint, as if drawn by some mysterious force.

Kwaku lost no time in fleeing from the room. The couple found him leaning out of one of the front windows.

"Is not so bad when you accustomed to it," the man said, encircling his shoulders with a muscular arm. "Is a great relief for us, you know. A young woman should be married before her boat sail into the land of darkness. Tonight we'll leave the wedding meal next to the coffin."

"But ... what for?" Kwaku asked. "She can't eat it."

"Yes, Mr Cholmondeley," his host said. "Tomorrow it'll be gone."

"You believe that?"

"Where you come from?"

Kwaku did not answer. Instead, he stood before his hosts, wearing a meek expression.

"Thanks for all you do for me," Kwaku said of a sudden, smiling at the man and woman in turn. "I going now. I remember I got to send a telegram to my wife."

He took up his grip and tripod, but found his way through the door barred by the man.

"I going scream, Mister; so let me pass."

"You can go whenever you like," the woman said from behind him, "after we give her the marriage meal."

"When is that?" Kwaku demanded.

"One hour past sunset, Mr Cholmondeley. You can do whatever you like after that."

Watching the sun stream in through the window, Kwaku realized that many hours must pass before he would be allowed to leave.

"If you stop me I goin' scream," he threatened once more.

"Go on, Mr Cholmondeley," the man challenged him.

Kwaku put his head through the window and made as if to scream, but fear of what the couple might do restrained him.

"Well, Mr Cholmondeley, I did say you can do as you please," the woman told him. "Scream if you want."

Pretending that he had no intention of screaming, Kwaku faced them. "I'm not a ungrateful man. You did befriend me and I can't turn on you."

He put his grip and tripod down and, affecting indifference at the constraint placed on his freedom, asked, "Just tell me what part of New Amsterdam this place is.

"This place?" said the man. "It called Stanleytown."

Kwaku's heart sank at the sound of the dreaded name. When he was still a small boy he had heard talk of a notrious obeah murder that had taken place in Stanleytown. He recalled that the murdered child had been found in a latrine where she had been drowned, in order to satisfy instructions received in a dream.

"You ever hear about it?" asked the woman.

"No, Mistress. I don' know Stanleytown at all. But is nice to know I'm in a place with such a nice sounding name. Everything about this house so nice. An' your daughter got such a nice name. Adele."

"Your wife, Mr Cholmondeley," the man corrected him. "She's your wife now. It's the name of a flower or something beautiful like a flower. I never see one myself, but with a name like that it must be a flower among flowers. And she was a flower among young women. She walked like a queen, didn't she, dearest? The blood is now cold, but we'll remember her before she was married, when her blood was warm and she was growing into a woman and her hips did swell out like the petals of a flower. And d'you know, Mr Cholmondeley, she was a ugly child till she was about ten. Then her skin started to get smooth and she ... ." Choked with emotion, the man was unable to continue and, ashamed at his weakness, fled inside, leaving Kwaku with his wife.

"He's not a strong man ... in spirit, Mr Cholmondeley. Stay until tonight. He won't touch a hair of your head if you stay till tonight. People're frightened of him because he does keep to himself, but he's a gentle man."

The sight of his host in tears had already transformed the situation in Kwaku's eyes.

"As long as you don' ask me to stay for longer, Mistress."

"I give you my word, Mr Cholmondeley."

By afternoon the intolerable stench had penetrated into the rest of the house, and when the sun went down Kwaku was sitting by the open door, holding a wet towel over his nose. From time to time one of the neighbours in the house further on would appear on the porch and stare over at him, only to disappear inside when Kwaku looked up.

Now and then flocks of birds flew over, appearing first over the river, black specks in leisured flight, and disappearing minutes later, beyond the Public Road, and Kwaku recalled the late afternoons in his village, the shadows of circling crows and frogspawn in the trenches. There was no activity in the sawmill which, in the distance, seemed to be floating on the river itself, its huge corrugated roof a solid shadowy mass. Kwaku was disturbed by something ponderous in the shadows of the gathering night. Perhaps it was the thought that, once the hour after sunset had passed, he would still be unable to leave; or perhaps he was put out by the absence of the couple, who presumably were in the room with their dead daughter. He reflected on the remarkable circumstance that the death of a single person was capable of fouling the air to such a degree, that in the midst of what people accepted as normal the abnormal was on the prowl, caged by the restraint of custom and fear of retribution. When the stench reached the neighbours and the couple were found out, there would be an outcry, possibly as great as the one that followed the discovery of the girl in the latrine, in the 'forties. Yet here he was, in the thick of the occurrence, uncertain as to the outcome. He planned to pick up his grip and tripod and to flee when the ridge of light on the horizon disappeared. Everything depended on the sun, and, as in his own house, there was no clock in the strangers', only an awareness of the sun or the singing of birds at morning. One of his earliest recollections was the yellowing edge of a plaque of butter as it was melted by the sun, a recollection that became a fascination, which came before his passion for anything connected with the sea.

Suppose the woman's father arrived home before he left? Would he be expected to chat with him? Did the father exist? Or was he an invention to attract him to the house? The hour passed slowly, like those interminable Sunday afternoons before he came to know Mr Barzey. Here and there a light went on, now in a neighbour's house, now in the distance among the trees. And by the minute the awful reek grew, threatening to suffocate him.

Kwaku, with a sudden resolution, got up from his seat, crossed the large room and took hold of his grip and tripod; and in the twinkling of an eye he was in the street, heading for the Public Road where the taxi had dropped him. He walked as quickly as his grip would allow him, constantly looking back to see if he was being pursued by one or other of his hosts; and in his anxiety to get away he failed to notice how fresh the air was. It was the sight of a mangy dog sitting in a gateway that reminded him of the stench and decay. Had there been time he would have stopped to stroke the wretched beast.

Once on the Public Road Kwaku turned left, slowing down at the sight of the cars, the buses and the knots of people standing by the roadside, even stopping occasionally to recover his breath.

He came upon a group of people standing with their backs to the road, and as he went by someone began shouting. An argument followed, but no sooner was Kwaku far enough from the gathering for their words to be meaningless than a child's voice broke into song, like the sudden flight of an oriole. He turned back and joined the men and women screening the child from the road.

"Take it back, take it back,
The powder in the jar.

For some your talk
Might have the meaning
Of a gift.
But take it back

110

The powder in the jar.

I caught the lie
Inside your words,
So take it back,
Take it back,
The powder in the jar."

Kwaku took up his things and went on, beset by anxieties about his family and doubts as to the wisdom of his decision to travel to New Amsterdam. At the entrance to the shed beside the stelling he looked around him, and seeing no one about he went to the corner where he had slept the night before. But almost at once the folly of choosing the same shed occurred to him, so he got up and left it to find another shelter for the night.

18   How Kwaku acquired a reputation

KWAKU STQOD in front of the photographer's shop, the only one of its kind in New Amsterdam, according to his informant, the cane-juice seller stationed at the entrance to the stelling. In a miserable showcase strewn with prints curled by the heat of the sun lay, here and there, the inert bodies of flies which evidently used it as a graveyard. From what Kwaku could see of the prints, which were not too twisted to show off their photo-surfaces, the owner of the shop was less competent than he. The portrait of one young lady, with attractive features and a bold expression, exposed the deep lines of her neck cruelly.

"He don' know a thing about lighting," thought Kwaku with malicious satisfaction.

Pushing the glass door he entered the shop and enquired of the middle-aged East Indian man sitting at the counter if he could see the proprietor.

"Is me," came the reply. "Is a wedding?"

Kwaku explained that he was looking for work.

"Work? In photography? You don' see my display case? Even in the capital the photographers going to the dogs."

"I can develop. I know everything 'bout developing," Kwaku said hopefully.

"My wife does do that."

"I can take photographs too."

"My son does do that."

"I can...."

111

"I does do that too, whatever you was going to say."

"Oh," Kwaku muttered disconsolately.

"Things bad, eh?"

"Well, yes," answered Kwaku, with no attempt to conceal his desperation. "I want to work. Is not that I don' want to work. They got a lot o' lazy men in this world. I want to *do* something and ...."

"Why not do something else? Nowadays you got to know to do more than one trade. Look at my counter. Nobody would think I'm a photographer from my counter."

Kwaku picked up one of the number of paperback and hardback books neatly arrayed on the counter.

"Is Chinese?" he asked the proprietor, lifting the book he held in his hand.

"No. Korean. Those is Chinese," he declared, pointing to another set. "Who can read Korean an' Chinese in this country? But these books flooding in, though."

"Who does buy them, then?" asked Kwaku.

"Nobody."

"Then why you stock them?"

"Guess, ne," came the evasive reply. "Before we used to get only American an' English books, which din' got nothing to do with us. Now they remedy the situation by giving us books we can't read."

Most of the remaining space on the counter was taken up with second-hand books in English, novels, school books and even books with musical notation.

"They does sell good, the music. In fact all of them does sell good. The bookshops in Georgetown closing. Central Bookshop close, Argosy on its las' legs. All these in here are second-hand, except the Chinese and Korean ones. You want to buy a Korean book?" he asked facetiously.

Kwaku, preoccupied with his own problems, had already switched off.

"Things bad, eh?" the man asked again. "Where you from?"

Kwaku told him.

"If I was you I'd do anything, if you want work. Photography is a dead loss."

"I'm a shoemaker, too."

"Shoemaking? Well, why you din' say so? That's it! I keep telling my children .... Anyway, go an' see Barton; he'll put you right. He living in Winkle."

The photographer came out of his shop and showed Kwaku how to get to Winkle, an old quarter of New Amsterdam once famous for its blacksmith shops.

Kwaku wanted to seek occupation in shoemaking only as a last resort. He knew that the trade was expanding – what with the restrictions on the importation of shoes and the growing leather industry – but was equally aware that he could only scrape a living if he returned to making and half-soling shoes. Bitterly disappointed at the lack of opportunity in photography, he heaved his luggage on to his shoulder and set out for Winkle.

On the way the houses became smaller and more dilapidated, as if they were in competition for a neglect prize. Having walked the distance recommended by the photographer he asked a little girl standing on one leg where Mr Barton the shoemaker lived.

"So!" she said, pointing to a broken-down house a few yards on.

"But where's his shop?"

"He in' got shop. He does work there!" she exclaimed, amazed at Kwaku's ignorance.

Not believing the little girl, he left his luggage on the grass verge, jumped the narrow gutter and looked around.

"Mr Barton!" he called out.

"What?" came a gruff voice.

Kwaku followed the sound of the voice and found an old man so perfectly camouflaged in the half-light by his dark clothes that he might have stood there all day without seeing him.

"The photographer send me. He said you would help me find work."

"Which photographer?" came the gruff question. "He had his lights fix in the same place for twenty years. *In* you go an' out you come an' he want ten dollars fo' pressing a button. He in' no photographer."

"He say you can find me work in shoemaking."

"Is who you? I don' know you. Every sore-ass want to become shoemaker 'cause he kian' pass his school exams. I don' know you."

"That's a fine shoe, Mr Barton," said Kwaku, in an attempt to butter up the shoemaker.

"Is Italian," came the abrupt answer. "Is what you want, I ask you?"

"I looking for a job."

"This in' no Employment Exchange. You looking? Look, ne. Nothing to stop you looking. Finding's the thing. Look till you y'eye fall out. I been looking for peace for seventy years an' all I find is strife. Nobody stop you from looking."

Kwaku turned to go, but the shoemaker said to him, "Words never kill. Sit down."

Finding nothing to sit on Kwaku settled on a tiny stool about five inches off the ground, which would have been too low for an infant. But the shoemaker seemed to care not at all that it was uncomfortable. Kwaku watched him work without attempting to address him. He watched him place a half-made shoe on a piece of leather, which

113

he then marked out with chalk. He watched him cut along the line laboriously until the sole was ready to be sewn to the shoe. And during this time neither exchanged so much as a grunt.

When at last the shoemaker spoke it was with the same bitterness as before.

"You don' come from New Amsterdam, I can see that. I did born an' grow here an' all my life I been dying to get away. An' every time I try something happen to keep me. When I was fifteen I hear two girls talking 'bout me. 'You ever see his nose good?' one of them say. 'No, what wrong with it?' the other girl ask she. 'Well, the nex' time you see him you look up it.' That's how I become conscious of meself. I get a handmirror and do what the girl say. I couldn' see nothing special. It was the same nose as I always had. But obviously the women din' like it. I was so hurt I decide to stop working at school; and when I lef' I decide to get a lowly job, so as not to get above the condition of me nose ... I tell you this story 'cause I don' know you and 'cause you don' come from round here. I been dying to tell it for years ... I get married to the ugliest girl in Winkle 'cause I thought that everybody I pass by was looking up my nose."

It was all Kwaku could do to suppress his laughter. For a while it was on the tip of his tongue to say, "Bend back you head let me look up your nose," a request he would have been unable to resist in happier circumstances.

"If you want you can live here an' help me," declared the shoemaker after a long pause. "But all I can give you is tea in the morning an' a meal at twelve o'clock. You don't got to say yes."

"I say yes," Kwaku snapped eagerly before the old man could change his mind.

And that is how Kwaku Cholmondeley, shoemaker from C village, inveterate liar, would-be photographer, near bigamist and father of eight children, came back to the old but despised occupation of shoemaking, of making leather-wear for other people's feet.

After sharing the man's midday meal, Kwaku went and lay down in a hammock which he dragged out of a trunk with a curved top.

"Sling it up there," Mr Barton told him. "The wife used to sleep in it."

Kwaku surveyed the room – the house consisted of one room. The absence of chairs and tables gave it rather the appearance of a shed than an inhabited room, and the thick pile of dust in the corners, typical of those homes with a single occupant, reminded him of the way the old man ate. Every mouthful was followed by a champing and grunting issuing from a mouth that opened occasionally to give Kwaku a clear view of the state of the food before it was finally swallowed with a pronounced gulp. Mr Barton was decidedly no intellectual, thought Kwaku. He was no Mr Barzey. If he had a zip down his belly he would have opened it to give a practical demonstration of the fate of the food he swallowed so violently. He was one of those people who had never heard of privacy and who, in full company would probably lift himself off his chair in order to discharge a powerful, malodorous fart and immediately afterwards continue his interrupted contribution to the conversation as if nothing unusual had occurred.

The room was about ten feet long by eight feet broad. From the rafters hung three empty birdcages to add to the confusion of cluttered boxes, trunks, discarded shoes, lasts, balls of twine, lumps of wax and other unidentifiable objects lying about. Lit by a single shuttered window opening out on the road, the room reminded Kwaku of the interiors of houses he imagined were inhabited by women accused of being Old Higues, except that he always imagined them guarded by a malignant parrot, feeding on bananas by day and more offensive fare by night.

Yet, in that dirty, ill-tended room, Kwaku fell asleep readily, despite his long uninterrupted rest of the night before. The sun, which had crept over the house, now shone through the open back door, magnifying the bits of dust that floated like plankton on the current of some ocean in a continual state of restlessness.

Suddenly Kwaku sat up, awakened by the sound of a violent quarrel that was almost certainly coming from under the house. Thinking that the old man might be in danger, he leapt from the hammock and shot through the back door.

Kwaku found him alone, his head raised like a fowl-cock about to announce the dawn. He was singing. Just as it was impossible to arrive at such a conclusion from the sound of his voice, so it was impossible from the unintelligible words. It was the expression of utter elation on his wrinkled face that gave him away, an expression that could only accompany this distant cousin of talking. Watching Mr Barton perform, one readily understood why stammerers no longer stammered while singing, why hearts distressed by the coils of sorrow found solace in song and why strong men foundered in the collective emotion of low-church chanting. Over and over Mr Barton sang the same stanzas until, from the stresses and an odd word that escaped the repeated exclamations Kwaku discovered the source of the chant.

"From heaven He came and sought her
To be his holy bride,
With His own blood He bought her
And for her life He died."

"I thought you was quarrelling," Kwaku said mischievously.

And, little by little, Kwaku learnt about Mr Barton and his eccentricities, which made Mr Barzey look like a conformist minister.

115

Between the hours of twelve and two in the afternoon the man was invariably seized by an attack of ecstacy, only to fall back into his surly silence between two and half-past two. Even the fit of confiding that had prompted him to tell Kwaku about his nose proved to be exceptional and was never repeated.

The next day Kwaku wrote Miss Gwendoline to inform her of his permanent address and to let her know how he was faring in New Amsterdam:

> Beloved Wife,
> I hope this find you as it leaves me, by the grace of God. Things going very good with me and I working in a photography shop. I am the owner right hand man and already he cant do without me. Well, you see? The first night I get taken in by some nice people who wouldnt take any money. They had a daughter but she pass away when she was three or four and I had to console them and tell them that death is in the midst of life. The woman say I bring joy to there house. I didnt see them since that first day, but I got the feeling I leave a deep impression. I sending this postal order for twenty dollars which use to buy yourself and the children clothes. If I had my life to live over I would buy land, land, land. Now that things not too good and people standing in line all over the country to buy food is people with land that laughing. I been to see the new Canje Bridge. You should see it. It dont got to lift up like the old one to let boats go pass. I hear they build a new bridge cross the Demerara river at Bagotstown. Bridges everywhere. Look at that. We moving forward and going sideways at the same time. That is how crab does walk. I living by a old man who so fussy I got to bathe three times a day in his big bathroom. It got tiles and all. You go in the bathroom in the morning and you want to stay there all day. I got to go now. Give the children my love and let them know I send money for them. Soon you can go and get Clayton and Irene from their grandmother. I going to try and send more money next time.
> Your loving husband
> Kwaku.

Kwaku's lies did not strike him as being odd. Indeed, they were no longer lies, but necessary additions to the dull fare of day-to-day living, like casreep to pepper-pot, or coconut to cook-up rice.

The next day he went to the post office to stamp and post his letter, only to recall, just after he had dropped it into the post-box, that he had forgotten to mention that he had not yet seen a water-tank, only rainwater barrels which, to his way of thinking, were unmentionable substitutes for the swelling belly of an iron tank, symetrically riveted along its joints and resting lengthwise on two supports. Anyway, the letter was irretrievably resting on a pile of hidden mail in a letter box that bore a striking resemblance to a water tank and only needed to be laid on a horizontal plane to complete the resemblance.

Kwaku, on his way back to his lodgings, wondered what the old man would give him to do when he got back. He had only allowed him to wax a length of twine that morning and, at his own suggestion, to pick some breadfruit from the tree at the back of the yard.

"I don' eat it. Is slave food," he grumbled.

But he had no objection to cooking it for Kwaku who on no account was to touch the big iron pot, which had belonged to at least three generations of his people.

For three weeks Kwaku lived with the old man, doing little he considered to be work, learning little more about him than he had learnt in the first few days, except that he took in hardly any work and lived barely at subsistence level. His only entertainment was his afternoon flights of song. No one came to visit him, he went nowhere, and business with his customers was conducted in so few words that they had to be supplemented by gestures, a. nod, a questioning look, a raised eyebrow, a pout of impatience or some other from his wide repertoire.

In the weeks that followed, Kwaku's irritation with his situation grew. His money was running out; the little work there was left him with a great deal of time to reflect on his idleness; and worst of all he had established hardly any contact with people who lived in Winkle. His life in C had not been much different; but there was his friendship with Mr Barzey and Blossom, achieved despite his character, accidents of time as it were. "Every mouldy biscuit got he own voom-cheese", the saying goes. And for the people living in the vicinity Kwaku was indeed a mouldy biscuit, ill-clothed, wild-eyed, erratic in his greetings and reticent to the point of rudeness. They had no idea that he would have grasped the slightest opportunity to make friends with anyone, if only he knew how. Should he say "Howdyedo" to those he met? Or "Hi"? Should he stand with his hands in his pockets, affecting a relaxation he never experienced? Should he repay hospitality with hospitality? The first time he was invited into a neighbour's home everything went well until the moment came to leave. Then, overwhelmed by the attentions of his host, he said, "Thank you! Thank you very much. Thank you very, very much." But the host, wounded by Kwaku's effusiveness, declared, "Don' give me all them 'thank you' and 'pleases', understand? We don' got all of that nonsense round here." Kwaku took fright and hurried away, vowing to seek vengeance on the man. He would set a trap for his dog or throw his scruffy pigs in the trench.

But it was at the point when he recognized his situation as desperate that an unusual circumstance arose. The self-same neighbour fell ill, apparently the victim of a heart attack. He lay on his bed, unable to get up, hardly able to speak for the pain in his

117

chest. Kwaku listened to his wife tell of the seizure, her fright at the sight of an active man like her husband sitting on the stairs, speechless. The shoemaker, in the manner of the people of Winkle, listened without a word of consolation. Then, in a fit of inspiration, Kwaku suggested to the sick man's wife that he eat a feg of garlic every day.

"Garlic'll cure him," he said confidently, backing up his remark with a description of his father before he began taking garlic and afterwards. The lady hastened to communicate his advice to her husband; and within a few days he was up and about.

A blind man, hearing of the miracle, consulted Kwaku about his blindness, which fell upon him the day after he refused to attend his third cousin's funeral. Kwaku took hold of the man's head, stroked it gently and said, "On the twenty-third of July 198x you will be cured." That was four years hence.

As a result of these two incidents, fame came to Winkle. And, quick to discover the advantages of his popularity, Kwaku suggested payment for his services to a hypochrondriac lady, who gave him fifty dollars, as much as he used to earn in a week in C.

The transformation of Kwaku's condition, coming out of the blue as it did, took him unawares, so much so that he was not certain how he should conduct himself. The face he presented to the world was no longer appropriate; of that there was no doubt. On the other hand he was unwilling to relinquish the bearing to which, at least, he was accustomed. But one night the matter was decided for him by the shoemaker, who remarked that he could not maintain his reputation in clothes that would disgrace a beggar.

So Kwaku bought several lengths of cloth and gave instructions to a tailor to dress him like a gentleman with a reputation to maintain. And four weeks from then he strode through Winkle bearing a new walking-stick and a brand new appearance.

The same day he wrote Miss Gwendoline to tell her of his good fortune. She must go at once and fetch back Clayton and Irene from her parents, bedeck them in the finest clothes and tell them it was all their father's doing. He enclosed a money order for one hundred dollars in the envelope, enjoining her to spend it wisely. He knew the value of money, because he had never had any. Besides, its source was inexhaustible.

Miss Gwendoline wrote back promptly, complaining that she had no one to foop her. And Kwaku, dutiful husband that he was, replied in a sympathetic letter that he was in the same situation and understood. In two or three months' time when his reputation was unassailable, he would come home for a week or two and they would foop to their hearts' content.

Kwaku's reputation grew and inevitably the day came when he

was obliged to seek larger premises for his consultations. The shoemaker was not in the least moved by Kwaku's decision, and that afternoon lifted his voice to the sun and shouted his song for everyone within a mile to hear. The public clocks of New Amsterdam chimed the hours almost simultaneously; but for those living in Winkle, far from the town centre, the shoemaker's cantankerous imitation of a joyful voice was the most reliable way of telling the time.

So Kwaku left the street which evoked for many the days of jangling harness, horses waiting to be shod, discarded cart-wheels and the sound of hammer on anvil. He moved into a modest house a few streets up, ten minutes' walk from the market and the line of taxis waiting for the ferry to arrive from Rosignol.

19   A change of fortune

KWAKU WAS reluctant to take in a housekeeper, however old, for fear that Miss Gwendoline would not approve. He would not dare to lie about a thing like that, despite the distance that separated them.

He held his consultations in the afternoon, allowing himself most of the morning to do his shopping and cooking. At first his prescriptions were straightforward and confined largely to the use of garlic concoctions he prepared himself. But he gradually widened his knowledge of herbs from the patients themselves, who often had wide experience in the use of congo pump, burra-burra, mora bark and many of the easily available herbs and leaves. Furthermore, he soon learned the importance of ritual, which he prescribed according to the herb to be taken. The middle-aged women suffering blood pressure were to prepare the infusion of burra-burra at the start of the full moon; while the men who were afflicted with pains in their joints had to mix Kwaku's lime concentrate with high-wine and repeat a certain incantation seven times before drinking it.

The request of a man in his early thirties alerted him to possibilities of his practice far beyond the rewards earned by his medical practice. The man complained that for eleven years he had received no promotion in his work. New employees had come long after he was taken on, only to overtake him and look down on him as if he were a cockroach or a crab-dog. His resentment had grown so much that his home life was soured and his marriage threatened. Kwaku told the man that he could do nothing for him.

"But people say ...."

"What people say about me?" enquired Kwaku, eagerly.

"They say you got magic in your hands; and you know about

119

things other people don't know about."

"You think they like me?" And as the man appeared taken aback by the question Kwaku said, "I mean, I don' come from New Amsterdam and I not sure whether they accept me, you see."

"They accept you, yes."

"When they say howdye in the road they mean it?" Kwaku could not conceal his desire to be liked, which called a contemptuous look from the man.

"They're all talking about you."

Then Kwaku, anxious to rehabilitate himself, said, "Everything is in these." In saying this he raised his hands for the man to see.

"And here," he continued, tapping his temple. "And I *see* things, even before they happen. You hear 'bout the fire at the Rice Marketing Board?"

"Yes."

"I *see* that two days before it happen."

The man opened his eyes wide. "You saw that?"

"I see it. Now you know who you dealing with. I not one of them Wish-Come-True men going up and down the country selling wishes and disappearing before people can buttonhole them. I don' sell nothing. People pay me for results they know they going get."

"You can get me promotion then?" the man asked.

"I can get you anything," affirmed Kwaku, clicking his tongue impatiently, "if you want it bad enough."

The man sat watching him expectantly across the consultation table which was decorated with a white cloth and a turned purple-heart container with a round lid.

Kwaku would rather have continued discussing people's opinion of him, but was afraid of the man, who spoke so well and was quick to doubt. But what could he do for him? If he had failed to get promotion for so many years nothing he might do was likely to help him.

"Go home and plant a mango seed."

"Do what?"

"Go home and plant a mango seed, I say. And stop blaming your wife. She din' do nothing."

The man got up. "How much is it?"

"Pay me when you get the results. You going get promotion before the tree start bearing."

"That may be years."

"No. It depend 'pon how much faith you got."

The man left, impressed. And Kwaku watched him go, fully aware that his chances of an assured future might well lie with him.

How easy everything suddenly was! His back had become permanently stooped over his shoemaker bench, his ambitions had all

120

but died and his family was for a time under threat of dispersal. Now, at a stroke, his fortunes had changed. If he knew how to harness chance, what ambition was capable of resisting him? What freedom would he not conquer? His pride, which he saw as being constantly under attack, would become unassailable. Looking out on the white-painted paling surrounding his rented cottage he experienced, for the first time, the full satisfaction of his new-found position as healer and the security it brought him, like the delayed effects of rain on a parched field. He must get in touch with Blossom and tell her all he felt, and how he was convinced that he was on the threshold of an inner change so profound that he quivered with excitement just at the thought of the transformation. The move to New Amsterdam was probably its background, as was his overnight success as a healer. Yet, he could not escape the thought that Mr Barzey was behind it all; that he had endowed him with a consciousness he never before experienced, an awareness of things and people round him; that he had pushed him off a precipice and forced him to fly. His camera and tripod, useless to him now, were symbols of his journey into the labyrinth. If he accepted money from sick people without having been trained to cure them, most of them were nevertheless cured. Besides, guilt never flourished in his soul as self-esteem did, or affection. Those who dispensed drugs from a surgery smelling of carbolic soap and indifference were no better than he was. His patients were encouraged to talk and stay until he closed in the afternoon. They made their own diagnosis and compared them with his. He did not live apart from them.

Kwaku looked down at the street and the lengthening shadows, the crowns of a group of tall trees soaring above the houses on the other side, dark green in the mysterious glow of the setting sun.

He found that he was standing with his hands behind his back, involuntarily adopting the pose of those accustomed to success in their encounters with others. Yes, he would seek out Blossom and describe the fullness of his soul. He had once rejected her offer to secure a job for him with the Public Transport, declaring at the same time that he was made for better things. He intended to remind her of his prediction. Miss Gwendoline did not like to hear him boasting, but Blossom did not mind. It would be good to share the same house with the two women, experience an orgy of satisfaction in his relations with them and his children.

Kwaku closed the open window against the cooling wind blowing across the Canje river. Turning round, he surveyed the furniture. His aversion to using other people's furniture was such that he only sat in one chair, and treated the others as if they were enemies.

"I'm not going use you!" he used to say to one inviting easy-chair. "No use spreading out you hands like a woman. I in' using you and

121

that's final! I don' even know who sit in you before. Don' look at me like that, I just not using you!"

He intended to ask the landlord to take away his furniture and allow him to furnish the house as he wished. None of this solid, heavy stuff for him. He would buy light, modern furniture, even though what was sold in the shops did come apart in a couple of years.

The wind had risen imperceptibly and was howling through the louvres of the jalousies. The feeble light from the street lamp, insufficient to relieve the darkness in which the house was engulfed, fell on the bushes and castor-oil plant near the bridge, making rapidly changing patterns as they twisted and shuddered in the wind.

Kwaku sat down on the chair he had singled out as his, afflicted by a loneliness that came upon him without warning. If a moment ago he had been plotting the course of his future life he now began grubbing about in the past, calling to mind the fact that his mother had died in giving birth, that his father had abandoned him, and that his uncle, once he had married him off, took no further interest in what he did or the people he mixed with. Then he recalled that only the day before he had been reminding himself of his good fortune in his friendship with Blossom and Mr Barzey, and in his choice of a life's companion. But the sombre thoughts came back, and with every gust of wind he started up from his chair.

Then, as if all the gusts had come together in one mighty wind, the house shuddered in the onslaught; a sharp, long crack, like the report and echo of a firearm, rang out above every other sound, causing Kwaku to leap into the air.

"What is this at all?" he asked himself, admitting to himself that he was afraid.

He went inside, undressed hastily and put on his new pyjamas. Before getting into bed he knelt down and started praying, half-heartedly at first, but with a stern fervour, when a multiple flash of lightning lit up the bedroom.

"I'm not a bad man, God ...."

Suddenly his prayer was interrupted by a rapping out front, a persistent noise that continued through the intermittent lulls in the screaming wind. Unable to stand the suspense Kwaku got up and felt his way in the darkness, hugging the partition in order to avoid knocking over any furniture. Standing beside the front door he looked down through the slats of the Venetian blind over the sash window, but could see no one on the porch, though the rapping persisted. Then, with trembling hands, he undid the top and bottom bolts securing the door, which flung open under the violence of the wind. But before he could raise his arm to protect himself Kwaku was struck full in the face and fell to the floor, gasping in terror. "Take anything you want! Anything!" he shouted, grovelling in the doorway.

On looking up he was confronted with a branch which had been all but ripped from the tree growing between the porch and the door and was swinging back and forth in the storm.

"O God!" Kwaku groaned with relief.

When he had recovered sufficiently to use his legs he set about trying to wrench the branch from its trunk, only to give up in disgust. He locked the door once more, went back to his bedroom and changed into a dry pair of pyjamas, all the while thinking that he could not survive another night like that. He made up his mind there and then to seek the services of a companion. And, once more enwrapped in the warmth of his blanket, Kwaku started to reflect on the nature of terror; and that on every occasion when he had been in the grip of an experience which lamed him, there was nothing behind it but his over-heated imagination. At the age of four he had seen his aunt's corpse laid out on the bed. He recalled a number of details of the silent watch in the bedroom, the grave faces of his aunts and uncles, his grandmother nodding off, and the night light flickering and casting elongated shadows on the wall. Yet, despite his vivid recollection of the scene, he understood, at the time, little of what was amiss. It was later, at the age of fourteen that a similar occurrence held him in a state of unrelieved terror until he and his uncle departed. And thereafter, the very thought of a visit to a death-house aroused in him the greatest resistance. The envelope of death, the pallid, rigid negation of life was in no way threatening to him, a fact that was demonstrated by the gathering around it and the festivities in certain homes. But in his imagination its spirit was lurking somewhere in the house.

Kwaku duly fell asleep while the storm roared and the broken branch rapped against the door. The next morning he awoke to the singing of birds and a bright day which penetrated the Demerara window on the far side of the bedroom with oblique rays. The contrast of the weather with that of the previous night was so striking that he got up and pushed open the shutter. Through the open window the sky stretched away to an invisible horizon beyond the roofs of the low houses; the leaves on the fruit trees in the neighbouring yard fluttered in a light breeze that cooled his face and neck, still warm from a night beneath the woollen blanket. To the right, a stream of water was falling into the yard next door, from what appeared to be a hole in the floorboards; and indeed, from the squeals of children coming from it, the water was escaping from a bathroom with a derelict floor.

Kwaku thought with satisfaction that he would soon be able to buy his own house and keep it in good repair. But at the sight of a restless monkey tied to the back porch of the house, just beyond the leaking bathroom, Kwaku's face clouded over. He remembered that he had dreamt the night before, no doubt as a result of the anxieties about the storm. He had dreamt that there was a knocking on the window of the room in which he was sleeping, a room with a blindless sash-window. He woke up and saw a troop of monkeys grimacing through the panes. One of them was trying to open the window while two others were searching in a hysterical, preoccupied way for an aperture. There was an inevitability about the monkeys' entry, which occurred suddenly when, having managed to raise the window, they stood on the ledge grimacing and watching him. Then, without warning, they threw themselves on him in a body and began devouring him.

He detested monkeys and could never understand why people were fond of keeping them as pets. Parrots, yes, and even filthy animals like dogs. But monkeys! With their hairy, grimacing heads and jerky, puppet-like movements! Kwaku withdrew his head and went to lie down on his bed, perhaps to fall into a second sleep. Now he was his own master he could sleep to his heart's content until eleven o'clock or thereabouts, when he liked to take his shower, drink his bowl of boiling coffee, eat his buttered cassava bread and fried gilbacker, then start preparing garlic cakes and herbs for his customers.

Who would his first customers be? he thought. He had already learned that the men were more superstitious than the women in matters of healing. And even those who prized medicine above all else, who took their laxatives once a week and imposed a regime of enemas for their ailing children, cocked their ears at the mention of chalk lines to keep away spirits or gave themselves away by reacting with an unseemly violence at the accusation of superstition.

He had also learned that, apart from ailments of the body, there were two main sources of the distress: love and anxiety about the future. And much else as well; that women who had lost interest in sex often smothered their husbands with attention; husbands beat women they loved deeply.

Women came in to seek relief for their numerous aches and, because he listened without ever intimating that he wanted them to stop talking, they spoke at length, disclosing the secrets of their hearts, like those misshapen hand-made bottles that had lain at the bottom of canals for two hundred years, to be fished out by the scoop of a dredge, dripping and covered with a mysterious incrustation.

Kwaku loved his work, the freedom it had brought him, and the respect bestowed upon him by people who had no idea what he was really like.

A client suggested that he had a sign put up, "Kwaku – consultant"; but he no longer saw advertisement as necessary, since people came to consult him in any case. The immediate problem was to seek out someone to share the house with him and attend to repairs.

Kwaku sprang out of bed and was tempted to sing out loud as the old shoemaker was in the habit of doing. But until his neighbours got to know him he would conduct himself as befitted a healer, a man of the people. Perhaps the days when he could be himself were over. Time alone would tell.

20   The healer

KWAKU'S ENQUIRIES concerning a helper bore fruit. Only two weeks went by before a suitable applicant presented himself, a retired Customs officer, reputed for his honesty. Of his seven children not a single one lived in New Amsterdam, and, in his own words, "his wife had gone to meet her maker". The man, a Mr Chalfen, applied for the job because he imagined Kwaku to be an intellectual. Disappointed, at first, at his unaffected manner and his raw speech, he was none the less swayed by the status Kwaku's popularity had brought him, and by the elegant house in which he lived. Having settled for a hundred and fifty dollars per month he moved in a week later, on the day his own tenancy ran out.

Mr Chalfen was a man of medium height, decidedly taller than Kwaku, and who tried at all times to look superior. He had looked forward to his retirement only to discover that idleness was a curse that weighed heavily. Convinced that his Customs' colleagues were all mad and that he was the only sane officer in the department, he had few illusions about Kwaku's character, which was bound to display its true nature with closer acquaintance. God had put him on earth to seek out and find the weaknesses of his fellow men, and he had learned not to judge them too harshly.

Kwaku had taken on the man just in time, for a few days later he was asked to go and treat a boy of twelve who lived with his parents in a village between Albion and Port Mourant. The boy's father had written, in reply to Kwaku's letter accepting the commission, that he expected him any time during the following week.

Kwaku left the house early one morning in a taxi, his mind free of any anxiety about a burglar robbing him of his garlic tablets and garlic paste, which he kept in a shed at the back of the yard. Mr Chalfen had the best credentials and was not likely to have choke-

and-rob relations or loose women visiting him. Customs officers might be notorious for their drinking habits, but everyone knew them to be honest as the day was long, or whatever honest people were like. It was true that they were not averse to accepting a few dollars to free dutiable goods or liquor in bond. But there was dishonesty and dishonesty. Who would bury a man's reputation because he had fiddled his tax return? Or ostracize an accountant for devoting half his life to playing his customers' violin for a fee? One had to see these things in context. Mr Chalfen was as honest as the night was dark. And with this comforting knowledge Kwaku travelled the many bumpy miles to the village accompanied by other reflections, thoughts that centred on his absent family, Mr Barzey and his extraordinary encounter with the bereaved family in Stanleytown.

The taxi-driver's vehicle evidently anticipated the time when no cars or spare parts would be imported into the country, as had been rumoured. The various dials and gadgets which normally decorated the panel beside the steering-wheel of cars were gutted, leaving gaping recesses, out of which peeped wire-ends or jagged bits of bakelite. In fact, only the glass dial of the speedometer was intact. But the needle, normally trembling like the hand of a young woman about to touch for the first time what young women had always been nervous about putting their hands on for the first time, was inert, unmoved by the sudden spurts of speed or more predictable accelerations on the approach of one of those constructions that local villagers call bridges, but which the Public Works Department know perfectly well are a challenge to orthodox engineering and were put up simply to demonstrate the insufficiency of European mathematics.

On arriving at the home village of the East Indian gentleman whose son he had come so far to see, Kwaku settled with the chauffeur before getting out. His memory of the experience on the one occasion when he got out first and tried to settle in the tiny space between the edge of the road and the trench, and when he was rescued from the alligators that were alleged to inhabit it, to the accompaniment of the barking of all the village dogs, more numerous than the people, was sufficiently vivid to deter him from yielding to the temptation of tearing himself away from the naked springs of the ramshackle vehicle.

"Where Mr Kumar living?" asked Kwaku of a barefoot boy.

"Kumar? They got Kumar dere an' dere, and dere. All over they got Kumar," said the youngster, spreading out the fingers of both hands to illustrate the various direction of the Kumar dwellings.

"This Kumar got a sick boy. His son sick."

"Dat's Kumar Kumar. One of he fowls born with three foot the other day. He got a lot of fowls an' sheep dat look funny. They look like dog."

"All right, where he live?" Kwaku asked. "This Kumar Kumar with three-foot fowls and dog-face sheeps?"

"That's the man. I did tell you that was the man. How you know 'bout him? You don' live round here. I know you don' live round here 'cause I see you coming out o' the taxi with you batty stickin' out in the air as if you dancing."

Kwaku took a ten-cent coin from his pocket to give his informant, who whisked it out of his hand so swiftly that Kwaku stood staring at him.

"You not shy, eh," he told the youngster. "You better take me to Mr Kumar house."

The boy led Kwaku down the main village road and stepped in front of the fourth house from the highway.

"Is here. You wan' me wait fo' you? 'Cause sometimes is hard to get taxi and the drivers does always stop fo' me. Always! Ask anybody."

"Wait then," Kwaku agreed. "But I don' got any more money to give you."

"Who say I want money?" objected the boy. "I's you friend."

He stood beside Kwaku, grinning broadly.

"All right, friend, wait. But you might have to wait a long time, 'cause ...." Kwaku was on the point of saying why he had come but stopped just in time, remembering the rules of professional etiquette.

"He got a lot o' money, y'know," the boy confided, nodding towards the house. "He father dead an' lef he money, money, money."

"Plenty?"

"I telling you."

"Well, I gone," Kwaku declared, taking leave of his informant.

Then, as he was about to cross the bridge he turned round to ask the youngster if Mr Kumar had a dog.

"He got dog, yes. But it does only bite bone."

"Truly?" Kwaku said smiling, for the boy reminded him of his own youth and his anarchic attitude to the people and things around him. He was tempted to invite him in, but thought better of the idea. Mr Kumar would no doubt be acquainted with him and might not approve of a healer who arrived with a mud-spattered waif of his own village.

"Don't forget to wait," he reminded him instead.

Kwaku, on opening the gate, had to step aside to avoid treading on a compost heap of goat dung and leaves, from which a column of vapour was rising. The front yard was a wild mass of fruit trees and flowering shrubs which half obscured the staircase with its painted balustrades and decorated porch.

"Anybody there?" Kwaku called out from the stairs.

"Shout out more loud!" the boy called. "Sometimes the whole family in the back yard."

But just as Kwaku was about to follow the advice a man's head appeared at the window.

"You want something?"

"I want Mr Kumar."

"I'm Mr Kumar."

"Ah," said Kwaku, mounting the stairs, "I'm Mr Cholmondeley, the healer."

"Oh, me loss! Why you didn't say so?"

In a trice the door was open to welcome Kwaku, who thrust his little bag ahead of him, believing that the gesture was appropriate to his status.

"Sit down. Sit down! Make yourself at home. I didn't expect you so early. Well, well!"

The man, in his late thirties, was wearing a pair of short pants and a flower-patterned shirt with all the buttons undone. His face was smooth and his teeth brilliant white. In short, he was the picture of health and good humour, and his large drawing-room the picture of prosperity.

"Unusual place for sickness to visit," thought Kwaku.

"I really didn't expect you," said the man. "There's a doctor living twenty miles up the road, but it's no use sending for him. With all the clients he's got all over the place he thinks he's doing you a favour to come in a month's time. He does go round telling people 'Learn to accept death!' So round here we only does call him for death certificates. An' that's another story."

Then, stepping back to take a good look at Kwaku, Mr Kumar exclaimed once more: "So you come." And then, turning round towards the back of the house he commanded, "Kill a sheep!"

Kwaku saw no one, heard no one, but did not think it seemly to enquire whom his host had addressed, especially as he had promptly turned back to face him once more, smiling cordially.

"I hope you like mutton."

"Oh, yes," replied Kwaku. "Is my favourite meat. What about your boy?"

"He's bad, you know. Yesterday we been dangling cow heel in front of his nose. That boy would go miles to eat cow heel. But he just turn away as if was bitter coreilla. Anyway, now you come."

And Mr Kumar continued talking as if Kwaku's presence alone was enough to make his son well again. He talked of his early marriage, when he was still in his teens, of the local celebration, of

128

Kali Mai Poojah when the temple was filled with people and offerings of flowers, and the expectation of the sacrifice of a healthy goat. He complained of his younger brother, who was forever travelling in search of work, and left his wife and children to sponge on him. People had seen him in betting shops as far afield as Georgetown. When the shops closed a few years previously he, Mr Kumar, thought that would bring him to his senses. Far from it! He went away as usual, to turn up three or four times a year with trinkets for his wife and five children, only to leave again when his wife became pregnant.

"He's just gone. Soon after the boy get sick he left. He said he couldn't stand seeing sickness and worry. It does break his heart. His heart? What about mine?"

Mr Kumar was brought back to his son's illness by Kwaku.

"What're the symptoms?"

"Symptoms? If you ask me," he declared, for the first time with a severe expression, "the symptoms are all those dollies he does play with. Is *he* does make the dresses for his sisters' dollies! *He* does design them. Not the girls, but he. All day during the holidays he does sit down on the floor with scissors cutting out patterns and designing dresses. He says he wants to be a dress designer when he grow up."

Mr Kumar lifted up his arms in exasperation.

"I did tell him he'd get sick if he carried on like that. And that's exactly what happen. Man wasn't made to cut out dresses. But nowadays you got to expect anything."

Mr Kumar was interrupted by a faint voice behind him. It came from a girl with large eyes, a frail child of about five.

"Ma say the sheep kill."

"Good. Tell her I'm coming," said Mr Kumar. "Go and make the healer a cool drink."

Mr Kumar got up.

"Make yourself at home, Mr Cholmondeley. The wife can kill a sheep, but when it comes to the rest they can't do without me. The little girl'll bring you something to drink."

Kwaku was left to wonder about his host's family, an invisible brood, as discreet as they were silent, a sick child for whom he was urgently summoned, but who was ignored. Who had answered the call to kill a sheep? Where were the numerous children of Kumar and his brother's household?

The young girl brought him an unidentified iced drink, without a word gave it to him, and just as silently withdrew.

It occurred to Kwaku that if he managed to cure Mr Kumar's son he might build up a thriving business among the well-to-do East Indians of the coast. After that it could even be Georgetown. How was he to negotiate the fee? And when? Usually clients came to his house and were at a disadvantage. He went straight to the heart of the matter, or just said after the session, "It will cost so-and-so." Mr Kumar had already killed a sheep! Would it not be too much to say, "You kill a sheep which put you back one hundred and fifty dollars, but I still want my fee of fifty dollars. After all you had the benefit of the part of it I didn't eat," Kwaku wondered.

Kwaku looked down at the unpolished floorboards. Greenheart, at a dollar a foot. His eyes followed the sunlight flooding through the skylight. Roof of silver-balli wood. Here was a man who did not stint himself. "You won't surprise him on a bed of nails," Kwaku thought.

No, the best course was to charge him a moderate fee and get him on his side. In a few years, he could have as much money as Kumar and could then be himself, find out what he was really like. Even now he was obliged to skin and grin with everyone in order to ensure his livelihood. If he had been rich like the doctor of whom Mr Kumar spoke, would his attitude to him be the same? Would he sit and listen to him unburden himself, endure tales about boy-children playing with dollies and a brother doing a moonlight flit as soon as responsibility threatened?

The silence in the large house, broken only by the hum of an unseen refrigerator, was that deep silence of the countryside. Kwaku got up and went to a window that overlooked the road and a wide stretch of shrub-grown land beyond the drainage canal, in which two cows had sought refuge from the morning heat. To the left was a recently cleared sugar-cane field, for it was the season of grinding, when the factories worked through the night to deal with the endless deliveries from the fields on the coast-lands.

"What do I want?" thought Kwaku, taking in the expanse of country.

He had longed to escape poverty and now that he had he was driven by some unquenchable urge to be rich. He was not like that, nor was his wife. His character was satisfied by simple things: his family at ease, the respect of others, laughter, a full stomach. Yet he could not deny a prompting that most assuredly came from without, the whispering of a collective voice swamping his own desires.

Then his thoughts turned to Mr Kumar once more, who would have ignored him a year ago. Now his reputation was everything; it enveloped him like a luminous garment, drawing people's attention to him, covering the nakedness of his character. Possibly this was the reason for his unease, for his need to accumulate money while his success lasted.

Kwaku felt better at the thought that he had found a motive for his desire to make more money.

"Yes. It could end next week or even tomorrow."

Things change. A dead uncle, who used to be a cooper, was put out of work with the introduction of the Pure Water Supply Scheme. And the uncle who brought him up was, years earlier, a fisherman on the Courantyne, until the Surinam river police confiscated his boat for fishing in the river without a licence. With these recollections Kwaku's self-confidence returned and he decided there and then that in a couple of weeks he would go back to the village and arrange for his family to join him in New Amsterdam.

Voices from the back alerted him to the return of Mr Kumar who arrived beaming.

"Had to carve it up for the deep freeze. In a couple of hours we'll be dining on curry mutton and Irish potatoes. Shh!"

The importation of these potatoes was banned and Mr Kumar must have bought his from the contraband dealers of the Courantyne river.

"What's wrong?" asked Mr Kumar, who noticed that Kwaku kept looking through the window.

"I just remember a little boy who showed me the house. He did say he goin' wait outside, but I can't see him."

"He's under the house. The lil' scamp. Want to sweep the yard for fifty cents .... Why not come in and have a look at the boy while we're working up an appetite?"

Kwaku finished his drink and left the glass on a window ledge.

"Come, ne," his host said, inviting him to follow.

The youngster was laid up in the first bedroom, adjoining the drawing-room.

"Hey, good-for-nothing," his father bantered. "This is the healer."

Mr Kumar's son, no more than ten years old, raised himself on his elbow and stared at Kwaku, who placed his bag on the floor, then sat on the bed next to his patient. He put his hand on the boy's forehead, looking round the room at the same time to give the impression that he knew what he was doing. And in a flash he hit upon a course of action: he would give the patient a garlic enema and hope that nature would take its course.

The idea had occurred to him when he caught sight of an enamel enema cylinder hanging on the bedroom partition, its rubber tube neatly folded round it. Such a cylinder used to hang on his uncle's bedroom wall when he was a boy; and he lived in mortal dread of it, knowing that whatever his ailment, his uncle's lady friend would unhang it and administer to him an enema of her own concoction.

Mr Kumar's son must have guessed Kwaku's intentions, for he began to groan.

"Is what, healer? Is anything serious?" asked Mr Kumar, not knowing what to make of Kwaku's silence.

131

"It could've been," replied Kwaku gravely. "But we goin' banish the sickness with a special enema."

"O God!" groaned the boy, who, although he had no personal experience of an enema, had always regarded the cylinder as a threat, like those whips dangling from a nail in the houses of people with lofty principles.

"The healer knows what's good for you," his father said severely, as Kwaku handed him a packet of garlic powder.

"Boil the water and dissolve this in them," Kwaku counselled Mr Kumar. "I'll stay with your son."

"Don't stay with him!" Mr Kumar said sharply. "Is this house of women that do it to him, and all them dollies he does play with. Let him stay by himself and learn to be a man."

Then, addressing his son, he said, "You can see for yourself that what I used to tell you was true. You see?"

The boy nodded and, left alone once more, began to study the rounded form and the plastic tap of the cylinder which his father would reach for in a short while.

Kwaku went downstairs by the front staircase to see the youngster who had shown him the house.

"I din' know you'd stay so long," he said, jumping up on seeing Kwaku.

"I din' know either."

"What you doing up there?" And Kwaku was happy to talk to the boy as if he were a man and possessed a wisdom beyond his years. "You don' go to school?"

"Wha' for?"

"To learn to read."

"I know to read," the youngster declared.

"Good?"

"I's a powerful reader. You can read a book upside down? I can read a book upside down."

"You can ..." Kwaku began incredulously, for he exaggerated the talent of anyone who could read long words.

"You know what a enema is?"

"'Course! Is a tube you stick up people batty to get the shit out of them. I get one every birthday."

"Is impossible talking to you," said Kwaku, who was unable to tell if the boy was making fun of him.

"You not giving Mr Kumar Kumar a enema, eh? East Indian people don' have enemas. Just like they don' whistle."

"Where you get all this ... this talk from? What's your father do?"

"He's a drunkard," the boy replied promptly.

"I mean for a living. You know what I mean."

"He's a grinder."

"Sugar?"

"Yes. What other sort of grinder is there?"

Kwaku looked thoughtful, but did not answer. He was glad to have discovered an innocent side of the boy, after all.

"You wait here. Don' forget!" Kwaku warned the little boy. "I want to see you when I come out of this house."

Kwaku stormed upstairs as if he were angry. The discovery of such an unusual intelligence in a boy disturbed him to such a degree, he felt he had to collect his thoughts. He peered at him through the closed shutter. Such a person could teach him to spell and read expertly without his feeling ashamed at being instructed so late in life. He had bought a medical text book, but was unable to get to the bottom of it because he had never been taught how to use a dictionary. The huge volume lay on a small table in the drawing-room of his New Amsterdam home, a symbol of his incompetence in a world where every Tom, Dick and Harry knew how to read well.

Kwaku made up his mind. He would move Heaven and Earth to take the boy to New Amsterdam with him.

Mr Kumar returned with his wife, who was carrying two kettles. Behind them traipsed nine children, normally banished to the back of the house when visitors came, but now encouraged to witness the consequences of perverted conduct. Mr Kumar was determined that his other son should never meddle with dolls or dolls' dresses.

Kwaku surveyed the group of children, concluding that the dougla ones were the children of his brother, who had no doubt married an Afro-Guyanese woman.

"Now," explained Mr Kumar, "allyou going see an enema. Or else the healer's going to get vexed. And when he's vexed he can't heal. Understand?"

He was assured by the chorus of voices that they understood.

The patient was cowering against the wall, at the head of the bed, too frightened by the imminent assault on his dignity to be ashamed in front of his sisters, brother and cousins.

As Mr Kumar reached for the cylinder the first scents from the kitchen arrived in the bedroom. His sister-in-law had once witnessed the administering of an enema and, not wishing to relive the experience, remained in the kitchen to prepare the midday meal.

"The water too hot," Mrs Kumar protested.

"Serve him right," declared Mr Kumar, with a show of heartlessness that was not taken seriously by the others.

"Mamie," the mother ordered her eldest daughter, "go and throw cold water over the kettle then."

And the daughter, a nubile, compliant creature, left with the aluminium kettles held outwards from her legs.

"The weather hot, eh?" Mr Kumar said to Kwaku, wiping his

forehead with his hand.

"The children in the room make it worse," Kwaku replied.

But the host did not take the hint.

"Eleven of us in the room at the same time," Kwaku pursued.

"Yes, it's hot bad."

"And when your daughter come back," continued Kwaku, "it'll be twelve." To emphasize his concern he took a handkerchief of enormous proportions out of his pocket and wiped his streaming face. "Think of the boy," he urged, moving over to the window and gasping for breath.

The children and Mrs Kumar did not appear to be suffering, while Mr Kumar, hot as he was, could not let the opportunity slip by to make the little ones aware of the outcome of an alarming aberration.

As soon as Mamie came back, husband and wife set to work. Having tacitly agreed that she should hold the chamber pot while he performed the manipulative part of the operation, Mr Kumar seized his reluctant son, reminding him that there was an audience and that he must not make a fool of himself.

"What kind of example you're setting? You don't make all this fuss to cut up little pieces of cloth and fit them on plastic dollies!" he exclaimed.

He dragged his son to the edge of the bed, where Kwaku was holding the cylinder and his wife gripped the pot in readiness to apply it to the agitated backside. And as soon as there was a lull in the struggling, Mr Kumar inserted the tap and turned it on. The boy, whether from exhaustion or the calming effect of the warm tide up the lower reaches of his intestines, remained quite still, while his brother, sisters and cousins gaped at the prowess of adults. They had seen the mysterious cylinder on the wall, but none of them had bothered to enquire as to its purpose. And now, at a time of crisis, it was being used with that magical skill they had come to associate with grown-ups.

"That's it!" Kwaku declared suddenly. "Turn it off! Don' take it out until I tell you .... Now!"

And Mrs Kumar, holding the pot on a plane that would allow her to catch the you-know-what, while ensuring that it would not promptly flow out again, stood like a policeman on the ready at the entrance to a den of thieves who were about to be flushed out by colleagues. At the shout of "Now!" from Kwaku she responded with a lightning twist of her wrist, only to miss by a whisker as her son chose that very moment to adjust his aim.

Well, there are some things that defy description, since they offend the norms of decency. Besides, this was not Georgetown or some other sink of iniquity, but a little village on the Courantyne coast, where people were as pure as the sea-breezes that come from the north-east. They were all good Christians – even the East Indians, who had been converted to the joys of Lutheranism and the expectation of bliss in an after-life on East Coast honey and the milk of their wretched cows. It is enough to say that the portrait of the Mahatma which hung so high up on the wall that even a tall man like Mr Kumar would have been obliged to climb on to a chair to get it down, suffice it to say that the portrait of the Mahatma lost its smile that bright weekday morning as a result of the unpremeditated assault. And what is more, the children, uncertain as to what the remainder of the operation entailed, fled as a man, leaving the grown-ups to complete their work.

A quarter of an hour later Kwaku and Mr Kumar emerged from the bedroom panting and sweating like men who had survived an encounter with a deer-tiger.

"He's going to be better, Mr Cholmondeley?" Mr Kumar enquired anxiously, believing that his experience could not have been all in vain.

"He better already, Mr Kumar," Kwaku replied, waving his damp handkerchief. "He just need a week or so rest .... But I did warn you about the heat. The children shouldn' have been in the room."

"It's not the children, Mr Cholmondeley. It's the boy's nervousness. He's nervous like a little girl. What d'you expect, with his sisters for company and all?"

The two men went off to the back of the yard to wash their hands. On the way back Kwaku waved to his waiting friend and made his host promise to send him down a plate of food at meal-time.

The sun had shifted to the other side of the house and the rays of sunlight that managed to pierce the trees in the front yard embroidered the window ledges of the casement windows, which alternated with the shutters above the balustraded staircase.

"Nothing does ever happen down here, healer," said Mr Kumar, who was sitting in the open doorway. "Nothing. It's a fact. Your visit is a big event. If the boy get better we'll remember your visit."

Kwaku saw his chance to enquire about his friend under the house.

"Him?" said Mr Kumar. "He's always in trouble .... Ah, the food. Let's go and eat."

And at that point Mr Kumar and Kwaku were called to table to a sumptuous meal, served up by Mr Kumar's wife and children.

After they had eaten, the rest of the household gathered at the table, where Mrs Kumar said Lutheran grace and gave the sign for them to begin. Kwaku and Mr Kumar retired to the front of the house. Kwaku was trying his best to restrain himself from mentioning the subject that occupied his mind, namely the cost of his visit.

"Was a good enema, eh?" he remarked in an off-hand manner.

"So-so," Mr Kumar agreed.

"I mean effective."

"Very thing I was thinking."

"The sixth this week, you know," Kwaku confided.

"Yes?"

"Yes. It's coming back into fashion. Enemas. Doctors starting to realize it got its uses."

"The sixth! ... I couldn't be a doctor or a dentist though," said Mr Kumar. "Especially a dentist. All that hand-washing. I got a cousin who went to the States to study dentistry in ... let me see .... When did Mukerjee go away?" he asked aloud.

His wife's hardly audible voice came back in a sing-song Courantyne lilt. "In 'seventy-two, I think. Or 'seventy-three.'"

"I think it was 'seventy-two," Mr Kumar said, turning back to his guest. "He had dry hands and couldn't stand too much washing. And who tell him to choose dentistry, of all the professions. Just the idea of spending half my life with my hand down people throat would be enough to put me off. And dry hands into the bargain. This cousin of mine choose to study dentistry, and of course he had to give it up when the real action start and he had to keep washing his hands. Years down the drain! He's only a cousin by marriage, but that thing hurt me, I can tell you. If you are going to spend money, spend it on food. But to waste thousands of dollars looking at people teeth and not getting anything to show for it!"

Mr Kumar talked his head off until Kwaku, seeing that there was nothing for it but to take the bull by the horns, interrupted him and declared, "I got to go now. Look how low the sun getting."

"You right, you know," Mr Kumar agreed, although the sun was not low at all. "You right. Goodbye then."

"I can't understand him," Kwaku reflected. "He kill a sheep, feed me up, give me drinks and everything; but when it come to forking out money it's a different story."

And his sensitive nature would not allow him to mention the word "money". But then the memory of the journey, the mishap with the chamber pot and the thought of the trip back in a rickety taxi made him angry.

"As I say, I got to be going. My visit cost you sixty dollars."

"Six .... That's a little hefty."

"For you I'll make it fifty"

Now that it came to it Kwaku's embarrassment vanished, especially with Mr Kumar's resistance.

"I could make twice as much staying in my house," said Kwaku, hoping that his host would sense the irritation in his voice. "I bet when I get home there'll be at least ten customers waiting for me. I must've lost another ten customers that come and gone home 'cause I wasn't there."

"Sixty dollars to do what me and my wife could've done alone!" exclaimed Mr Kumar. "After all, you did only hold the cylinder."

"Look, Mr Kumar, I'm a professional man. I don' *argue* for my fee. But since you ask me what I do to earn it I going tell you."

Kwaku got up and stared down at his host.

"Is *me* that prescribe the enema. *I* prescribe. You had it, but you didn' know when to use it. And you don' know what powder to put in it. They got ginger enema, asafoetida enema, lemon grass enema, piaba enema, this enema, that enema. I could write a book on enemas. And you tell me I only *hold* the cylinder. Because I *devalue* myself and *hold* the cylinder you can't think straight 'bout the professional part of the job ... . You paying me my fifty dollars or not?"

Kwaku, now his old belligerent self, was prepared to go through fire for his fee. The smooth, round face staring up at him irritated him no end, as did the recollection of Mr Kumar's irrelevant talk of dollies and dry hands. He had never in all his life met such a cross, stingy idiot.

Mr Kumar, saying not a word in answer to his guest, only attempted to stare him down, but Kwaku would have stared at him all day long, till the sun went down and rose again.

"Good! I'll give you your fifty dollars. But I want a receipt," Mr Kumar said at last.

Kwaku, who once before had been asked to furnish a receipt, had memorized the requirements, which he now went over in his mind. Date, signature, amount, name of party and description of services rendered. Laboriously he penned a receipt for his host, signed it and waited while the latter fetched the money from inside.

Neither trusted the other and they stood holding the ten five-dollar notes with one hand and the receipt with the other. Eyeball to eyeball they stood, until Kwaku pulled the money from Mr Kumar's hand, letting go of the receipt at the same time.

"You-all see," shouted Mr Kumar, turning to his family and relations, who pretended to be unaware of the scene being played out in the front of their eyes. "You- all see that I paid Mr Healer."

He then turned to address Kwaku. "I thought you were a gentleman. But you only have to look at your handwriting to tell you never go further than fourth standard."

Kwaku was deeply offended by the remark, but smiled as if his host had spoken like an idiot.

"I don' quarrel, Mr Kumar. My profession don' permit me to quarrel. Goodbye."

She pushed her son away, saying, "Go out and play. I talkin'. You can't see I talkin'?"

Once the boy was outside she looked Kwaku up and down.

"Is just that he father always making promises, mister. Nothing but promises. An' he wouldn' admit he got another woman besides me and he wife. That's what I don' like. And *he*! He does go to school whenever he feel like it. Just 'cause Kumar children stay home today ... they got a sick brother ... an' they don't got to have education ...." She fell silent, aware that she was trying too hard to show her gratitude.

Kwaku moved towards the door, his mortification at the humiliation he received at the hands of Mr Kumar now seeming a little thing, a grain of dust he had transformed into a rock simply by contemplating it.

On the way to the Public Road he reflected that he was once poor like the bird-woman, that perhaps he was just as repulsive to women as she was to men; and for a moment all the suffering of his youth, when first he became aware of his unprepossessing appearance, came back to him and merged with the misery of the boy's mother. Was every person not one of God's children? Yet they all looked different, suffered differently ....

The sun, milder now, was sparkling between the trees. Voices in the stillness of the afternoon, suffused cries of children living out the chaos and make-believe of a private world, grains of dust, a golden mist above the village road, mutterings among the shrubs bending to a gust of wind .... Tomorrow the same longings in the wake of an experience that moved him immeasurably. Was it not so? Would it not always be so?

On the journey home, past the ravaged cane fields, the taxi drove by Rose Hall estate with its soaring chimney. Grinding was in progress, and its hundred lights like beacons hanging in the air dripped yellow into the gathering night.

21 A quarrel

KWAKU HAD sent half of the money left – after the gift of ten dollars to the boy's mother – to his wife, in a letter in which he promised to come home the following weekend. He decided to look Blossom up before he went, one afternoon that week, when there were not many clients. He was apprehensive as to the way she would receive him, for the better part of a year had gone by and he had not so much as enquired at Rosignol stelling about her.

On Thursday, always the slackest day of the week, he asked at the bus station if she was on duty, only to be told that she was not expected before five o'clock, the time her bus was due from Georgetown.

Kwaku knew no one in Rosignol and could do nothing but spend the three hours – it was two o'clock – waiting to see the ferry boats arrive and depart. He noticed that the vehicles that were taken on first and assigned the corner of the boat under the cabins would be the last to leave, when it docked on the other side. When the boat came back he watched cars and lorries stop on the turntable, which slowly swung them round to face the gangway so that they could drive off. Marvelling at the crowds coming and going, he became convinced that the town was a much superior place to the country, even though, during a gasoline or kerosene shortage, townspeople were at the mercy of forces they could not control.

As the tide changed, the boat approached in a much wider arc, drifting slowly towards the stelling it had deliberately overshot. Kwaku stood gaping in wonderment at the almost unnatural skill of the captain, who directed the manoeuvring from the bridge, accompanied by the jangling of bells and other more mysterious noises.

"You been lookin' for me, mister?" someone spoke to him from behind.

It was Blossom, smiling broadly.

"You mean you actually come to see me?" she asked jokingly.

"But you lost weight," Kwaku blurted out, astounded at the smallness of her waist. And he could not keep his eyes off her, as much on account of her slimness as because he had forgotten how much she was an albino, how she stood out in the crowd.

"Why you staring at me?"

"I must stare," he answered. "You change!"

"What we going do?"

"I don' know Rosignol. You want to come over to New Amsterdam?"

"No!" she said at once.

"Why?"

She took time to reply. "I ask Miss Gwendoline for your address and she say no, she not giving it to me."

"But she not here."

"No, I say."

"You're still the same," he rebuked her.

"You too," she countered. "You still so stupid. If Miss Gwendoline hear I been to you house ... ."

They had only been together five minutes and they were quarrelling. Kwaku, annoyed at her candour, waited for her to speak first.

"I know somewhere we can eat," she said, in an effort

141

to be conciliatory.

He walked beside her and Blossom reflected that since his school days he had not widened the circle of his friends, apart from his wife and Mr Barzey. Flattered that he clung to their friendship, she prided herself on the fact that no one else would dare offend him as she did.

"Where we going?"

She did not answer, and walked slightly ahead of him, brushing the wayside bushes, a single mass in the dusk. Furtively he watched the back of her head, her coarse albino hair that made a quarter circle on her neck. In their youth she often spoke to him of her father, but not any more. He fathered two albino children, and after the birth of the second he put his wife on castor oil during the third pregnancy; but to his dismay the third child was like the other two. His father taunted him with his incapacity to breed dark children, and saw his remark vindicated with the birth of the fourth, fifth and sixth daughters.

Kwaku's brief repatriation of their childhood was interrupted by Blossom.

"You din' even write."

And so their conversation began again. She spoke of Wilfred, who had become even more jealous of her, and described at length their latest quarrel.

"All these men who does give their woman diamond this and diamond that!" Wilfred had told her. "No wonder their women does leave them."

"I goin' leave you 'cause you *don'* give me nothing," Blossom had answered.

"Women don' respect a man for showering she with presents."

"I glad to hear that I respect you. Is news to me," she replied dryly.

And Wilfred, losing his temper, had threatened to leave her.

Kwaku laughed. Glad to find him in a good mood, she started testing him on the latest addition to her collection of riddles.

"What does die in March and then bear children in December?"

As usual, he had to be told.

"You never does know," she chided, more gently than before. "Is the silk cotton tree!"

She struck him on his shoulder playfully. "What's a bridegroom in rags?" she went on.

"Don' know."

"Is a donkey that going mate with a horse. That's a old one."

They were standing in front of an old two-storeyed house, which, from its neglected condition, was not lived in by the owner.

"Is here," Blossom said.

142

"You know the people?"

"Yes. The bus drivers and conductors does eat here in the day when they got time."

At the door, ajar despite the evening air, Blossom called out, "Miss Ruby!" She did not wait for an answer. "Come, ne?"

She and Kwaku entered through the open door and stood waiting in the middle of the drawing-room.

Miss Ruby appeared at the front door.

"I been in the bottom house, chile," she said apologetically. "You eating?"

"What you want?" Blossom asked, turning to Kwaku.

"Anything you taking," Kwaku said, embarrassed by the woman's company.

Blossom ordered boiled shrimps, brown rice, fish sauce, cucumber and two beers.

"What you gone so shy for?" she asked Kwaku when Miss Ruby had gone.

"You don' understand. Since I'm a healer I got to be careful. People does talk."

Blossom sucked her teeth in scorn, and Kwaku knew very well what she meant. He looked the part of a well-to-do healer and she could not admire him for that.

Miss Ruby brought them two opened beer bottles and went back at once to the kitchen to prepare the meal Blossom had ordered. Kwaku sat at one of the round metal tables and Blossom drew up another chair from a table in the centre of the room.

The front of the house was dark, for the burned-out bulb of the street lamp had not been replaced. But the tilley lamp hanging from a nail on the partition opposite the wall against which Kwaku and Blossom were sitting filled the rest of the drawing-room with its light.

Miss Ruby came out from the kitchen to find her two clients sitting in silence. She herself, a bowl in her hand, sat down on a chair under the tilley lamp. The deep silence of the night, the humming of the lamp, Blossom's company and the spectral, noiseless presence of Miss Ruby shelling peas under the garish light consumed Kwaku's rancour. The change that had been operating in him, since his success as a healer and the respect shown him by his clients, was complete, it seemed. Blossom did not approve of his careful dress, but that did not matter. Besides, what could he do about it? A force without him obliged him to put on the expensive shirt-jac, the creased trousers and buff shoes. Rags were for poverty, just as his present outfit told the world where he stood.

In a corner of the darker part of the drawing-room Kwaku could make out two mutilated dolls. There must be a child in the house, he thought. And almost at once there was the sound of an infant whimpering and Miss Ruby put down her bowl on the floor beside the chair, then hurried into the room behind the partition. She came out hoisting a small cradle which she placed near the chair, went back inside once more and returned with a small child in her arms. She placed it in the cradle and began rocking it gently while singing in a soft voice, all the while lowering her into the cradle. Finally she took up her bowl once more, only interrupting her work from time to time to nudge the cradle with her arm.

Blossom, who often came to Miss Ruby's house when the drawing-room was full of bus and ferry staff, had only once before visited it at night. She had once lent Miss Ruby money and a friendship had grown between them. Miss Ruby served her the best cuts of meat, while Blossom brought her things from Georgetown, which she was unable to buy in Rosignol.

Blossom had taken Kwaku there so that they could talk freely. There was so much to tell him, about herself and Wilfred, for instance. She loved him as much as she had ever done, but she did not want to bear his children. Her children would have to be someone else's, someone responsible, on whom she could rely. No one would understand her, or her urge to be intimately associated with more than one man, each of whom responded to a different need. She had heard her mother say on a number of occasions that hers was a family in which the women loved once, and for life. This axiom had acted on Blossom like a lid on a simmering pot. Her desire to be married to more than one man had been felt even before she met Wilfred. But living with him had only confirmed what she always knew; and the guilt at what she had known all along and her inability to share it with someone else had caused her to suffer since she got married.

When she heard that Kwaku had been asking after her, she rushed to meet him, believing that his fame as a healer was only the light given off by a profounder transformation. Instead, she had found the same companion of years ago, the same vulnerability, the same need to be protected.

Blossom looked over at Miss Ruby and the cradle with the sleeping child, who did not seem to mind the bright light from the tilley lamp. She was envious of this woman and her daughter and, unaccountably, of all the accoutrements of her household, the chairs, iron tables for her customers, the dolls mutilated by the infant and even the rusted wrought-iron window-guards put up in the middle 'sixties against the desperadoes, who had grown in number with the political turmoil.

Miss Ruby occasionally stole a glance at the couple. She liked Blossom because the younger woman did not take long to confide in

144

her, just as if she were an aunt or an old friend. But she found her strange, even eccentric. Whenever she set eyes on her she remembered something Blossom had told her: at the marriage fête held for one of her sisters Blossom had danced with her father, who held her so close to him and in such a manner that there was no doubt as to his intentions. To Miss Ruby's question as to her reaction, Blossom confessed that she had been flattered.

Miss Ruby could not decide whether she liked Kwaku or not. He was obviously someone important, possibly a member of the Party. He probably had his fridge stocked with foodstuffs no longer available in the shops, as some Party affiliates were rumoured to have. Probably, through him, Miss Blossom could get hold of some margarine for her. Miss Ruby recalled how Blossom had once told her, "All I want is for my husban' to behave himself." Now that he was behaving, she was still not content with him. Perhaps this man with her was the rival, the one to make her content.

She got up. "A few minutes now only," she said to the couple before going into the kitchen.

"You hungry?" Kwaku asked Blossom.

"Yes. You?"

"Telling me!" he exclaimed softly.

"Your children growing up."

"You see them a lot?"

"Yes. All the time."

Kwaku instinctively felt that he should not talk about his children, in the same way that the subject of Miss Gwendoline was banned in conversation between them.

Blossom leaned over and kissed him on his cheek, then, as he did not seem to mind, full on the mouth.

"Now you can write and tell Miss Gwendoline," she mocked. "Tell she I interfere with she property .... You not shame to leave she alone so long? You know your big daughter growing up? She got little breasts."

Kwaku was embarrassed by her talk, but she went on.

"When you goin' back to your wife, eh? Mr Healer, when you goin' back to your wife? You men!"

At her last words Kwaku remembered the woman in the village to whom he had given money. "You men!" she had said, speaking of no one in particular. He had heard the expression before.

Was Miss Gwendoline as angry that he had stayed away so long as Blossom suggested? Starved of love these long months he put his hands on Blossom's leg, but she went on talking.

"You men! Healers and ministers, bus-drivers, policemen .... Is where you taking us? I don' want to go nowhere with you, you know ...."

145

She looked down at Kwaku's hand on her leg, which had pushed her dress as far as it could and was stroking her left thigh, slowly travelling back and forth, back and forth.

"Every day," said Blossom, "I travel up and down the coast and see things; and yet women sit down outside their house in the afternoon as if nothing gone wrong .... If I talkin' stupid, is because I stupid. I not like you, with your healing and everything."

Blossom placed her hand on his and began caressing it. "You never did want me at school. What you want with me now, eh?"

Kwaku put his hand in her panties and she opened her legs to allow him easier access.

"My father did dance with me one time, years ago. And I feel ... how he couldn' control himself. He been drinking ... and afterwards he couldn' look straight at me .... And in his eyes you could see everything, like in a looking-glass. You could see your face, the furniture. Everything was black. And that night I did wait for him ... but he didn' come. One thing I know: when I go to see my maker and he ask me to say .... Nobody does understand when you talk. Kwaku, you silly boy! What you doing to me? What you done to me? I'm talking to you. All them wrecked cars by the roadside, sinking in the flowers, sinking, sinking under the moon. I'm talking to you. Kwaku .... I'm talking to you!"

She shouted the last words and, jerking herself away, slapped him full in his face.

"I'm talking to you," she said softly.

Then she fell silent, for with Kwaku words lost their power, unlike Wilfred, with whom she found a delicious aversion in abuse. Already in childhood she knew Kwaku better than she did her brothers, his fear of horses and crowds, his passion for cards, and his disappointment that no card-playing company would tolerate him for long. She knew him well enough to resent his desire to sleep with her, for, when all was said and done, he would not love her that way. Her father was a Taurus as well, whose loyalty was little more than an incapacity for arousal.

Miss Ruby came back with a dish of food and her two guests sat at table opposite each other, while their hostess went back and forth until everything had been placed at their disposal.

"If I ..." began Blossom, when she was certain that their hostess was remaining in the kitchen.

"You goin' shut your mouth?" Kwaku intervened, standing up as he spoke. "You think I did want to see you so that you could drivel all over me? You in' got no right to talk to me like that. Nobody does talk to me like that any more. I changed. You can't see I changed?"

She sucked her teeth in derision; but before he could say a word their hostess arrived with a tray on which were two wine-red glasses full of refreshment. Kwaku sat down again and waited until she had disappeared once more into the kitchen.

"If you want me to insult Miss Gwendoline to please you, you might as well jump in the Canje, 'cause I not doing it. What go on between you and she is all-you business."

Blossom had started eating, just as if nothing was wrong. Occasionally she even looked up at Kwaku; and for all the world he might have been relating an incident that did not concern either of them personally.

"Since you been pushing them passengers around 'pon them yellow buses you get so overbearing people'd think you was the General Manager. I not the first to notice that ever since they had that United Nations Women's Year business all you women does walk about with you chest push out as if you own the country."

Kwaku fell upon his meal and consumed it at such a furious pace that Blossom was only halfway through hers when he threw his spoon on to his empty plate. Their hostess must have known that they were having words, although they had taken care to keep their voices down, as much on account of the baby as from a concern to conceal the fact that they were quarrelling.

"You see, she stay in the kitchen," Kwaku remarked.

But Blossom was not to be appeased. "I sleeping here tonight and you can't sleep here, so you might as well go, seeing as you done eating."

"You stupid she-goat!" exclaimed Kwaku, rising from the table once more.

"You don' have to pay. I'm a independent woman. I work for my money and spend it."

But Kwaku did not leave, as she had expected. Instead, he hung around the front door. He had intended, earlier on, to invite her to go with him on an excursion up-river to Mara, before his family came to join him. Now that was no longer possible. He was annoyed, not so much by her show of ill-temper, or even about her obsession with Miss Gwendoline, but rather because she had not said or done anything to show that she recognized him as a new man, a healer of repute. He wanted to shout out, "I am the healer of New Amsterdam. Dozens of people does recognize me when I walk past the market and the post office and the fire station. You come and meet me, just as if it was years ago when I was a laughing stock and every crab-dog did wash their mouth 'pon me."

Kwaku left, full of resentment towards his childhood friend and all those in the village who were certain to act as she had. And, halfway to the stelling, he stopped and turned, undecided whether he ought to go back to the house. After all, their quarrels never lasted. Should he not return and be the first to forgive?

"Come to Mara, ne. There's a excursion by boat. We'll laugh and talk, as long as you don' call Miss Gwendoline name."

But he could not beg a woman..

22 Talk and drink

KWAKU'S RETURN to his village was a triumph. He did not know that it was Blossom who, having heard of his successes at the Rosignol Transport Depot, had lost no time in spreading the news. People kept dropping in all day to see him and ask if all they had heard was true. Was he now a big man in the Party and partly responsible for government policy? Was it true that a street in New Amsterdam was named after him? Kwaku resisted the inclination to say "yes" to these questions, but did not say "no" either. Then, when he thought there was a large enough number of people in the house, he sent Philomena to buy him a box of cigars, just to demonstrate the way money talked.

Miss Gwendoline took on a girl to do the housework for the day, so that she could supervise Kwaku's conduct and organize the feeding of so many visitors. As for the children, they gawked at their father so shamelessly that Miss Gwendoline allowed them to stay away from school in the afternoon.

One woman demanded to see the presents Kwaku had given Miss Gwendoline, who, with Rona's help, spread out on the bed the fifteen dresses Kwaku had brought.

"None of them does fit," said Miss Gwendoline dryly. "That's a man for you." And with Kwaku's approval she gave away the dresses to whichever of their guests they fitted.

"Is how long you been away, Kwaku?" asked an old woman who had installed herself on a stool since early morning.

"More than a year," he answered.

"We miss you, boy."

She it was who, when Kwaku was still a little boy, had told him, "You uncle should put pepper 'pon you an' feed you to the alligators! You in' good for nothing else." Now here she was eating his food and behaving as if she had predicted a brilliant future for him.

But his thoughts were mostly for his children, the boisterous twins, Mona, who at thirteen had the breasts of a grown woman; his favourite daughter Philomena, a wisp of a child at eleven, as beautiful as the twins were repulsive; Damon the quiet one who, bored with sitting around, went off to school in the middle of the afternoon. Clayton spent much of his time keeping Irene in order, for since their return from Miss Gwendoline's mother she was well-nigh unmanageable.

When the men came, towards evening, they were given cigars and rum and began making jokes of which Miss Gwendoline disapproved.

"You looking fresh since las' night," one man observed to her.

"All you men so lawless! You don' think of nothing else," Miss Gwendoline replied, hoping that her show of displeasure would put them off.

"All I say is you looking fresh," the visitor protested. "You want me to say you looking stale when you lookin' fresh?"

"Don' say nothing at all," suggested Miss Gwendoline.

"All right, I going keep my mouth shut. I in' going say nothing like that, 'cause I not a prying man. An' I not going to say that I could hear the groaning and moaning all the way from my house. You satisfied?"

The visitor had said this with such a straight face that, had he not been betrayed by the meaning of his words, an onlooker might have thought him serious.

"It's the floorboard," Kwaku remarked.

"Floorboards don' groan," declared the man, enjoying Miss Gwendoline's discomfiture. "An' in any case is who does walk about after they put the light out?"

"Is how you know what happening in this house when you living down the road?" Miss Gwendoline retaliated. "You been prowling round the house las' night, ne?"

"I in' been prowling about nowhere," the visitor said, not in the least put out. "Is the noise that was loud. Everybody must've hear it, 'cause people start putting they light on and looking through the window like that night when Mr Gordon find a family of yowaree stinking out he house and he set his dogs 'pon them. Now look at that! You must've been making a big, big lot o' noise. Admit it, ne? There in' no shame in welcoming you husband back!"

Miss Gwendoline, furious that she was defenceless against the visitor's humour, looked at Kwaku for protection.

"Leave she alone," he put in. "You don' do nothing so you never make no noise, that's all."

Far from being angry, the man answered calmly. "My wife is the sighing kind," he said. "She does make so: 'Haah! Ahhaah!' like the sea breeze early in the morning. That's why you don' hear nothing ...."

Miss Gwendoline was saved by the arrival of the visitor's wife. He got up and offered her his seat and showed her a deference that surprised everyone. And it was clear that he had no intention of pursuing the subject he had been so eagerly discussing.

As the house filled, both Rona and Miss Gwendoline were obliged to help the girl in the kitchen, appearing only now and then to distribute sweets to the guests and to collect the plastic paper plates in which the chow-mein and other food had been served. The back and front doors and all the windows were open, yet the large room reeked of tobacco smoke and liquor. No one's conversation was intelligible except to those in the immediate vicinity, for the room was full of people talking aloud, children running from one room into the other and men who, uncertain as to their allotted span on earth, had drunk too much too quickly, and were sitting on the floor, their backs to the wall.

Mr Barzey had sent a message to Kwaku, inviting him over to Mr Gordon's house. He hoped Kwaku's uncle would come over as well when he returned home from work.

Kwaku was so delighted at his welcome he would have liked to make a speech expressing his gratitude for the villagers' conduct. Indeed, his gratitude was so profound he wanted to confess that it was he who had damaged the Conservancy and beg forgiveness for all the misdemeanours of his delinquent youth. Had he followed his inclination he would, given his state of mind, almost certainly have admitted to crimes he had not committed, and even invented imaginary crimes, in order to provide his confession with that solid basis which lends to repentance the quality of martyrdom.

"All these people come for me! For me!" he thought. There was Bruck-Foot Johnny, whose right leg made geometric patterns between its rising and falling to the ground. He had gone abroad with two sound legs to fight in somebody's wars and had come back with an embossed medal and a leg that had developed its own mind. Some years earlier Bruck-Foot Johnny had tried to chase Kwaku up the village road, but as soon as he had worked up speed the leg swivelled round; and before he knew what was happening he found himself running in the opposite direction, as if it was *he* who was fleeing from Kwaku. Then there was Crow-Bar who, rumour had it, had left his foetal home with a posture so stiff that he was promptly nicknamed Crow-Bar by the midwife, who at one time had been his father's mistress and had no love of her former lover's wife. Crow-Bar was standing with a glass in his hand, as erect now as he had been at birth, if rumour were to be believed. He had never shown Kwaku any affection and was even heard to remark that the militia could do worse than use him for target practice at point-blank range.

Now, Kwaku reflected, all these people admired him. All had been forgiven. The unsavoury memories of his youth had been rubbed out, forgiven – no, forgotten. And here was the manifestation of people's attitude towards him, their admiration and respect. They were drinking his rum and eating his food as proof of their generosity and the Christian power of forgiveness.

Kwaku was on the verge of tears when he discovered the true significance of the gathering. Riding Miss Gwendoline the night before was nothing compared with the discovery of the spirit of affection which had wandered into his house and was now roistering amidst the smoke. If *he* could not forget his youth, at least *they* had.

Kwaku sought out his wife and told her he was going over to see Mr Barzey. If anyone asked after him one of the children could fetch him from Mr Gordon's house. Miss Gwendoline thought it was too early to leave his guests, but gave in when he repeated that she could send for him if he were needed.

So Kwaku left by the back door and called out at the foot of Mr Barzey's stairs.

"I'm ready!" a voice called back, while the front door opened promptly.

Kwaku was deterred from coming up by his friend's gestures.

"It's she! She's sleeping," he declared.

"Who?"

"Who else?"

Kwaku had forgotten the state of war between Mr Barzey and his daughter-in-law. The improbable conflict had lasted throughout the many months of his absence and the old man showed no less relish for battle now than at the time of his going away.

When they reached the Public Road Mr Barzey stopped and shook Kwaku's hand violently as if he had only just seen him.

"You're looking fine! Fine! The terror of drug doctors – you're looking fine! It's dark and I don't have my glasses, but you're looking fine. Let's go."

Suddenly the thought occurred to Kwaku that they had forgotten to pick up his uncle. But there was no light in the low cottage.

"He hasn't come home yet," Mr Barzey remarked. "We'll shout over later if we see light in the house."

They crossed the Public Road and arrived in front of Mr Gordon's gate.

"Oh, ho!" Mr Barzey called out, banging the latch of the wrought-iron gate.

Immediately a furious barking broke out and, no sooner had the front door opened than a hound leapt out, yelling with such fury that it seemed certain it would strangle itself.

"King Kong!" shouted Mr Gordon, to which the hysterical animal reacted immediately. It shrank past its master and into the back yard, through a smaller iron gate which gave access to the extensive kitchen gardens and the bull pens.

"Come in, gentlemen," said Mr Gordon, opening his gate just enough to let his visitors through. He showed them into his gallery, which was dominated by a piano with candle-holders and a large television set.

"You've got a television set?" Kwaku could not help saying.

"Oh, I just brought it from England. It can't pick up anything. Just for show."

"I hear there's television in Venezuela," said Mr Barzey. "You've ever tried?"

"No, only lines come up," answered Mr Gordon who, despite his deprecating air, was proud of his television set.

Kwaku had never before seen Mr Gordon so close up and had not imagined him to be so short. The permanent grin, reserved for over-the-wall socializing, had gone and was replaced by a show of quiet authority, as if to let his guests know that here, in his new house with its easy-chairs, its spiral staircase to the storey above, and its sumptuous dining area, he was master.

Soon after the three men had taken their seats a young girl came in with a bottle of whisky, two bottles of soda water and four glasses.

"The fourth glass is for your uncle. He said he would come," explained Mr Gordon.

"He hasn't come home yet," Mr Barzey told him.

At first there was some constraint in the conversation, no doubt because Mr Gordon hardly knew Kwaku. After congratulating him on his success as a healer in New Amsterdam he enquired about his work. Kwaku took care to make a favourable impression and related only those incidents which, he believed, were suitable for superior company. Mr Gordon, in turn, told his guest of his experiences in England, of the importance of television in people's day-to-day living, of snow, ice on the panes in the depth of winter and the explosions of spring.

Kwaku urged Mr Barzey to relate the incident of the funeral procession to the Bourda cemetery. On hearing this Mr Gordon appeared extremely interested and insisted that he hear the story.

"Goodness, goodness!" Mr Gordon kept repeating, apparently disturbed by what he had just heard. "They travel, you know. They wander about the earth."

"What?" asked Kwaku.

Mr Gordon then told them why he had come back to Guyana, given up the nightly television programmes and the fat wages of overtime work. One evening, he told them, he went down the escalator to the underground platform, where he took the train daily to his house in a London suburb. He stood among the crowd thronging the platform, waiting for the train to come in.

"All I was concerned with," Mr Gordon continued, "was jostling my way into the carriage when the train arrived. At last it came and the pushing started. Then, as I was elbowing my way forward, I

152

looked up to see where I was going. And what I saw .... I stopped ...
I couldn't believe .... The carriage was full of ghosts! Dead people.
They were all sitting next to one another, motionless. The crowd
round me didn't seem to mind. They kept on pushing and shoving to
get their standing room in that carriage. But I couldn't bear to
watch and shut my eyes until the doors closed and the pushing
stopped. I hurried out of the station and went home by bus. I was
tired, you know: all that overtime, day in, day out, to make more
money to pay for the car and the colour television and holidays and
God knows what else.

"To cut a long story short, I went to the doctor and got some tonic
from him and a doctor's certificate for a week's holiday. I didn't tell
him what was wrong, mind you. Those people put you away if you
look funny; you don't have to see things. You just have to say 'Boo!'
or even go round in rags, and off with you in an ambulance screaming 'Ah hee! Ah hee ! Ah hee!' like a motorized jackass. So I stayed
home and got up at twelve o'clock the next day, spoiled myself with
food and drink. The Monday I went out to work I was fresh and
ready for anything. I plunged into the underground as if I was born
there, man. And when work was over I stood on the Holborn escalator that kept going down, down into the bowels of the station.
The platform had more people than ever waiting to elbow your ribs
out and trample over you to get on the train when it came in. Then
we heard it coming, 'Zhooooo!' getting louder and louder. And even
deep down there people's breath came out in a mist from the cold,
breathing over you, as if they wanted to soften you up. Hm! But
before the doors opened and the pushing started, when the train was
just coming to a halt, my eyes were fixed on the carriage slowing
down in front of us, a carriageful of dead bodies with their eyes
gouged out. This time I couldn't even close my eyes, but had to
watch them every second until the train pulled out, taking them
Christ knows where .... Listen to me! The next day I went to the
airways and booked my flight back to Guyana – one way. And the
same day I made arrangements to take the maximum amount of
money I could out of the country at the time."

"You've ever seen them again?" asked Kwaku.

"We don't have underground over here," came Mr Gordon's
reply.

Mr Barzey asked Mr Gordon about Guyanese living in England;
and now the conversation was well underway. He related, in turn,
how the shoemaker had once taken up with a young woman who, at
one time, was always to be seen in his shop, perpetually sweeping it
out. She became pregnant at the same time as the shoemaker's wife,
and when her condition began to show he installed her in a room on
the edge of the village. One day he sent the apprentice to do shop-

153

ping for both his wife and mistress; but the stupid lad delivered the mistress's shopping to the wife's house and the wife's to the mistress's. The shoemaker was unable to explain to his wife why she received coconut oil instead of cooking oil, lard instead of butter and a long list of inferior goods. Nor dared he confess to his expectant mistress that the bagful of expensive provisions was meant for his wife.

Kwaku felt more and more out of place in the company of these two men, who conversed with facility on every conceivable subject, from the mass murders at Jonestown to the arrival of a ship with a cargo of garlic. It was not until his uncle's arrival that the conversation took on a character that was more to his taste.

His uncle – who the night before had welcomed him back with little show of enthusiasm – told the story of a friend of his who was arrested by the police for being drunk and disorderly. The friend, who suffered from bad breath, kept protesting that he was not drunk.

"I not drunk," he kept shouting.

"You drunk!" the policeman did say. "And you disorderly!"

"I tell you I not drunk. Smell my breath!"

The policeman craned his neck forward to inhale the breath from the man's mouth, which he obligingly opened wide.

"He did so!" said Kwaku's uncle, making a puffing sound with his mouth. "And the police did so!" exclaimed the uncle, falling back on his chair as if he had been struck a fatal blow.

"They had to take the policeman to hospital and put him in a oxygen tent. And this friend with the bad breath, they changed his charge from drunk and disorderly to grievous bodily harm."

Kwaku, while taking part in the company's laughter, was thinking that he had contributed nothing to the conversation. He racked his brains to find something amusing to say, and seized his chance when Mr Gordon told them of his favourite television programme, "The Sky at Night", on which he had heard about the most recent discoveries in astronomy. One of them especially intrigued him. Described as the Black Hole, it was a burnt out star that had collapsed and become so dense that it exercised a tremendous attraction on every other body in its vicinity.

"Not even light escapes from it," Mr Gordon ended his description of the collapsed star.

"A Black Hole?" said Kwaku. "It sound like Blossom pussy!"

But for all his pains to contribute to the conversation, he received a withering look from his uncle. However, neither Mr Barzey nor Mr Gordon seemed to mind. They had been drinking for the better part of an hour before the uncle arrived and were already in high spirits.

"When you're going back to New Amsterdam?" demanded his

uncle, as a warning to Kwaku to keep his unseemly remarks to himself.

Kwaku, encouraged by the smiles of the other two men, and wishing to avenge himself on his uncle for putting him down in company, gave his account of the enema he administered to the boy on the Courantyne coast. And, as Mr Barzey's and Mr Gordon's amusement grew, Kwaku's uncle began devouring himself with rage.

"But wait," said Mr Barzey, "did the boy get better?"

"I don' know."

"When all is said and done," remarked Mr Gordon, "how many young people die?"

"I dunno," Mr Barzey took him up. "Only yesterday my son was reading the 'In Memoriam' page of the paper and he handed it to me to show how many of the photographs were of young people."

And for a while their conversation centred on the life-expectancy of Guyanese. Mr Barzey said that when he was a youth a good many people used to die as a result of a wound caused by stepping on a rusty nail. During the conversation Kwaku's uncle watched him like a chicken hawk, until, soothed by the whisky, he began to relax and take an interest in Mr Gordon's tales about England. He showed them the bric-à-brac he had collected while there, the crockery, the old books, the rugs with which he had decorated his walls and all the objects that testified to a lengthy stay in a foreign land.

The men drank and talked until Philomena came to fetch her father, because some of the guests interpreted his absence as an insult. So he bade the company goodbye, to his uncle's relief, promising to see Mr Barzey the next day.

He went out into the night to meet Philomena, and hand in hand they crossed the road.

"What you did in Mr Gordon house?" she asked, for she had never been beyond his gate.

"Talk and drink."

"You stink of liquor. I don' like you drinking."

"I been drinking whisky."

"It does stink, just like rum .... Did you carry on?" she then asked him when they reached the foot of the steps.

"How you mean carry on?"

"You din' make a fool of you'self?"

"No!" he exclaimed. "I don' do that any more."

She tightened her grip on his hand and he wondered what it was about this child that made her his favourite daughter.

23 The children

KWAKU LAY down to sleep, befuddled with the liquor he had been drinking. He had begun with rum, continued with whisky at Mr Gordon's house and come back to his own home to find the twins' godfather waiting for him, an unopened bottle of local gin in his hand. The twins' godfather made him promise to put them out as apprentices as soon as possible, for he could see that they would come to no good if allowed to behave the way they did.

Preoccupied with the twins' possible fate as delinquents Kwaku lay down to sleep after nearly all the guests had gone home. But instead of falling asleep at once he was kept awake by recollections of his visit to Mr Gordon's house, into which he would surely not be allowed to penetrate after his unseemly remarks. Above all he saw distinctly before him the photograph that hung on Mr Gordon's partition with the inscription: "*Ni vous sans moi, ni moi sans vous*". The sultry head of a woman with half-closed eyes must have been in some way conntected with him. Did the words mean anything? Was it another language? Or a code of some sort? Was the woman his wife, his mother when young? Had Mr Gordon ever been married?

Kwaku's fascination with Mr Gordon's home, deepened by his exclusion from it since it had been built, was such that he made up his mind to get into it once more, somehow, on some pretext; probably through his friend Mr Barzey, who would no doubt let him know the next day what had been the effect of the remarks that had put out his uncle.

When he lay down, day was already showing on the horizon in faded colours. Somehow, by the following afternoon he must manage to have slept long and sobered up, for he had promised Crow-Bar to come and see his wife, who had been afflicted with fainting spells ever since his brother came to live with them. Kwaku was surprised that he was consulted, for he had convinced himself that however much the villagers honoured and fêted him they would never consult him about an illness, as the people of New Amsterdam did.

Everyone knew the story of Crow-Bar and his wife and everyone knew the remedy, as Crow-Bar himself did. Her brother must be put out of his house if his wife was to get well again. Crow-Bar had consulted him in all likelihood only as a matter of form. Why else? He could give him no better advice than everyone else with whom he had discussed his domestic affairs.

Late the next morning when Kwaku woke up, Miss Gwendoline insisted that he should go and see the fisherman who lived near to the mangrove trees by the creek mouth.

"Go and see them first 'bout the apprenticeship," she said firmly, but with an indulgence that was never absent from her voice when she addressed Kwaku. "Go and see them first, because somebody might go before you." She advised him to promise to send the family a set of hooks from New Amsterdam.

"Suppose they sleeping?" Kwaku asked his wife. "They does work nights, don't they?"

"Them people never sleep! At least nobody ever catch them sleeping."

So he set off reluctantly. In the time of his absence the twins had got worse but he had no idea why Miss Gwendoline and the twins' godfather should make a to-do about the matter.

He turned left at the creek, walked past the church and kept on until he came to the last house, built perilously near the sea, Kwaku thought. In the yard a half-built boat, abandoned some years earlier, was lying upside down, its untarred hull resembling the roof of a quaint building.

Kwaku hesitated. Perhaps he should have brought the twins with him. On the other hand who in the village did not know them?

Before he could decide how he was to approach the family about his sons' apprenticeship a voice called out to him, "Aie! Famous people don' come this way, brother!"

The speaker appeared on the porch of the cottage grinning broadly.

"Morning, brother," Kwaku greeted him. "Praise the Lord!"

"Praise the Lord, brother," came the answer. "But is wha' bring you this side? When I see you comin' down the road I say fo' meself, 'He reach? He reach so far?' Well, come up, ne. You think we got teh-teh or something?"

Kwaku shook hands with the speaker on the porch, before following him into the cottage, which was utterly devoid of decoration, ornament or furniture. On the floor was spread out a great net, while in a corner a number of calabash floats were strewn.

"Sit down, man," offered the fisherman, pointing to nowhere in particular.

Kwaku sat on the floor, almost in the doorway. Convention required him to keep the object of his visit to himself until the talk was well underway. The fisherman was the storyteller of the village, a slim, muscular man who moved as though he were jointless, an impression emphasized by the short trousers he wore. His three brothers, their wives and children were never seen in any other attire, which facilitated handling of the fishing tackle and in any case helped to reduce the expenses of their occupation.

"I see you got a show-boat, man," Kwaku opened the conversation, nodding towards the yard.

"Is true. But wha' fo' do? The man say he not finishing it till we pay him the full money. An' when we get the money he say it going cost more. So we buy the silver-balli wood weself and go to him. 'We got the wood,' we say. 'Come and finish the boat.' But then he say the labour cost gone up. So we tell him, 'We going help you and you can charge the same as if you was working alone.' Then he say he going think 'bout it. And he been thinking 'bout it ever since. See these people! See how we people does stick together!'"

"Where your brothers?" enquired Kwaku, making a pretence of picking his teeth.

"All over the place."

"An' the women and children?" Kwaku asked, thinking it was polite to ask after them, although he was not in the least bit interested where the fisherman's wife, brothers, sisters-in-law and children were.

"All over the place. If you wait they could be back some time."

Kwaku turned this remark over in his mind, but could make nothing of it.

The fisherman's home was notorious among the villagers for its lack of hospitality. No one was ever known to have been fed there, not even with a piece of fried fish. But then all their time was devoted to making ends meet. At that very moment the other members of the family were probably out collecting sea-food among the mangrove or snails on the banks of the creek. Their father was from the north-west and had brought his knowledge of sea and river food with him. No other family in the village could stomach the idea of eating snails.

It was on the tip of Kwaku's tongue to ask if it was true that none of his relations ever slept, and if they did, where they all bedded down. There must be a good eighteen of them, he thought.

"I hear you's a big man now," said the fisherman, "healing ministers and big people."

"I never had no minister patients," protested Kwaku. "Who tell you so?"

"So I hear. An' they say you expecting a minister from overseas. Is true?"

"Naw," said Kwaku, eyeing the fisherman to see if he were not making fun of him.

"So I hear," repeated the fisherman, who did not appear to be joking. "Chicken hawk does fly, so I don' see why you kian' heal a foreign minister or two."

"How you fishin' going?" enquired Kwaku, not wishing to commit his sons to an indigent apprenticeship.

"Go-long, go-long. Not like the old days."

"Is a job for young people?"

"If they got money to buy the tackle is a job for anybody."

Kwaku's mind was set at rest. He sighed and immediately brought forth a protest from the fisherman.

"Don' do that, man. It does bring bad luck!"

He began to hum a tune, to show the fisherman that he did not mind being reminded that sighing brought bad luck.

"I really come 'bout the twins," said Kwaku at length.

"Why?"

"I want them to learn fishing with the best fishing people. And everybody know you and you brothers is the best."

"You boys? Learn fishing. You know what you saying? Them boys would head for Mickerie and end up in Africa. Naw! Fishing not fo' them. High-jumping or comfa dancing, but not fishing."

Although the fisherman had summarized the general opinion as to the twins' unreliability, Kwaku was annoyed and hurt that it had been expressed in such a forthright manner.

"They're changing for the better," he told the fisherman.

"The twins? Not the twins. Only las' week they catch one of we fowl and put it under the boat with a stray dog. And the fowl in' lay a single egg since then. It does go about limping and shitting all over the yard. Naw, naw. Is not fishing they want to do. They should become policemen and torment the criminals. Naw, naw. Fishing not for them."

"If you don' help them," said Kwaku, "they goin' got to do it theyself."

"Well," said the fisherman, after reflecting for a long while and scratching his head, his ears, his testicles and under his arms, "it's up to you. If you want two corpsees 'pon you hands you kian' make me responsible for that."

"All right, but what I goin' do?" asked Kwaku.

"I tell you already."

"Those boys givin' their mother nothing but trouble. I thought you could help me."

The fisherman did not reply, for he felt that he had said the last word on the matter.

"Suppose I was to give you fifty dollars when they start an' another fifty when the apprenticeship done?" suggested Kwaku. "In any case they can't start for a couple of years yet."

"Ah," said the fisherman, rising from a sitting position to squat, aborigine fashion. "Money, they say, does talk. Well, it sound as if it singing now. You's a rich man, Kwaku. Everybody know how much money them foreign ministers does pay you. I hear they got people in the States who does pay they wives to give them foop. Is true?" And here he burst out laughing.

"Imagine paying you wife to get a lil' piece of the star-apple. It in' enough that people got 'to pay fo' food, they has to go asking they wife fo' foop in exchange fo' money. 'Please, me dear, what about a piece o' foop?' " Here his voice changed to that of a wheedling female: " 'And is how much you goin' pay me?' " Then back to a man's baritone: " 'Ten cents.' 'What? I worth ten cents?' Then she go an' put on she nice dress and red-up she lips and perfume she hairy cunt then present sheself to she husband, who by this time got he tongue hanging out. 'Is how much I worth now?' 'One dollar,' he say, not caring 'bout he pocket no more. So he grab she and lay she down 'pon the floor. But before he could put the spoon in the food she say, 'Bring the dollar first!' An' the poor husband rush inside as if he running to ketch the last bus. When he come out she get up and tek the dollar note to the window for see the light shine 'pon it. 'Cause them Americans is counterfeit generals. By this time the man groaning and looking at she like a dog in dog season. 'Is good money. I tell you,' he say. And she say, 'So you tell me, but I got fo' see fo' meself.' 'O me God! Come, ne?' he groan, stretching out he hands. And is only when the woman sure the note genuine she lift up she frock and skin up sheself 'pon the floor. Somebody who been living in America for years tell me that does happen. Truth o' God!' "

"You goin' take the twins, then?" Kwaku asked eagerly, having listened with great patience to the fisherman's story.

"I going tek them, yes. So when they coming?"

"I tell you, in a couple of years."

"Oh," said the fisherman, disappointed.

Then, after a short pause he continued, "You see how money does talk? An' how it does mek you talk? Money. I don' know why the government does get so vex when people mek they own money. *They* does do it, and nobody does complain. I in my thirties and if I could find the time I couldn' go nowhere 'cause I in' got the clothes .... You know wha' wrong with this country? It crawling with worms and foreign preachers. Foreign preachers, not foreign worms. The worms is we very own. Some of them even like talking 'bout Africa, as if is they discover it. And what they don' know is they got people that know more about Africa than them. My family don' live no different from we great-grandparents. But it don' stop these people preaching 'bout Africa and things like that .... You know one time a few years ago I did travel. Yes, man! One time I travel. I been all the way to Kurupung to see me sister family. She married a miner. An' I been to Kurupung and I see t'ings I din' know exist in this country, in the world. You ever see rock 'pon the coast? You never see rock on the coast. But in the interior they got rock, rock father and rock mother. And you look 'pon them mighty things and you see how small man is 'pon this earth and how the forest can squash him jus' like that!"

The storyteller clapped his hands together.

"Like that! Fact is, I did go to this God-forsaken place to see me sister family. Family? She cóme from a family that does stick together like glue. Try prising we apart. We family call Glue! So she married this bush-man living at Kurupung where the diamond mines close and they in' got work, even for donkey. They does get up at any time of the day 'cause they in' got no work to do. And everybody demoralized 'cause there in' no work. Man make to work. Look at this family! We poor, but we does work, work work. Today I only home 'cause is my turn to watch the house. Look at me hands. Look. Is not mooning about did make them like a mora plank. I know 'bout work. You should see my sister three children, three nice girls, pretty girls. On a Sunday afternoon they does dress up in all they finery and stand about the house 'cause they in' got nothing fo' do. They does move from one room to the nex', back again, like travellers 'pon the road. In the end a bottle of rum does appear, like magic – 'cause my sister and she husband in' got money fo' buy rum. Then in no time you see them tottering about, drunk to the world, kicking at anything in their way, pitching from side to side like a fishing boat when the wind ketch it! Young girls – one's only ten – drunk, staring as if they don' got mother or father! I say to me sister, 'Let the girls come back and scrape a living with we.' 'With you? Ketching and scraping fish and stinking up they body? These girls got education.' I in' say nothing, more 'cause that sister always had a hot mouth. She in' want she daughter to stink of fish, but she don' mind them tottering about the place in all they finery, when all o' them unemployed lay-about men watching them like chicken hawk watch them baby chicken. What you got to say 'bout that, Kwaku? You with all you experience treating ministers and kings from abroad and healing people who never do a hard day's work."

"I see," said Kwaku, adopting a pose suitable to the deep reflection the fisherman expected of him. "That is a profound matter: drunken children in the bush."

And Kwaku thought to himself that this was no garlic matter. The fisherman was not a fool. His whole family were known for the independence of their ways, their strange habits and lack of religion. Mr Barzey had remarked the day before that the black man had endured two disasters in the last few hundreds of years, slavery and Christianity; the one an attack on the body, and the other an attack on the spirit. Kwaku saw the fisherman's family as the embodiment of an ideal.

"You sure the children been drunk?" asked Kwaku, not knowing what to say.

"Kwaku, they was drunk, I tell you; and they was carrying theyself without shame."

"If you did bring them to live with you," Kwaku remarked,

161

following the spoor of a sudden inspiration, "they would've bring trouble in your house. What'd you do with girls who does wear fine clothes?"

The fisherman drew his fist under his chin, while looking past Kwaku. When he spoke his voice had changed.

"You's a healer, Kwaku .... You know how to find a man character? Eh? That man, my sister husband, he pass through this village like a whirlwind and take her away. He did come with sweet words. You remember them actors that come here 'bout fifteen years ago? And the one that play *all* them parts? Was he. Is he me sister married. They put on they plays in the school hall, remember? This man could make a audience think he was anything and me sister follow him about the village. He did tell her that he was rich and had property all over the place; and look where she end up? At Kurupung."

While the fisherman was speaking Kwaku was turning over in his mind the possibility of making him a client. He had asked if he was a healer. There was no possibility of getting money from him, but the twins' future might be thereby assured.

"I hardly does go out on the sea no more," continued the fisherman. "I been losing me grip since that man bewitch me sister and carry she away so far from she family. Now, is me does stay home with the nets and watch the house."

"What the rest of you family say 'bout you?" asked Kwaku.

"Nothing. They don' say nothing. Is not only the wind and the dark ... is the water. Even the swamp water where they does find the oyster 'pon the mangrove roots, even the swamp water does do somet'ing to me. I not a coward, you know. Besides, I's the head of the family since me father dead and gone."

The fisherman, who had meanwhile settled on the floor next to Kwaku, jumped up and skipped over a corner of the net. He took up a conch lying on the floor under a window.

"You see this conch? If I blow it, the family'll come before you could get to the gate."

Staring at Kwaku, he was holding out the conch towards him in such a way that Kwaku shuddered momentarily.

The fisherman put the conch to his lips and at the same moment Kwaku shouted, "All right! I believe you."

And the fisherman lowered his hands. He burst out laughing.

"You frighten! I gone an' frighten you .... People say men is brothers. If men are brothers they won't got to keep repeating it. 'Men is brothers! Men is brothers!' But men not brothers. But wha' fo' do? Life is life. My sister gone 'cause that Kurupung man put on a mask and carry she away from she own family."

"I can heal you," Kwaku blurted out, without knowing why.

162

"O Kwaku," said the fisherman, "you musn' say things like that ... . That man din' only take me sister away, he work obeah 'pon me 'cause I did curse him and say he wasn' a man, with his actor make-up and powder 'pon his face."

"I can heal you, I say," insisted Kwaku. "If you do as I tell you."

The fisherman placed his conch on the ground and came over to Kwaku.

"But I in' got no money to pay you."

"You don' have to pay me. Jus' look after the twins when they take up they apprenticeship. You serious 'bout the apprenticeship, then?"

"Serious? I very serious. I telling you, Kwaku, if you can get my sister and this man out of me mind I'd do anything fo' you. I'd tell the family to make you twins the best fishermen on the coast. They'd know all 'bout seine nets, pin-seine nets, cadell, mending them, everyt'ing. They got secrets that if a man know he family would never starve. During the locust plague you see we children starving? No. We gather crooda bush and live 'pon shrimps and oyster and fish. Kwaku! You in' ...?"

"I say I can heal you. I going make up something and send it with one of the twins. I going send enough to last a year. But you got to do jus' what I tell you."

"Come to the back o' the house," the fisherman said. "Words does fly out of the door and window them, and does settle in people ears, and they does end up knowing more 'bout you business than you yourself."

Kwaku followed the fisherman, skipping over ends of the net spread out on the floorboards.

Kwaku hurried away to escape the early afternoon sun. He could feel the heat from the road through his casual shoes, on the back of his neck and on the top of his head; and he regretted having left the house without a hat. Two sheep were grazing in the churchyard between the graves of villagers who had died long ago, their matted wool like improbable, dun-coloured greatcoats. The calabash tree standing sentinel at Blossom's gate was in flower and the stench of its blossoms filled the still air, causing Kwaku to look up at his old playmate's house, the windows of which were closed against the heat of the day. When he had already gone by, a voice shouted out:

"We not talking? You don't know your friends?"

He looked up and saw Blossom's head appear through a half-open window; and before he could answer, Wilfred was standing behind her, his shirt front open.

"Mr Healer himself!" exclaimed Wilfred in a mock-welcoming tone. "Is what bring you to this lil' village?"

"Is all right for all you," said Kwaku, shading his eyes from the sun, "you inside, but I outside."

"Come in, ne?" Wilfred said. "You frighten or something? I know is not me you frighten of."

"I been out since early morning time," Kwaku excused himself. "Another time."

"Where you been? I see you coming from the church road, and I know you not a church-going man, like Miss Blossom."

"I been to see the fisherman 'bout the twins," answered Kwaku, who had already dropped his superior pose, what with the relentless sun and the long session with the fisherman.

"You want learn to fish, ne?" said Wilfred.

"Shut you mouth," Blossom said sharply.

"I got to go now, or I going end up with sun stroke."

"When you going back to New Amsterdam?" Blossom demanded.

"Tomorrow."

"Tomorrow? Already? Come tonight and eat then."

Kwaku agreed, while seeing little possibility of keeping his promise.

He left with a brief wave of his hand, smiling with satisfaction at the way Blossom had handled Wilfred, who was only the second person in the village to show him as little respect now as before he went away to New Amsterdam.

Out of courtesy he dropped in at his uncle's for a chat before walking the few yards to his own little house in the back yard. They sat in silence, neither caring to start a conversation. What was there to say to this man who had brought him up because it was his duty and had not concealed his relief when he married and set up house on his own? His life was dedicated, it seemed, to the search for peace, peace from his neighbours, from Kwaku, and from women; for Kwaku had never seen a woman in his house, had not once seen him in conversation with a woman. His house was spotlessly clean, the only evidence of an extravagance being a length of fly-paper hanging from a metal projection attached to the partition that divided the single bedroom and drawing-room.

Kwaku could never ignore his uncle; nor could he keep away from the house in which he had spent much of his childhood and all his youth. And in spite of his uncle's contempt for him he felt bound to him by an unspoken affection, undiminished by his disappointment that the older man did not acknowledge his status as a healer.

"You going tomorrow, I hear," his uncle said.

"Yes, is tomorrow."

"Hm."

He then lay back in his Berbice chair, turned his head to one side and closed his eyes, determined to get the most out of the few hours of quiet that lay ahead.

Kwaku bade him goodbye and thoughtfully left the door open to facilitate the circulation of what little air there was.

"Close it!" came the laconic order.

He did as he was told, leaving his uncle to the sleep that never failed to overtake him once he closed his eyes.

Early that evening Miss Gwendoline cooked fried chicken, and the whole family sat around the drawing-room talking or playing. Philomena was half-lying, half-sitting on the floor at his feet, with Rona next to her, more girlish than she in her deportment. The twins and Damon were racing tanks made of cotton-reels discarded by their mother, while Irene and Clayton were lying full-length on the floor, unwilling to retire to the bedroom with Fabian their baby sister, lest they missed a story of New Amsterdam or some unexpected treat.

Occasionally Rona had to serve clients who had come to buy her mother's black pudding, so that there were often more than a dozen persons sitting or standing around in the tiny drawing-room.

Shortly after seven o'clock the church bell began ringing; the soft, cracked notes mingled with the sound of the surf and the engine-roar of a passing car. And Kwaku wondered whether he was really going back to New Amsterdam the next day, away from his family, his uncle, Mr Barzey and all those villagers he had known since childhood. Had he ever been to New Amsterdam? Did he actually live in a rented house there, a short walk from the new Canje bridge and the smart quarter of the town?

Every time he looked at Philomena she smiled. She and her mother made life worth living, he told himself. Intoxicated with the discovery that he was loved by his family Kwaku chose a moment when no clients were about and then told them the story of Mr Semple's farting horse, which people came from all around to see. It used to break wind on command and the air would reek of grass. Adopting some of the fisherman's mimicry he imitated the horse's nonchalant air while munching grass, and Mr Semple's outrage on the occasion that the animal refused to co-operate when he invited his drinking companions to witness a demonstration of its prowess; then his delight when his friends, about to leave, were taken aback by the long-drawn-out explosion and the fetid smell that followed.

The family demanded more stories and descriptions of New Amsterdam. And Kwaku told of its numerous churches and the public clocks that started striking all at once. Then one by one the children fell asleep, first Clayton and Irene, until they were all lying on the floor in every conceivable posture.

"When Clayton and Irene come back from my mother," said

165

Miss Gwendoline, "they go on as if they din' know me or the others. They did get so close to their grandmother they din' want to come back."

Then because he was not impressed by what she told him she said, "Philomena got man." She watched closely to see what effect the remark had had.

"What you talking?" said Kwaku. "She not even twelve yet."

"She got man, I say."

And Kwaku called to mind the way Philomena dressed, dwelling on her earrings and painted nails. "I don' believe you."

"She got man," Miss Gwendoline repeated unrelentingly. "She don' want to wear she ribbons to school no more."

"You make her?" asked Kwaku anxiously.

"I make her, yes. Rona does still wear ribbons and she nearly fourteen. Before you go you must tell she to come home straight from school; she going listen to you." Miss Gwendoline's last words were spoken with some resentment.

"Children nowadays," was all he could mumble, marvelling at the same time how a woman so capable should ask his assistance in something so small. Yes, he would speak to Philomena. He reflected that he had brought Rona a length of cloth as a present from New Amsterdam, while his gift to Philomena had been a necklace. In future he had to be careful. It was not right to encourage her, as Miss Gwendoline surely felt he was doing.

"When you buy house," she said, "make sure it got a veranda. I did always want a house with a veranda."

She was sorry she had been so sour, and wanted to make amends.

"It going have a lot of rooms," he promised. "You mother can come and live with us if she want."

Lasting disharmony was unthinkable between them. It was as though, having passed through hard times, nothing could mar their happiness in each other.

She told him that she did not believe he had done the right thing in going to the fisherman's house, after all. The family was odd, different from everyone else in the village. But she agreed that the twins were so backward at school and so cantankerous that fishing might be the only thing to keep them out of trouble.

She was never tired of asking him about New Amsterdam and whether the women there were good-looking. But the conversation always came back to the children. Rona was attending classes in needlepoint, patchwork and candle-making. And every time she called Rona's name he understood her to mean: "You only got eyes for Philomena. Why you bring necklace for she when you only bring a piece of cloth for Rona?"

Miss Gwendoline left her husband to go and feed the youngest,

166

who had fallen asleep too early. After years of living together he *knew* what she was doing behind the partition: while holding Fabian in one arm she was making her cradle with the other. From the sharp sound of the cloth, followed by an almost inaudible rustling, she would put her down in a moment, before coming out to join him, carrying a plate with crumbs stuck to the fatty remains of the child's meal. He could not fathom this mystery of living, this feeling of body for body and deep appreciation of a slight gesture. Would he have felt the same way about any other woman who had given him eight children?

Kwaku and Miss Gwendoline had only been able to make love once since he came home, for the children fell asleep all over the place, unwilling to retire to the bedroom when they felt drowsy. When she reappeared he intended to take her to the back of the yard behind the locust tree.

But as soon as she came out Miss Gwendoline spoke of Philomena once more. The night before he returned from New Amsterdam she dreamt that she, Philomena and he were sitting on the back stairs in the moonlight. Kwaku was sitting between them. The moonlight was shining on Kwaku and his daughter, who was wearing a red dress. Miss Gwendoline, however, was in the shadow, on the right of her husband. Angry at this, she got up and made Philomena change places with her.

"And what I do?" asked Kwaku, evoking his daughter's languid gestures.

"You in' do nothing. You jus' sit there, like nothing happen."

"But nothing happen," Kwaku protested.

"I din' say something happen."

Kwaku was sure they would quarrel, thus spoiling the harmony of their last evening together.

Miss Gwendoline brought him a portion of souse from the kitchen and started to lay out his clothes for the following morning. But Kwaku, impatient with her constant activity, made her sit next to him and told her an obscene story. He then began stroking her head; and when she objected that one of the children was bound to wake up he dragged her out into the back yard behind the massive locust tree. In the distance the fronds of an ité palm imposed on the darker sky its fan-like contour, floating, it seemed, above an invisible trunk. Scattered at random intervals behind the line of back yards were tiny bouquets of fire, night lights lit as a protection against the spirits of darkness.

No sooner had Kwaku achieved a climax than he hustled his wife away from their hiding place against her will.

"Two married people with children foopin' in they own back yard!" mocked Miss Gwendoline, pushing him fondly as he entered the house. "You in' shame?"

"You can talk," Kwaku replied, "working from foreday morning till night time. But when I alone with all that time on me hands I don' get nothing else to think about, except you smooth skin and the thing 'tween you legs."

"You ever do it with anybody else since we married?" she asked, thinking of Blossom.

"Me? Even if a woman skin up sheself in front of me, and even if she look like the Queen of Sheba and even if she put a gun to me head, I wouldn' do it."

"You sure?"

"If I sure!" he declared emphatically.

"Well, you know Blossom did come one time to enquire where you does live in New Amsterdam," said Miss Gwendoline, not certain whether she had written him about the visit.

"You tell she?" asked Kwaku, assuring Miss Gwendoline by his expression that he knew nothing.

"What I going tell she for?" she said indignantly. "She got she own man. What she want to come visiting you for in town? Especially when you in' see a woman thing for so long. According to what *you* say ...."

Kwaku felt as if he had never been to New Amsterdam, that he had never practised as a healer; and he thought on the weeks ahead with trepidation. Seized with a sudden nervousness as to his work, on which his family's new-found well-being depended, he talked incessantly.

"You know how so much people changing their names to African names?" he said to Miss Gwendoline. "I had to treat a man wife for she bad foot. Well, the husband did change he name from Smith to Uba. She was vexed 'cause she didn' want she name change. And is only afterwards she find out what Uba does mean. It mean: 'Man with a bag in which Winds is kept and does open to let out the Westerlies when the Moon come out after the end of March ... and does go back again in November ... every Leap Year.'"

"That little word mean all that?" asked Miss Gwendoline incredously.

"I telling you."

"Well, I never!"

She let him talk, although there was much she could have told him as well. While he was drinking with Mr Barzey and Mr Gordon she had thrown out a guest single-handed because he had made an insulting remark about Kwaku's dead mother. "So Kwaku is a healer now!" the man had said. "I used to bounce his mother." And Miss Gwendoline, who had known the man for years, would accept no apology for the offending remark. Menacing the guest with her bulk she pushed him, protesting, towards the door and out into the yard, where he remained for several minutes, complaining loudly at the bad reception he had been given. Miss Gwendoline had forbidden the children to mention the incident to their father. Now she sensed his nervousness and knew him to be as vulnerable as he ever was. People never changed, deep down, she told herself. If he was less excitable, if he was more easily contented, it was only because things were well with him and she was his anchor. Conscious of her responsibility she discharged it without giving him cause to suspect how well she understood him.

"You tired?" Kwaku asked her.

"You don' want to do it again!" Miss Gwendoline exclaimed.

Those few words of protest were, in a curious manner, an expression of his own contentment, his delight in his family and home. They belonged to him. And was not love a kind of possession? The one book in the Bible he could read without difficulty was the Song of Solomon, on account of its simple language and directness. And in it he had read, "My beloved is mine and I am his." Love *was* possession. He possessed Gwendoline and his children and they possessed him. He did not love Blossom, for neither possessed the other. And it was this demand on her part that he had resisted in the house at Rosignol. They were like sister and brother, and the deep affection he bore her contained nothing of the possession that ravages when it is lost.

Miss Gwendoline was wearing a pair of new slippers Kwaku had brought from New Amsterdam. Until then she had always gone about barefooted, even in the yard. Shoes were only to be worn when one went out on the road, or on occasion, when strangers came to the house. And Kwaku got to thinking of the shoemaker and his new mistress and regretted his impetuous behaviour on the eve of his departure for New Amsterdam.

"Yes," he sighed.

The couple could have talked all night, surrounded by their sleeping children, the furniture, the thick shadows pressing against the window panes, the streets and fields, and the wandering vehicles that offended the quiet village night. But in the end they went to bed and were soon breathing as deeply as their children.

The next morning Kwaku went away while his children were still asleep. He left Miss Gwendoline drenched with his odour and words of regret. In a box stuffed in the corner of his grip were bol-de-mel cakes she had made for him, saffron coloured, the things he liked best, and which Miss Gwendoline claimed she made even better than her grandmother.

169

And during the early part of his journey in the yellow bus his thoughts centred on Philomena and Damon, his quiet son, who had hardly spoken a word during his stay. It seemed that he had sought refuge in silence, the very opposite to Clayton and Irene and the cantankerous twins.

Miss Gwendoline had promised to send one of the children over to see Crow-Bar and apologize for his being unable to come round as he had promised. There was so much for him to ponder on during the journey, not least the jealousy his success had aroused in some of his neighbours and his inadequacy in the company of Mr Gordon and Mr Barzey.

But Kwaku soon fell asleep, half-hypnotized by the rocking bus, the drone of its engine and the unbroken flat-lands grown with courida bush.

24 The hollow ball

THREE WEEKS after Kwaku had left for New Amsterdam with a promise to send for his family before year-end, Miss Gwendoline was visited by the fisherman, who appeared behind Kwaku's uncle's house one afternoon when she and the girls were sitting on the front steps. They were laughing at the antics of Fabian who, in an effort to walk, kept running in short bursts, only to be caught by Rona or Irene as she was on the point of keeling over on to the hard, sun-baked ground.

"You come to see Kwaku?" Miss Gwendoline asked. "He gone back to New Amsterdam."

"I know. Is you I want to see," he said, managing with those few words to banish merriment from the yard.

"Me? Wha' you want to see me for?"

"I want you to send he a message. Tell he is weeks and me sister in' come back yet. And I still kian' forget. Tell he he kian' go round making promises an' not keeping them. Tell he ... tell he what I say."

"I goin' tell him," promised Miss Gwendoline. "But why not go to his uncle?"

She pointed her chin towards Kwaku's uncle's back stairs.

" 'Cause this business in' got nothing to do with he uncle. What I going go see his uncle for?"

The fisherman looked down at the company, and especially at little Fabian sheltering behind Rona's protective hands.

"Write he. Tell he soon," said the fisherman, turning as he spoke.

The company saw him duck under Kwaku's uncle's house and

then cross the bridge before turning left on the Public Road.

The children waited for their mother to speak, not knowing what the exchange of words was about.

"What Pa promised him to do?" asked Philomena.

"Something 'bout his sister," replied Miss Gwendoline. "The sister was like you. She did like wearing high-heel shoes and acting like a big woman. When the actors from town come to the village she go away with one o' them. She did like high heels and rouge and painting she nails, like you. And look where she end up – in the bush!"

Fear had put the bitterness in Miss Gwendoline's voice. Fear of the fisherman's family, who respected nothing, and were not even intimidated by the police.

"What you goin' do?" Rona pressed her.

"What I can do? I goin' write you father. You goin' write him for me."

Miss Gwendoline wanted to have the letter written at once but, so as not to alarm the children, took Fabian from her eldest daughter and began dandling her on her knee. But the others were not fooled.

"When we goin' go and live in New Amsterdam?" asked Irene.

"In a few months, God willing," answered her mother.

The children had never seen their mother so subdued.

"Why everybody frightened of the fisherman and his family?" Rona enquired.

"People say they never been in a church," Philomena said, finding her tongue, "an' that when one of them dead the church not goin' bury them."

This innocent remark comforted Miss Gwendoline, who regarded her own faith as a protection. Only recently Philomena had been confirmed.

"Don't go talking 'bout the village that your father did promise to do something for the fisherman," Miss Gwendoline warned.

"Why not?" Philomena spoke up boldly.

"Because I say so."

Eventually Miss Gwendoline got up to warm the black pudding for the customers, who would start coming after dark. There was no need to slave from morning till night now that Kwaku was sending her good money; but she had become accustomed to the coming and going, the village children loitering on the steps and in the yard long after consuming what she had made with her own hands. If she had nothing to do at night she would be obliged to turn to church work or sewing. Unlike Philomena, whose presence now oppressed her, Rona had walked in her footsteps, accepting without question her role as helpmeet and organizer of the household, so that, should she ever be let down by a man, the skills she had acquired at her mother's

171

elbow would stand her in good stead.

Miss Gwendoline kept Rona up that night in order to write her letter to Kwaku. If she could find or borrow a stamp from a neighbour one of the boys could go to the post office in the next village and slip it into the letter box. But no stamp was to be found and she was obliged to keep Rona away from school the following morning so as to despatch the letter as quickly as possible.

A few days later Kwaku's reply came. She must assure the fisherman that he had done his best by praying that his sister would come back from the bush and that, if not, her brother would get over her absence. He could do nothing more. Kwaku warned her to keep him away from the house. Luckily she and the children had been sitting on the stairs when he came. Miss Gwendoline herself went round to the fisherman's house the same afternoon and delivered her husband's message. All his numerous family came to the windows and out on the stairs to hear her tell him what Kwaku had written.

The fisherman's legs must have been oiled, for they glistened in the late afternoon sunlight. The children and the women, who had come out on to the stairs, all long-legged and barefooted, were staring at Miss Gwendoline silently, waiting to hear the head of the family speak.

"You tell you husband he got to keep he promise. That's all I want. We don' mek promises we don' keep."

Miss Gwendoline began to speak, but he interrupted her.

"He got a week. Seven day and night. Me sister going walk in this house in seven days' time."

Miss Gwendoline's anger was roused by this threat.

"Don' threaten me husband, fisherman. 'Cause whatever you do to him I goin' do you back. They got plenty of you, but I got eight children who growing up, and lots of family in the villages along the coast."

Miss Gwendoline started down the stairs, trembling with rage at her reception on strange premises.

"Miss Gwendoline!"

She turned round.

"Tell he I say seven days."

"And I tell you touch him if you want to see who I am."

She raised her fist at the house and the fisherman and his family looking at her through the windows of their house or standing on the stairs in their short pants. It was her fear of these people and her anxiety on her husband's account that had roused her anger. If they wanted to harm him all they need do was enquire after Kwaku in New Amsterdam and they would be directed to his house.

She wrote her husband that night and warned him of the fisherman's uncompromising manner.

172

Miss Gwendoline posted her sons as look-outs on the seventh day after her visit to the fisherman's house. It was the evening of Divali, a public holiday. The houses of the few East Indians living in the village were darker than on similar nights in the past, for a brisk wind had begun to blow as soon as the sun had set, putting out many of the lamps on the porches and stairs.

The twins had taken up position under their grand-uncle's house, while Damon stood at the window, looking at the meagre display of lights. The whirring of cicadas came from the grass across the trench, undisturbed by the swift passage of a taxi rattling by.

Miss Gwendoline's house was unusually quiet, for she had made it known that nothing was on sale that night; but children still came from time to time and had to be turned away by the twins. In the end, tired of waiting, they went out on to the Public Road to join the other children playing games in the warm night air.

Damon, alone at his post at the window, did not give the twins away to their mother. He strained his eyes to catch sight of any familiar figure that might come along the path beside his grand-uncle's house or emerge from under it.

The stranger's voice caught Damon sleeping, for he had nodded off momentarily, his head resting on his arm.

"Is where you mother?"

But before Damon could react he found himself holding a ball which the fisherman had thrust at him.

"Give you mother this."

"Ma?"

But the fisherman had already vanished among the shadows.

"Ma?"

"What?" she asked anxiously, hurrying up to see if anyone was there.

"It was the fisherman. He say give this to you."

Miss Gwendoline took the hollow ball – hardly larger than a cricket ball – from her son, who made a show of being alert.

"Take it back quick!" his mother ordered him. "Throw it in his yard."

"Suppose ...?"

"I goin' come with you then," Miss Gwendoline said. "Wait."

In no time she had slipped on her slippers and was hurrying by her son's side towards the fisherman's house.

"Is where them good-for-nothing boys?" she asked, remembering that her twins had been posted on the look-out and were now nowhere to be seen.

"I don' know," Damon said untruthfully.

"How you mean you don' know? Was three of you. Two gone and you don' know. O me God! You know what I got in me hand here?"

Damon looked at the ball, half-knowing the answer to his mother's threatening question.

"If I had to rely on all you children! This is obeah story. I don' know why you father din' leave these people alone."

Damon's legs nearly gave way under him at the mention of the word "obeah".

"I did tell you plain that you father did write not to take nothing from him," Miss Gwendoline reminded her son.

"I thought you say not to let him in the house."

"Is the same thing," snapped Miss Gwendoline.

A faint light glimmered deep in the fisherman's house, but no one was to be seen.

"Throw it! Quick!" Miss Gwendoline whispered to her son.

Damon hurled the ball into the yard, where it fell with a thud on to the unfinished boat. And in no time mother and son were hurrying away.

"Your father heart would drop out if he did know what happen tonight," Miss Gwendoline declared, panting in an effort to keep up with her son, for whom even the houses in the fisherman's street had become objects of terror, with their steep staircases and shuttered windows.

On the way home they came upon the twins, in conversation with a group of boys.

"Bring you ass here!" Miss Gwendoline shouted, grabbing hold of one of them.

In full view of his friends she belaboured him with blows while his brother fled up the road, less afraid of the power in his mother's arms than at the shame he would have to endure if beaten in front of his teenaged friends.

"Two big ugly brutes like you kian' even watch the house!" she bellowed at her son. "Get you tail home!"

And while he walked away unprotesting, Miss Gwendoline turned her attention to the group of friends standing about silently.

"All-you in' got nothing better to do than loll around the road?"

No one dared answer her, but once she had turned into her yard they began laughing about the twins' fate and comparing their parents' tempers.

Late into the night Miss Gwendoline was sitting alone in the darkness of her front room, wondering what the hollow ball had contained. The fisherman had tried to put something on her and her children. She had no doubts whatsoever about this.

She sat listening to the droning wind, the monotonous, trailing tones that threatened never to end, and became all at once aware that she was a mother of eight, as if it had happened in a single day,

174

crept up the night before and took her in the morning: "You're a mother of eight!" And childhood was forgotten in a night. She had had no youth, as she recalled, not like Philomena; like Rona she had known only work before she was given away in marriage. Work was satisfaction; and everything could be put right with work. Except obeah, which dragged up centuries of terror and fear of night-time, fear of water, of leafless trees, hollow receptables, flowers, gifts and the silence of neighbours. Her mother, mortally afraid of its possibilities for evil, had communicated this dread to her.

Kwaku, with his rash promises, his words like horses that had slipped their bridles, had chosen the right one: the fisherman would be content with nothing less than the fulfilment of a promise. And who was this sister? A good-for-nothing whose habits had been a constant cause of dissension in her family and whose going away had been welcomed by all her relations except him. Why should he use this meagre excuse to persecute Kwaku and her?

The business had had at least one good result: there was no longer any question of the twins' doing an apprenticeship with the fisherman's family. God knows what might have happened to them. Miss Gwendoline thought it best to send Irene and Clayton back to her mother, at least for the while. She would ask Kwaku to come at once and they would decide what should be done.

An unexpected fall in the wind startled her and she looked outside into the night, but could only see Kwaku's uncle's house and the bushes shuddering under a troubled sky. Filled with unease Miss Gwendoline retired for the night, after testing the bolts of the doors and windows.

25 Miss Gwendoline's affliction

VILLAGERS WERE leaving the little whitewashed church with its disturbing needle-sharp wooden spire. Some lost no time in crossing the bridge that led to the road, while others stood on the stairs or in the church yard, talking to acquaintances or waiting for relations to join them. A few better-off women opened parasols against the morning sun, but most of the others – the congregation consisted almost entirely of women – were protected by broad-brimmed white hats.

Miss Gwendoline and her eight children were among the last to come out, for it took time to gather her brood from the various parts of the church where they preferred to sit. The twins brought up the rear, while at the front Miss Gwendoline sauntered along with Fabian, her youngest. No one spoke. Once on the main road only a

175

few of the congregation were ahead of them, for most of the others had turned left.

From within the village came the sound of wet garments being beaten against wood. The wind, less brisk than the day before, lifted the dresses of the girls, who placed one hand against a thigh and the other on their head to prevent their hats from being blown away. The trench water, ruffled by the fitful gusts of breeze, was moving slowly, drawn to the main drainage canal and the sluice gate.

"Look, the koker mus' be open," Damon remarked, pointing to the water. But no one answered him.

At the approach of a car the whole family stepped off the road on to the sloping grass verge and there waited for the vehicle to go by.

On arriving at their yard they hailed Kwaku's uncle, who was sitting at the top of his staircase reading the Sunday newspaper.

"All right," he said, returning the greeting in a drawl, as though it were an effort to speak in the morning heat.

Only Miss Gwendoline and Rona took the pathway by the fence, the others preferring to use the short cut under the grand-uncle's house.

"Ma, what wrong?" Philomena asked her mother, who seemed unwilling to follow her children into the house.

"I can't see," Miss Gwendoline replied softly.

"How you mean?" Rona asked.

"I don' see anything."

"Ma!" Rona whimpered.

"Take me in the house."

"What happen, Ma?" one of the twins pleaded, for he saw his mother probing about the room with outstretched right arm.

Rona and Philomena began to wail and the younger children started crying as well, for the occurrence was beyond their comprehension.

"Go an' get your father uncle," Miss Gwendoline told them in a calm voice.

And within the minute Kwaku's uncle was in the doorway.

"Miss Gwendoline?" he called to her.

"Is my eyes, Uncle," she said, turning towards the sound of his voice.

"You don't see anything?" he asked, changing his position.

"No."

"I can see you, Ma," Fabian said, tugging at her mother's Sunday dress.

"Listen," Kwaku's uncle said, addressing the children. "All you change your clothes. Rona, you do the food .... I say go and change!" he ordered one of the twins, who stood gaping at his mother.

"And you listen!" he added, glaring at him. "If I hear you or your brother giving your sisters trouble I'll give you the belt myself."

He pulled up a chair and helped Miss Gwendoline sit down.

"Don't worry," he comforted her. "These things happen. They come and go just like that. Wait. I'll go and get Mr Barzey."

"Miss Gwendoline?" said Mr Barzey, who was breathing heavily from his dash across the yard.

"Yes, Mr Barzey."

"Listen to me," he said, dropping his voice. "You have to wait until the morning. It might pass; it might not. In any case you won't get a doctor today."

"I got something to tell you," she said. And she proceeded to tell the men about the fisherman's visit and the ball he left.

"All right," Mr Barzey declared. "I'll go to the police now. I'll come back and tell you what happened."

The two men left Kwaku's house and went over to the uncle's.

"That fool!" the uncle burst out.

"Well, you can't do anything about that now."

"If it wasn't for her and the children," continued Kwaku's uncle, "I'd wash my hands of the business."

"At least he's earning money," Mr Barzey reminded him.

Once Kwaku's uncle had changed into his road-shoes, he and Mr Barzey took up a position on the bridge to hail a taxi.

The girls had put Fabian, Irene and Clayton to bed for their afternoon nap and were doing the washing up when the door opened.

"We've come back," said Kwaku's uncle, behind whom two uniformed policemen were standing, each on one side of the fisherman.

Miss Gwendoline was still sitting on a chair in the middle of the drawing-room, dressed in her Sunday clothes. Only her hat had been removed.

One of the policemen, a small man in khaki and peak-cap, stepped forward.

"I'm Police Constable Drayton, Mistress," he said respectfully, taking his cap off. "Can you tell me what happened on the day the fisherman came to see you? Don't be afraid, Mistress."

Kwaku's uncle bent down and whispered into her ear that the fisherman was standing in the room. at which she drew back with a start.

"Don't be afraid, Mistress," the other policeman reassured her, "he can't do you anything."

She began talking, and as she talked her words became less agitated.

"When you shook the ball you heard a noise?" P.C. Drayton asked.

"A slight rattling sound," she answered.

177

"You mind if we search the house?" asked the policeman.

"Why?"

"He might've left something else, Mistress. The ball might've been a sham."

At that point Mr Barzey came back and told Miss Gwendoline that his daughter-in-law had offered to help if she needed anything. But Miss Gwendoline claimed that Rona and Philomena could manage on their own.

"What's happening?" he asked Kwaku's uncle, who answered that one of the policemen was searching the house to see if the fisherman had left anything behind.

At this reference to himself the fisherman gave Kwaku's uncle a contemptuous glance.

"I going visit you one night," he said boldly, giving the threat all the greater weight by the lack of expression on his face.

"You're not *visiting* nobody!" the policeman standing beside him exclaimed.

"Why not put me in handcuffs an' get it over with?" demanded the fisherman. "All all-you jokers in uniform! Where you was when that man take she away, dress up like woman with powder and rouge 'pon he face? You din' do nothing then!"

"What's he talking about?" the policeman asked, addressing Mr Barzey and Kwaku's uncle.

"He tell my husband," Miss Gwendoline spoke up, "that his sister run away with a actor from town. And he vex 'cause my husband promise she would come back. And 'cause she din' come back he blaming him."

The policeman made a note in his notebook.

"That's a motive," he then declared, satisfied with the discovery.

"Motive?" sneered the fisherman. "You's a servant. You got fo' do what you told like a lil' boy. 'Cause they put you in long pants you think you's a man."

"Shut you mouth!" ordered the policeman.

"Hit me, ne!"

The young policeman looked round at those present in an effort to restrain himself.

"Go on, hit me!" exclaimed the fisherman. "Put handcuffs 'pon me an' brutalize me!" Saying this, he joined his hands at the wrist and offered them to the policeman, who, judging by his expression, would have struck the fisherman if others had not been present.

"All-you got to crawl fo' you daily bread, like dog ...."

"I say shut you mouth!" the constable exploded, raising his arm threateningly.

Then P.C. Drayton returned. "What's happening?" he asked.

"He's shooting off his mouth," his colleague replied.

Turning towards Miss Gwendoline P.C. Drayton said, "Mistress, we're going have to release the fisherman if we don't find the ball on his premises. If he come round here again let us know. Send one of the children. We gone now. I hope your eyes get better."

Embarrassed by his fruitless search and his inability to do no more than offer words of consolation he left abruptly, followed by his colleague, who was pushing the fisherman ahead of him. And the fisherman, before he left, uttered an indescribable noise, a high-pitched snigger that seemed to come from the back of his throat.

Miss Gwendoline, Kwaku's uncle, Mr Barzey and Philomena – who had slipped in from the kitchen on hearing the young policeman threaten the fisherman – remained in silence, as if the policemen's departure had left them exposed to as much uncertainty as before.

"You're sure you don't want my daughter-in-law to come and help?" Mr Barzey asked at length. "On Sundays she doesn't have a lot to do."

"No, thank you, Mr Barzey. The girls big enough and can manage."

"I think you'd better let the twins sleep by me," Kwaku's uncle said.

Miss Gwendoline nodded her approval at the suggestion.

The men left and Miss Gwendoline listened to their footsteps on the stairs and on the planks in the yard, sounds that seemed magnified since her affliction.

At first the two men stood at the foot of Kwaku's uncle's stairs, not knowing what to do next.

"Come up, ne," offered Kwaku's uncle. "I haven't cooked yet, but I got some coconut water in the fridge."

"What you think of the story?" Kwaku's uncle asked, after he had placed two glasses of clouded drink on a low table at which his guest was sitting.

Mr Barzey sighed, unwilling to give an opinion at once, for he had not had enough time to reflect on the manner in which Miss Gwendoline had come by her affliction.

"When Kwaku came back," he replied finally, "he had a big welcome. At least it looked so. People streamed in and out of his house congratulating him."

"I know what you mean," put in Kwaku's uncle.

"Quite! A lot of people still got it in for him. And besides, in a small community like this, envy is like food and drink to some people. Fall down and they'll help you up; but don't rise above them!"

Kwaku's uncle winced at these words without knowing why.

"You got to admit, though," he said, "Kwaku does cause confusion wherever he goes."

"True," agreed Mr Barzey.

"Even now he's away things happen. To tell the truth I wouldn't be sorry to see the back of him."

And Mr Barzey was surprised at the vehemence in his voice.

"Anyway," he remarked, "if the fisherman caused Miss Gwendoline's blindness he's not going to try anything else. The important thing's to cure the poor woman ...."

"And after that," Kwaku's uncle interrupted him, "to get Kwaku to hold his tongue. You've got influence over him; make him hold his tongue!"

Mr Barzey wanted to leave. It was impossible to carry on a conversation with this man, he thought, for everything he said was tainted by the dislike he bore his nephew.

"Whatever we think of the matter," said Mr Barzey anxiously, "you agree we've got to do something to help Miss Gwendoline."

"Yes, yes," Kwaku's uncle agreed.

They came to the conclusion that there was no urgency in consulting a doctor and that it was best to wait for Kwaku to return. Mr Barzey would then accompany him and Miss Gwendoline to a doctor recommended by the clinic.

After that was settled their conversation became less tense. Mr Barzey mentioned that Mr Gordon had just bought a piece of land about three miles aback for grazing his cattle. The farmer to whom he used to pay an agistment fee had turned to sugar-cane planting when the price of sugar rose and Mr Gordon, obliged to sell most of his cattle, was taking no chances this time.

"You think sugar prices will go up again?" enquired Kwaku's uncle, affecting an interest entirely foreign to his nature.

"It goes up and down, doesn't it?" replied Mr Barzey.

The conversation of these two men, as incompatible as any two humans could be, was only kept alive by the demands of civility.

When Mr Barzey rose to go, saddened by the inability of two grown men to get on with each other, vaguely anxious about the future of the Cholmondeley household now that Miss Gwendoline had lost her sight, he threw caution to the winds and said, "If you don't stand by them, Heaven knows what might happen."

Kwaku's uncle hesitated, then in a more conciliatory tone said, "I did marry him off more than fifteen years ago. Fifteen years! Isn't it understandable that I want peace after all this time? Try and understand."

"I know," Mr Barzey answered. "Believe me, I understand. And, after all, his girls are big enough to run the house .... But do whatever you can for Miss Gwendoline."

Satisfied at Kwaku's uncle's implied promise to stand by his

180

relations, Mr Barzey left him on the threshold of his home, reflecting on the discovery of a furious jealousy of his nephew's success.

The sun had fallen halfway towards the horizon and in the next yard a young woman was pounding paddy in a mortar, surrounded by chickens and diminutive pigs. Behind her rose a tilting, shingled house, its single shutter wide open, revealing a gaping, unglazed window.

Kwaku's uncle sighed, closed his door and went into his kitchen to prepare his lunch.

BOOK 3

26 A dream of monkeys

KWAKU CHOLMONDELEY had started to wind up his affairs in New Amsterdam two years after his wife became blind. He and Miss Gwendoline had decided that in two years' time he should have made enough money to come back home and set up shop in an extension to the rented house the landlord had permitted them to construct. Miss Gwendoline had chosen not to move to New Amsterdam in her condition. Besides, it was far from certain that a shop selling cooked food would thrive there.

Having built up a lucrative practice that took him all over the Courantyne and the East Bank Berbice, Kwaku's main concern was to work as hard as his health would permit him and put his savings away in the bank.

The two-year period was coming to an end none too soon, for his fortnightly weekend visits to his family revealed a state of affairs that called for the presence of an adult with a firm hand. Though Irene and Clayton were now living away, at their grandparents' house, Miss Gwendoline's authority over the smaller household had declined. Challenged at first by the twins, who often made fun of her, their example was soon followed by Philomena, at first cautiously, then more openly. Kwaku's uncle had thrashed the twins several times, but as they grew and finally surpassed his height they resented his interference. And one night, the night after Mashramani, they dragged him back into his cottage when he was about to go out and vented their rage on him. Kwaku could not get a word out of his uncle as to what had happened exactly. The latter contented himself with expressing the hope that Kwaku's house would perish soon.

Rona, haggard-looking for her fifteen years, had given up school to look after the house and her mother; and even her father's fortnightly visits had ceased to interest her.

"You know what I would do with your twins if I was you?" Mr Chalfen, Kwaku's assistant, said one day. "I would give them an ultimatum. It's the only way." He was pounding garlic, the smell of which filled the house and reached as far as the gate.

"It would break they mother heart if they had to go away," Kwaku told him.

He himself had turned over the idea in his mind more than once, just as he had thought of bringing them to New Amsterdam. But he dared not risk losing customers.

The house in which Kwaku lived looked no different from the way it was the day he had moved in, except for the glass jars containing powdered garlic and dried herbs for infusions, congo pump, ginger, camomile, sweet broom, daisy and many others. Mr Chalfen had labelled them in his careful, italic hand, so that they resembled pages from ancient, illuminated manuscripts, cut out and bordered with lines drawn in red, green, magenta and black.

"I would ultimate them, Mr Cholmondeley," remarked Mr Chalfen, speaking about the twins. "Then everybody would be better off." And in saying this he ground his wooden pestle into the stone jar with a vengeance.

"When I was a boy my father did ultimate me," he continued. "Up until then he only used to look up from his newspaper and say, soft, like a woman, 'You're wasting my money at school. You're not learning anything. You're just wasting my money.' Soft, just like a woman. Year after year whenever I brought home my report he would look through it then say the same thing. 'You're wasting my money at school.' Soft-soft, gentle-like, just like an old woman. Then the day in July when I brought home my fourth-year report – I remember the day good, because the school team did lose nine-two at football and I was the goalie – when I brought home the report and sat down to drink my cocoa the old man say, 'Come and stand here while I read your report.' Soft, soft, pussy-foot soft, like when he was turning the page of a book. Mr Cholmondeley, I wouldn't like to tell you what happen to me. When that man suddenly came to life, just like arapaima fish when he swallow bait. All I know is that when my father did finish ultimating me I was already praying for the new term to start so that I could eat up my books. That's children for you!"

Mr Chalfen's passion for labelling was equal to his passion for pilfering. He sold Kwaku's garlic and infusions at half-price in Mara and other villages distant enough to reduce the risk of detection. He would set out on Sunday mornings – a day Kwaku did not practise – on the pretext that his work as a catechist required him to officiate at a wedding or a funeral. Kwaku, believing him to be the personifica- tion of honesty, used to watch him leave early in the morning, holding his strapped suitcase as if it were in danger of flying away from him.

Kwaku admired Mr Chalfen, above all for his restraint and his ability to detect the scent of immorality in others. His loyalty was such that he often begged Kwaku to take him back to the village with him when he left for good.

"Nobody would come to me if I practised in the village," Kwaku had explained more than once.

Kwaku's faith was such that slanderous tongues only served to confirm him in his trust of the old Customs officer. According to one patient Mr Chalfen's first wife had left him because he was untrustworthy. She went off to live with a school teacher who had been giving her free Geography lessons for seven years. He got married again when he was fifty to a girl of sixteen from Port Mourant. But he was so jealous of her that he used to come home unexpectedly during the day and hide on the ground floor of their house in order to catch her red-handed if she took it into her head to misbehave. And, according to the slanderous patient, the poor creature had to endure the humiliation of being followed to the toilet by her jealous husband on weekends when he had so much time on his hands. Frightened by such a display of possessiveness she ran away, back to Port Mourant, and gave birth in her mother's house to a boy-child.

"Tch!" Kwaku had told the patient, "all he does have to do is pound garlic and dry bush-leaf for tea. What I care if he can't keep his wives?"

And so Kwaku refused to be influenced by people who did not have enough work to last them through the day. He saved as much money as he could, went to visit his family every fortnight and on public holidays, and kept himself to himself, secretly turning over in his mind Mr Chalfen's suggestion that he should practise in his own village.

The morning before Kwaku's departure he went to settle with his supplier. On the way back to his cottage he had to skip about to avoid the puddles in Stanleytown, the district he first became acquainted with through the dead girl's mother. Vaporous streets smelling of rain gave way to the pitch road skirting the waterfront. He would miss the interminable chimes of white-faced clocks at midday, the elegant houses in the quarter where he lived and the dininutive monkey tethered to a perch in the yard of the neighbouring house. New Amsterdam was an affront to village life.

Breaking a rule he had followed strictly until then he entered a rum-shop to buy a drink. When he was able to catch the eye of the barman he ordered a schnapps-glass of rum and a local soft drink, which he took to a table near the door and fondled, while customers came and went. The badly ventilated room reeked of stale liquor and the air was full of insects, numbed by the heat and the heavy atmosphere. Most of the customers dropped in for a short time, as a welcome interruption of their work, market porters, butchers in blood-stained overalls, women who had abandoned their stalls and transport workers in discreet uniforms.

Almost immediately after taking the first sip of his rum mixed liberally with the maroon-coloured soft drink he had bought simply for its appearance, Kwaku's head began to swim. The town dwellers around him moved in a saffron cloud, as in a dream. And it was from that dream that a woman emerged and sat at his table without uttering a word of greeting. Kwaku, uncertain whether he was in a condition to converse with anyone, smiled at her, but turned away once more to contemplate the cloud in which his fellow citizens moved.

"I wish they'd do something 'bout these flies," the woman said.

"Right," Kwaku agreed, not having yet overcome after his two-year stay in the town his feeling of inferiority in the presence of New Amsterdamers.

"You don' recognize me?" the stranger asked.

"Me?" asked Kwaku, turning to look at the woman. "No."

"You wouldn' normally talk to people like me. Women who does drink in a rum-shop, I mean. But you know me, you can take my word for it."

"No, lady," declared Kwaku, after submitting his table-companion to as close a scrutiny as his mist-covered eyes would allow.

"You remember the East Indian man in the Courantyne and the boy who did show you the way?"

Kwaku looked at her, perplexed, trying to single out from the numerous journeys he had made up and down the coast the people who fitted the woman's description.

"Mr Kumar!" she exclaimed, nudging him in the ribs. "The enema! My son tell me you give the Kumar boy a enema an' nearly kill he."

"Of course. You're the lady ... the boy mother!"

"Eh, you see, you remember now."

"But is what you doing here in New Amsterdam?" Kwaku asked, remembering her as one of those women who, like his own wife, must have been born working.

"I come visiting ... and to misbehave meself."

She laughed out loud, and as she did so Kwaku recalled that she had a backside that did not go with her skinny body. Involuntarily he looked downwards to see if the appendage had grown smaller or larger.

"When I walk in the door I say to meself," continued the woman, "that's the man that did give me money an' din' want nothing for it. That's the crazy man."

Her laughter drew attention to the table, the last thing Kwaku wanted.

"Anyway," he told himself, "tomorrow I'll be gone. To hell with what they think."

Then to the woman he said, "Keep your voice down. How's the boy?"

"Him? His father tek him away. His God tek him away. You men all the same. When it come down to it you don' want no woman, except to soak you whip an' keep house fo' you. But companionship?

At leas' that's not what he did want. All-you prefer one another company."

She seemed quite different to Kwaku, who remembered only her bitterness.

"At leas' I understand now," the woman said without emotion. "The nex' time I'll know wha' fo' expect."

"He's a nice boy. I wish my children was brainy like him."

"His father is somebody, you know," the woman told Kwaku, sticking out her bird chest to make her point. "A much respected man. I don' know what he take up with me for."

She told Kwaku that Mr Kumar's son was worse than ever after he left and only recovered weeks later. Mr Kumar himself was fined two thousand dollars for buying garlic in Surinam and selling it off at a prohibitive price.

From the way she kept putting her hand on Kwaku's arm he was in no doubt that she liked him; and, despite her ugliness and strident manner, her youth and the discovery of this attraction inflamed him.

"You want to take a walk up the bank?" he suggested.

She understood at once. "Le' me done me drink firs'," she answered, and took nothing but a sip.

Kwaku's companion remained silent, overcome with a modesty that seemed strange to her nature, he thought.

Then, when she had finished her drink, they went out into the blinding sunlight, set out on their way side by side on the pavement, separating occasionally among the jostling wayfarers before coming together again. They walked towards the south, away from the throng of the market until they came to the outskirts, dominated by lush vegetation and dead grass. Fewer cars went by on the dusty road and the space between the cottages became larger, while here and there a tethered goat tore at the undergrowth. A woman sweeping her yard called out at them, only to be sociable.

Kwaku was looking for a spot where he was certain they would be undisturbed.

"Where you takin' me?" she asked.

Was it her docility that gave him brutish thoughts, the desire to throw her to the ground and release his sperm all over her? He did not mind to answer her question, and for that she took his arm.

Unable to find a suitable place Kwaku chose a piece of open ground behind a tuft of bushes.

"We stopping here," he said.

"I in' even know your name," she declared, full of despondency.

"Wha' you want to know my name for?"

He pulled her to the ground and began fumbling with her blouse. "Undo it," he said impatiently.

186

"Let's talk a little, ne?" she pleaded, while unbuttoning her taffeta bodice.

But Kwaku, driven by a sort of rage, took out both her breasts and applied his hands to them as if he were kneading lumps of dough.

"I get him when I was fourteen ... this man used to come with his wife; an' he uses to kiss me an' press me to him in front of her ... he uses to kiss me 'pon me mouth. Is so men stay ... in front of his wife. An' she din' think nothing, 'cause I was so little, I suppose. One night I get up from my dream; I was workin' meself up just like I was under a man ... and nobody did ever touch me before ... ."

"Take your clothes off," Kwaku ordered her, "I want see your body."

"Here? Please, not here! If somebody ketch us?"

But she began undressing while protesting. She sat on the ground, mesmerized by his manhood.

"Le' me put back on me clothes, please," she begged, never taking his eyes away a moment from his open trousers.

Kwaku, even at that moment, was struggling with himself against the desire to humiliate her, although she had done everything he asked. And he pressed his mouth against hers, lay her on the ground and fell on her as ruthlessly as the stallions in the fields, with bared teeth pressing against the flanks of a sweating mare.

He was looking away into the clouded rim of the horizon; and she was staring at him, wondering why he used her like that after the day of kindness long ago. Was it because she had no man? Because her son had run away and she was defenceless?

Kwaku took out his wallet from his hip pocket.

"No! I din' do it for that .... No! I come to town to misbehave, not to pick fair."

Kwaku replaced his wallet and got up, inviting her with a look to do the same. But she only rose slowly, reluctant to leave.

"Do something fo' me instead," she told him.

"What?" Kwaku asked, moved by her refusal to take his money.

"Write me a letter."

She took a pencil from her handbag and wrote her name and address on a crumpled bill Kwaku found in one of his pockets.

"I in' get a letter for months," she said.

"Oh," Kwaku muttered, scanning the rounded, carefully written letters.

"You better leave me here," she said, stopping abruptly.

"Why?"

"You go on. I goin' stand here by the tree till you go out o' sight."

"All right. Tell you boy hello when you see him."

She watched him move away in the immensity of a landscape of

187

buttressed trees, of patches of brown and the yellow flight of orioles.

Kwaku had promised to give Mr Chalfen an answer that afternoon; but he still had not decided whether to take him to his village as his assistant. He would have to pay him while he looked around for customers. That consideration alone would have been enough to decide Kwaku against the idea, had it not been for the equally important fact that the retired Customs officer was indispensable.

Just as he was despairing of ever finding a solution to the problem it occurred to Kwaku that he could not transport his store of garlic and infusions in one trip. Mr Chalfen could come to the village and stay a few days until Kwaku decided what he ought to do.

But Mr Chalfen had hit upon a better solution. Since he was on pension Kwaku need not pay him anything for three months. It would by then be evident whether the people in the surrounding villages would be prepared to take Kwaku's reputation, acquired in the Courantyne and New Amsterdam, as a qualification for practising among them.

Kwaku accepted the proposal, not realizing that Mr Chalfen had cooked up his plan weeks before, but had held it back in the hope that Kwaku might decide to take him away while paying him the wages he was already receiving. Kwaku was in no doubt that Blossom would agree to put up his assistant in her drawing-room, overriding any objections Wilfred might have.

Mr Chalfen arranged his stock of jars on the bedroom floor, the sweet-broom with the sweet-broom, the lemon grass with the lemon grass and so on. And long after Kwaku had retired for the night he was occupied with his labelling and bottling, stopping from time to time to smoke a cigarette and watch the monkey in the yard next door in its endless journey, back and forth on its horizontal pole, like a spirit in torment.

Under a bright moon the shadow of the Demerara window louvres lay upon the ground like a row of seats on a motionless boat.

About an hour or so after he went to bed Mr Chalfen was awakened by a piercing scream. He sat bolt upright in his bed and in his terror called out, "Mr Cholmondeley!" at the same time fumbling for the switch on the partition.

"Is what happened, Kwaku?" he asked when the bright light revealed Kwaku leaning on an elbow, his head buried in his hands.

"Go to the window," Kwaku pleaded softly, as though afraid of being heard by anyone beside Mr Chalfen. "Peep out an' tell me what you see."

"Was it you then?" whispered Mr Chalfen.

Kwaku nodded, and then, gesticulating with his right hand, urged Mr Chalfen to go to the window.

"What you see?"

"Nothing," Mr Chalfen reassured him, "the moon's gone and the yard's dark."

"You don' see nothing else? Look again."

Mr Chalfen stared out of the window for a good half-minute, to get his eyes accustomed to the darkness.

"There's nothing, Mr Cholmondeley. Only the monkey walking up and down its perch."

"Close it! Shut it!" exclaimed Kwaku.

"The night's so warm, Mr Cholmondeley," Mr Chalfen objected.

"Close it!" Kwaku whispered, with such violence that Mr Chalfen complied at once.

"Is what wrong?"

"Was a nightmare. I dream they been scratching at the window."

"Who?"

"Monkeys. A whole band of monkeys was trying to come in, fighting an' scratching at the window. I dreamed the same dream one time long ago."

"And that's all?" Mr Chalfen asked.

"In the end one monkey just lifted the window an' they burst in in a frenzy. Then ... then they began eating me ...."

"Eat ...? Well, it's only a dream. If I was you I'd wait a little bit before lying down again. The neighbours would think we're murdering somebody if you scream like that again."

"Don' turn off the light," Kwaku said, seeing him reach for the light switch. "Let's talk ... you see, let's talk."

"Why you keep saying so?"

"Let's talk. I did do her a bad thing. And she say, 'You go on and I going watch you *out of sight*.' You hear them words? *Out of sight*. She say she was going watch me out of sight, and that does means getting smaller and smaller .... The first time I meet that woman –"

"Who, Mr Cholmondeley?" enquired Mr Chalfen, scepticism having given way to a worried expression on his face.

"A woman I did meet in the Courantyne an' give money to when I been to heal a boy. The firs' time she was all irritable, so crotchety that you feel like running away from her. This time she laugh all the time ... an' I take advantage of her, jus' because she was so nice .... What you think she mean when she say, 'I going stand here and watch you till you go out of sight'?"

"It doesn't mean anything particular," Mr Chalfen answered. "Not as far as I can see. She was going to watch you ... it's a kind of goodbye she was telling you."

"Nobody can watch you out of sight," Kwaku said with vehemence, now growing bolder as he drew comfort from Mr Chalfen's presence, the lighted room and the closed window.

189

"What you think she meant, then?"

"I don' know," replied Kwaku. "God only knows. I do so many bad things in my life. An' she even did want to know my name."

"It's natural, Mr Cholmondeley. If the two of you had a frolic you didn't expect her to want to know your name? Put yourself in her place ...."

"Go to the window again, but don' open it."

Mr Chalfen was prevented by the window-panes from getting a wide view of the yard below, where the monkey was perched.

"I can't see properly."

"Never mind. It still there .... You coming back with me to the village?"

"We agreed," Mr Chalfen said. "Can't you remember?"

"Yes. I wanted to know if you did remember."

With that, Kwaku lay down, feeling that Mr Chalfen had no idea of the way his nightmare had affected him. He feared that a period of his life had come to an end, that he was dragging Mr Chalfen back to the village out of fear that that period would no longer be accessible to him. He had made no friend in town, for anxious to maintain his status as healer he had kept to himself. These absurd thoughts he could not get out of his mind; how could he tell Mr Chalfen about them?

Unable to fall asleep Kwaku changed his position in bed several times. The silence and the knowledge that the monkey was not far away made him restless. He had treated patients for insomnia, and one especially, who thought that the room in which she slept was crawling with centipedes, had aroused his pity, for on the face of it she was a stable woman and a good mother. He thought of her and consoled himself with the reflection that a monkey outside the house must be less threatening than centipedes in it.

He would not have reduced himself in Mr Chalfen's estimation by admitting to being terrified of living within a stone's throw of the fisherman. His hatred of the man and his godless family was exacerbated by his anxiety about the twins' future and the feeling of guilt towards Miss Gwendoline who was bearing her cross without complaining. Before he had become somebody, a member of the community to be reckoned with, he would have repaid the fisherman and his family in kind. They did not possess a water tank, only two barrels to catch the rainwater shed by the roof of their dilapidated house, just like most other families; but that dilapidated house could be set on fire. In those days his pride was intact. Now, whenever Kwaku was home at weekends, he avoided going out lest he met someone from that house. "Look how we blind he wife and he walking there as if he is fowl-cock self. He don' even know to protect he people. Hi hi! Look how he turn away 'cause he kian' bear fo' look at me."

They were like that, wrong and strong. Kwaku nearly wept from shame and frustration. Of all people Miss Gwendoline! She said nothing, gave him no reason to believe, by word or deed, that she thought any less of him. But was it possible for a woman to respect her husband when he was incapable of protecting her? As a healer he had heard enough from wives and husbands about their lives together to realize that a man had to be protector to his wife. When she gave the word he had to go and face even an army of malefactors, armed perhaps only with a stick, even at the risk of being brought down like a dog. For at the sight of that dog lying on the road, with its gums and teeth showing and blood oozing from its mouth the wife could say, "Now that's a man!" And she could tell her next husband how *he* died for her. Yes, he had no doubt that women were like that.

Had it been possible Kwaku would have slipped into his village by night unheralded, and rapped on Blossom's door, just as on that night after he had breached the Conservancy. Then, were it possible, he would remain hidden for the rest of his life, coming out only at night to watch from the window; to watch the cars go by, the holiday celebrations, Christmas night, Divali, Pagwah, Mashramani, and spot his children from time to time, judge how much they had grown ... from a distance, out of shame. He knew deep down that his practice as a healer was at an end, yet he was dragging Mr Chalfen back with him.

At times he could hear the jangling of the monkey's chain as it abandoned its itinerary and slid down its pole to stand on the ground, and then again when it clambered back up to its perch, where there was enough room to resume its fruitless journey to the limits of a circumscribed world.

The next morning when Mr Chalfen woke him Kwaku had slept only a few hours, and his bloodshot eyes stared at his assistant as though he was looking at him for the first time.

27   Family troubles

BACK IN HIS village Kwaku lost no time in putting up his board:

K Cholmondeley
HEALER
9 a.m. to 6 p.m. except Wednesdays
and Saturdays.

In the six weeks that went by he treated one customer, an old cart-driver who pretended to be ill so that Kwaku might treat his donkey at the same time.

Mr Chalfen, who was lodging at Blossom's, was of the opinion that his landlady's more presentable residence was likely to attract customers. Wilfred objected violently to the proposal that his wife's house should be used for Kwaku's business but Blossom agreed. And within a few hours most of Blossom's drawing-room furniture was put in storage under her house while all the accoutrements of Kwaku's practice were transferred from his home to his benefactress's.

Wilfred ceased speaking to Mr Chalfen and took to grinding his teeth whenever he passed Kwaku on the stairs.

"One more infringement of my married rights and I leaving you," he warned Blossom the morning after.

"Go, ne," she answered, adjusting an earring. "Is not me going come and fetch you back again."

"And since he come back to live in the village you getting more uppity, flouncing you'self about the place as if he is you bridegroom."

"At leas' it going make you look at me now an' then," she answered insolently.

"I watching. I jus' watching, I in' warning. But I watching."

"The more you watch," she began singing, "the less you see. The less you see the better fo' me."

"God!" Wilfred declared, grinding his teeth.

"If you keep grinding you teeth like that," she told him, apparently bent on provoking him, "you goin' get that gum disease. You know the one I mean .... An' you remember what happen in the church when the preacher say, 'There shall be weepin' an' gnashin' of teeth!' An' the old woman in the front pew say, 'Thank God I in' got none.' An' the preacher say, 'And the gums shall feel the strain!' "

Wilfred, provoked beyond his patience, raised his hand to strike her, whereupon Blossom drew back, knocking over the powder tin and a bottle of lotion. But he restrained himself, so that his hand remained poised above his wife's head.

"Is only 'cause is against my principles to hit a woman, that's why."

Blossom, half-dressed in front of her mirror, was trembling, and could not bring herself to speak.

"Look how you ready to risk we marriage," complained Wilfred, "jus' to please your boyfriend."

But Blossom, so apt with words a few seconds ago, was now too shaken to reply.

Despite Blossom's sacrifice and the new board Kwaku had had painted in red, no one gave him custom, and he sat all day at Blossom's window, silent and morose.

One morning after hard words from Miss Gwendoline about the hours he was spending in Blossom's house he told Mr Chalfen that there was no chance of his receiving a wage; and the same day he took down his board and transferred his garlic and bottles of dried herbs back to his own house. The idea of building an extension at the back of the house was dropped for the while for, according to Miss Gwendoline, eventually the children would move away and a larger house could only be justified by a business. To Kwaku's objection that her black-pudding business would benefit she replied, "We'll see."

During the August school holidays Kwaku took to spending a couple of hours each day in the new beer-shop, where unemployed young men were in the habit of passing much of the day playing pool. Philomena had orders to fetch him if a client called; but in September, when the children went back to school no client had come. And Kwaku, instead of resuming his watch at the front window, kept visiting the beer-shop, on the understanding that Rona, who no longer went to school, should fetch him if a client came.

The weeks and months went by and Miss Gwendoline fell back on the simple fare she was used to preparing for her family in the early days of her marriage. At the end of one such meal, one of the twins, now seventeen, said, "Is what we gettin' now for food? You call this food?"

"Get up!" Kwaku shouted at him. "Apologize to your mother!"

"Leave him, Kwaku," Miss Gwendoline said quietly. "Leave him."

"I say apologize," repeated Kwaku, ignoring his wife's plea.

"I in' do nothing ..." he began with a sneer.

But before he could finish what he was saying Kwaku was upon him and had brought him to the ground. The boy was rather taller than his father, but the frenzy of the attack had taken him by surprise.

"Apologize! Apologize!" Kwaku screamed, raining blows on him.

"All right!" the twin shouted, so as to be heard above his father's screams.

Kwaku, almost out of breath, stamped out of the house, leaving the family at table and his meal unfinished at the empty place.

He remained standing at the entrance to the beer shop. The loud strains of music from a coin-operated record-player could be heard a good hundred yards up the road.

"Tears on my pillow,
    Pain in my heart,
    You on my mind ... ."

193

Something was keeping Kwaku at the entrance. The forty-five cents for a bottle of beer, the absence of men of his age at that time of the day, his growing fondness for alcohol, perhaps all these things weighed together on his mind. But what else could he do, apart from looking up Mr Chalfen who, for some unknown reason, had put off his departure to New Amsterdam? Blossom did not mind. In fact she was glad to have someone in the house while both she and Wilfred were out.

For a couple of minutes Kwaku hesitated between deciding either on entering the beer-shop or going a bit farther to Blossom's house. In the end he crossed the new concrete bridge, bought a beer and took a seat near the end of the counter, so that he had a clear view of the street through the open shop front. The young woman behind the counter, a stranger from another village, sat unsmiling on her high stool. Kwaku had never seen any of the youths successfully engage her in conversation, and it seemed that they were somehow afraid of her. In New Amsterdam there were many of the old rum-shops left, with cubicles and a preponderance of older people. In them most of the customers drank rum, rather than weak beer. Moreover the bartenders were friendlier.

Kwaku stared at the road, out of reach of the cue-butts and the conversation. No one took any notice of him. Occasionally he would be roused from his reflections by an outburst of laughter or a quarrel, but he would soon withdraw into himself again, his eyes fixed on the road.

Blindness had transformed his wife. He could no longer pretend it was not so. It had reduced her to an inactive being who depended on a stick or the shoulder of anyone at hand. It broke his heart to see the impatience on Damon's face when she asked him to interrupt whatever he was doing and help her about – Damon, the most long-suffering of his children. Because of the black-pudding business and the children she had never had any time to go visiting, so that her circle of friends, small in the beginning, was reduced to two women when her two closest friends went to Georgetown, one to get married and the other to work. Besides, the two who had remained lived deep in the village by the pasture lands, and could only look her up on a Sunday or drop in on the way back from shopping in a neighbouring village.

"Miss Gwendoline got her children," people used to say.

Kwaku smiled bitterly at the recollection of this remark.

It would have been easier if she had accepted Blossom's offer of friendship, for she would have stood by her. Fabian could have spent a few hours in her house from time to time; and Philomena, who admired her, might have accepted her guidance.

"Tcha!" he said softly, and put his empty bottle on the counter as a sign that he wanted another.

While the young woman got up to serve him he took out forty-five cents from his pocket, using the loose change he had received from a dollar note when he bought his first beer. Taking the new bottle he went back to his seat to continue his reflections.

When Miss Gwendoline said, "Leave him, Kwaku," it had only redoubled his fury, so that he fell upon his son. He knew exactly what she meant. Kwaku was certain that she meant, "Leave him. Is Philomena you should be putting in his place!"

And she was right, thought Kwaku. The night before, Philomena had climbed through the window to get back into the house, both doors of which Miss Gwendoline had ordered Rona to bolt when her second daughter had not come in by eleven.

The other night there had been a terrible row after Miss Gwendoline seized her daughter and wanted to see if she was still a virgin. Kwaku, determined not to interfere, went into the kitchen while the rest of the family looked on. He remained doggedly by the back door even when his wife shrieked his name.

Kwaku took it all out on the twin when he fell on him. And if he had had his way would have chased him and his brother out to go and look for work, with the same stick his wife used to feel her way about the house and the yard.

Now the days were so long! Each morning he had to get up with the birds, just like everyone else, dress as if he had a destination, and then finally take his place at the window to welcome clients who never came. He detested his fellow villagers. If a stranger settled there and put his board up they would patronize him *because* he was a stranger. Through the sound of canoning pool balls he picked them out as they went by on the road, cursed them heartily, each for some defect or something from his past. One did not know who his father was and another came home the day after the big Georgetown fire, laden with goods he had plundered from a shop.

While he was in the middle of his sixth beer he saw a man waving to someone in the shop.

"Somebody waving to you, Mister," one of the youths said.

"Me?" Kwaku asked, and tried to make out who it was. He got up, taking his bottle with him.

"You kian' tek the bottle away," the young woman behind the counter said gruffly.

"Tcha!" Kwaku said, waving the bottle in her direction as he tottered towards the door.

"Bring me bottle back!" she screamed at him.

But Kwaku ignored her and went out to meet the stranger.

"Is you!" he exclaimed, recognizing Mr Barzey.

"Come out of that shop, man!" Mr Barzey told him. "Finish your beer and come home to my place."

Kwaku did as Mr Barzey suggested. And when the young woman complained about his behaviour he said, "Every bare-assed lil' girl want to tell you what to do nowadays."

Content to have retrieved her bottle she turned her back on him.

"Why haven't I seen you all these weeks?" Mr Barzey complained, as they approached his house.

"I got troubles," Kwaku answered. "Little troubles an' big troubles. New Amsterdam troubles and village troubles. I'm a town man now, you see."

"Troubles, my tail!" Mr Barzey sneered, pushing him up the front staircase.

"I was buying a house like this in New Amsterdam," Kwaku told him. "With stairs higher than this and two verandas. Two! Your house don't got verandas."

"You'd better behave yourself," Mr Barzey said as they sat down. "My daughter-in-law's due home soon and you know how you're afraid of her."

"Me! Frightened?" protested Kwaku. "... Yes, brother, it happen since I go to live in town."

"So it's town that's frightened you?"

But Kwaku did not answer.

"You hear the noise in my house at twelve o'clock?" he asked at last.

"Yes," Mr Barzey said.

Kwaku then told him of the twins and Philomena and of Miss Gwendoline's loss of power in her own home; and Mr Barzey did not interrupt him, even during the long pauses, when he was trying to recollect events that occurred weeks earlier.

"If I were to tell you," Mr Barzey said, when he had come to the end of his account, "that you don't have troubles, you'd get vexed."

"You don' see the way Miss Gwendoline does feel about the house with her stick; and how even Fabian does make fun of her in front of the lil' children in the village .... You ever hear of a woman sticking her finger up she daughter to see if she's a virgin?"

"Yes," Mr Barzey replied.

"My godfathers!" declared Kwaku, disgusted at his friend's apparent callousness.

"Why don't you go back to New Amsterdam and take the twins with you?"

"And what about Miss Gwendoline?" Kwaku asked.

"She'll manage ... without the twins."

"And Philomena?"

"Philomena, Philomena, what's wrong with Philomena?" Mr Barzey broke out angrily. "Not one of your children're bad.

196

Nothing's wrong with the twins and Philomena."

"You know they beat up my uncle? They lie in wait for him an' beat him up, like if he was a lil' boy; they own flesh an' blood."

"You weren't there when he flogged them with a belt and all the little children in the village used to run after them shouting, 'I goin' cut your tail, like you uncle cut you tail.' Your uncle is out of his time."

"He used to beat me," protested Kwaku, "an' it din' do me no harm."

But when Mr Barzey only looked at him for an answer Kwaku did not understand.

"An' what I'm going to do with them in New Amsterdam?" Kwaku asked.

"Let them look for work, ne?"

"A lot of people with paper qualifications kian' find work. How I goin' find them work?"

"When you start up your business again," Mr Barzey said firmly, "you'll find them some sort of work. And if you can't, buy them a piece of land and wash your hands of them."

Kwaku wanted to thank his friend, but restrained himself because he felt humiliated that he could not have worked out such a simple plan. He changed the subject and talked of the long queues in the New Amsterdam shops and of a Guyanese who came back on holiday from the States with a suitcase full of goods that were unavailable in the shops.

"He made hundreds of dollars."

"It takes all kinds," said Mr Barzey dryly.

In the last couple of years he and Mr Gordon had become thick and visited each other's house regularly, which was one reason why Kwaku kept away. A few minutes in the company of the two men were enough to emphasize his inadequacy.

One evening he saw them speaking at Mr Gordon's gate and joined them. But when Mr Gordon – during a conversation in which Kwaku took no part – remarked that television was the ultimate evidence of cultural anaemia, Kwaku felt as if he had been dealt a blow on the head. He recalled the boy who spoke so intelligently, and was near to tears for the little he could offer his children. So it seemed to him; for his success had imbued him with an exaggerated respect for book education.

"Let me tell you a story," Mr Barzey said, interrupting Kwaku's reflections. "There was once a family of five, mother, father, two sons and a daughter. When the children were in their teens their mother died; and the sons, now that the mother was out of the way, openly made advances to their sister. The father threatened to put them out of the house; but the sons were bold as brass, because they were two. So they warned their father not to interfere. One day when the father came back home from the fields he found the older son making love to his sister in their parents' bed and struck him a blow on the back. 'You dog!' he shouted. 'In my own bed! Get out of my house and don't come back.' The other brother, hearing the commotion, came running in from the back. Seeing that his father and brother were about to come to blows he took his brother's part. He circled the father from behind while the older brother attacked him from the front; and it was only when the father lay still on the floor that they stopped cuffing and kicking him. Believing him to be dead they waited till late that night, wrapped and tied up his body in banana leaves and carried it aback to a dark part of the forest. Next morning the father was awakened by the howling of the monkeys and finding his eyes covered and his hands unable to move he thought he was buried alive. But he soon managed to tear himself free of the twine his sons had tied him with. You can imagine: being a farming man he didn't know anything about living in the forest, so that in no time he was near to starvation and began to eat his own excrement. One evening when he could hear the stirring of animals coming out of hiding he thought that he was having his last glimpse of the sun going down; then he saw a yowaree stop near him. It stank like carrion and was surrounded by a swarm of flies. 'What wrong with you, Mr Man?' the yowaree* asked him. And the father told him the story. You know how people don't like yowaree because of its stink. So, seeing an opportunity to make a friend, yowaree said he would help. He went to the man's house and asked to see the eldest brother. 'If I tell you something you ought to know, promise you won't kill me.' The man's son promised, so the yowaree said, 'Your brother and your sister does laugh at you behind your back, because your sister say you got a bent penis.' 'Me? That's a lie!' 'So she say, though,' said the yowaree. 'Tobesides, they planning to kill you because your brother don't like sharing his sister with you.' The yowaree ran back to the bush and waited till the next day. Then he crept up to the house and saw the older brother and his sister wrapping up the younger brother in banana leaves. He ran back to the bush to report to his friend the goings-on. The man lost no time in going to his house, where he found his eldest son eating out of a tin plate. When he looked up and saw his father standing in the middle of the room he dropped his food and started whimpering, because he believed that it was the dead man come back to kill him. The father took one step towards his son, who bolted through the back door, leaving the house to his father and sister. And since that day yowaree always like living near humans, stinking up their houses

* Opossum.

198

whenever they get a chance."

"What the story mean?" Kwaku asked, disgusted by the crude details of the tale, the last thing he expected from the mouth of a man like Mr Barzey.

"It means a lot," Mr Barzey declared. "You've got to find out what it means for you. You've got wife and children and can't afford the luxury of dignity. For me, dignity is the only thing worth living for. And it's the one thing I can't find in this house. I bet you don't see my troubles as important, but for me this house is hell. One morning I caught my daughter-in-law in my room.... Oh, what does it matter anyway? ... If you went to practise in Georgetown I would come with you and start up as a photographer again, even at my age. People can't help despising you when you sponge on them. It's a way of enslaving somebody. They enslave you with their generosity and despise you for being a slave."

Kwaku saw the story as a warning to take the twins away, something the old man had not intended.

"You been a good friend, Mr Barzey," he said.

"I've got something for you." He went to his room and came back with his album of photographs.

"You're joking!" Kwaku said, stunned that the old man was prepared to part with the thing he prized most.

"Go home now, because my daughter-in-law's coming at any time and I'm just not up to facing her."

Kwaku left, taking his gift with him. And in truth, as he descended the long staircase he saw Mr Barzey's daughter-in-law pushing her moped along the road.

28 A conversation overheard

KWAKU KEPT putting off the date of his departure until the day when one of the twins, together with about a dozen others, was picked up by the police for loitering. Although he was released later, with a warning to keep off the streets, Kwaku at once began making preparations to go off to New Amsterdam with him and his brother.

Mr Chalfen, less enthusiastic about going back than Kwaku imagined he would be, took charge of preparing two suitcases of infusions. They would have to wait until they got back to New Amsterdam to buy garlic from their supplier who, in turn, would need time to obtain his supply from a Surinamese with a shop on the Courantyne river, where contraband goods were openly sold.

Kwaku insisted that Miss Gwendoline should accept the invitation of a friend to spend the day at her home deep in the village. He himself took her on the Saturday morning before his departure for New Amsterdam. He hired a taxi specially for the occasion; and despite Fabian's screaming they set off, over the rutted village road towards the stretch of land where the clay soil gave way to pegasse.

Back home he sat down on the lowest step of the back staircase. He pulled off his shirt, contrived a makeshift fan of it and began fanning himself languidly. The voices of Philomena and Rona came from the kitchen and he heard a note in his eldest daughter's voice that was new to him, an unconstrained, almost flippant tone. And Kwaku realized that he had never known Rona to be away from her mother's supervision.

"...You know," he heard her say, "the one who does borrow other people clothes."

"You love him?" Philomena asked.

"Yes," replied Rona, accompanying her confession with a burst of laughter.

"You ever do it with him?" Philomena pursued.

"Only one time."

"But he mus' be about twenty-six!"

"You ever do it?" Rona asked her thirteen-year-old sister in turn.

At this Kwaku cocked his ears, anxious not to miss a single word of what Philomena was to say.

"No. I won't let none of them touch me. When I go to live in Georgetown an' I'm a model I .... "

Rona interrupted her, "Model? Models got to wear fancy clothes. Where you goin' get money to buy fancy clothes?"

"Pa going get rich this time in New Amsterdam. He say so. And he goin' send for me."

"Who say so?" asked Rona scornfully.

"I say so."

After a short silence Rona asked, "What you want most in the world, after clothes and going to Georgetown?"

"I wish we'd get a new bathroom, one in the house, like at Blossom house."

"What for?" Rona asked, with laughter in her voice.

"'Cause that old fool living next door who does sit staring over here all day does peep through the crack in the wall when I bathing."

"You see him?"

"He does put he one eye to the slit," Philomena said indignantly, "and when I throw water at him he does go round the other side. Men so stupid!"

"He old enough to be your great-grandfather."

The girls laughed aloud and one of them must have struck her arm against the one half of the shuttered window which was still closed. The window flew open so that the girls' laughter attracted the attention of the old man of whom they had just been speaking. He came to the fence and began sniggering as though he had been taking part in the girls' conversation. Kwaku, afraid that he might be detected by his daughters, rose quietly and went to sit on his uncle's back stairs instead.

He wondered at Rona's confession.

"Where she get the time?" he reflected. "The man who does borrow other people clothes? Who's that?"

His delight on learning that Philomena had never been intimate with anyone was so intense, he experienced a near physical relief. What was more, she had not admitted to loving anyone. Indeed, if her words meant what he thought she was contemptuous of the boys and men she met. He must remember to tell Miss Gwendoline of Philomena's innocence. But it might be better to say nothing, for his wife's dislike of their younger daughter had nothing to do with the girl's apparent experience with boys, Kwaku thought. Even if she believed her to be a virgin she would resent her love of fashion magazines, of make-up and earrings.

That morning he had gone out with Miss Gwendoline alone for the first time since the twins' birth; and that when she was blind! On arriving at their destination a group of children came up close to see her and Kwaku felt her grip tighten on his arm when she became aware that they were being watched.

"Lil' bastards!" he muttered.

Suddenly an urge to hear what his daughters were saying overcame Kwaku. But this time he remained standing at the foot of the stairs, for by now the girls were speaking loudly and one of them even shouted occasionally at little Fabian, who could do no more than stand about and listen to their meaningless conversation.

"One day before Ma was blind," Rona was saying, "she been out and he come. He slip in through the back door when he did think I was alone."

And for some reason they both laughed.

"We started talking an' talking; and, child, I don' know what get into him, but he go to the window and look out and see Damon playing dice by himself in the back yard. 'Who's that?' he say. 'That's my father,' I tell him. 'O God!' he shout, an' bolt for the front door. 'Is only Damon, stupidy,' I shout out. 'Come back.' And you should see his face. So I say to him –" and here she was seized by an uncontrollable giggling – "I say, 'Is sunglasses that make jackass eat bottle!'"

After the giggling that followed this last remark Philomena said, "Tell me 'bout the time when he sing."

201

Rona obliged. "Well," she began, in a simpering tone used by those who are telling a story that was a proven success, "well, child, it was the same day. He stop sulking when I say I love him. 'Is what we goin' do now?' he ask. I pretend I didn' know what he mean and I tell him, 'Sing for me, ne.' 'Sing? What I goin' sing?' And I say, 'Sing "Jesus want you for a sunbeam".' Hoo, hoo hoooo! He start singing 'Jesus wants me for a sunbeam'. He so stupidy!"

"And you still love him?" asked Philomena.

"Yes."

And the girls laughed more loudly than ever, so that Kwaku's fears that the old man would come back were realized, for at the height of the rumpus he reappeared. Kwaku, forced to abandon his post again, slipped through a gap in the fence. The old man, taken aback by the unceremonious manner in which his neighbour penetrated into his yard, stood gaping at him.

"What you want?" he asked.

"You in shame?" Kwaku said, grabbing him by the collar.

"Leggo me!"

"You in' shame? Listening to young girls with you tongue hanging out? You got one foot in the grave ... ."

"Loose me!" groaned the old man. "I goin' tell me nephew you brutalize me. When he done beating you up ... ."

"You nephew! He just like you; he blind in one eye and does see double from the other. Beat me up? He can't even beat a drum."

Kwaku let go of the old man's collar and strode away towards the Public Road. Then, reflecting that the old man's nephew – even with the disadvantage of his fawfee eye – was capable of thrashing him, Kwaku turned round and said, "You bring you nephew in this and I going tell everybody in the village how you does peep at the girls bathing, how you does put you good eye at the chink in the bathroom. Go on, tell you nephew, ne. Tell him and you not goin' dare show you face in public again."

With this parting remark Kwaku went off, feeling less uneasy.

"I don' even know my own children," he told himself. "I don' know Rona or Philomena. I wonder if I know Damon. If somebody come and ask, 'Who is that boy playing dice in the back yard?' all I can say is: 'He's my son.' But I don' even know what he like."

Kwaku was more disturbed by the discovery that Rona had a secret life, secret from her mother and from him, than by the disclosure that she had been intimate with her young man. Moreover, the side of her character that prompted her to make fun of him was a revelation, which might have been easier to understand if it had been Philomena, whose candour, like her love of clothes and make-up, was there for all to see.

"Jesus," he thought, involuntarily crossing the road when he was approaching the liquor ship, "you worry 'bout children when they small, you worry 'bout them when they big ... and I'll probably be worrying 'bout them when they married and got children."

Kwaku turned in at Blossom's yard. He decided to go and see Mr Chalfen about their trip to New Amsterdam the following day. He had intended to do so in the afternoon on his way to bring Miss Gwendoline home; but the events of the last half-hour had put him out of sorts, and the last place he wanted to be was in his yard or lying about the house.

Three suitcases, placed one behind the other, were lined up against the partition dividing the drawing-room from a bedroom in Blossom's cottage. Kwaku, on entering through the unbolted front door, was glad to see that everything was ready.

"Mr Chalfen?"

"I here in the kitchen."

Kwaku found him in Blossom's company, dressed in one of her aprons and holding a metal ladle in his hand. She was wearing a head-scarf decorated with parallel yellow lines.

Already irritated by his encounter with his old neighbour, Kwaku sneered at his colleague.

"If you not careful she'll got you sweepin' the house too."

"Leave him alone," Blossom said, placing herself between Kwaku and his assistant.

Surprised at his venomous tone she kept staring at him.

"You come here in a bad mood the day before you goin' away," she said. "What happen? We not talking?"

He could not treat her badly. It was so long since they had had a satisfying conversation he was prepared to put up with a lot rather than offend her. The sight of Mr Chalfen apparently at home in her kitchen seemed to him an intolerable imposition, for it did not occur to him that she might have invited him to assist with the cooking.

"If you sit down and behave yourself," she said playfully, "I going feed you. Chick, chick, chick, chick! Bidi, bidi, bidi!"

"Leave me alone," Kwaku protested.

"I goin' leave you alone if you stop sulking."

"All right!"

And with that he went back into the drawing-room, followed by Mr Chalfen, who had taken off his apron. Carefully, Blossom undid her scarf and with a shake of the head let her hair fall onto her neck. And it seemed to Kwaku that she had undressed in front of them, throwing about her a scent of crushed flowers and notions of beauty.

Kwaku's resentment at Mr Chalfen's presence escaped neither Blossom nor her guest.

"What's he got against me?" wondered Mr Chalfen.

"You finished cooking?" Kwaku asked him.

"The food's simmering now," he answered.

"So it simmering!" Kwaku exclaimed sarcastically. "You sure that's all you learn in this house?"

Blossom enquired after Miss Gwendoline and Kwaku told her about the trip into the back of the village. When she heard that the twins were going with him to New Amsterdam Blossom asked where they were going to stay.

"At a guest house," Kwaku said. "But we'll find a place soon."

"You can always stay at that place we been to in Rosignol, if the worst come to the worst," Blossom told him. "You remember her?"

Kwaku nodded; and once more his irritation at Mr Chalfen's presence assailed him.

Blossom took a bottle of rum and three glasses from a cabinet filled with crockery. She had intended serving them with alcohol after the meal, but changed her mind when she sensed that there was the possibility of unpleasantness between Kwaku and Mr Chalfen.

The men drank their rum straight while a noiseless drizzle spattered the window-panes and the scent of cooking came from the kitchen. Mr Chalfen, restrained by Kwaku's presence, looked away in the distance, his thoughts back in New Amsterdam, where he remembered Kwaku as a man with a faint air of mystery about him. But even now he did not put his conduct down to jealousy.

Kwaku called to mind Blossom's home when she was still at school and living with her parents, whose house was pervaded with the same peace; and he recalled the bright afternoons there, when he would play girls' games with her. Often he would spend hours over litty, the game of six pebbles, and share in the family's meals, which were served in chipped enamel plates. If his uncle and Blossom's father had taught him to be a man, it was her mother who was the source of affection and a shadowy power, the one whom he had once discovered standing behind Miss Gwendoline in a dream. Her stories were spellbinding and during their telling Kwaku would sit with his chin on his knees and steal glances at Blossom.

"And this donkey," reflected Kwaku under the influence of his second schnapps-glass, "come here, don' know Blossom from Adam, and settle in her house like monkey 'pon a star-apple tree."

"I not ordinary, you know. Blossom, I telling you. I not ordinary. I can't read good; I don't know 'bout labelling 'cause I'm no cheap sign-board painter. But I got something people in New Amsterdam and on the Courantyne know 'bout. Tobesides, them people know 'bout suffering. I drink bush rum with them and while we was drinking this illegal rum we sing, 'To hell with the police!' I mean look how they drag my son to the station for loitering. Loitering! That's a way of life for us. If we not loitering we not living. When it come

204

down to it the police telling them, 'You change your way of life 'cause some of you does lie in wait for people and rob them.' But in the Courantyne they does make bush rum and drink it. You ever hear rich people drink bush rum? You ever hear rich people curse the police? Rich man don' curse God. No, sister. You know why? 'Cause God is a policeman who does drink X-M rum. If you give him the smoothest, oldest, richest bush-rum he going say, 'Is a law-abiding citizen who don't like loitering, and does approve of finger-printing. And all of you bush-rum drinkers and loiterers not only got to carry identity cards, but you got to be computerized. One day I going know everything you does do, when you does take a shower, and when you does make love to you wife.' Yes, I telling you. I ... I forget what I was saying .... Ah, oh, yes! The police! They din' arrest the fisherman 'cause they din' have evidence. But when it come to my son all they need to arrest the boy was that he was doing what people been doin' since Christ know when."

Kwaku stopped in order to pour himself more rum.

"Instead of calming you down it only make you worse," Blossom told him.

She locked the rum bottle away in her cabinet and sat down once more.

Kwaku got up, lifted his schnapps glass and said in a loud voice, "I drink to all loiterers, whores, bush-rum drinkers and lovers of freedom."

Mr Chalfen, sitting opposite Kwaku, remained silent with pursed lips. Kwaku knew that he was a catechist and that his remarks about religion had offended him deeply, and was disappointed that he had not protested.

"All you men alike," Blossom told him. "We look at you as if you so all-powerful; and then when we get to know you, is something else."

"Women in' no different," Kwaku retaliated. "How many of you don' lay down under your men and think, while he fighting himself up, 'For Christ sake, hurry up an' get it over with!' I know one woman who does plait she hair while she husband doing it. You don't tell me 'bout men. At least men like a open book."

"Not so as you notice," Blossom said.

Kwaku delivered a mighty suck-teeth and advised her to look after her pots. "You in' smell something burning?"

"It mus' be your top lip," Blossom said angrily, annoyed that he should speak to her like that in front of a stranger. The very thing she wanted to avoid had happened. They had ended up quarrelling. She got up and went into the kitchen, near to tears.

"You satisfied now?" Kwaku asked Mr Chalfen, as if he had been responsible for upsetting Blossom.

"If you don't want me to come back with you why not say so?" Mr Chalfen asked. "You keep throwing hints about as if you're frightened to talk your mind."

"I don't got nothing 'gainst you, Mr Chalfen."

They both looked forward to Blossom's return, not having anything more to say to each other.

"You don' know what it is to be left-handed," Kwaku eventually remarked, "in a world where everybody's right-handed."

"How d'you mean?"

"Not even being blind," said Kwaku, "but just being left-handed. Not even that you want to write from right to left when everybody else writing from left to write. No. I talking 'bout being different. But to get blind! She does hear everything round her now. When we talking alone she does stop all of a sudden and say, 'Listen! Somebody in the yard. He passing the house now. Must be somebody going from the back to Mr Barzey or your uncle.' And I wanting to console her and don' know how to ... . But the hardest thing to understand is why I don' feel no malice for the fisherman. You ever hear anything like that? A man blind the woman you love and you don' feel no malice for him. Sometimes I going along the road and see somebody for the first time in my life and I get such a rage inside me, only 'cause the man wearing funny trousers or he got a small, small nose. Something stupid like that. And I want to go up to him and say, 'If I was a judge I would hang you.' One day in New Amsterdam – it was the day after the month of Ramadan and all them Muslims that been fasting come out 'pon the road dressed in white; them fathers and their boy children who did come out to buy them balloons and sweets. And a balloon-seller was standing at the street corner with his long blue balloons and shouting, 'Balloons! Balloons!' And every time he open his mouth you could see his gold teeth right round the top of his mouth. And it vex me to see him flashing his gold teeth. I shout out, 'Is what you clean them with? Brass polish?' The man give me a murderous look, brother. But you see what I mean? I did feel malice for the balloon-seller, more than malice even. But I don' feel nothing 'gainst the fisherman. How you explain that?"

"Look you sons passing," said Mr Chalfen, who had got up to stretch his legs.

Kwaku rose from his seat, and through the window he saw the twins ambling by, each with a birdcage in his hand.

"Well, they not taking no birds to New Amsterdam, I can tell you," he announced with a smile.

It had not escaped Mr Chalfen that Kwaku had been trying to make amends for the insults he had directed towards him earlier. Now his smiling face reassured him completely.

When the food was brought in the two men sat down again at table. Blossom had put on the transistor radio, which was now giving out popular music with a tinny sound.

"You hear something?" asked Mr Chalfen.

"Go and see, ne," Kwaku said to him.

But Blossom went instead, leaning out of the window, then drew back at once.

"Is what?" Kwaku enquired impatiently, and as she would not answer him he went to see for himself.

If he intended saying anything the words died in his mouth, for standing at the foot of the stairs was Miss Gwendoline, her head tilted backwards and her eyes moving restlessly from side to side.

Kwaku and Blossom stood staring at each other, neither knowing what to say or whether anything should be said. Mr Chalfen, who was about to get up from table, was waved back violently by Blossom, who then took Kwaku by the hand towards the back of the house.

"I wonder how long she been standing there?" she whispered into his ear.

He felt her trembling hand in his. "I don' know."

The rain had stopped, but there was the smell of damp everywhere, like the smell of sodden fruit and wood embedded in the earth. A silence sat on the house so heavily that Blossom stood quaking beside Kwaku, piercing him with her look to see if he understood the riddle of his wife appearing in her yard. At last the silence was broken by the crying of a child next door, a sudden violent outburst.

"She know you here," Blossom whispered.

"I don' think so. She still listening."

At the sound of Miss Gwendoline's retreating footsteps Blossom said, "You better go. If you hurry ... ."

"What?"

"You could get home before her," Blossom whispered, as if Kwaku's wife was still listening to them.

Kwaku rushed off to overtake his wife and arrive home before her.

As Kwaku listened for the tapping of Miss Gwendoline's stick, it occurred to him that she must know he had to go to Blossom's house in order to make last-minute arrangements with Mr Chalfen. He could easily have gone out to meet her openly. It would be much worse if he pretended that he had been home all the time, if indeed she had heard him talking. He tried to recall the conversation at Blossom's house after the twins went by with their birdcages, for she could not have taken up her position before that. As far as he could remember he had only spoken about something insignificant.

Tap, tap, tap came the sound of a stick on the paling fence next to his uncle's house.

"Eh, eh," Kwaku called out. "Is you? I was come for you at five o'clock. Wha' you come back so early for?"

"She got sickness in the house," replied Miss Gwendoline. "Her husband fall sick las' night an' I din' want to stay. So car bring be home. What you been doing all day?"

"Nothing," Kwaku said. "I been over to see Mr Chalfen 'bout the luggage tomorrow."

"You been over? When?"

"Ever since!"

"And what you do the rest of the time?"

"You questioning me like policeman now," Kwaku said with a nervous chuckle.

"The girls done their work?" Miss Gwendoline enquired, allowing Kwaku to lead her up the stairs.

"In between their chatting they been working," Kwaku declared, in an effort to give the impression that he had been at home most of the time.

Miss Gwendoline had put on weight since her affliction, for she was unable to dart about the house and yard as she had been in the habit of doing. She sat down carefully on her chair in the middle of the room.

"Why you like sittin' in the middle of the room like that?" Kwaku asked her.

"So that I can hear better what goin' on."

"Oh." Kwaku waited for his wife to accuse him, for by now he was certain that she knew his whereabouts a few minutes before.

"Rain, rain, as if the dry season kian' come," Miss Gwendoline remarked.

She was in the habit of sitting out in the afternoon shadows with the sound of her children's voices round her and imagining who might be in the cars that went by on the Public Road. The afternoons used to pass like that, in small, insignificant talk, until all the children came home. Now she could hear the steps of her eldest girl children, and, as they arrived at the door, the abrupt interruptions of their conversation.

"Is where you been?" Miss Gwendoline challenged Rona.

They, too, had gone out, thinking that their mother would not be back before sundown with her threatening stick.

But before Rona could answer Miss Gwendoline bawled her down, insulting her for having dragged Fabian out when her cough was not yet better. Then she turned her attention to Philomena.

"You been with them all the time?" she asked. "Is you I talking to, Philomena."

"Yes. Ask them. I was with you, wasn't I, Rona?"

"Yes, Ma; she been with me."

"All you go out of the room an' leave Fabian with me," Miss Gwendoline ordered the two older girls.

"Fabian, come to Ma."

Fabian approached slowly, afraid of her mother's temper, which she often displayed in her quarrels with the intractable Philomena.

She passed her hand over little Fabian's body, then whispered into her ear, "She been with you all the time?"

"Yes, Ma," Fabian protested, surprised that her mother should have doubted her sisters' word.

"Where you been?"

"To Duty-Free, down the road."

"What you been doing there?"

"Philomena and Rona been talking to Duty-Free an' I been next door to Miss Claris."

"So you weren't with them all the time," Miss Gwendoline declared triumphantly.

"No."

"No," her mother repeated, letting her go. "You tell your sister to come in here."

"One day," Miss Gwendoline told Philomena when she came back into the room, "I going cut off all your hair an' you going know to behave then ... ."

Kwaku, distressed at his wife's meanness, did not intervene, but signalled to his daughter to remain silent, for he imagined that the very thing which Miss Gwendoline feared might be brought about by her own injustice towards Philomena.

When they were left alone once more he told Miss Gwendoline what he had overheard Philomena telling Rona. But, far from admitting that she had misjudged her daughter, Miss Gwendoline remarked, "And where she does get lipstick from? And why when she was only ten Duty-Free catch her walking about her house in she high-heel shoes? She man-struck!"

Night came and the girls went to bed earlier than usual, their spirits dampened by their mother's bad mood, which crept about the house like the humidity that deposited a fungoid growth on their towels. Then the three boys came in and retired, leaving their parents alone in the small drawing-room.

As Kwaku was about to retire and leave Miss Gwendoline alone in her perpetual night world – she had got into the habit of going to bed in the early morning hours after Kwaku's move to New Amsterdam, even before she became blind – she said to him, "I coming to New Amsterdam with you. We all going."

Kwaku could not believe his ears. She was facing the bolted doors and looking upwards as she always did since the onset of her affliction. Her stick was on the ground within reach of her right hand, like an appendage laid aside for the night. In an odd way it resembled her, by some trick of association, no doubt.

"But I going tomorrow," Kwaku said at last.

"You can wait a week or so."

"I was goin' stay at a guest house. Where we going stay with everybody?"

"You could send Mr Chalfen to get a place for us," Miss Gwendoline explained, unruffled by his objections.

And every additional objection was parried by a practical suggestion; so that in the end Kwaku was obliged to agree.

"I going to bed then," he said, laying his hand on her head affectionately.

While in bed Kwaku relived the scene, starting from her unexpected announcement, and recalled that for a moment he had peered into an abyss. Indeed, it was he who had wanted the whole family in New Amsterdam, when he began to make money. But now, he felt instinctively that it was not the right thing to do. He had no idea how long it would take to build up his clientele again, and might regret abandoning the cheap rented house. Besides, clients who came to be treated would find a house full of children, in contrast to the cottage in the smart quarter where one could even hear the humming of the bees. That morning he had got up full of anticipation of taking up again a lifestyle that had brought him a measure of dignity. Then came his irritation at the way Blossom's hospitality had been extended to Mr Chalfen; and then, as if that were not enough Miss Gwendoline's appearance at the foot of the stairs, materializing like an unexpected presence. And now this!

Kwaku could not bear to think of the problems the move of his whole family would bring with it. A school would have to be found for the younger children And how could his practice prosper in a house where a black-pudding business was carried on?

Inwardly he cursed Mr Chalfen, whose behaviour had detained him at Blossom's house longer than he would have stayed under normal conditions, and thus allow Miss Gwendoline to creep up on them. Tomorrow when he went to tell him of the change in plans he would do some straight talking. On the other hand if the retired Customs officer was to prepare the way for their settling in New Amsterdam he could not risk offending him.

Kwaku twisted and turned in his bed, chagrin mounting, until he seized hold of Mr Chalfen in his imagination and strangled him slowly so that his eyes popped out of his self-satisfied head and he fell, lifeless, face down on the floor among his labelled jars of herbs.

Miss Gwendoline smiled bitterly at the thought that her family had retired while she alone remained up, sitting on her stool, reflecting that there was no darkness to signal the coming of bedtime for her. Early that morning while she and Kwaku were travelling along the bumpy road she reflected on the strange circumstance that the only faces she could recall with certainty were those of Kwaku and Blossom. Blossom, rather than her own children, her own little Fabian, who no longer came to sit on her lap and who became restless whenever she knelt before her to have her hair plaited. Apart from those, she recalled only the faces of the dead, which offered themselves to her imagination with extraordinary clarity: her grandmother, an aunt and a sister-cousin who, like Damon, had never seemed to belong to those around him. In the car she had called to mind Blossom, and, unable to see anything around, could not put her out of mind. Therefore she resolved to come back early and try to catch Kwaku out. The taxi-driver was told to put her out in front of the calabash tree, an unnecessary instruction, since he knew the house of the woman who worked as a conductor on the yellow buses. She had only half-believed in her plan, for too many things could work against its success. Blossom, whom she knew to be on holiday, might be at the window when the taxi stopped, or she might even hear it pull up in front of the house. As soon as the taxi door opened Miss Gwendoline heard Kwaku's voice, speaking the way he did when he felt at home in company. Filled with rage she tapped her way across the bridge, intending to go halfway up the stairs to hear whatever was being said. But she understood him from the yard, and listened, only to find that she could reproach him with nothing. Yes, he must be happy in her company to talk like that, she told himself.

Miss Gwendoline thought back on the scene, the sudden silence following the footsteps above her head, and finally her retreat, leaving her husband in the house of that woman. From now on the family would stick together, for she no longer had her two eyes to see what everyone else could see. Blossom – so she was told by a friend in the village – did not want children. That was the most dangerous sort of woman, the kind who got in the habit of breaking up marriages because they could not bear to produce offspring as nature intended. In any case Blossom had always struck her as being sly and all too ready to gorge herself on her memories of her childhood and Kwaku's. The day she came to ask for Kwaku's address in New Amsterdam she told her how, as a boy, Kwaku was afraid of her father, because he believed that he used to take off his face at night before he went to bed. As if the story would endear her to Blossom! Such evocations of their childhood, which Kwaku had learned to keep to himself, only stirred up her fury against the childless woman. *She* had several healthy children and was rearing them successfully. *She* had done her duty and did not need to ogle at other women's husbands or parade herself on a bus like a man. Yes, she and the lot were going to accompany Kwaku to New Amsterdam. They would get rich there or perish there, whatever God intended. She had prayed to be relieved of her affliction, but He had seen fit to bind her more securely with it. Now He was unlikely to deny her the wish to see her husband and children prosper.

29 Rain in the night

MR CHALFEN assured Blossom personally that he would be able to rent a large house for Kwaku's family through a distant relation who was an estate agent and knew the town like the back of his hand.

Kwaku, in an uncommon display of courtesy, persisted in calling him *Brother*, and reminded him of the time when they shared a house in New Amsterdam.

"Remember the rum-shop?" he asked. "The one opposite the market?"

Mr Chalfen knew the rum-shop well. But he and Kwaku had never drunk there together. Kwaku even pushed his bonhomie so far as to remind him of their outings in Stanleytown, the district of New Amsterdam where he had been introduced to the dead girl.

"We've never been there together," Mr Chalfen said, knitting his brow.

"You're sure?" Kwaku asked. "Isn't that where we did go walkin' together?"

"No!" said Mr Chalfen hotly, certain now that Kwaku was making fun of him.

"And the Winkle. Remember the Winkle?"

"What about the Winkle?" Mr Chalfen asked, his eyes flashing.

"You know the Winkle! You can't deny you know the Winkle," declared Kwaku feverishly, searching for some activity in the Winkle with which he could connect the retired Customs officer.

"Course I know the Winkle!" Mr Chalfen shrieked, a wild look having replaced his normally fowl-cock confident air.

"You remember the women in the Winkle?"

"Which women?" Mr Chalfen demanded, ready to fall on Kwaku and teach him not to provoke him while Blossom was in the house.

"The women, man," Kwaku whispered, winking and nodding towards Blossom's bedroom.

"I don't know any woman in the Winkle. The Winkle's a slum and I've never been for walks down anywhere. And I'm no womanizer. You'd better apologize for .... "

212

Blossom, who had been listening from inside, appeared in the doorway.

"What the two of you at one another throats for?" she asked, surprised at Mr Chalfen's violent manner.

"Is nothing," Kwaku said.

"It *is* something," Mr Chalfen objected. "He's dragging me around New Amsterdam to places I wouldn't set foot in."

"I get carried away sometimes," Kwaku said. "I sorry, man. You can't even take a little tantalize."

"Well, I thought you meant it," Mr Chalfen said, pleased that Blossom did not miss Kwaku's apology.

An hour later he went off with the suitcases full of herbs and the promise of a bonus if he managed to secure a suitable place for Kwaku's family.

Blossom remarked that she would miss him. "Even Wilfred did like him, in the end."

"I din' like him, though," Kwaku declared flatly.

"You don' like nobody except your family .... Kwaku, I want you to give me a child."

"What?"

"You hear me. You not deaf!"

"And Wilfred?"

She looked away, apparently unwilling to discuss Wilfred.

"What about Wilfred?" Kwaku asked again.

"The doctor say he kian' get children. Why you think we does quarrel all the time like that?"

"I din' know."

"What you think?" she said angrily. "I does go round broadcasting that he kian' give me children? Don' get vex, Kwaku. Don' let's quarrel again."

"We not quarrelling."

"I want you to give me a child, I tell you. I don' want to die childless."

"Childless, fatherless, landless, moneyless," said Kwaku reflectively.

She left him and went inside; and he could hear her shuffling about in her bedroom.

Blossom came out finally, dressed only in her thin petticoat. She walked to the kitchen then went back into the bedroom, so that Kwaku could see her breasts and the hair above her legs through the transparent material. Back and forth she went, now with a cup, now with nothing in her hands, as if her house were empty and the windows of her house were closed.

"The people nex' door goin' see you," Kwaku remarked.

"Shut the windows, then," she answered nonchalantly.

Kwaku got up and followed her into the bedroom instead, where the single window was open as well. He closed it.

Blossom sat on the bed and watched him.

"Don' come and sit nex' to me with all you clothes on," she warned.

He took off his shirt without undoing the buttons, then, having stepped out of his trousers and underpants, stood before her as naked as she had first seen him when they had a shower together in her mother's house. He was then seven, a thin, undernourished waif, skin and bones, on whom her mother had taken pity.

Blossom stood up and pressed her body against his, opening her mouth so that he might kiss her and know, from the warmth and softness of her lips, that she had desired him since childhood.

Kwaku slept with her and discovered in her a part of his wife and a part of himself. He hid in her hair and her hands, and their enfolding was the culmination of that long, ambivalent relationship that wound its way from childhood to adulthood, and which neither fully understood. And if Wilfred had walked in at that moment she would have been incapable of stopping, like a horseman in a headlong ride. Kwaku wept at this mystery, as affecting as the clocks in New Amsterdam that chimed all at once, as the pale, pale face of the dead girl in Stanleytown and the ugly, abandoned woman from the Courantyne.

"You coming back?" she enquired.

"When you next day off?"

"I on holiday. I did tell you."

"The day after tomorrow."

Kwaku came back again and again the following week, to *flog* her, as she said, in one of those crude expressions she occasionally used.

"You not going come back from New Amsterdam, you know," she told him one afternoon.

"How you know?"

"You all not coming back."

"I don' know," said Kwaku. "In any case I can't live in the same village with the fisherman while Miss Gwendoline blind. I feel like everybody talking 'bout me."

"People talking 'bout you, yes. But they always been talking 'bout you."

"I feel bad for Miss Gwendoline sake, 'cause I know that she did want me to do him something back. But what I going do against people like that? I in' no obeah man."

On the last visit to Blossom's house – two days before the departure for New Amsterdam – Kwaku got first-hand knowledge of what he had heard a great deal about: he received a hair-cut, a wound on his penis from Blossom's coarse pubic hair. Only the day before,

214

when the rain fell continuously, so that little Fabian could not even go out into the yard to play and had to remain at the window watching the deluge, the cattle standing about in the field and the empty Public Road, she kept repeating a rhyme she had heard from one of her sisters:

"Rain in the morning,
Rain in the night,
Kian' get a hair-cut,
Kian' fly me kite."

He had heard Blossom tell a woman friend that she was *flying kite*, and somehow knew that it meant that her monthly period had come on. Kwaku was suddenly aware that the verse his youngest had been singing was full of sexual allusions. Now that Blossom had *marked* him he understood why he had treated Mr Chalfen the way he had.

"You going miss me?" Blossom asked him.

Such questions embarrassed him. They were not necessary.

"How you mean miss you? I going see you sometimes in Rosignol."

"Don' lie," Blossom said without emotion.

"I telling you," he insisted, believing that he had taken from her something that would last him a lifetime.

"Anyway ... anyway, Kwaku ... ." Choking with emotion she could not say what she wanted to say.

"Go home!" she ordered him when he tried to console her.

As he got dressed she unfolded the blanket at the foot of the bed and covered herself with it, so that when he spoke she pretended she could not hear him.

Kwaku looked out on to the street to make certain that no one he knew was passing, then slipped through the door.

The teacher's house was half-painted – the operation was interrupted because of the rain – and at the window a middle-aged man was sitting. People said that she had got married to someone she did not care for, only to have a man in the house for her son's sake.

Kwaku had a sudden urge to look up Mr Barzey, who had not been seen at his window for several days; but as he was about to knock on his door he changed his mind, restrained by a premonition of unpleasantness. He had taken it into his head that his old friend would be disagreeable and even imagined a conversation between them in which Mr Barzey would begin by saying, "So you're taking the family after all!"

"Yes; you think is the best thing?" Kwaku would ask.

And to this Mr Barzey would reply that he was an idiot.

So Kwaku turned away from the door and went home to his wife and children.

215

The next day his uncle came to say goodbye and to distribute sweets. He joked with everyone and laughed so heartily that Miss Gwendoline put aside her despondency, and even the twins joined in the merriment. Only Kwaku stood apart, suspecting that there lay behind his uncle's manner an intense relief that he and the twins were moving away from the village and in all likelihood would not return.

As he was about to leave, his uncle invited him to go to the beer-shop with him, but he declined, feeling that he had been let down by his unusual display of mirth. Whence could a man of such a sour disposition call up such gaiety? All his insults, his indifference in the past years, had not affected him like this show of mirth. Since Miss Gwendoline's blindness came upon her he had not once invited her over, only because he did not want him in his house, Kwaku was certain. Yet it was common knowledge that he was no longer wild, that he was now as responsible as anyone in the village.

On the following day — the day of the family's departure — Kwaku woke up, still preoccupied with his uncle's conduct. But when he mentioned it to Miss Gwendoline she remarked that he was incapable of seeing the good in anyone. Had he forgotten that his uncle had brought him up, just like a father? That he had brought them together? After what he had put up with from him and the twins it was surprising that he bothered to speak to them at all. Kwaku had forgotten all that in his obsession with his recollection of his uncle's mirth. Miss Gwendoline was right, after all.

But even as the family filed past his uncle's cottage with its flaking paintwork, its chintz blinds and the fret-worked cornice of its porch, Kwaku could not suppress a new surge of resentment.

The same taxi that had taken Miss Gwendoline into the village drew up on the grass verge. Kwaku helped the driver to load the three suitcases into the boot — he had left the bulk of his possessions with his uncle — before assisting Miss Gwendoline to get in at the back.

Then the car, registered to carry five passengers, drove off with Kwaku, his wife and six children, along the coastal road that led to Rosignol, past the courida bushes of the sea shore and the coconut groves of Mahaica and Mahaicony.

"If Irene and Clayton been with us," said Kwaku, "we couldn' all hold in the taxi, eh?"

But Miss Gwendoline made him no answer.

30 Destitution

KWAKU RETURNED to New Amsterdam to find that another healer, using his garlic technique, had established a practice there. This man's popularity had grown when he announced that he was a faith healer as well and backed his claim up by healing a woman who suffered from pains in her stomach.

Though no one came to Kwaku there was nothing left for him but to continue in occupation of the two-storey mansion Mr Chalfen had hired for him in the quarter where he once had his successful practice. In the space of a few months the exorbitant rent had eaten into his savings alarmingly, and Kwaku, who had been afraid of the damage a black-pudding business might do to his potential practice, now allowed Miss Gwendoline to sell the rice-filled black entrails in a stall behind the house. But the commerce was short-lived, for an employee from the municipality came to inform him that no business could be carried on in that quarter.

Mr Chalfen, who had not been paid for three weeks, deserted them when he heard that the family would not even be permitted to earn money from a black-pudding stall in their back yard. Kwaku had noticed how shoddily he had been labelling the jars of new herbs, but dared not say anything since, to a certain degree, he believed his fate to be in Mr Chalfen's hands.

And within six months of residing in New Amsterdam Kwaku and his family faced destitution with but two hundred dollars in the bank.

One twin had been found work as a post-office messenger by the husband of a woman Kwaku had once treated; and every afternoon he came home, surly and intransigent, because his salary was barely enough to buy his lunch and pay what Kwaku demanded from him as a contribution to the family resources. At night he and his twin brother went out and came home after midnight, defying Kwaku to raise his voice in protest. They teased Damon mercilessly, calling him their parents' "*darling son*" and challenging him to go out with them at night. One night Damon, nearly thirteen years old, accompanied them, but declined to go after that, for what reason neither of his elder sisters could extract from him. Even Philomena and Rona were glad to see the backs of their eldest brothers when they went out after dark and left the mansion to them. They would then stand at the gate and watch the young men go by, promptly repulsing them if they attempted to approach the gate.

Town life was filled with endless possibilities, but Rona and Philomena, fifteen and nearly fourteen respectively, were cautious about encouraging the young men's advances before they were

217

acquainted with their new surroundings. Hearing that they would almost certainly be moving to a much smaller house they felt that their parents had let them down. Philomena in particular, unaccustomed to restraining her feelings, undertook to speak to her father about the move.

Kwaku told her everything, down to the sum that was left in the bank. He brought the bank-book out and showed it to her.

"See, child," he said indulgently. "I don' keep nothing from you, do I?"

"Can't you work?" she asked.

"At what? I too old to get a job as a shoemaker. They only want apprentices so they can take advantage of them." He told her of his unsuccessful attempt to secure work as a photographer.

"And why you come back to the village when you were making money, then?"

"I had to come back because you all was leading you mother a dance. If the twins did know how to behave we would've be rich by now. You-all and the twins din' treat her good."

But no sooner had he uttered the words than he regretted them.

"Not you, child .... One day I goin' make money and I'll take you to the jeweller shop and let you choose what you want from the trays of bangles and necklaces in gold, and rings with them dark red stones .... You like it here in New Amsterdam?"

"What's it matter if I like it here, when we can't buy anything? I getting big, you know ...."

"I know, I know. Don' think I don' know. You're a big girl now. Don' think you mother don' know."

But at the mention of her mother Philomena's expression changed.

"She love you."

"You right," she said sarcastically. "That's why I can't do nothing right. If I was Rona I wouldn't stand for how Ma does make her work from morning till night. I would've gone long time."

Kwaku, saddened by his daughter's blunt observations turned away.

"You and Ma think she stupid," Philomena continued, "'cause she always sweeping and washing and looking after Fabian."

Annoyed that the insinuation seemed to be lost on her father, Philomena added, "Since Ma gone blind she been carrying on in front of her eyes. Why you think she was always putting Fabian to bed when we was in the village? In the morning, in the afternoon, in the night; Fabian always had to go and lie down."

Kwaku wanted to hear no more, but did not know how to formulate his objection. It pained him to hear his favourite daughter expose her own sister to his wrath. He would have liked to say that he knew all about Rona, and that he had no intention of passing on what he knew to her mother.

"If you did know what you mother been through when we was young you wouldn' talk like that. Is because of the way Rona help her that you could go to school every day and learn to read and write."

"Even when you been sending home a lot of money Rona –"

"I don' want to hear no more," Kwaku said violently. And immediately he regretted his words.

"Don' touch me! You always want to paw me," Philomena burst out, as he tried to stroke her cheek.

They were standing on the porch, she with her white dress against the door, whose old, cracked paintwork gave it the appearance of an untilled field at the height of the dry season. Her thick hair, untameable, even with the help of pins and comb, gave her the appearance – from a distance at least – of a woman. Up to a year before then, she would lie down on the same bed as her father and think nothing of it. She had lately become aware of his presence in a physical way, of the things that belonged to him, of the smell of his shirt, and resented the manner in which he left his underclothes lying around, just as if she and Rona were still little children. A year ago she had felt deeply for him; today she found it almost impossible to contain her irritation at his behaviour, his indolence, his very presence. Why did he lack the authority of Mr Barzey? Why had his role in the business with the fisherman been so passive? And now he tried to paw her whenever he had the chance.

"Why you eyeing me like that?" Kwaku asked.

"Nothing," replied Philomena, and turned her back on ⸲ .ı to enter the vastness of their new home, a vastness unrelieved by four chairs, a table and three beds, bought since they arrived in New Amsterdam.

Kwaku looked at the wide road and thought of the eight clients who had visited him since he came back.

Just a few yards from his house Kwaku spotted him. Although he was lost in thought as to his predicament with the house – he had received a note to vacate, which was to expire in three days – he recognized him at once. But before Kwaku could turn away and reduce his chances of being seen he heard the friendly call, "Mr Cholmondeley! Mr Cholmondeley!"

Kwaku threw his shoulder back and turned to face his acquaintance like the man he was.

"Hello, Mr Gordon!" he shouted, as though he had just recognized him.

"Well, I never! Where're you off to?" Mr Gordon asked.

"My home. There."

"Where?"

"Over there. That huge house with all them windows and the double staircase."

"That's yours?" Mr Gordon asked.

"Only just, though! I don' like mortgages, so I pay for it cash."

Mr Gordon expected to be invited in, but Kwaku stopped at the gate, while gesticulating towards the mansion.

"Eighty thousand he was asking," Kwaku said excitedly. "But I beat him down. His own agent tell me to beat him down. You don' know what these agents like, Mr Gordon. I beat him down to seventy-nine thousand, five hundred and ninety-seven, and he say he had another purchaser waiting 'pon the sidelines. 'I don' care where he waiting,' I say. 'He could be waiting 'pon the roof. I don' intend goin' higher than seventy-nine thousand five hundred an' ninety-seven dollars!' And all the time I had my poor blind wife and my six children waiting on the stelling with nowhere to go. But in this life it does pay to be firm. So now it's all mine."

Mr Gordon was flabbergasted. In fact he was so flabbergasted he was expecting Kwaku to lead the way up the stairs and set before him a carafe of rum.

"So you're making a lot of money!" Mr Gordon said.

"It jus' rolling in, Mr Gordon. 'Pon wheels."

"Let's go for a drink," Mr Gordon said, nodding in the direction of the market. It was obvious that for his own reasons Kwaku had no intention of entertaining him.

Kwaku would have jumped at the invitation a week earlier, but he owed for his last drinks.

"All right," he agreed, after weighing up the possibility of a public humiliation against that of the barman's absence.

On the way Mr Gordon told him that his plan, when he came back from England, was to settle in New Amsterdam. But the town held youthful memories for him which had not been laid after so many years abroad.

Kwaku, not to be outdone, confided that he intended to travel as well.

"Don' say nothing to anybody," he said, "but I got plans to go to Siam, the place with all them cats."

"Ah," Mr Gordon managed, convinced now that he knew how the wind was blowing.

Kwaku led the way through the swing doors and invited Mr Gordon to buy him the first drink. He remained in the background, scanning the faces of the customers standing round and the barmen behind the bar to see if the man he owed money was there. But he was nowhere to be seen.

"Terrible thing, eh?" Mr Gordon declared, on joining Kwaku, a bottle of fruit-cured rum in one hand and two schnapps glasses in the other.

"What?"

"Mr Barzey," Mr Gordon replied, believing that Kwaku was up to his tricks again.

"What happen to him?"

"He hanged himself!" Mr Gordon exclaimed.

In his dismay Kwaku could only recall Blossom, the wound she had inflicted on him and the bleak summits of her breasts.

"So you didn't know?"

"No. No, Mr Gordon. If I did know you think I would've gone on talking 'bout myself? I swear to God I din' know."

"Everybody thought his daughter-in-law was afraid of him; in reality he lived in mortal dread of her. But worse than anything he couldn't stand having to go to table when he was called and ask for the key when he wanted to visit me. One night she locked him out when his son was away."

"So he gone," Kwaku muttered disconsolately. "Is like if I lost a hand."

"She came home one afternoon, locked her moped to the back stairs, and as she went up she saw him through the window, spinning slowly as if somebody was turning him. What I can't understand is why he should choose that way to go; and why he should hang himself in their bedroom rather than his. People's actions are a mystery, however much you think of it."

"Yes, Mr Gordon, you right. You and Mr Barzey always right. He did give me his album."

"A photographic album?"

"Yes."

"He never spoke to me about that," Mr Gordon said.

Kwaku was glad that his dead friend had not shared all his secrets with Mr Gordon. He wanted to confess that the grand house, work of one of the great carpenter-builders, with its exuberance of windows and ornate porch, did not belong to him; but he was restrained by the desire to keep something from Mr Gordon, whom he did not know well. Instead, he talked of his family, of the twin who nearly lost his job because he had carried out the orders of his superior, who had insisted that the receipt for every telegram should be signed legibly. On delivering a telegram to an important official at the Town Hall he asked him to sign the receipt once more because he could not make out his signature. The official complained and the twin had to wait several days before he knew that he was to be let off with a warning.

Mr Gordon, too, spoke a good deal. He spoke of his prize bulls and the servant girl in his house. He confessed to Kwaku that he would never have said much to him in the dead man's lifetime.

Then the two men sat in silence, banished by the identical grief into the anonymity of the noise and conversations around them. People came and went, others sat alone, with the apparent intention of staying until the rum-shop closed, while other groups grew or lost a member or two before being joined by yet others.

It was the first time that Kwaku had drunk here in the company of another – except for his encounter with the woman from the Courantyne. The rum-shop was the resort of poor workmen and inveterate drunkards who came bearing the marks of the previous day's hangover, and of women who no longer cared about their reputation. Sometimes the swing-doors would fly open and everyone would turn in the expectation of witnessing a fight. At other times a woman would come in looking for her husband among the rusting iron tables, which had the appearance of having been retrieved from a rubbish heap. It was here that the damned, the sick and the hopelessly lost drank and bled; here was the last port of call for those from among the working people who would end up in the home in Canje, where the inmates' souls were pillaged as their food-parcels were, and the visiting dental surgeon had lost the art of filling teeth. Here, in the stench of urine from the passage and stale liquor from the counter, Mr Gordon and Kwaku sat facing each other in the wake of Mr Barzey's death.

"I went and found her sweeping the house after they took his body away," Mr Gordon told Kwaku." 'I didn't do him anything,' she told me. 'Why're you telling me that?' I asked, knowing how guilt was working her up. 'Because you were his friend.' Her face was all bloated with crying and I felt sorry for her. You know that two weeks after the autopsy she was her snooty self again? ... But I tell you something, that room she's been dying to let all these years she won't let now. Nobody'll take a room in that house .... You notice how many couples don't have children nowadays? Or can't. People have possessions now, like abroad. Sometimes they're married ten, fifteen years before they decide to have a child. And meanwhile they collect things and bring their dogs to live in their house and even share their bed. Then in three, four years they get tired of the furniture and throw it out and buy a new set. And it doesn't stop them from complaining about the high cost of living .... This slow descent to the plains of Armageddon ...."

"I know, Mr Gordon," said Kwaku, who did not know. The comparison of Guyana with countries abroad was entirely lost on him, for he had travelled no further than a carrion crow ever flew in its life.

"Imagine," went on Mr Gordon, "spinning slowly. Circling. If you understood the circle you wouldn't need to understand anything else. Do you realize that, Mr Cholmondeley? We wear them on our fingers, our wrists, our ankles, in our nose, but we don't realize we're fascinated. Beautiful, isn't it? Why should you realize it? Tell me, Mr Cholmondeley. If I were to demonstrate to you that you're better off dead than alive would you kill yourself? Of course not. You'd find all sorts of reasons for continuing to live. That is the second secret. You're not in control. You all used to laugh at me over my garden wall. Oh, I know. Don't deny it. You used to laugh at me, at what I wear, at the way I kept grinning as you went by. But did you ever ask yourself why I was smiling? No. I won't tell you. But I'll tell you this: in my house I break every law I can break. Behind my walls I break laws with relish, Mr Cholmondeley. I've been watching you. You're a law-breaker yourself, but you're unaware of what you're doing. If I were to disclose to you what I do behind my high walls you'll only be devoured by an itch to tell someone else. That's your great weakness: you can't keep your mouth shut."

Mr Gordon was now speaking with a controlled rage, which kept Kwaku's eye on him, as if he were a magician.

"Another weakness you have is to care too much about others. Oh, yes, you do! You breached the Conservancy, but deep down that's not what you wanted. Me, I'd never do anything like that, not because I care, but because I value my liberty. No pompous fool calling himself a magistrate is going to take away my liberty on the excuse that I broke the law. But how do you think I came back from abroad with all that money? You ever thought of that? Course not! Where I was working everybody was on the fiddle. So I just went straight ahead and did in London what the Londoners do. And here? I pay my Party dues and grin with everybody. When you were in New Amsterdam making money you came back so that your family wouldn't collapse. You're so damned self-centred you believed they needed you badly. You came rushing back to the village, and when that didn't work you returned to New Amsterdam to buy a house. You buy a house! With peanuts? If you had the nerve I'd show you how to buy a house, starting with nothing, just giving yourself two years. But you're a blabberer and a misfit. And worst of all you care for those around you too much. You know the person I admire most in the village? Not the teacher or the shoemaker, nor Blossom. No! Your uncle. He doesn't care, but it didn't prevent him from bringing you up. The minute I set eyes on that man I said, 'Ah! That's a loner, a man who doesn't care. The true intellect. A man who would give a woman ten dollars a week not out of sentiment, but out of conviction, and wouldn't even ask anything in return, not even gratitude.' "

Now why did such a calculating man like Mr Gordon choose to

confess to him that he was a thief, thought Kwaku? To him, a blabber-mouth? He was disgusted with Mr Gordon, with his attitude to life, with the fact that he was a self-confessed thief, with the manner in which he spoke of Mr Barzey's death, "spinning at the end of a noose". To think that he had placed him on the same pedestal on which he had put Mr Barzey, a hundred times his superior. Had it not been for the free rum he dispensed he would have got up and left him in the foetid noisy atmosphere of the rum-shop, the entrance to which was now spattered with rain.

"So," continued Mr Gordon, "every society *generates*, yes *ge ... ne ... rates* crime, so why this odium attached to committing crime? I agree that if you didn't punish people they'd be encouraged to break the law. But we should say openly, 'There's nothing wicked about law-breaking; it's just stupid to do something that'll deprive you of your liberty'... the slumber of fools."

Mr Gordon paused for breath. A man standing by the table had been listening intently and showed his disappointment at the interruption by turning to look at him. Believing that he had attracted Mr Gordon's attention he made a show of drinking from his glass.

Kwaku, not knowing what to reply to the torrent of words, said the first thing that came into his mind.

"You ever heard 'bout the man who could only make love to the jingling of bells? *Ting-ling, ting-ling*, slow and soft. One night he been making love while his wife was tinkling these lil' bells near his earholes, slow an' nice. and all of a sudden the fire engine pass by with its bell clanging 'Bang-a-lang-lang! .... That was the end of him."

Mr Gordon looked at Kwaku as if he was a worm. He shook his head slowly in a gesture of such utter contempt that Kwaku was offended.

"I going buy you a beer," said Kwaku, who had made up his mind to use up the change in his pocket.

"We haven't finished the rum yet," Mr Gordon retorted, grasping the neck of the rum bottle, two-thirds of whose contents were still undrunk.

"That won't las' long," Kwaku declared, jumping up from from his seat.

At the counter the man who had been listening so attentively to their conversation spoke to him, but his words were lost in the noise of voices, so that Kwaku did not even realize that he was being addressed.

"I know your friend, you know," the stranger repeated, bending down to shout in his ear.

Kwaku, thinking that he had inadvertently offended

him, stepped back.

"Your friend, I know him."

"Mr Gordon?"

"Yes. Used to live in the same street in London."

"You don't say!" Kwaku exclaimed.

"Yes, man," the man said. "I nearly killed myself laughing when I heard him shouting at you. We used to call him Opium because he was a television addict. If his wife did hold a gun to his head he wouldn't have moved from the set. She even had to bring his food to him on a tray while he was watching television. It's only when he heard there was a programme on immigrants that he'd break out in a cold sweat and go to bed for the night. His wife and mine were friends. If I was to ... ."

"Two beers," Kwaku said, giving his order to the barman who was leaning forward, his left ear slightly cocked to pick up the order.

"From what I understand he's living in a village," continued the stranger, as the barman turned and with a swift gesture plucked two bottles from the shelf behind him. "I'm surprised."

The stranger had to wait for his answer while Kwaku counted out his money in five-cent and one-cent pieces. He did not intend to buy anything more expensive than a beer for a man who had been abusing him.

"Why you surprised he living in a village?" Kwaku asked, eager to hear further revelations about Mr Gordon's past.

"If it's one thing he likes as he likes television it's making money."

"He does make money all right," Kwaku informed him, disappointed that the stranger had nothing more interesting to say. "He does keep bulls and thing."

"Doe he live in a big house?"

"It big, yes. Concrete. A big, concrete house ... with a wall ... and iron gate. And a girl to serve him. She come with the concrete house."

"Listen," said the stranger, bending once more towards Kwaku's ear. "Ask him where his partner is,"

"What partner?" Kwaku asked, his interest flaring up once more.

"Yes. Ask him where the chap who was his partner is."

"Why?" asked Kwaku, annoyed that the stranger would not come right out with the whereabouts of Mr Gordon's partner.

"You just ask him."

"See you," Kwaku said with a nod, leaving the stranger standing at the corner of the counter, an amused smile on his face.

And Kwaku, with the discretion of a mongrel in the dog season said, even before he sat down, "Is where your partner, Mr Gordon?"

"What?" the breeder of bulls asked, taken aback by Kwaku's impertinence. "What's that you said?"

225

"Your partner, where he is? I mean, that lil' girl in your concrete house not a man, is she?"

Mr Gordon looked long and steadily at Kwaku and then, seeing that there was little likelihood of intimidating him, got up slowly, brushed the sleeves of the jacket he was wearing, and without so much as a goodbye, left Kwaku standing with the two bottles of beer in his hand.

Kwaku thought of the money he had just spent and cursed Mr Gordon heftily.

"The low-down dog! The stinking, no-good yowaree! Blasted fart-smelling expatriate! What I going do with the beer now?'

Catching sight of the stranger from the corner of his eye Kwaku hurried away to avoid having to offer him one his bottles.

Kwaku stood in the doorway, clutching his bottles. On the street a ponderous vehicle passed by, to be swallowed by the shadows. A blinking candle-fly ahead of him went out suddenly, like the noiseless snuffing of a flame. Stepping into the road he nearly trod on a half-dead, mangy dog, which managed to raise itself for a moment on its four legs, then fell back into its lying position.

It was only after Kwaku had gone some way up the road, pursued by the voice of a drunk shouting obscenities, that he realized that he was going the wrong way, west instead of east. Muttering to himself he turned back and tottered into a night that stretched like a corpse beyond the Canje bridge.

At the entrance to a wretched hovel he passed two pregnant women, talking belly to belly, and felt an urge to say something to them. And, his eyes still on them as he went by, it occurred to him that he was capable of loving a thousand women ... the same nakedness, the same mystery

In the confusion of houses massed in the shadows it seemed to him that morning was unfolding like a bale of cloth. Then the sight of his mansion brought back the reality of his living somewhere, a house clad in shutters, of his children and his blind wife who had singled out one child to dislike for no reason, since its childhood; one child who had come out of her womb like the others.

Kwaku climbed the stairs, holding on to the banisters. He knew that Miss Gwendoline was waiting up for him, sitting in the corner of the long gallery. The house was too big for her to keep in touch with the goings-on in it, as she used to do from her vantage point in the middle of the drawing-room in their village home.

"Hee, hee, heeeee!" Kwaku began to laugh softly. "When the bailiffs come to levy on me fo' non-payment of rent they going get a shock. I don' got no furnitures. How they can levy 'pon me for non-payment o' rent when I in' got no furnitures? Heeeee! O me God, how they goin' get a shock! Oh, life! Levy? Levy, ne. Bring you

226

bailiffs and they four men to levy 'pon me. Come ne, come in and take all you want. I got two bed and a couple o' chairs. And the law say I got to keep the bed them. Heeeee! Look story! That in' no levying. That's non-levying. Bailiff, bring you four men and non-levy 'pon me, please, I willing! Look, I opening me door to you. You want some water? Look, drink straight from the goblet, ne. All-you mus' be tired from carrying me non-furniture. I tell you, non-levying is not easy work. I know! That's one work you won't catch me doing. Hee, heeeeeeeeee! I never laugh so much in me life. O me God, me sides bursting and me temples hurting me. Bailiff, you kian' say I don' co-operate. Anyway ... ."

"Is what you making all that noise for?" Kwaku heard Miss Gwendoline saying to him. Her voice came through the jalousies below the casement windows and the louvred shutters that could not be adjusted, which let in all the air and sounds from outside and were the hallmark of the old mansions.

"I coming, Miss Gwendoline," Kwaku called out. "I coming, darling, 'pon a starling. I coming, me cooing pigeon, me lil' ground dove."

He pulled himself up the bannister as he spoke.

"Look how I coming to you. I flying in the air to you, me little God-bird. One time I did promise you a parakeet, but I did forget. You remember, lil' blue-saki? A parakeet with a lil' curved beak. Remember when we went visiting how I say to your friend parakeet, 'Give me a kiss, lil' bird.' And you remember what this parakeet do? He turn his back and shit 'pon me nose .... Ah, my little tawa-tawa, those were the days!"

Kwaku, instead of pushing open the door, sat down on the top tread of the stairs.

"You been and leave me all alone all these hours," Miss Gwendoline complained through the shutters. "And the girls been talking in whispers. I don' even know if they gone out or in bed. I don' even know whether is day or night. They only tell me when I ask."

"The sun's gone black, lil' God-bird," Kwaku said, his voice falling as if he was carrying a burden. "Mr Barzey dead."

"Who say so?" Miss Gwendoline asked.

"Mr Gordon tell me so. We been drinking together. Remember Mr Gordon, the man who uses to live opposite us in the village. Remember? The one who does fuck his little servant girl?"

"What he died from?" Miss Gwendoline asked.

"A rope."

"Somebody hit him with a rope?"

"No, he hang himself."

Miss Gwendoline groped for the rosary round her neck.

They never discussed Mr Barzey's death again and Kwaku was to bury his camera and tripod in the back yard of the mansion, on the edge of a garden of nettles and spore-laden fern.

"You better come in," Miss Gwendoline told him. "I smell rain. Rain goin' fall again."

Kwaku was nodding off and just managed to grab hold of the bannister before he pitched forward.

"You hear 'bout the beggar who the rich man give a dollar note to?" he asked her, more concerned about keeping awake than entertaining her. "This man give a beggar a dollar note. The beggar was begging from a telephone booth where he used to spend the night. The nex' day the beggar turn up at the man house and tell him he din' have nowhere to go. 'All right,' the man say. 'You can spend the night here, in the kitchen.' The nex' morning when the man wake up and go into his kitchen to get some water he find the beggar ... I kian' remember the rest of the story .... You know we going have to move? If push come to shove I suppose we could get the old shoemaker to take us in."

"Which old shoemaker?" Miss Gwendoline asked, believing that he was talking about the village shoemaker.

Kwaku suddenly recalled that he had not told her the truth about the singing shoemaker with whom he once lived in Winkle.

"Oh, was a shoemaker I uses to know in Winkle, not far from here. He used to bleat when the sun come up or go down, I kian' remember."

He got up and went inside, fearing that he might commit another indiscretion.

"Come to bed," he told his wife. "You remember las' night you couldn't find the way. Tonight I going be so sound asleep I wouldn't hear you when you call."

Miss Gwendoline raised herself ponderously from the straight-back chair which, miraculously, had borne her weight all these hours. She held on to Kwaku, who guided her up the stairs to the storey above, where the bedrooms were. They had to pass the room in which Rona, Philomena and Fabian slept, and then the boys' room. There were two unoccupied bedrooms, for none of the family would have dreamt of sleeping alone, even the twins, who were now seventeen.

In a brass jardinière which stood on a piece of furniture just outside the adults' room drooped the remains of potted plants which the family had allowed to die, partly because Miss Gwendoline was unable to do anything in the larger house and partly because it was believed that the former tenants would come to reclaim the jardinière. Kwaku put himself on the side where the partition was in order to prevent his blind wife from knocking over the plants. The

door of their room gaped to reveal a bed from which at least one of
the cross-boards that supported the mattress – cross-boards cut for a
narrower bed – invariably fell to the floor with a terrible noise and
woke the rest of the household, who would come running to see what
devil was attacking their parents.

Kwaku lay down beside his crippled wife, who, he knew, would
not fall asleep before two or three in the morning. It was her
incessant turning in the bed that managed to dislodge the support
cross-boards. He kept telling himself that Mr Barzey could not
really be dead. Mr Barzey and his uncle were the only two men in a
crowd of shadowy males, who were for him the male principle of the
world. While he was making money and acquiring a reputation as a
healer, his mounting pride had often taken the form of a dialogue
with them.

"You see," he would address his absent uncle, "I not a good-for-
nothing."

And on another occasion to Mr Barzey, "I goin' learn to talk like
you. I got the money now. I goin' learn not to lose me temper, and
how to crush people with a look."

His was a plague of men. Mr Barzey had been the first man to
respect him, the only one. Even a sponger and crab-dog like the
Customs officer would have peed on him, given half a chance, only
because he possessed the secret of letters and a fine handwriting. Mr
Barzey had been his God, a towering mora tree, a dacama giant
among dacama giants, rising from a pile of unrotted leaves beyond the
cluster of lianas, the clutter of relationships. But what was the good of
his strength and intellect? He ended up dangling from a noose. Even
his daughter-in-law would not have dreamt up such a punishment.

Kwaku was haunted by the fear that without his mentor he would
be exposed to the most terrible dangers from a hostile world. His
thoughts leapt from one possible disaster to another, disasters
heaped on him or brought about by his own conduct. He saw
himself freeing Mr Gordon's bulls, encompassed in a large corral.
Creeping up to the corral he would open the gate, then swiftly
clamber up a tree for safety. With a shout he would alert the
animals, one of which would, with a brusque twitch of his head, look
in his direction. One by one the bulls would rise and follow the one
that was standing by the open gate, then realizing that they were
free they would file out one by one, to appear unexpectedly in
people's yards, in early morning.

He also saw in his imagination areas of refuge, like the rum-shop,
and the company of a mangy dog that had been trampled underfoot
so frequently it could no longer resist the company of humans; the
boy singing by the wayside at night-time, a death-house in
Stanleytown, ravaged by the stench of a rotting young body

bedecked with flowers, waiting for its bridegroom. And at the foot of the stairs of that house a guava tree heavy with fruit as large as pomegranates. A shoemaker living in Winkle alone, who cared nothing for money, whose thoughts flew like butterflies on an iridescent wind, So came his thoughts from deep within him, charged with colours from the slumber-time of childhood. The short space of time when he could provide his wife with slippers and his children with sweets wrapped in paper from the jars of shop-holders was like a stain on the gravel, soon washed out in the primordial water from dark clouds.

31   Blossom's visit

RONA WAS sitting on one of the drawing-room chairs she had brought to the kitchen. At her feet, astride a minuscule stool, was her little sister, who grimaced whenever Rona passed the comb through her hair to mark off a square to be plaited. Neither of them spoke, nor did Philomena, who was washing the plates and spoons they had used for lunch – "breakfast", as they called it.

A great silence filled the house, a silence that, in a strange way, was not disturbed by the noise of the plates and spoons, nor by the desultory chirping of birds inhabiting the trees that seemed part of the house, so hard did they press against its flanks.

Philomena was anxious about Rona's reticence, about the fact that she had just bathed for the second time that day, as if she were determined to take all that the house had to offer before they were evicted. The electricity had already been cut off; and when night came the family gathered at the front to talk or brood by the light of the street lamp, a hallucinatory excretion to which the family, bred on kerosene illuminations and the light of the moon, had succumbed.

Fabian raised a hand in protest at Rona's vigorous use of the comb, but was slapped for her insolence.

"An' if you start crying I going put you to bed," Rona warned.

"I can't do nothing now!" Fabian protested.

"I say quiet!"

"Why you so irritable?" Philomena asked, without turning round to face Rona.

She received no answer.

That morning there had been a violent quarrel between Kwaku and the twin who was not working, in which their mother had made no effort to intervene. She sat on her chair looking upwards as though she were deaf as well or listening to a voice from without the house. It had been a day of threatened violence and portents.

"We going get a visit tomorrow," Miss Gwendoline had said. "Three people going come."

And it was this remark, made over a bowl of coffee, that had precipitated the quarrel. The twin had rebuked his mother.

"Why not say something 'bout my future? You always … ."

But before he could complete the sentence Kwaku had ordered him to shut up. The girls held themselves at the ready to spring between their brother and father, who seemed to welcome the opportunity to deal with his son. Rona, standing next to her brother, saw his clenched fists, the pale skin on his knuckles contrasting with the darker skin round it. Then, unexpectedly, he retreated through the back door.

After some time had passed, Philomena asked her sister once more, "Why you so irritable?"

"I not irritable."

She longed for the village and the predictable behaviour of her elder sister. The last few days she was nearly reduced to tears by her silences and the way she treated Fabian, who followed her around the house from morning till night.

It was Saturday morning and Philomena had put on her most attractive skirt over which she had tied a cloth before she started washing up. Her brassière formed a white rim round the edge of her blouse, like foam on the ridge of a brown wave. Having finished the washing-up she stood watching the embers in the coalpot, now surrounded by a circle of ashes. She looked into them and saw the features of the fisherman's sister who had run off with the powdered actor and was now perishing with her children in the bush. The image could not be that of anyone else, with its raindrop earrings and cold-pressed hair. Her mother had often enough repeated the story as a warning, but had only managed to rouse a slumbering desire to do what was forbidden. She kept staring at the cooling embers in the hollow of the coalpot

When Rona had finished plaiting Fabian's hair she made her fetch the shopping basket.

"You taking her?" Philomena enquired.

"No. I want to come back quick, and she does walk too slow."

"You going bring home something for me?" asked Fabian, who came back, holding the basket with both hands.

"With what money?" Rona asked sharply. But she bent down and kissed her all the same.

She left by the back door, perhaps to avoid being questioned by her mother, or because all the children had taken to using the back staircase, for a reason that was clear to no one.

Within the hour a stranger came bearing a message that Rona had left home for good. She took Kwaku to the spot where she had spoken to her, a few paces from the fire station; but despite the stranger's assistance in searching the market and enquiring in the shops she frequented his efforts to trace her were fruitless.

"Don' worry too much, Mister," said the woman when they gave up searching. "She mus' go to the market to buy. All-you mus' go to the market. Is man she gone to live with; and when girl children do that sort of thing man don' respect them. She going come back, take it from me. I did try to get her to go home. Is not that I didn' try."

Kwaku walked absently in the direction of his home.

"Rona," he reflected, "how she going live on her own?"

Unaware of the irony in his questioning he stumbled along, persisting in the delusion that Rona could not manage on her own.

"No, is Miss Gwendoline and Philomena alone," the thought forced itself on him when he arrived at his house.

Probably the woman was right. Rona would be back soon, tomorrow even. For of his teenage children she and Damon were the least able to manage without the family. That was as certain as the imminence of their eviction.

He found Miss Gwendoline with Philomena, Damon and Fabian. They were so stunned by the news that they were huddled together, Damon standing next to his mother and Fabian on her lap.

"She been acting funny since yesterday," Philomena said.

"How?" Miss Gwendoline demanded. "What she say?"

"She been hardly talking. And when she talk to Fabian she could only shout."

"She din' say nothing 'bout a friend or so?" her mother asked.

"No, Ma," Philomena answered, unusually subdued.

The family spent the afternoon in the gallery, suggesting clues as to Philomena's whereabouts; and with each promising suggestion Kwaku or Damon would rush out to hunt her afresh. They stayed in the gallery until evening and the endless calling of the cicadas began.

Miss Gwendoline pondered her dislike for Philomena, which she no longer denied to herself. She was in no doubt that her second daughter had been responsible for Rona's disappearance. All the whispering, the insolence had not been for nothing. Her mother had not come to assist her at Philomena's birth. Small wonder! How distressed she had been that her mother had kept away, when her birth pangs had lasted all day and the whole night that followed. Philomena had tortured her even before she was born, and she had never been able to forgive her.

Now that the running of the home was to be in her second daughter's hands she would be forced to show a more obliging face,

232

like the white-robed mummers at a country wake. In place of her anguish had grown an anger so consuming she dared not speak lest it be noticed.

Kwaku had arranged that they should move in with the old shoemaker in Winkle as soon as they were put out. Another season of suffering! But at least Fabian would never be far away in a house as small as that.

There had sprung up in Miss Gwendoline a craving for Kwaku's company, and once she had even persuaded him to take her to the rum-shop where he spent so many hours.

No, she should never have left the village. Yet, could she have stayed apart from Kwaku who, sooner or later, would have fallen a victim to Blossom's shameless intrigues? She was bound to come by his address in New Amsterdam, and, God knows, a lonely man could not be expected to resist the advances of a barefaced women.

From one of the neighbouring houses came singing, a brief outburst that died no sooner than it had begun.

When Miss Gwendoline trusted herself to speak she said, "Philomena, get the broom and sweep the house."

"At night-time? Is night-time, you know. And I sweep it this morning."

"Well, sweep it tomorrow morning as soon as you get up," replied Miss Gwendoline.

Kwaku knew what his wife had meant. A house was swept thoroughly after a funeral. She had wanted to offend Philomena, who had not understood. It was a warning to Damon as well, that they were not to follow in Rona's footsteps.

The children's presence prevented him from consoling Miss Gwendoline, whose only thought was to offend. Her blindness and the children's indifference, born of fear of their mother's condition had soured her. But for Kwaku she could do no wrong.

Kwaku, in the long silence that followed, imagined the bailiffs' arrival the next day, and feared above all his humiliation in front of the children. He even imagined the bailiff gesturing peremptorily in his act of dispossession, and himself going down the stairs, his wife on his arm, the long descent to the weed-covered garden and the warning never to return; and his hesitant look backwards and the exit through the iron gates. And like someone who is not content with his triumph, the bailiff would pursue him into the road and manhandle him in full view of Philomena, who would look on silently.

The wan light from the street lamp seemed to have faded since the day before, thought Kwaku, whose mind then went back to his nightmare about the malevolent monkeys, and the incessant journey of the solitary monkey on its long chain beneath his window.

Then came the urge to weep, on account of his impotence in face of a fate he could not control and the growing hostility of his twin sons. One had begun to have violent dreams, which he recounted with a truculent air, while the rest of the family sipped their black coffee and spoke as if muttering in their sleep.

All that night Fabian whimpered, even when she fell into a brief sleep. Philomena had warned her that if she pronounced Rona's name once she would not come back; but, unable to prevent the little one from crying, she lay down, her head in her hands, reconciled to the fact that she would not fall asleep for some time. Like Rona, she was not one for brooding. Like her she saw the break with her village boyfriend as another unexpected event, like a drought or a death, and was infinitely more distressed by the rending of a garment or the loss of her bead necklace, which went astray during the move to New Amsterdam.

Philomena was certain that Rona was now at the house of a man in his late twenties whom she used to allow to fondle her at the gate, even when their mother was at the window. From the top storey of the house she had seen this man stroking Rona's breast in the hot early afternoon sunshine, and she kept talking to him as if nothing were happening, as if what he was doing did not concern her. The man never came at night, but Rona never saw anything wrong with this.

"She's gone to this man's house, I'd bet my bottom dollar," thought Philomena.

How different was her attitude to this New Amsterdam man, whom she had met a short while ago. There was no teasing, no tormenting; and as soon as he went away she would insist on being alone, in some corner of the big house, usually in the shadow of the jacaranda or the back stairs.

One day, thought Philomena, she would go away too, away from the twins' persecution, from her father's cloying admiration and the demands of Fabian. But when she left it was to be with someone superior, who did not disrespect her.

Miss Gwendoline got up later than everyone else, took the calabash from the window ledge and felt her way to the bathroom, in order to get washed and prepare herself for the day.

After the first meal of coffee and unbuttered bread she took her place at the window as was her custom.

At mid-morning, when the bailiff was on everyone's mind, there were visitors. Miss Gwendoline raised her head higher than usual. "Is who, ne?"

"Is me, Wilfred, Miss Gwendoline."

"O Lord! Come in, ne? What you standing on the stairs for?"

"Is Blossom at the gate," Wilfred said. "She can come up too?"

"How you mean she can come up? Bring her up!"

The couple did not expect that welcome and had planned how to make Blossom's visit acceptable to Miss Gwendoline.

"Allyou come!" she shouted out. "Philomena! Is Blossom and Wilfred!"

Miss Gwendoline recognized Fabian's footsteps.

"Go and get your sister, child. Tell her Blossom come."

And no sooner did the couple enter the house – Wilfred had waited for his wife to come up – than Philomena appeared.

"Is you?" she asked, never able to conceal her admiration for Blossom.

They kissed each other, and whether it was that the gesture escaped Miss Gwendoline or she did not mind, she continued smiling.

"Go and get you father," Miss Gwendoline called out. "He somewhere at the back. No, bring a chair from the dining-room first. Fabian, you tell Pa we got visitors."

"When you come back," Blossom said to Fabian, at the same time half-stifling her with an embrace, "I got something for you."

Blossom drew out gifts from a plastic bag, a pair of sun-shades for Miss Gwendoline, five pounds of garlic powder for Kwaku and trinkets for the girls. There was nothing for the boys, for it was not seemly to bring presents for boys in their teens.

"Yesterday," said Miss Gwendoline, "I tell them we going have visitors. They din' believe me. You see? But I did say three would come, and is only you two."

Blossom and Wilfred exchanged glances.

"I expecting," Blossom said quietly.

"You ... at last!" exclaimed Miss Gwendoline with evident relief.

Kwaku came back with the chair and a large tin can.

"You're the last people I did expect to see," he declared. "We lend out the chairs. Which one of you going sit 'pon this thing?"

Wilfred took the tin can from him and sat down carefully on it.

"You hear?" Miss Gwendoline said. "Blossom expecting. She wait till we leave to get pickney."

"We hear things bad," Wilfred said to Kwaku, "so we bring food."

The two men left the room, Kwaku carrying the bag with the food.

"So you expecting!" said Miss Gwendoline. "Come le' me feel your belly."

Blossom got up and allowed herself to be examined by Miss Gwendoline, who felt the contours of her stomach, while Blossom stared unwaveringly at Kwaku, who had come back without Wilfred.

She only looked away when she realized that Philomena was watching her.

"I stop working although it not showing yet," Blossom said.

"It in' showing yet. You right," Miss Gwendoline remarked. "And what if it showing! My mother work right up to the week before I born and it in' do me no hurt."

"Is the jolting in the bus," Blossom declared. "And I was always having bad feelings .... Is where Rona? She gone out?"

Damon had just entered the drawing-room, barefoot and dirty, as if he had been catching crabs.

"Rona gone," Miss Gwendoline answered softly, her voice quivering with emotion. "Only yesterday."

"You mean she leave home?"

"She sixteen," answered Miss Gwendoline, "so she's woman, you see. Nowadays you's woman at sixteen."

"She was so obedient," said Blossom halfheartedly.

"She leave, and the bailiff coming today, at the latest tomorrow. Is so children stay nowadays."

"All right," said Kwaku, embarrassed in the presence of Wilfred, who had meanwhile returned. "Don' work yourself up. She gone. We going sleep today. Tomorrow's a day for talking. Plum-tree wood don' rot, but we made out of flesh and blood."

Then, after a pause, Kwaku continued. "You know what Mr Gordon did tell me? He say the first thing he notice when he come back to Guyana was that there wasn't any second-hand shops. In a poor country like this and all."

"Three come as I did say," declared Miss Gwendoline, taking no notice of what Kwaku had been saying.

"How you mean?"

"Yesterday I saw three people was going to come and three come. Wilfred, Blossom and the child Blossom carrying."

"Oh, yes," Philomena said with surprise, casting an involuntary eye at Blossom's waist.

And everyone felt uncomfortable, as though a secret had been revealed.

"I wish I did live in a big house like this," said Blossom.

"It got two toilets an' a bathroom with tiles," put in Philomena.

"You mus' show me before I go."

"Come now, then," Philomena offered.

She and Blossom went off to see the tiled bathroom, accompanied by Wilfred.

Miss Gwendoline seized the opportunity to ask Kwaku how Blossom looked, and was pleased to hear that she had become ugly.

"Soon she goin' be big," said Miss Gwendoline, her face transfigured, "and no man will want to look 'pon her."

236

"True," agreed Kwaku. "She wasn' much to look at before. But when you come to think of it, how many of us is much to look at?"

Miss Gwendoline did not reply. Her first recollection of ugliness was as a very small child, when a visitor materialized, a well-dressed man with gold teeth, which, in her young mind made up for his repulsiveness. Ugliness could only be cured with gold. In her early teens she discovered a well of vanity within herself and was unable to abide her indifferent appearance; and she came to believe that her lack was redeemable with gold and jewellery. Then when, as a mother with big children, her husband presented her daughter with jewellery the gesture seemed to her to denote an equivocation beyond the bestowal on the child of a token of affection. Philomena was a beautiful child.

A few minutes later, Philomena and Blossom came back with food from the package, and the latter was touched by the immoderate appetite of Kwaku and his family, and by the way Miss Gwendoline left a debris of rice around her chair on the floor. The children, hunched forward on their boxes and a tin can, were facing different directions and, like their father, took no notice of the way Miss Gwendoline was eating.

"You ever hear a organ play?" Kwaku asked Wilfred.

"Only on the radio."

Wilfred, who thought he hated Kwaku, felt such pity for him now that he listened intently whenever he spoke. Besides, his suspicions as to Blossom's infidelity now centred on a bus-driver. Kwaku had lost weight more rapidly than the others and his elongated skull had the effect of emphasizing his haggard appearance.

"I don' know why I ask," remarked Kwaku. "They got so many churches in this town. Churches and clocks. Well, I hear a organ in a church here."

"It wasn't a organ, Pa," Damon corrected him. "Was a harmonium."

"Was a lil' organ; but it's still a organ," Kwaku insisted.

"A organ got reeds," Damon said.

"Boy, you telling me 'bout organ?" Kwaku asked scornfully. "I been christened in a church with organ. If you look in that harmonium you goin' see small pipes. Is a organ, I tell you. In fact the name harmonium mean 'harmonious organ'. Now you put that in your pipe and smoke it!"

"He right, you know, Pa," Philomena said.

"Child, listen to me. You know any instrument you does play with you foot?" Kwaku asked, turning to Philomena. "Is only organ you does play with foot. A harmonium you don' play with you foot, so is a organ. Now that is logic! You does play drum with you foot? You does play violin an' guitar with foot? Answer me! You does play clarinet with you foot? When last you see a foot-playing trumpeter? You ever hear a man footing the trumpet? You see him lipping it, but I sure nobody ever see him with his toes curl round a trumpet mouthpiece. Don' bother with Damon; he in' got experience and what's more he in' got logic."

Then, prodding Damon in his back, Kwaku said, "Admit you wrong, ne? It in' a crime to be wrong."

"But I right!" Damon decalred.

"Admit it, I say!" exclaimed Kwaku, leaping up from his seat. "Admit you don' got logic, you numbskull!"

"Is what wrong with you?" Miss Gwendoline asked.

Wilfred restrained Kwaku, who was glaring at his son as if he had done some terrible wrong.

Just then there was a banging on the front door and the company looked at one another, struck dumb by the sudden, portentous knocking which reverberated round the enormous building.

"Is him!" declared Miss Gwendoline.

"And I did forget to bolt the door," Kwaku said.

The knocking started again, a loud, hostile assault on the door. Kwaku rushed out of the drawing-room and Wilfred followed him.

They found three men in the gallery itself.

"Who give you permission to come in my house?" Kwaku demanded.

"I'm sorry, I thought no one was in," the man in uniform said.

"Well, get out again!" Kwaku ordered with a sweep of his hand.

Instead of complying, the man took a folded piece of blue paper from his picket and insolently thrust it under Kwaku's nose.

"Go on, then!" Kwaku shouted. "Take it, ne. Take what you can find!"

Miss Gwendoline appeared in the drawing-room, led by Damon.

"Is the bailiff," Kwaku told her. "Christ and his two disciples."

"You don't shame?" she screamed. "You in' got a family? We living on what my son does earn. All-you don't provide work, but you take away the roof from over people head. Let me tell you! If you put us out you going eat raw food for the rest of you life and everywhere you turn you going find broken glass."

The three men ignored her and went into the drawing-room, to the back of the house, followed by Philomena and Fabian.

Miss Gwendoline made Damon take her to the gallery and she waited there until he came back with her chair from the dining-room.

Kwaku, in his humiliation, went to hide at the back. The footsteps trampling the floorboards of his house, just as if he were the stranger and the strangers lived there, obliged him to press his hands to his ears. Then he closed his eyes, the better to induce the storm of

238

images that drove him to do foolish things in childhood and the early days of his marriage. He saw a pleated skirt, a man on a short-tailed horse and a sky covered with kites at Easter time, swarming over the blue like coloured tadpoles. There was sweet-smelling urucu smeared on an aboriginal Indian face, and spread out beside it a pack of playing-cards. The fisherman had something to do with his plight, he was now certain, the keeper of the dogs, all because he did not fulfil a promise to bring back his sister. O God! How could they all share that tiny house in Winkle? ... And Philomena with her soft, moss-like lips, was she to live in the same house as the mad shoemaker? A creature so twisted from living alone? What were they ferreting about his house for? They were not permitted to take his beds, his clothes and cooking utensils. All they could find was the chair, an axe and a brace of stone eagles.

In his despair Kwaku sneaked into the drawing-room to see if he could catch sight of Philomena. But she was not there. She must have taken Fabian downstairs to shield her from her parents' distress.

Blossom touched Miss Gwendoline on the shoulder to let her know that she had joined her.

"I sorry, Miss Gwendoline," Blossom said.

"Yesterday was Rona ... now this. If Rona was here I could've stand it. You see, I don' trust Philomena, with all her airs. Nobody in my family ever had them airs, and in Kwaku family neither. He uncle don't get them airs."

"Some people born that way, Miss Gwendoline," declared Blossom. "But she's a good girl."

"You say so, 'cause you don't know her. When she in company she always got to take somebody aside and whisper; she can't join the conversation with everybody else. She's sly, I telling you, and don't think of nobody excepting herself."

"If you want," said Blossom, "I could take one of the children to live with me till better times."

Miss Gwendoline tried to find with her gaze the place from which Blossom's voice came.

"Irene and Clayton been with their grandmother such a long time," Miss Gwendoline declared, "I don' even know what they look like any more. Children should know their mother .... You're a good woman. I always did see that, but I couldn' bear you hanging 'bout Kwaku, you understand? Is not that I don' like you. You don' got a ounce of malice in you. Is this long, long friendship I can't favour, like if the two of you know something I don' know. Sometimes I does feel like walking round the house and touching everything, the partitions, the banisters, the window-sills; but there's always somebody home, watching what you doing. When I had me eyes I didn' care for privacy ... . So many things gone and change. I does jump at the slightest noise now. What I going to tell Kwaku for? He got enough on his mind with the wild men ... is the twins, shouting, banging doors late at night. I sure they does bring women in the house when the rest sleeping, 'cause more than once I did smell perfume. Kwaku know, but he frighten to say anything .... You sure Wilfred won't mind if you take Damon? He like children?"

"I don' know if he like children," Blossom replied, "but if he don' like them he going got to pretend."

"All right, take him. He won't give you no trouble."

"He'll want to come?" asked Blossom.

Miss Gwendoline nodded.

"You think so?"

"I know so."

The bailiff and his men could be heard pounding the boards in the room above them.

"What they doing so long?" Miss Gwendoline demanded.

"They going shake all the mattresses to see if anything hide in them," Blossom informed her. "But they can't put you out."

"Who say so?" asked Miss Gwendoline urgently.

"The order is to levy on you. They got to get a court order to evict you. Is not the same thing."

"Call Kwaku quick, then," Miss Gwendoline urged her. "He at the back or downstairs. Send one of the children."

Miss Gwendoline, left alone, listened intently to the sounds in the house, and believed she could hear four men upstairs. She did not know that Wilfred had joined them.

Her thoughts turned to Blossom and she regretted having treated her badly in the past for, after all, the friendship with Kwaku had borne fruit. What was more, there had been no intimacy between them. She was convinced that this was so.

The trampling on the stairs announced the approach of the bailiff and his men.

"Where's your husband, Mistress?" the bailiff asked.

"I don' know."

Kwaku had slipped away. Now, while the men were discussing what to do next, he came through the front door.

"You know it's against the law to hide any chattels that can be distrained," the bailiff said pompously.

"He didn' hide anything!" Miss Gwendoline said defiantly. "We're poor people."

"Poor people living in *this* house?" the bailiff sneered.

He looked at his colleagues and then, repressing his anger, said to Kwaku, "We'll be back, Mister. And you better have some chattels."

240

He stormed out of the house, followed by the other two men.

Kwaku, watching them go from the window, shouted out, "Bring six bailiffs, you jumped-up crab-dog! Bring you mother and you father and you decrepit grandparents ...! "

Kwaku's voice got louder as the men increased the distance between themselves and the house.

"Come on, you knock-knee, cross-eyed battican! " he screamed. "Nex' time I going throw you out with my bare hands! "

Philomena was in tears on the back stairs, and Fabian, who had cried for so long after Rona went away, could only stand by her sister, bewildered at the events. She could not understand why her father and mother had allowed three men whom they did not know to do as they pleased in the house, and believed that Blossom's visit was connected with the untoward happening.

Miss Gwendoline told Kwaku what Blossom had said about the unlikelihood of eviction that day and he calmed down.

"Blossom want to take Damon away till things get better," she said to Kwaku. "What we goin' stand in his way for?"

"Who's goin' stand in his way? Not me."

No one had asked Wilfred, who stood aside in his sullen manner, trying to catch Blossom's eye. First Kwaku, then Mr Chalfen. Now Damon. He could no longer pretend that he had any control over the running of his home. He had believed that the loss of Blossom's job would make her more dependent on him, but she still did as she pleased. The threats he used to utter soon after their marriage proved to be hollow, and he was reduced to contemplating her self-willed behaviour with a show of mute consternation.

"Why they din' take the axe?" asked Miss Gwendoline.

"'Cause I hide it." Kwaku said. "It right there, 'pon the roof of the porch .... We not make to live in town. We's village people .... Look at it out there, all them houses, all them people drinking and shouting and evicting other people. Look at it; it like a snake with red eyes, calling you, calling and whistling like comoodie snake, 'Phew, phew, phew. Come, I going put meself round you. Go to sleep, lil' village man.' And when you wake up you see the snake love you so much he squeeze you till you guts come out, slow, slow, till you got no pride and you go to sleep for good .... You see how the twin learn 'bout using the telephone, 'bout electricity and all? And they tell him if he good at studying he could become a engineer. But this place frighten the life out of me, I can tell you."

While Damon was getting ready to go with Blossom, Miss Gwendoline sat Fabian on her lap and explained why her brother was going away. Then she began singing, to console not only the child but herself for a dwindling family. And all the while Philomena could not keep her eyes off Blossom.

"They think because I can't see ..." said Miss Gwendoline reflectively, addressing no one in particular. "Last night I dream Rona cut off all her hair and send it to me by post. When she was a lil' girl people used to wonder how she did manage to plait her hair fine, fine, fine, and tuck the plaits under for the night. Kwaku used to say, 'Look how she doing she gardening.' She was a glutton for work. How I was to know she fed up?"

"Who say she was fed up?" Kwaku said, trying to take the blame from his wife's shoulders.

"If she was fed up she should've say so," continued Miss Gwendoline. "She only had to say so and I would've understand."

"I tell you is not your fault," Kwaku put in. "Is the town. They got town trouble and village trouble."

At last Damon was ready. Although he was nearly fifteen he was still in short trousers, and his long legs seemed incongruous in the company.

"Don't give Miss Blossom or Wilfred no trouble, you hear?"

Damon said goodbye to his mother, who made him bend down to receive a parting kiss.

"When you father business flourishing we going send for you," Miss Gwendoline said. Everyone but her saw the gesture of contempt he made.

"Be respectful to your uncle," Kwaku added. "He's the only family you got in the village."

Damon hurried out of the house, ahead of Wilfred and Blossom, to avoid the rain of advice that was about to descend upon him, while the latter set about making their long goodbyes.

Blossom lifted Fabian high into the air and spoke to her.

"You want to come and stay with me one day? During the holidays? Eh, feetee?·I going make you a dress and we can go for a walk on the back dam. An' we could get Uncle Wilfred to take us to the pictures."

But Fabian did not know what to make of these words after the turmoil of a while ago, and just stared at Blossom with watery eyes.

"Promise you going come?" Blossom asked.

Fabian nodded in a show of compliance and involuntarily turned around to see if Philomena was still there.

Blossom embraced Philomena in turn, aware of the impression she had made on the strange girl.

"You come too, one day," she told her.

The whole family leaned out of the window to watch them go, and even Miss Gwendoline turned towards the street, her mouth slightly open and her eyes flickering in the afternoon sunlight.

The others saw Blossom, Wilfred and Damon turn the corner and go out of sight where there was a row of signs printed in thick capital letters: STICK NO BILLS.

"She join the Seventh-Day Adventists, you know," said Miss Gwendoline, only to hide her emotion. "No pork, no trousers, no dancing, no work on Saturdays."

"She tell you so?" asked Kwaku.

"Yes, when we was alone she say she join them. But on Mashramani she wear her trousers and Wilfred get vexed. He say she in' not Seventh-Day Adventist if she wear trousers."

In the end Miss Gwendoline was left alone. The silence in the house brought back her youthful days, the days of dependence, and the first party she attended, when she was thirteen years old. She and other girls her age remained upstairs, hankering after the freedom of the older ones, who mixed freely with the young men and danced to their hearts' content. Yet, when two youths came upstairs the girls were tongue-tied. Then one girl who picked up courage to address them spoke harshly and the young men retreated, believing they were not wanted.

She recalled her first encounter with death. Her grandfather died soon afterwards, an old man with a full head of hair, his Portuguese ancestry betrayed by his bloodless complexion. An old woman bent down to wipe the corpse's sweating forehead before she, Gwendoline, was permitted to kiss him for the last time. And her revulsion was deepened by the hair on his face, which had continued to grow after he died. The body had been turned to the east, but no one could say why, nor why the blinds of the houses in the village were drawn and the windows closed when the procession set out for the village cemetery. These were the mysteries of life to which the villagers attached so much importance. In town, instead, there were big houses, signs with Stick No Bills and a terrible isolation. She had been happy in three different homes, her parents', her grandparents' and that of an aunt by repute, whose husband collected pictures of horses and endowed his children with a legacy of equine names. In retrospect her childhood had been a long preparation for the present time of sounds and perpetual darkness. She had accepted the changes that came with her blindness and wished only that she should die before Kwaku, for life without him would be intolerable.

Evening fell, and the gentle hours; the street lamp came on, paler than the morning star, smothering the porch and windows in an eerie, oppressive light.

Once more the Cholmondeley family went to bed in the belief that they were spending their last night in the mansion they could not afford, and which, despite its attractive appearance, had only seen seventeen clients to test their father's prowess as a healer.

243

The twins were the last to retire, having come home after eleven at night with friends, who left long after the sound of traffic had died away.

32   Kwaku and Miss Gwendoline

NEW AMSTERDAM was smothered with rain, a massive downpour that had begun late at night and continued throughout the morning. The vehicles silently creeping by the rum-shop appeared to be straining through the water, as incapacitated as the men and women obliged to make their way home or betake themselves on some urgent errand. Overhead the electric wires swayed and tossed in the gusts of wind that blew up the street in the direction of Stanleytown.

Kwaku sat at a table with his wife, looking out of a side window of the rum-shop, where the charred greenheart and more timbers of a burnt-out building could be seen and, beyond a low tenement range obscured by the extraordinary precipitation of water.

No one could be heard speaking, not even the customers who from time to time went up to the counter to order a schnapps glass or a bottle of local beer. The noise of money given as change was the only sound that competed with the rain, a sharp explosion, like the crack of a whip.

When, after a long interval, someone pushed the swing doors, his entrance was like an intrusion into a private world of boredom and despair. And on each of these occasions the mangy dog – it had kept vigil in front of the shop for more than a year – slunk in, in the shadow of the customer, but was driven out into the rain by someone who had seen or smelt it.

Empty tables were separated from their chairs by a gap that was larger than usual, as if the customers who had been sitting at them had left in extreme irritation, thrusting them back as they got up. Although the rain had not penetrated into the rum-shop everything was covered in a damp film and the walls themselves seemed to ooze water from their insides.

The sound of a clanging bell got lounder, and as a vehicle thundered by, everyone raised his head. It was indeed the fire-engine! On another day the occurrence would have been greeted with laughter, but no sooner had the mystery been solved than heads were bowed again.

Kwaku got up, but Miss Gwendoline held him back.

"No more."

"One more."

"I say no more!" she exclaimed.

Kwaku shrugged his shoulders, felt his trouser pocket with his right hand, and with difficulty pulled a small, round bottle from it. He unscrewed the top and put the bottle to his mouth. Miss Gwendoline began mumbling.

"What you say?" Kwaku asked.

"The twins going to get you," she repeated aloud.

The night before, the twins had called him out of the Winkle house he now shared with the shoemaker, he, Miss Gwendoline, Philomena and little Fabian. They had enticed him out on the pretext that someone needed a healer and they would take him to the house of the sick person. They had dragged him by force behind an old blacksmith's establishment, where abandoned cartwheels were rotting on the damp ground, and there thrashed him for several minutes.

"We got a decent place for Ma!" one of them kept saying with every blow.

They left him propped up against the wall of the derelict building, like one of those ventriloquists' dummies that appear in American films.

"The twins going get you 'cause you don't hear," Miss Gwendoline repeated.

Kwaku put away the bottle, and Miss Gwendoline could not say whether he had done so on account of the warning or whether the two shots he had drunk had satisfied him. He turned, contemplated her as though he had seen her for the first time, then looked away again.

One of the barmen came over to them, a cloth in his hand.

"Is what happen to you?" he asked, alarmed at the condition of Kwaku's face.

"I fall down the stairs. Is that big house. I does get giddy jus' by looking down them stairs."

"Look," said the barman, "everybody know you not living in the big house no more. Everybody know you living in Winkle."

Then, irritated by the effort of speaking in the heavy atmosphere, he left Kwaku with the words: "As long as you don't tell people you get that face in the rum-shop."

"It big, eh?" Kwaku said to his wife.

"What?"

"That burnt-out house," he declared, as though his wife were capable of seeing. "Funny how they got big and little things .... I know a woman once had one big breast and a lil' one. She inherit the big one from she mother side and the .... "

Kwaku scratched his head. "Me mouth hurting me," he complained.

"Then shut it," Miss Gwendoline declared.

He had an urge to do what the others around him were not doing and to say whatever came into his mind; but after a few words his mouth began to pain him even more.

"I hear that in America they got lil' pieces of metal that can do the work of hundreds of people. They say millions of people going be out of work and there going be a revolution."

"We always had· that sort of unemployment," said Miss Gwendoline absently, "but there in' been no revolution ... . The twin that out of work in' revolt yet."

"I know," said Kwaku, tensing himself with pain, but unable to let Miss Gwendoline's retort pass. "But the twin is only one person. Tobesides, what you call that? The way he and his brother tear me to pieces last night? If that not a revolution then I'm a monkey's uncle."

Miss Gwendoline had already lost her way in her husband's words and failed to answer. She accompanied him to the rum-shop, she told Philomena, to see that he did not get into trouble, but had begun drinking herself, though the taste of rum revolted her.

The rainy season had followed an exceptionally long dry season, at the height of which Philomena had announced that she was pregnant. She was barely sixteen. Blossom had replied promptly to her letter asking for advice, declaring that she would come and see them, and urging Philomena to put off telling her parents until her visit.

Blossom came with her four-month-old son, a beautiful child wrapped in pink gauze. And it was while Kwaku was rocking it in his arms and whispering endearments into its porcelain ears that Philomena announced that she was expecting. Kwaku had suspected her condition but dared not say anything to Miss Gwendoline, whose dislike for her daughter had increased as she came to depend on her more and more.

"I getting a child," Philomena had said defiantly. Her words were accompanied by a burst of laughter from the house next door.

Kwaku, who found the silence that followed unbearable, said loudly, "It in' a crime, is it?"

"God give us children to destroy us," Miss Gwendoline intoned, as if singing. "So you getting child! We savings run out and we living off your brother, who got to keep his brother too and can't even go out at night because he must save his shoes. And you getting child."

Miss Gwendoline called to mind the young man with sweet words who visited and talked of clothes and relations abroad, who talked incessantly. Philomena had fallen for his impeccable manners and sartorial elegance. Miss Gwendoline did not like him. No one liked him, not even Philomena who, having waited too long for an encounter with her ideal, now deceived herself that Ivor was a cut above the other men and youths who called out or tugged her when darkness had fallen.

"Is who own?" Miss Gwendoline had asked.

"Is Ivor's! Who else I does see? Who else I can see here? Who would come here? Your darling Rona din' want to come here 'cause her man-friend would've up and left her. She did spread her wings; but I remain!"

Philomena stood defiantly in the centre of the room. "I stay 'cause of Fabian."

"I know!" shrieked Miss Gwendoline.

Blossom took her son from Kwaku and went out into the yard, where the neighbours, who had done the same on hearing the quarrel, were listening intently.

"Well, now you know!" Philomena shouted at them.

Miss Gwendoline, thinking that the words were meant for her, said, "If I had my eyes you couldn't a talk to me like that."

"If you had your eyes," Philomena answered, "I wouldn't be here!"

Kwaku had stood by, torn between loyalties. When the quarrel came to an abrupt end he went to the door and told Blossom to come back in.

Now in the oppressive silence of the rum-shop, longing to speak, but prevented from doing so because of his injuries and Miss Gwendoline's strictures, he recalled the injuries with mortification. In that room on that October day were the women he loved most and his infant son, Blossom's child. As he rocked it in his arms he wanted to shout out his claim to the little creature with clenched fists, but was saved from an indiscretion by the quarrel between his wife and daughter.

Was not Miss Gwendoline right? He had never seen so many babies before, just at a time when the country seemed to be sinking under its weight of debt and ambitions. He saw disaster everywhere, and the man who had laid claim to the telephone booth, was he not a portent of worse to come?

These last few weeks the belief grew in him that Miss Gwendoline would fall ill, and every morning he enquired of her health.

"You sleep good?" he never failed to enquire.

One night he woke up to find Philomena lying on her back, displaying the flower of her nakedness where her dress had ridden up as she slept. He stared at the tuft of hair, crossed himself and lay down again. But, unable to drop off, he crept across to kneel over his daughter. And it was only when she turned in her sleep that he went back to his bedclothes on the floor and feasted on the memory of her youth.

Kwaku no longer wanted to work, for despite his family's deprivation and the threat of his sons' brutality he had become accustomed to the complete freedom he enjoyed. He had laid up a hoard of large rum bottles to be sold for drink when his savings ran out, with the first three of which he had paid for his rum three hours previously.

The rum bottle in his pocket had been bought for the shoemaker, who had given him the money before he left. Kwaku, intending to replace what he drank with water on his way home, drew the bottle out of his pocket once more and took a long draught from it.

"You mustn't steal," Miss Gwendoline said reproachfully.

"I know. I can beat you, fornicate with a whore, watch me family go to the dogs and not work. I can do anything. Anything! But I musn't steal."

He gave a long suck-teeth then took another draught from the bottle.

Soon after the move to Winkle, the twins moved in with friends who had started a commune in a derelict house, the owners of which had emigrated. Philomena said that they and their women spent the evenings smoking ganja and singing Rastafarian hymns. She had said this with disgust and Kwaku recalled the night she had gone out accompanied by Fabian and returned with glazed eyes and dilated pupils.

"I musn't steal," declared Kwaku. "You are right. I won't steal, just for you and the two children we got left. And for the grandchild *on the way*. Aha! It might get lost, our grandchild on the way. Funny how we does talk. I on my way too, and you on your way ...."

"You mouth not hurting you no more?" Miss Gwendoline asked sarcastically.

"No, I put it to sleep with the shoemaker rum," replied Kwaku. "But I ask you something. I on my way, you on your way to the place all these infants come from. And what I want to know is why we don't meet. You can answer that? By rights we should meet. And how all these children on their way know the road? Lil' children, crawling *on the way*, how they know what turning to take?"

"You talking stupid," Miss Gwendoline remarked, dismissing his enquiry.

Kwaku passed the shoemaker's rum bottle to Miss Gwendoline, for the bump it made in his pocket kept reminding him of the need to wet his dry throat. Now that the rum was out of reach Kwaku felt a twinge of conscience, remembering that the shoemaker had moved into the little kitchen at the foot of the back stairs to accommodate his family.

"Tcha!" he thought. "To hell with all that!"

But in his slow decline into a sort of idiotic bliss the one thing that worried him constantly was his longing for drink and the lack of means to satisfy it. Even the possibility of being waylaid by the twins held no terrors for him, nor the coming birth of his grandchild.

No one entered the rum-shop, even after four o'clock when clerks went home, or five o'clock, when municipal employees ceased work. And with the departure of the odd customer into the deluge Kwaku and Miss Gwendoline were the only customers left, apart from two notorious alcoholics, who were always there to enter the rum-shop before both leaves of the door were open and had to be helped out of it at closing time.

The mangy dog had slipped inside and was shivering under an empty table. At the slightest sound it raised its head, ever ready to obey an order to get out or an encouraging kick in its flanks.

When dusk fell, Miss Gwendoline gave the signal that it was time for them to go. Kwaku picked up her stick and helped her up.

Once outside they were drenched before they were on their way.

"The taxis stop running!" a voice called out from the other side of the road. "Everything stop running."

Kwaku and Miss Gwendoline walked through the rain as though it was the most natural thing to do, she with her head held high and he seeking out obstacles on the pavement. Two clocks began to strike six almost simultaneously, with a ghostly ringing sound which, according to old people, can still be heard on the sites of once thriving blacksmiths' shops in Winkle on the eve of Pentecost.

The warm rain lashed the couple's faces, at times driven in a spray by a horizontal wind and at other times in swollen drops that fell diagonally. In the distance the downpour seemed to fall upwards into the emptiness of an invisible sky. Houses came and went in the evening mist like shadows, and as the couple went by the mansion they once inhabited Kwaku could not resist casting a longing glance at it and reflecting on the shelter it must afford those who had come after them.

The long road to Winkle under an ink-black pall of clouds, the shuddering trees, the empty side streets from which nothing escaped, and flocks of birds returning to land with a jerking flight....

Kwaku, without telling Miss Gwendoline where he was going, left home one afternoon with a sugar bag. He made for the street in which the mansion stood and there took the lid off the dustbin of a house with a broad drive. The plantain, sweet-potato and other skins he found in it were transferred to his coarse hessian bag, together with any other food remains he could find. He went from house to house, from dustbin to dustbin until his bag was full. Then he took the side streets across the town to a house on the edge of the

Canje creek where lived a pig-breeder with whom he had come to an arrangement. After collecting two dollars and fifty cents he went back home to fetch Miss Gwendoline, for they had taken to drinking at night, to allow Philomena and her man-friend some privacy.

"You coming?"

"The birth pains start," his wife told him. "Blossom say she would come today, but she in' come."

Kwaku went next door to beg the neighbours for help. And when the room was full with the neighbours and her women friends he made off to drink alone, for the first time in more than a year.

He came back when the rum-shop closed, but fled at the sight of so many lamps burning in the room. When he returned, after sleeping for a couple of hours under the Canje bridge, he took courage and went in, to find the women sharing a hot meal with Miss Gwendoline. The conversation stopped, for they had been trying to persuade her to leave Kwaku for good and go home to her mother's village.

"Is a girl, Mr Cholmondeley," the neighbour told him. "And that man who does visit your daughter not going marry her."

"Is a beautiful child," one of the neighbours' friends added, in a more conciliatory voice.

The women got up to go at the first light of dawn and Kwaku could then take his grandchild up for the first time and admire its well-formed body.

But, as the weeks went by it was evident that the child was not normal, just as his suspicions about Philomena's pregnancy were gradually confirmed by the thickening of her waist. His heart went out to his daughter, herself little more than a child, and he hoped fervently that one day he would be able to do something for her, bestow on her a gift more precious than a gold necklace. Mr Barzey had once said that all women had a secret urge to return to their mothers' home. Philomena had never left hers.

Blossom came, after a lengthy illness. She brought her son, who was now walking. Kwaku had written that his grandchild was a mongol, and she brought a book for Philomena, an old book of pictures illustrating Guyanese folktales, because, as she thought, any present that appealed to her vanity would have been inappropriate. But Philomena was not expected home until late that night.

She longed to talk to Kwaku about their son, about Wilfred, who had taken to the boy as if it were his own. The child had united them and had brought peace to their house. But, on account of his wife, Kwaku took care never to be alone when Blossom came visiting.

Less than an hour later Philomena came in, dressed in an armless blouse and a short skirt.

"Well, well!" she exclaimed, like a woman of the world.

The young woman embraced Blossom with such sincerity that she had to hold back her tears. She had expected to see her dejected, ill-clad, cowering in a corner. Instead, her clothes were well-made and her handbag, decorated with a sculptured metal clasp, came from abroad.

Philomena took Blossom's boy to show him off to her neighbours, pretending that he was a relation! And when she came back she offered to accompany her to the stelling.

Miss Gwendoline knew that her daughter intended telling Blossom about her secret life, about the source of her money with which she bought the expensive clothes hung up on the walls in plastic coverings, short skirts and long ones, dresses buttoned down the front, blouses with ruffled sleeves like those worn by women in Columbia, and other elegances.

And Philomena told her idol much, that she had a longing to wear men's clothes, that she did not feel she could ever love a man. But she could not speak of what she wanted to confide most of all. She told Blossom that she had always known where Rona lived, but had promised not to tell. Yes, Rona was happy.

They said goodbye on the stelling and Philomena waited to see the ferry-boat depart, across the Berbice river.

That night Kwaku and Miss Gwendoline left Philomena and her man-friend with their child and went off to the rum-shop, armed with the money he had made from disposing of the pig-food. It was Republic Day and everywhere there were revellers, young people in fantastical dress, shouting greetings and slogans. The entrance to the mansion in which they once lived was decorated with red bulbs and Kwaku saw again the lights of Albion Sugar Estate on his journey back from the Courantyne when he was a successful healer. He saw the lights now, like clotted blood on the night's dark skin.

Further on they had to make a detour to avoid tripping over the legs of the man who had taken over the telephone booth. He was sleeping with his head turned aside, so that his breath had clouded the glass where he enhaled.

The rum-shop was overflowing with people, most of whom would never have dreamt of drinking there in normal times. They even stood in the side street with their glasses in their hands. Kwaku, who found great difficulty in passing through the crowd, nudged his wife to go ahead. Miss Gwendoline changed the stick she was carrying from her left to her right, and the men gave way in front of her, Kwaku keeping close behind.

Inside, the customers were even more densely packed, and Kwaku despaired of finding a seat for Miss Gwendoline or of reaching the counter to buy his rum. He left her standing by the wall, promising to be back as soon as he could.

When at last he returned, grasping a half bottle of rum, Miss Gwendoline was no longer there.

"Miss Gwendoline!" he shouted.

"If you looking for the blind lady she sitting over there," said an old man he had never seen in the rum-shop before.

Kwaku pushed and shoved in the direction the stranger had pointed, until he stumbled against the table at which Miss Gwendoline was sitting.

"How you get it?" he shouted above the din.

"Is a man bring me to it," she replied.

He poured a shot of rum for her and they drank an unspoken toast to the years they had been together and to the children they had brought into the world. He began stroking her head, and while doing so thought of Damon.

"Blossom din' say nothing 'bout Damon," he said.

"She din' want to tell you that you uncle refuse to take him, that's why."

Kwaku did not understand what his wife had said and the couple gave up any attempt at conversing in the noise around them.

The shirts of the men standing about were drenched with sweat, as if they had been dancing, despite the wind through the open swing doors, which had been latched to the wall.

Of late Kwaku needed only a couple of shots to make him unsteady on his feet and Miss Gwendoline was determined to keep the rum bottle until he could sit next to her. She made no attempt to stop him drinking altogether, for she herself could no longer do without the daily ration of alcohol, nor the sorties from the dreary room in Winkle. Unable to see the eccentric shoemaker, she attributed to him a monstrous face that haunted the afternoon silences after his weird outbursts of song. And, even after she could judge with some accuracy the time of the outbursts and prepare for them, she was always caught by surprise. All this and the fact that Philomena had wrested from her the role of mistress of the house obliged her to seek solace in the evening outings in town, a town she only knew by description.

"Kwaku," a youth whom he had begged for money a few days earlier shouted in his ear, "is true you sons had to haul you out of the gutter a few days ago and take you home?"

No sooner had he said this than he was gone, shouldering his way through the crowd, which had dwindled somewhat in the last quarter of an hour.

"What he say?" Miss Gwendoline asked, tugging at his arm.

"He only did want to borrow money."

The crowd got smaller by the hour, and at last Kwaku was able to take a seat at his wife's table when two men got up. Thereupon he wrenched the bottle from her hand and poured a glassful.

"You going kill you'self, you wait," Miss Gwendoline told him.

Someone began blowing a mouth-organ in the far corner, where the bar joined the wall, but no one listened, even though the din had subsided and people's words could be heard distincly.

Kwaku kept mumbling to himself unintelligibly. His head was bent forward so that his chin touched the table.

"Don't drink no more, Kwaku," Miss Gwendoline urged when she put her hand on his shoulder.

Like an obedient child he passed her the bottle, saying, "You not vexed, eh?"

"No, I not vexed."

"Hi, Kwaku!" a man called out to him. "Do a dance for we, ne?"

Kwaku shook his head.

"Look, man, you getting this if you dance."

The man held up a dollar note and turned round to show the company what Kwaku would earn if he danced.

Kwaku jumped to his feet before Miss Gwendoline could restrain him and tried to take the note from the man, who teased him by holding it above his head.

"After you dance, not before," he said, turning round to seek approval from other customers. "Hey, everybody, Kwaku goin' do a dance. You with the mouth-organ, play, man. Sh! Sh! Everybody, Kwaku goin' do a dance."

Kwaku started dancing even before the music began and someone began clapping to provide him with an accompaniment.

"Go on, Kwaku!" another customer encouraged him. "Look!"

Kwaku looked and saw another note being waved. He contorted himself, jumped as high in the air as he could, then, having recovered his balance, stuck out his backside while swivelling round. More people began clapping and shouting, "Come on! Come on!"

Miss Gwendoline sat, impassive at her table, pretending she did not know what was going on, until she closed her eyes tight in a grotesque grimace which caused her lips to disappear between her teeth. Then tears appeared below her eyelashes, coursed down her puffed-out cheeks and disappeared under her chin.

"Yea! Yea! Yea!" the customers were shouting in unison, drumming and clapping as Kwaku twisted and turned in his comic improvisation.

In the end, exhausted from his display, he stopped to take breath. But the spinning had brought on a bout of giddiness which he only now felt. He stood for a while, held his head, and then fell to the ground, drawing from the customers howls of laughter. First, the man who promised him the money bent down and put the dollar

253

note into his right-hand trouser pocket, so that half of it stuck out. Then the second man, who hesitated before following suit, placed his note into Kwaku's left side pocket, so that he looked as if he had sprouted wings below his waist.

The sound of laughter died away when Kwaku got to his feet and stumbled to his wife's table.

"Is where you character now?" she managed to say.

"What you crying for? Somebody do you something?"

"No, I just remember," she answered.

"What?"

"From when I was a lil' girl, that's all."

The bartender went and undid the catches which held the door back, for the night air had become cold. And just after he did this a young man entered the rum-shop, singing as he did so, and cast a gloom over the company with his song, which the harmonica player began to accompany.

"Take it back,
  Take it back,
  The powder in the jar,
  For some your talk
  Might have the meaning ...."

Kwaku recalled the dead girl dressed in bridal clothes lying in her coffin and shuddered at the thought of his precarious existence.

"Let's go, ne," he said to Miss Gwendoline.

She got up, gripping her stick with her right hand and taking Kwaku's arm with her left.

That night she dreamt that an army of worms was crawling from her mouth as she lay prostrate on the floor. The next morning when she woke up she could not communicate to anyone her dream and her conviction that she would die soon. And after her bowl of boiling coffee she sat out in the shadow of the house, dreaming of the village where she reared her children and of the stench from Blossom's calabash tree in flower.